"DOES THE SEA WITCH ___
SWORD WHEN SHE MAKES LOVE?"

Seaghan MacNamara's voice touched her like a tongue, as if he were kissing her freely and malevolently.

"It depends on the man," Arrah challenged him.

He took her arm, and she allowed him to lead her down the beach a way, behind a large boulder. She knew she shouldn't be here with him, yet the force of him was as unrelenting as the whirlpool into which she had sailed.

"Do you know that the great storytellers of old said that once land and sea, evil and good, dark and light, man and woman were one."

"What does that have to do with me?" she asked.

"You're a woman of great courage. You dared to take a pirate's ship from him and to navigate the Dragon's Mouth. Now I give you another dare." He reached out and touched her face. She didn't draw away. "Dare to dream of love. Not just a lad's love. But a man's love. Dare to dream of what it is like to make love with a man until you feel completely and utterly possessed by him, until you lose all sense of yourself. I dare you!"

He grabbed her shoulders with a power that made her wince, then he kissed her as if she were the first woman in the world and the last woman in the world.

"The ocean is cold, Arrah," Seaghan whispered, "but in it is the hottest blood of all."

TEMPTING THE FATES

A shadow moved behind a granite boulder at the edge of the beach.

"Show yourself," Arrah ordered.

The shadow moved again, came closer. It was Seaghan MacNamara.

"Is the sea witch frightened of the dark?" he mocked softly. In the shadows his face was impenetrable as granite.

Yes, she wanted to say. *I'm frightened of you. But more than that, I'm frightened of myself, of my desire for you.*

"Someday Arrah O'Donnell will tempt the Fates once too often," he whispered, taking her arm.

He was enormous and powerful. He intoxicated her. Never had the overwhelming presence of a man heated her so.

She stepped back, but he grasped her to him and closed his mouth on hers with a fierceness that demanded her surrender. Something told her she must not yield, but her body wouldn't listen. She allowed him to press her down to the sand. She was hot, open and waiting for him, elemental in her intense desire.

She wanted him to take her.

Also by Elona Malterre

The Celts

MISTRESS
OF THE
EAGLES

Elona Malterre

A DELL TRADE PAPERBACK

A DELL TRADE PAPERBACK
Published by
Dell Publishing
a division of
Bantam Doubleday Dell Publishing Group, Inc.
666 Fifth Avenue
New York, New York 10103

ISBN: 0-440-50308-6

Printed in the United States of America

April 1990

10 9 8 7 6 5 4 3 2 1

BVG

No novel is ever written solely by one person, and this book is dedicated to the people who helped bring about its completion:

Graham Young, whose stories of the sea echo throughout these pages;

Pat Allan, who weaves her own Irish charms beside the ocean's edge;

Mark and Alexandra, whose unfailing patience and support shore me when the waters are troubled;

Maggie Lichota and Jenny Delson, whose editorial expertise guided me through the rough passage of rewrite;

And to the crew of the *Golden Hinde* (wherever you sail now), I'm especially grateful for the magic afternoon we shared. May your sails rise again.

To all of you I say thank you and good journey.

PROLOGUE
Ireland, 1425

The Island of the Eagles lies off the west coast of Ireland. Cliffs and shards of rock thrust up to pierce the sky. It is a windswept place of stark, fierce beauty, exposed to the violence of the sea, a place where the curses of dying women carry the venom of prophecy. The family of the O'Donnell had been cursed by a dying fishergirl: they would have no male heirs until a woman was hanged by her lover.

This night the wind howled like a woman driven mad by the loss of all her children.

High in the Castle of the Eagles, the mistress, attended by her women, cried out in childbirth.

In a lower part of the castle, a servant woman lay in childbirth as well. She was alone, hidden in a dark corner, the wind slashing beneath the door. Lightning speared the blackness and lit it to stark brilliance. The woman's face twisted with pain. She pressed her knuckles between her teeth and bit herself to silence.

In the upper chamber a midwife, a scarf covering her face, bent to the mistress. The wind hit hard. A shutter slammed open, curtains flew. The shawl blew from the midwife, exposing a large purple birthmark. She instantly turned from the mistress, scrambled to retrieve her scarf, and covered her face again. A woman rushed to close the shutter.

Finally, after a long and painful labor, a girl child was born. The mistress, weak with exhaustion, fell to sleep. The other women left the chamber.

The midwife wrapped the child in swaddling and carried her to the chimney, laid her in a shovel and held her over a low fire. Wicked spirits attended women in childbirth, stealing away newborns, substituting their own evil kind. If the child was a changeling spirit, it would rush up the chimney: fire was the greatest enemy of every sort of fiendish creature.

"Burn, burn, burn," chanted the midwife, "if of the devil burn, but if of God stay safe from harm."

The midwife had her back turned to the sleeping mistress. Hastily she pulled a rope from beneath her apron and tied it to a loop she had made in the swaddling garments. She let the newborn down to the level below by means of a secret opening at the back of the chimney. The child was crying. The servant woman struggled to her feet. She kissed her child, untied the newborn of the mistress and replaced it with her own daughter.

Thus it was that the child of the mistress was exchanged with that of a servant.

PART I

CHAPTER
1
Ireland, 1446

Carbri O'Connor's stepsister, Finola, had a restless spirit. When Finola was but a babe, her mother had requested Finola's horoscope be cast. The astrologer said the stars pointed to Finola's becoming powerful and beautiful. Finola's mother, never one to trust to stars alone, made all the preparations so that the prophecy would come true.

First she murdered her husband, who was a member of a lesser sept of the O'Connor clan. She fed him poison mushrooms that she had ground and mixed into dulse. Then she married one of her dead husband's kinsmen, a member of a more elevated O'Connor sept.

When the seasons of the moon came on Finola, her mother gave her a sleeping potion and paid one of the male servants to climb into Finola's bed in the middle of the night and spread her thighs and touch her. Finola's mother threatened the servant with death if he penetrated Finola with his organ, for she had to stay a virgin for her marriage.

In her dreams, Finola felt the powerful body of a man, smelled the warm sandalwood scent of a man kissing her breasts, stroking her, and finding the center of her and touching her and touching her. Night after night she would have the same dream and would wake up with an intense aching.

During the day she moved her body and eyes in a hungry way that many men found appealing. She had no want of suitors.

As the stepdaughter of one of the senior chieftains of the clan, Finola was eligible for a lucrative match. Finola had no say in the choice of bridegroom. Her mother chose a wealthy, powerful widower of advanced years.

Finola had anticipated her wedding night with eagerness, thinking she would find relief from the hunger that had constantly tormented her. Unfortunately her husband became so roused by her desire that he spilled as soon he touched his manhood to her. Subsequently he had tried again, but when he discovered Finola's maidenhead was too unyielding for him to penetrate, he grew impatient, then tired, then limp.

The old woman, who was experienced with such matters, had to be called. She came carrying a jar of grease and a bull's horn. Finola's mother helped to restrain her daughter, first with her hands and then with ropes, as the old woman, using the bull's horn, attempted to pierce the maidenhead. Finally, amidst a great deal of blood and shrieking, it yielded.

The subsequent nights of Finola's marriage were vague repetitions of the first attempt. Her husband had little control over his manhood and spilled himself like a boy at his first encounter. The marriage bed, instead of bringing relief for Finola's unbearable aching, had only made it worse.

Then Finola's husband developed the first of a series of weaknesses and the aphrodisiac treatments of the sea holly and early purple orchid failed to raise desire in him.

Finola took lovers from amongst her husband's guardsmen, calling them to her chambers and making them undress in front of her, choosing her lovers amongst the most favorably built. But she was a difficult woman to love. No man had the stamina to last long enough to bring her to pleasure.

Seaghan MacNamara had arrived to visit her husband. MacNamara was the handsomest man Finola had ever seen, exuding a potent male virility like a stallion at a breeding pasture. During the dancing festivities, she slid her hands down his powerful loins and pressed her palm against his manhood. She felt his powerful grip tighten about her waist. She had taken his hand and led him by the stairs to her chamber. He was enormous, but he refused to enter her. At first he inserted only his fingers until she was raging and pleading with want. Finally he came into her, but slowly, his hugeness filling her. For a long time he moved very slowly, barely perceptibly. Then he began to thrust more quickly. She felt the hard, rhythmic push of his buttocks under her fingers. She pressed her nails into his flesh, and then his rhythm quickened, pumping and thrusting. He did not stop for breath or to change position, or because he had a cramp in his leg, all those excuses she'd heard from other men. He did not stop for anything, but continued, did not come to climax, but continued to thrust until she lay in his arms shaking with pleasure. That sharp beak of hunger that had eaten at her for so long was gone. She was a flower that had bloomed, a bell that had rung.

In the past, Finola's body had known only want, now it had tasted satisfaction, and the torment of wanting it again consumed her. Repeatedly she pleaded with Seaghan to take her away with him. But he refused, reminding her that she was already married.

Finola had gone to the witch and asked for a love potion. Carrying it home, she had dropped the jar in the courtyard, and the castle goat had licked up the contents. Thereafter he followed her around, bleating miserably. The servants laughed at Finola and she ordered a scullion to butcher the goat.

There had never been anyone like Seaghan, not before or after. He was a man among men, and sometimes Finola would take her pick of as many as five or six of her husband's guardsmen each day and still she was never able to rediscover the feelings that she'd had with Seaghan. The other men only inflamed the heat that burned inside her. Sometimes the men would bring her close to her pleasure, but then they would suffer from shortage of breath or they would spill themselves. The rhythm would be broken and they would have to start all over again. Their fingers, their mouths, their tongues, all touched the wrong places. "Here, you fools!" she would scream at them. "Here! Here!" And they would open their eyes wide with fright as though she were some banshee shouting at them.

Only MacNamara had known instinctively where to touch, where to put his fingers and his splendid manhood, so that his lovemaking was like a long song, moving inexorably and surely, patiently and certainly to a final, shuddering conclusion. Never since had she known such pleasure.

At eighteen, Arrah O'Donnell had no frail prettiness as other women did. Instead, her bold, strong beauty held both men and women in awe. When she walked past a group of soldiers or sailors, they would stop their talk and gaze with secret eyes on her waist and hips, hidden by chestnut hair falling in profusion.

For over three years the sons of neighboring chieftains had sought her hand in betrothal, but she declined them all. When Arrah was a child and her grandmother had been alive, the old woman often sang a melody, a tune she had made up called "A Song for Arrah." It began:

> Arrah of the distant eyes,
> The wind sings in your mind.
> Arrah of the distant eyes,
> You'll always choose the path
> that's wild.

Arrah amused herself with the fisherfolk, ran along the beach, and swam in the sea, untamed and free as a mermaid. She wanted nothing of the restraints of marriage.

She was often tempted by men. At feasts she would dance with them, and the heavy, hard warmth of their bodies raised yearnings in her, but she saw the life her mother led—sewing tapestries, doing embroidery, overseeing the dyeing of cloth. Arrah O'Donnell wanted no part of such confined tedium.

One day she had asked her mother what it was like to be with a man. Margaret looked at Arrah. "Surely, daughter, 'tis time you were discovering this for yourself."

Arrah had danced with Carbri O'Connor frequently during the feasts of the last fortnight. Now she danced with him again. He was in training as second in command on her father's ship. After he returned from his trip to Arabia, Carbri would be ready to captain his own vessel. He was a lanky, wiry young man with a full blond beard and mischievous hazel eyes.

The main hall was filled. Pipers played out their best music, forcing the air faster and harder through the squealing bagpipes. The bodhran players banged out their rhythms on the goat-skin drums. Cup bearers, refilling tankards, moved among the crowd of sailors. In the kitchen the bond servants jigged and hornpiped as jollily as the soldiers. Wine flowed. Men leaped and danced, and when they grew hot, they removed their leather jerkins, threw back their heads and drank more ale.

Carbri took Arrah's hand and led her away from the noise into a quiet alcove behind the feast hall. Arrah was aware she should not go with Carbri: he was betrothed to Agneis de Burgo, the daughter of a neighboring lord. His stepsister, Finola, had arrived that afternoon to tell him the engagement had been finalized. But Arrah had always liked Carbri O'Connor's easy, good-humored ways and the coolness of the alcove provided Arrah with a respite from the dancing.

Through a corner she caught a glimpse of Finola standing close to the far wall, her heavy-lidded eyes looking everywhere. Arrah had taken an instant dislike to Carbri's stepsister, a dark-haired woman whose eyes constantly moved as though watching for someone, and whose voice tinkled with false friendliness.

Arrah moved deeper into the alcove. In the shadows, she allowed Carbri's hands to pull her to him. She smelled wine on his breath and knew that he wanted to kiss her. She lifted her mouth.

But her mother's sharp tone interrupted the would-be kiss. "Arrah! You know what happened to your father's sister, playing with a man mated to another. Now, go and search him out!" Margaret ordered. "His captain seeks him!"

Arrah did as her mother told her.

Arrah's father, Reevnarg—a name meaning red circles, because of the bloody path by which he had taken control of his territories—was the most formidable chieftain on land or sea on the west coast of Ireland.

As a child Arrah remembered him being jovial, but since she had dismissed so many suitors he had grown unpredictable and harsh, often lashing out at her, bellowing like an enraged bull. His affections, his approval, depended upon her doing exactly as he ordered. The devil take him, she wasn't marrying just to stop his shouting.

She approached him with apprehension. Then the captain rushed by her and passed him some message. Reevnarg's head lifted as if he smelled blood. Arrah was relieved. She could return to the dancing.

A dark, looming stranger with a very black beard approached her. She knew immediately that he was a sailor: he had the unmistakable rolling walk of a man who was used to the pitching of a deck beneath his feet. Sailors always asked permission before they danced with Arrah, but this man took her hand without speaking a word. His fingers gripped hers like a carpenter's vice. Dark crescents like bruises shadowed the skin beneath his eyes.

Before she could ask his name or his position, he shouted for the sword dance, and pulling two swords from his girdle threw them down, crossed, on the floor.

Usually the sword dance was danced only after a major victory in battle. There had been no battle, but the pipers began to play without question. Arrah flung her arms with aggression and challenge as she kept time to the words of the dance:

Fire! Fire! Steel, oh, steel!
Fire! Fire! Steel and fire.

The stranger met her at every step. They were in perfect rhythm. The turns dizzying, her breath came quick and hot. Faster and faster they spun. The stranger confused her, for although he had the immense, powerful shoulders that only an oarsman could have, he wore a beard. Under Brehon Laws, which dictated custom and law, only a chieftain, his sons, brothers, or nephews could wear beards. But the stranger's beard was closely trimmed in the style of a foreigner, square about his jaw, whereas Carbri's and Reevnarg's beards were full. Faster and faster he moved like a dark whirlpool beside her.

Oak! Oak! Earth and waves!

She would not be outdone, so she stepped and twirled faster.

Fire! Fire! Steel, oh, steel!

Although the stranger was a Titan, he moved with an uncanny ease and quickness as they leaped through one step and then another.

Fire! Fire! Steel, oh, steel!

Arrah saw that the inside of his coarse green cloak was lined with green satin. She stopped moving in mid-step to ask him who he was. The stranger grasped her in that moment of stillness. He held her with such enormous strength that she was absolutely immobilized. Arrah had never been so overpowered by anyone.

The music stopped and she pulled away from him. Breathing exaggeratedly she pretended that she was out of breath. "Enough," she gasped.

"I wish to dance." He bit out the words. "More music," he shouted. The pipes and drums began again.

She pulled her arm away angrily.

He grabbed it back, holding her in a tight grip and spun and turned her. She deliberately stepped on his foot, but since she wore only *brocas*, soft heelless shoes made from deer skin, her stepping had little effect, except to make the stranger spin her even harder. She yelled for her father's guards, but the noise from the bagpipes and flutes and drums was deafening. No one heard her. The stranger pulled her against him, and she felt her breasts crushed against the huge heat of his body, felt his quick breath blown against her face. His hands imprisoned her, holding her absolutely still. He towered above her, his dark eyes dangerous and hard, and for a moment she didn't know what he was going to do.

But then Finola glided beside him and touched the stranger's arm, and although Arrah didn't like Finola, she was relieved to see her. The stranger frightened her, and Arrah, up to now, had rarely been frightened of anything or anyone.

Although the music hadn't ended, he released Arrah abruptly. He turned and walked away with Finola, leaving Arrah standing alone. The dark green of the stranger's mantle loomed above the rest of the dancing crowd as he moved through it.

Carbri grabbed Arrah's hand, his hazel eyes filled with teasing. The musicians began another song and the pipes played louder.

"Who is he?" she shouted over the screaming of the bagpipes.

She saw the stranger nod to her father, and then they left the feast hall together. Finola, suddenly ignored, trailed behind them, scurrying to catch up with their long forceful strides.

"Seaghan MacNamara," said Carbri, pressing his lips against her ear and then her neck. She drew back slightly, but his lips followed, gentle but persistent, and now she didn't draw away. Carbri led her back in the direction of the alcove.

"Why does a MacNamara chieftain sail with the O'Donnell ships?" she asked in the quieter alcove.

"He was the MacNamara tanaist, named to follow his father, the Mac-Namara chieftain, but he's been cast out."

"What reason?"

"A woman. MacNamara is a taker of women. He casts them off and discards them like soiled shirts. He did the same with Finola. Enough talk." Carbri pulled her close again. She felt the pressure of his lips against her neck, then higher, on her cheek, on her chin.

Steel struck steel. The music stopped instantly. Someone yelled "Attack! Attack! The MacNamara have attacked." Tumult exploded as men took to arms. Carbri gave Arrah a brief kiss on the lips then pulled his sword and rushed off.

CHAPTER
2

The battle ended quickly, for Reevnarg had been forewarned of the impending attack and ordered his men to lay in ambush. Beneath the air of festivity had been readiness of battle. The MacNamara retreated ignobly. The injured fighters left behind were treated, so they could be chained as oarsmen in the fleet of Reevnarg's ships. Those wounded past the point of recovery were killed.

News of the attack came to Reevnarg from Seaghan MacNamara, who had been secretly forewarned by his own kinsman, Bres.

A comely lad with hair like ripe corn and eyes like the blue lakes of Killarney, Bres had been stabbed in the fighting. Debrogail, one of the kitchen wenches, took an immediate liking to him, for he was saucy with his eyes. He watched her as she mashed the woundwort plants and applied them to his arm to stop the bleeding, and after that he held her hand and wouldn't allow her to leave him.

Unlike many of the other servants who were given to sullenness and anger, Debrogail was a cheery young woman who had a sublime voice. She whistled and sang with the sweetness of an angel as she kneaded the bread or churned the vats of butter.

Bres had seen Debrogail dancing on top of the table when the Mac-Namara stormed the castle. She was unabashedly lifting her skirts and entertaining the rest of the kitchen, her reddish blond hair swirling like a magician's silk about her shoulders. He had been charmed by her long legs and her singing. When the guards came to round up the MacNamara attackers, they were unaware that Bres was the one who had forewarned of the attack. He had taken an arm wound. "How can I fight," he said, leering openly at Debrogail, "when there's so much that's lovely and charming to be stealing away my eyes?"

It was absolutely necessary that no one know that Bres had been the spy, so he was treated as a prisoner for appearance's sake. But as he was being led away, Naira O'Donnell, Arrah's older sister, happened to see him. Naira had been recently widowed. The lean haunches of Bres, supple as those of a deer, had immediately appealed to her and she spoke with her father. "Keep him here manacled in my chambers. If you take him to the dungeon, he'll die as sure as the saints. He'll be no good to you at the oars. I'll take charge of him."

Reevnarg was agreeable to her request.

Naira called Debrogail and spoke imperiously to the servant. "You'll look after the wounded young man!" Naira always spoke imperiously. Because Arrah's unruly abandon always caught the attention of suitors and castle visitors, Naira was consumed by an overpowering jealousy of her younger sister. This jealousy had made her as sharp-edged as a sword.

Naira left Debrogail with pointed instructions to look after Bres Mac-Namara.

Debrogail was only too delighted to do so, for she found his charm seductive.

She washed the wound and cleaned it, glancing up at him coyly from the corners of her dark, wickedly sparkling eyes. Bres pulled her kercher from her head, spilling her almond-colored hair about her shoulders. When he tried to lean his cheek against her full, warm breasts, she gave him a light, teasing snap on the nose for his impudence. Bres exaggeratedly howled in pain.

"What have you done?" Naira's sharp voice pierced the chamber. She was on the verge of hysterics as she approached. She slapped Debrogail's face, sending her sprawling to the ground. "And what are you doing with your kercher off?"

"I wasn't intending . . ." Debrogail tried to defend herself.

But there was no defense. Naira slapped her again. "Quiet! Or I'll have you thrown in the dungeon."

Bres tried to intervene. "It was nothing. I was just crying out because . . . I had a muscle cramp in my foot."

Naira had fixed her mind that Bres would soon become her husband. She was not about to lose him because of the careless medicining of a servant. "If you ever hurt him again, I'll order you drawn and quartered, do you understand?"

"Yes, mistress," said Debrogail.

"She's done nothing," insisted Bres, "except to tend to my wound and attempt to make me comfortable."

"And if she does anything else I'll have her thrown to the sharks." Naira said this with a chilling certainty.

Debrogail and Bres exchanged a secret glance before Debrogail let her eyes fall to the floor again. "Yes, mistress," she said again.

After the defeat of the MacNamara, Reevnarg began preparations for his voyage to Portugal and Africa. The day before he sailed he was in a jovial mood, as he always was before a voyage. He asked Arrah what she wanted him to bring her. She didn't want anything, she told him. When he insisted, she asked for a pet monkey. One of the men had brought one back with him, but the sailors in their revelry had fed it heath beer. The monkey had fallen to the floor and in the riotous dancing had gone unnoticed and had been trampled to death.

But her father retorted, "You're past the years to be playing with pets. It's time you started playing with a man," and he winked at his wife. "Someone who can master your damn passionate will. Plant some babies in your belly and you'll stop your foolishness. I'll no longer have it—the daughter of Reevnarg cavorting with the fisherfolk like a common girl.

"The chieftain of the Joyce of Connemara has an ill wife, not long for this world. When he was here, your looks pleased him. He has lands a plenty for a cattle booley. He'll pay a hundred cows for you as the bride price."

"I don't want to marry anyone!"

"I told you, husband," said Margaret, "when Arrah was born it was ill luck to name her after your sister. She's of the same reckless nature."

Reevnarg ignored her remark. He'd heard it a thousand times before. "Don't let his silver hair be frightening you. The Joyce still has plenty of fire in his loins. He gave his last wife two babes. He'll be offering a seaworthy vessel in addition to the cows. When I return, I'll be taking you to his bed. Then if you show to be carrying his seed, there'll be a wedding to follow!"

"I won't!"

"I've allowed enough of your silliness!" he shouted back.

Arrah stormed out of the main hall in a fury. She ran out to the cliffs, where she always went to think. At the three hundred steps she looked down on the turbulent ocean smashing green and silver below. Arrah's eyes were as changeable as that sea, and now that she was angry, her gray-green eyes were silver as the sea-foam.

She tried to remember who the Joyce was, but could not. When her father was home there were always chieftains and captains calling at Eagle Island because of the trade in hides and wool. Because of difficult tides and winds, the coast was treacherous to navigate and Reevnarg's skills and the skills of his sailors were often in demand to pilot visiting ships. She couldn't place Joyce's face amongst the dozens and dozens. But it didn't matter who he was or what he looked like, Arrah was certain of one thing—she wasn't going to be his bride.

She wished her grandmother were still alive. Her muim with the silken white hair always had an answer for everything. Unlike Margaret, who wanted Arrah to act in a way befitting a chieftain's daughter, Muim understood that Arrah did not want to be cooped like a hen. The words from Muim's song returned to her:

> Down where the lonely sea gulls fly
> You'll find your way. . . .

Further toward the south of Eagle Island the cliffs rose more steeply. Birds nested in the crags: razorbills, cormorants, guillemots and gulls, as well as the eagles that gave the island its name. Always, too, there was the clamorous barking of seals, who sunned themselves on the numerous rocks. Arrah liked their sleek glistening playfulness and sometimes swam out to the rocks with them.

When Arrah was younger, she used to run up and down the steps, slippery with the surf, racing and playing with the children of the fisherfolk. It was the fisherfolk who had shown her how they dried the skins of sharks and used them as sandpaper to smooth the wooden ribs of their boats, so splinters didn't tear the hides that formed the boat shells.

She, Carbri, and Debrogail had built themselves a small boat, and pretending they were seamen, sailed it around the bay.

Reevnarg had come down to the beach. "Aye, daughter. 'Tis a pity you're female. I'd be making a fine seaman out of you, if your sex was to have been different."

"But I can be a seaman!"

"Nonsense!" He laughed. "The only mast fit for a woman is the mast of a man tipping inside her." She hadn't known what he meant then.

Now as Arrah looked out to sea she was surprised to see a ship off Wolf Rock. She saw it from broadside and immediately knew it was not an Irish ship. The west coast Irish ships were cogs, single-masted, square-sailed ships that could also be driven with oars.

The ship off the rocks had four masts, large sails, and a broad beam. The prow was a brutal-looking protrusion that looked like a battering ram.

And then Arrah noticed the guns. Never had she seen such heavy guns. She counted five cannons on the one side, which meant that there would be five on the other side as well. From where she stood, it looked as though the cannons could fire balls the size of calves.

Joyce or no Joyce, the safety of the island was paramount. She had to tell her father. He would be out somewhere for a last hunt before his voyage. She knew she had to find him, and began to run along the cliff.

The cliff offered a view of not only the sea, but of the green hills of the island as well. Sheep grazed tranquilly, their cream-colored wool like small spills of frothy milk against the green.

She began running and calling, her voice echoing in the hills. Other chieftains hunted with falcons, but Reevnarg had discovered a way of training eagles to take the lure. He was extremely proud of his birds.

Over the crest of a near hill a white dove flew, its wings scalloped pale against the blue sky. A large shadow flickered on the ground in front of Arrah. She looked up and saw the unmistakable wing flight of an eagle. She knew what was coming. The eagle climbed, then swooped down. There was no sound, no struggle as the two birds appeared to fuse. Then the eagle extended its wings, and began to climb again, the dove hanging limply from its talons. Arrah ran, following the bird.

When she was small, she constantly pleaded with her father to take her "eagling." Always he refused, but Arrah was persistent, and finally one day he gave in.

They went out on horseback, because Arrah's shorter legs couldn't keep up with Reevnarg's long stride. A chieftain always rode a stallion, and Arrah, because she was already an accomplished rider, rode a spirited young mare. They both rode with one rein only, and used an *eshlasc*, a stick made from yew wood with a short whip on the end which they touched to the horse's neck to guide them.

When Reevnarg and Arrah reached their destination and dismounted, she pleaded to hold the bird, and at first her father refused. It was still a nervous bird, he said, and hadn't been satisfactorily trained to lure. But Arrah was not one to give up easily. It was a splendid bird, a golden color.

"All right, then. But I warn you—don't let go! Put this on first," Reevnarg commanded, handing her a huge leather glove.

The inside of the glove, when she slipped it over her fingers, was moist from the perspiration of her father's hand. It was huge.

Carefully, very carefully, he handed her the bird. It shifted and balanced, stepped nervously from one clawed foot to another on her wrist. The bird was hooded, but Arrah sensed its agitation through her arm. Her father had to relieve himself so he went behind a stone. She saw him there with his back turned to her. She held the thongs tightly. Thinking that her father would be pleased when he returned and found the eagle ready for hunting, she unhooded it. The startled bird attacked Arrah's free hand with its beak.

She screamed, and without thinking, let go of the leather thongs which were attached to the bird's leg.

The bird flew up, the leather straps dangling uselessly from its legs. Reevnarg rushed back and immediately began twirling the lure about his head, but the bird flew higher and higher, off toward the distant mountain.

Reevnarg watched until the eagle was just a speck in the distance. In his hand he held his horse whip. He looked at Arrah. She watched his face, looking for anger there, but his face didn't really change expression. His mouth didn't move, and his eyes didn't blink. Not a single muscle on his face seemed to have changed, except that everything about it looked different. The gray-blue eyes grew imperceptibly, unmistakably dark, the way a blue bruise turns to black.

"Go home, Arrah!"

"I'll help you get it back."

" 'Tis enough you've done!" He picked up the rein of his stallion.

She felt the disgrace of disappointing her father. "Please," she said. "Let me help." Intending to ride in the direction the eagle had flown, she moved toward her horse.

Her father's voice stopped her from climbing up.

"Walk home!" he said. "And quick. Out of my sight."

"I'm going to help you find it," she said, holding her ground.

"I'll teach you to disobey me!" Rushing at her he began to strike across her legs with the whip.

"Go home," he shouted. "You'll never come with me again."

"Why are you crying so?" asked Debrogail when she saw Arrah.

Arrah related what had happened, and the servant girl, with her three years' additional wisdom, explained matter-of-factly: "Arrah, you're a stupid fool of Beelzebub. If you want to be playing in a man's world, you can't be making the foolish mistakes of a little girl. To make him happy you'll have to find the eagle. I'll tell your mother you're with me looking for herbs."

The next day Arrah went out by herself to where she had lost the eagle.

She called and whistled. She'd brought chunks of raw chicken with her, and these she attached to a lure. For two days she waited and whistled and called. And then she saw the golden eagle, flying with the leather thongs still tied to his foot.

She spun the lure and whistled, and the bird caught it in his beak before landing on her forearm. But she hadn't brought any glove with her. The bird's talons tore at her flesh, but she held tightly. Then a pheasant flew over and the eagle tried to take off, ripping Arrah's arm, its wings beating at her face, but still she held on. Her hands and fingers were greasy with blood, her forearms were raw, but still she held on.

At Eagle Castle she ran into the room where her father was standing, staring out at the sea, his legs apart, his hands on his hips. "I've found him," she shouted.

He turned and looked at her, looked at the eagle, then back at her bloodied arm. He reached out and took the eagle, then with the other hand he pulled her close to him. Hanging on the wall above his chair, Arrah saw the O'Donnell sword, with its large emerald the size of an egg. Small rubies surrounded the green gem. She smelled the leather of her father's jerkin and she tried not to cry.

Arrah's mother was horrified when she saw the wounds and immediately called the servants to dress them.

Debrogail washed the arm with an infusion made from dried purple flowers of the marsh woundwort, but the scars remained, a series of jagged lines on Arrah's arm.

Naira often jeered Arrah about them. "You'll never find a husband now," she'd say. "No man wants a woman marked like an old battle-scarred soldier for a wife. With your sun-browned skin, you look like a bog peasant!"

Arrah ignored her. She had never forgotten the look on her father's face when he saw her return with the eagle. He had taken her with him after that, except for the times that he had the company of men to go eagling with.

In the distance Arrah saw the outlines of two dark-cloaked figures walking toward her. She thought that Carbri had gone with Reevnarg. But as Arrah continued running, she realized that the smaller man was too broad for Carbri. The smaller man was her father, and the larger man was the stranger who had danced with her the other night—Seaghan Mac-Namara.

Her father spoke amiably as she approached. " 'Tis known the world over that Irishmen are the fleetest runners. Are you trying to make us believe that the same is true for Irish women?"

As quickly as she could she tried to explain what she'd seen, but she was out of breath and her speech was broken and staccato.

"What is it, Daughter, that you gulp at me like a fish out of water?"

She took two or three deep breaths and then repeated her words about the ship.

Out of the corner of her eye she noticed the deep frown that marked MacNamara's wide forehead, and the dark look of brooding, but she didn't want to look at him, so she kept her eyes on her father's face.

"Daughter! Why such frenzy? You have a look about you like you've seen a phantom carrying its head! Be calming yourself!" With two fingers he began stroking the hooded eagle at the base of its neck. The dove had been put into a game bag. Reevnarg's hand was streaked with blood.

"But"—Arrah was still out of breath—"this ship had guns. Guns"—and she tried to indicate the size by spreading her arms—"and so many."

She heard the stranger curse beneath his breath.

"Aye, the English are preparing to attack France again," Reevnarg said as he continued stroking the eagle. "The English King hopes de Burgo's magic can help him. Finola told me. Were you talking with her today, Seaghan? Her eyes were poking in every corner trying to find you."

MacNamara ignored Reevnarg's question. "There's nothing but trouble when they're asail. Henry VI wants to strengthen his position in Ireland."

"Strengthen his position in Ireland!" Reevnarg guffawed. "When he can barely keep peace among the Yorks in England. We're too bloody far from London for them to be concerning themselves with the likes of us," he said.

"You know the prophecy. There'll be Englishmen in Ireland as long as the magpies remain," said MacNamara.

The Norman English had come into Ireland in the 1100s. Devrogilla O'Ruaire, the beautiful wife of one Irish king, sent a messenger to her lover, Diarmuid, a neighboring king, to come to take her away and make her his own wife. But she suffered a change of heart. Disregarding her violent screams, Diarmuid carried her off. In retaliation O'Ruaire destroyed Diarmuid's lands, imprisoned Devrogilla in a convent for life to repent her adultery, and banished Diarmuid.

Diarmuid traveled to England where he promised lords a share of Ireland if they helped him reconquer his lands. They made large gains of territory, and in 1175, the English King, Henry II, was recognized as High Lord of Ireland.

When Devrogilla lay dying in the convent she saw a magpie sitting on her windowsill. "I fear we have undone Ireland, for the English will stay as long as magpies remain," she said.

But over the passing years, as Anglo-Normans began embracing Irish women, they also embraced Irish customs and language. England's control of Ireland shrunk to two small areas.

"They do no harm at Galway or Dublin," said Reevnarg.

"Curse the adulterous whore who brought them here!" MacNamara swore with such vehemence that Arrah looked at him. "Aye," he continued, "a woman's fault again. Like Eve with the apple. Every man's troubles begin with women."

"And women's begin with men," she shot back. "Devrogilla asked Diarmuid not to take her." She saw MacNamara's dark eyes glaring at her.

Reevnarg spoke. "Enough of this talk. I'll not have lines in my daughter's face."

Reevnarg tried to touch Arrah's forehead, but his fingers were smeared with the blood of the white bird, and she withdrew. He ignored her reluctance, put his arm around her shoulder and continued talking. "Now, my beauty. Stop worrying yourself. Aye, but you'd be a beauty if it weren't for your damned sun-brown skin. But what can a man do when his daughter thinks she's a fishergirl. I ask you, MacNamara. She's a splendid filly, is she not, brown skin be damned?"

"I was admiring her the night of my father's attack. And her graceful foot as well, but your beautiful brown-skinned daughter doesn't seem appreciative of admiration."

Arrah looked at MacNamara sharply. "I don't call holding one to a dance when she won't be wanting it, admiration."

Arrah saw her father wink at MacNamara. "Aye. She's a stubborn one." Reevnarg handed the eagle to MacNamara, and before Arrah could do anything, her father grabbed her arm and pulled up her sleeve. "See these scars!"

Arrah yanked her arm away. She wanted nothing to do with MacNamara, and she particularly didn't want him looking at her.

Her father continued, "When she was young, she let one of my eagles loose. I was fit to kill a saint, I was. But she went back. Stayed out in the hills for three days. Came home with the eagle and those wounds on her arm. Aye, she's a tempest for a man. 'Tis for that reason I've seen fit to marry her to the Joyce. He's had plenty of experience with women and he'll tame her passionate spirit."

"He'll need more than experience. He'll be needing plenty of breath as well to keep up with her," said MacNamara.

Arrah felt his black eyes fix on her, but she was too furious to heed them. She pulled out from under her father's arm. "I'll not marry the Joyce!"

"Daughter, we'll have naught of your high color in front of visitors."

"I'll marry whomever I please, when I please, if I please!"

But her father grabbed her arm back roughly. All show of good humor was gone from his face. "You're my daughter and you'll marry as I say. And I'll suffer no more disobedience!"

"What am I? A brood mare to be exchanged and bred for a few dozen cows—"

"You're a woman. 'Tis your duty to give children."

"So why doesn't my mother do her duty to you?"

Her father's stinging slap silenced her. "You'll do as I say." He reached into his game bag and pulled out the dead white bird, its head rolling limply from side to side, its neck ripped and bleeding. "Now, take this and tell the cook I'll be desiring roast pigeon tonight. I'll be eating enough fish when I'm at sea." He threw the bird at her.

Arrah's reflexes were quick and she caught the bird, but immediately threw it back at her father, aiming for his head so he had to jump away. "I'll not take your cursed bird!" Grabbing her skirts she ran off in the direction she had come.

She ran back to the cliff. She saw that the ship had already passed Eagle Island and was heading southward, its sails growing smaller as the wind carried it, like an enormous graceful bird, farther and farther into the distance. Be damned! She would not marry the Joyce.

CHAPTER
3

In his youth Brion, chieftain of the MacNamara, had been an immensely handsome man, but now his features were contorted with rage. He went through the main hall of Knockmoyle Castle in a fury, kicking at dogs and chairs and at servants. The Island of the Eagles had once belonged to the MacNamara, had belonged to them for generations, but many years previous Reevnarg O'Donnell had wrested it away in a bloody battle.

When Brion MacNamara reached the other end of his banquet hall, he slammed his fists against the stone walls until his knuckles bled. He should have killed Seaghan when he had the chance. He should have killed him as soon as he emerged from his mother's womb, and hung him out for the rooks and ravens to pluck out his traitorous eyes. So much treachery in a son. Who could have thought it possible? First Seaghan had committed adultery under his father's own roof, and now this final treachery. Alerting his enemy Reevnarg of the attack! Preventing him from retaking Eagle Island!

Brion went to the window and flung the shutter open with such violence that the hinge snapped.

Once, a long time ago, he had been a happy man. He and Reevnarg O'Donnell had been like two lambs running wild in the field. They and Cormac Joyce had learned the bow and arrow together as boys. Springs had been mellow then, summers gentle. And then had come youth. The killing of the first elk, and then the killing of his first enemy, and then taking pleasure with his first woman. The hunt, war, and women. That had always been the order of his life.

Later he had fallen in love with Arrah, sister of Reevnarg, his best friend. But Arrah was married to another. His rival wasn't even in Ireland, but in England to discuss the new earldoms being formed in Ireland. She was passionate, Arrah, and wild and headstrong, her face always lifted to the wind. He loved her, loved her more than he ever thought he could love a woman.

Their love was sinful and wronged all the laws of Ireland and of Christendom and of reason, and yet neither of them could hold it in check. They lived for the night when they could lose themselves in each other's arms. Love drove them to speak of mad plans. In hushed tones they spoke of killing her husband when he returned.

Brion trusted no one with the deed but himself. Arrah insisted on going with him. Together the two of them went out in the dark of the night to wait in ambush behind the group of large stones that marked the fork in the path. They had made love as they waited.

Unknown to Brion and Arrah, Reevnarg accompanied her husband home that night. When Brion tried to kill him, Reevnarg came to Arrah's husband's defense, and wounded Brion. Arrah, dressed as a servant, her face hidden by a hood, foolishly rushed out from behind the rocks to come to his defense. Reevnarg was a ferocious fighter.

In the dark it was impossible for him to see that he plunged his sword into the breast of his sister. She collapsed on the ground, her hood falling from her splendid face, her beautiful hair tumbling loose. It was then, holding his beloved Arrah's head in his lap, that Brion swore eternal enmity between himself and Reevnarg. The man who had been his best friend became his eternal enemy. There were constant battles between the O'Donnell and the MacNamara, looting, pillaging, murder. The MacNamara lost the Island of the Eagles to Reevnarg. And now Reevnarg harbored his own treacherous son.

Brion had married another woman, the mother of Seaghan. And when she died while Seaghan was still a boy, Seaghan became the focus of his love. God, how happy he had been when he saw his son ride the MacNamara stallions with such skill. How proud it made a father to see his son become a better and better swordsman, until he was virtually unbeatable. Day by day the boy and then the youth grew into a forbiddingly handsome man, grew to be a greater and greater hunter and warrior. Seaghan MacNamara was a god among men.

A third wife bore Brion a second and third son, but they were no match for their older brother. There was no doubt that Seaghan was to be named tanaist. It was a father's greatest honor to have his son thus chosen. Often it was a nephew or a brother who was named by the clans to rule as chieftain.

Wives were frail things, always vulnerable to some weakness, like his mares that were no match for his stallions. His third wife expired as well.

Brion didn't mourn her passing. His passion had been too great for Arrah to ever really love another woman again.

He married for the fourth time, a woman named Tiltiu.

Seaghan's beauty among men became the subject of women's talk. His sexual appetites and prowess were extolled in hushed conversations. Tiltiu heard the talk. Tiltiu and Seaghan. Did they think Brion MacNamara a fool? Did they think he didn't see the looks between them. The hooded eyes, the glances so quick, too quick!

There had been a storm that night, and the roll of thunder had covered Brion's steps as he stole into his son's chamber. It was then that the lightning had struck and he had seen Tiltiu astride Seaghan, sitting on his erect phallus, with her open-mouthed expression of ecstasy that he, Brion Mac-Namara, had not in five years of marriage been able to bring to her damned face.

Christ! The cruelty of God to give a man eyes to see his wife pleasured by his own son!

Brion MacNamara screamed at the sky. "I swear, in the name of God, I swear I will not rest until I have killed my eldest son."

As Arrah approached the castle she heard the sound of the piper, a sound she normally welcomed, for it signalled a visitor. Often she would walk down to the beach to greet whoever arrived, but feeling downcast she had no desire to speak to anyone.

The Castle of the Eagles was a high, four-story battlement surrounded by two-foot-thick stone walls.

Compared to some of the fortifications, with their twelve-foot-thick walls on the mainland, the Castle of the Eagles seemed small and vulnerable. But there had been little need for heavy fortifications because would-be attackers were reluctant to attempt the Atlantic swell.

Except for occasional patches of beach, the west was an unwelcoming coastline of severe, sharded rocks, jutting and sharp as broken glass. The sky could darken in a moment and a torrent of wind could catch a ship and crash it against the rocks before sailors could tie in their canvas. In the bad seasons it was a frightful wind that blew, a howling ravenous wind that seemed to be shrieking for sacrifice.

There was a saying at the Castle of the Eagles, that even though its walls weren't thick, the castle would never fall because a woman had been buried alive under its foundations. St. Columkille, the founder of Iona, in Scotland, had buried one of his monks alive under the foundations of his abbey. Many of the other castles and abbeys also had men and women, and even children, buried within the mortar to keep the buildings strong. Sometimes in the night, the ghost of the woman was seen wandering the ramparts of the Castle of the Eagles. Each time her ghost foretold a death. Arrah had never seen the spirit, but the guards spoke of it, as did her mother and her grandmother, when she had been alive. When Arrah had been small she had tried to imagine what it would have been like to be buried alive, to have the mortar pressing against her nose and her mouth, to try to fight the tightened ropes. Arrah could never cross the courtyard without thinking of the ghost.

Debrogail was working near a well in the middle of the courtyard. She stood in a large wooden tub, and with her skirts raised high, looked slightly ridiculous, showing lithe, blue-colored legs as high as her knees. She was giving the final rinse to a newly dyed batch of cloth. Bres, Seaghan MacNamara's kinsman, stood close by laughing and teasing her.

Arrah's mother took immense pride in dyeing cloth because she was able to make cloaks for her and her husband that were like no other cloaks in Ireland. Irish chieftains wore brightly colored mantles, often red or saffron, but the cloaks and mantles of Reevnarg and Margaret were colored with a deep, highly coveted purple dye.

Ordinary blue dye was made from bilberries, but Margaret would send her women out to gather certain rare shellfish called whelks. The women always squealed with excitement when they found one.

Margaret would keep the whelks alive in barrels in a dark, cool chamber in a lower part of the castle. Each day Margaret ordered fresh sea water brought for the whelks.

The process of removing the dye from the shellfish demanded so much precision that Margaret trusted no one but herself with the task.

With a needle Margaret probed between the shell and picked out a white vein, which yielded a drop of the coloring liquid. Then she put the creature back into a barrel and repeated the procedure in a few days until the dye in the whelk was exhausted. She threw the remains to the cats.

Early one morning when Arrah had been a child, Debrogail and Arrah's grandmother had sung a beautiful song about a prince and a princess who had fallen in love. Unfortunately their fathers were warring kings. The prince and princess had agreed to meet one night in secret. But a great storm came. Disregarding the tempest both the prince and princess set out in small boats from their respective islands. The lovers' boats were swamped by waves, and they both drowned.

Because of their courage, the gods took pity on the lovers and turned them both into the shellfish called whelks, because purple was a mixture of blue, which symbolized faithfulness, and red, which was the color of passion and courage.

All during that morning Arrah had thought of the courage of the lovers, of the way they had braved the storm to be with one another, of the way her mother's sharp needle pierced the white vein. She thought of the darkness of the dyeing room and of the whelks in the small oak barrels and of the smell of broken shells.

That afternoon when Margaret lay down for a rest, Arrah called Debrogail and together the two girls struggled carrying the barrels of whelks back to the shore. The prince and princess hadn't been turned into creatures of the sea to be stabbed with needles and thrown to the cats.

But the girls, huffing and puffing, had just managed to carry the first barrel to the waves when Naira saw them and ran screaming for Margaret.

Margaret was furious. She ordered both girls back to the dyeing room. She spread dried, hard peas on the stone floor. "Now, you'll both be kneeling there and asking the good Lord forgiveness for your mischief. And you won't be getting off your knees until you're called for the evening meal."

As soon as Margaret closed the door Arrah and Debrogail got off the peas.

"Arrah, you're a stupid goose of Beelzebub," said Debrogail. She rubbed where the peas had left sore indentations in her kneecaps.

"If I'm a stupid goose of Beelzebub, then you're an even stupider goose of Beelzebub for helping me," said Arrah, also rubbing at her sore knees. "And Naira's a cowardly sneak."

"Oh, I'd like to make celery sauce of her," said Arrah.

They immediately began to rearrange the peas for a game of *togaim*. They set the peas in a circle and tried to shoot them out as if they were marbles.

They had been playing that game when suddenly steam started to rise from the stones. Arrah was delighted with the mist and wanted to lift the stone to see where it was coming from, but Debrogail, who was terrified, began to scream for Mistress Margaret.

As soon as Margaret saw the steam, she forgot the girls' punishment and shooed them from the chamber. Arrah and Debrogail were delighted to be free and ran off giggling.

Arrah hadn't thought of the incident in a long time. Seeing Debrogail standing with her blue-dyed legs made her think of it now. The rising steam in all likelihood had something to do with the dyeing process, a procedure which Arrah hated. Secretly she was grateful that she no longer was forced to participate in it. Debrogail, as a servant, was not so fortunate.

When Arrah had begun her monthly courses, Margaret had insisted it was unbecoming for Arrah as a woman to keep servants as her friends. Despite Margaret's protestations, the two young women managed to keep their friendship until Arrah's fourteenth summer, when Margaret had insisted that Debrogail call Arrah, "Mistress." The distinction of "Mistress" had put an impassable distance between Debrogail and Arrah over the years. It was a distance that Arrah still regretted, especially when she saw Debrogail laughing and she remembered how as girls they had shared their joy.

Suddenly Debrogail and Bres stopped laughing. "Bres, Bres! Where are you?" Naira called.

Bres ran off, disappearing into the bawn, where the cattle were kept.

Naira came out from the chapel and approached Arrah with her customary aloofness. Arrah noticed that her sister wore one of her finest dresses, a high-waisted gown of deep purple, blue, and silver. Naira's eyes, unlike Arrah's, were an unchanging, unyielding blue.

"Have you seen Bres?" Naira asked Arrah.

Arrah glanced at Debrogail, who was vigorously churning the rinsing water with her bare feet, her face downcast. "I think I saw him leave with Father earlier to take his eagles hunting," Arrah lied, seeing the hint of a smile on Debrogail's lips. She churned her feet faster in the wash.

"Why is it," asked Naira, "that every time a man shows an interest in me, Father takes him off hunting?"

"You can have my man," Arrah said. "He's betrothed me to the Joyce."

"I've had enough of your aged cast-offs," Naira said bitterly. "This time I've chosen my own man." Naira's dead husband had first asked for Arrah. When Arrah had refused, he'd asked for Naira. Naira had accepted.

"You don't know what chance you'll be missing, Sister. Father says the Joyce has plenty of metal in his sword," teased Arrah.

But Naira had never had much of a sense of humor. "Then you keep him," she snapped, walking back toward the chapel.

Arrah winked at Debrogail.

"Thank you, Mistress, for not telling about Bres and me." Debrogail smiled at her. Arrah had never grown accustomed to Debrogail calling her "Mistress," and even now it grated unnaturally on her ears. *You're a stupid goose of Beelzebub for falling for a man that Naira likes,* Arrah wanted to say. She wanted to recapture some of their childhood camaraderie. She wanted to talk to Debrogail about having to marry someone she didn't want to marry. "You'd better be careful," Arrah said solemnly. When Naira went into a fury, her wrath was unequalled.

Debrogail was serious too. "I know," she said. "But he liked me even before Mistress Naira set eyes on him."

Normally Arrah would have gone in the front doors of the castle, where she would have stopped to talk to Legless Paddy.

Legless Paddy had lost both legs in a shark attack when he fell overboard from one of Reevnarg's ships. When Arrah was a child, she spent hours with Legless Paddy listening to his stories of the sea and wind and stars. He used to make her small clay shapes, ducks, geese, dogs, and pigs, and even sailboats, which the cook would bake for her. She and Debrogail used to play with the figures.

Each time Paddy saw Arrah he would ask, "Lassy, is dhat duck dhat I was makin' for ye, will it be behaving now?"

She loved Paddy's game. "Yes," she answered with excitement.

When Arrah grew older she stopped playing with Paddy's animals. But he continued molding the small shapes. "Arrah, lassie? That ship I was makin' for ye. It won't be sinkin' now will it, but sailin' proper like?"

She had grown impatient with the game. "I don't play with toys any-more."

Paddy's eyes had brimmed with tears. "Nobody will be wantin' anything dhat Legless Paddy will be doin'."

"I was just joking you, Paddy," she'd said and had taken the small clay sheep from his fingers. After that, she'd started lying to him. "Yes! The lambs are all eating and growing." "Yes, the ducks'll all be swimming. The mother and all her little ones . . ." And each time his wrinkled face, ugly as a monkey's, would smile. She never had the heart to tell him that the small figures had become a nuisance and she threw them all out to sea.

Today Arrah didn't feel like humoring Legless Paddy, and headed for the back door.

She didn't know this person she was supposed to marry, but she knew she wanted no part of him. In ancient times women didn't have to marry the men their fathers chose for them. Her father's flagship was called the *Maeve*, named for the warrior queen of Connacht. The bards sang of her, told she would allow no man to love her until first he'd defeated her at swords. And how, if she loved one man, she always had at least two waiting in his shadow. Another of her father's ships was the *Skatha*. Skatha, too, was a woman warrior, skilled in all manner of warfare, fighting not only with sword and shield, but battle-ax as well. Why was it that the women of old were allowed to choose their own lovers and husbands? To live as they pleased rather than doing embroidery or dyeing cloth as her mother did. God's eyes, how she hated the gray drudgery of it all!

One of her father's great wolfhounds, Bran, whined and wagged his tail when he saw her. Tethered outside the kitchen, he stood taller than a colt, a gray-colored creature with coarse fur. Arrah petted him and he thrust his damp, cool nose into her hand.

A magpie, half-tamed on kitchen scraps, stood pecking a short distance away at a kitchen midden. It flew up, then teasing the dog, swooped down, its black-and-white wings a hair's breadth from the hound's fangs. Arrah remembered MacNamara's words. *You know the prophecy. There'll be Englishmen in Ireland as long as the magpies remain.* The magpie swooped again, but this time it misjudged distance. The hound leaped up against the tether, snapped shut its jaws. Before Arrah realized exactly what had happened, the dog, his muzzle covered with feathers and blood, was ripping the bird to shreds. Arrah looked away.

A nauseating stink like the smell from burning hair, but wet and soggy, filled the kitchen. The focal point of the room was a huge fireplace, twelve paces long and hung with cranes and black pots.

A rustling came from beside it. Arrah saw bare buttocks thrusting vigorously back and forth at what at first appeared to be the wall—a man's buttocks, and from the mousy, tattered hair at the back and the thin, sloped shoulders, she realized that the half-naked man was one of her father's sailors. But he wasn't thrusting against the wall. On his shoulders Arrah could see small fingers, and she heard a woman whining excitedly as the man rutted into her.

Nothing about the scene surprised Arrah. The servants and serfs and soldiers copulated with whomever they wanted, almost whenever they wanted. They changed husbands and wives as easily as a cow shed her coat each year in spring. The scullery wench could choose her own mate. The very sparrows and rooks chose their own mates, yet she, Arrah O'Donnell, had to marry someone her father had chosen for her.

"Bridgett!" Arrah shouted angrily. Startled, the sailor turned, his mouth open. Slightly behind him stood the scullery wench, a sulky, dark-eyed girl whose head scarf was all askew. Her face had a flushed expression as though she'd just run a race. Her skirts had fallen back down around her knees when the man had pulled away from her.

"What is that stink?" asked Arrah.

"It's the chicken feathers I'll be boiling." Bridgett straightened her head kercher and rubbed her hand across one breast. The sailor moved away toward the door, but Bridgett grabbed his hand, and pulled him back. She had very small white teeth, like a child's, that showed as she spoke. "The mistress, your mother. She was getting a grease stain on her gown. And it being her red one and one of her finest, she was telling me to take the stain out. And there won't be a better way of doing it, than scalded chicken feathers."

The smell made Arrah hold her hand over her nose. As she left the kitchen, she heard the movement of bodies behind her and Bridgett's giggle as the two resumed what she'd interrupted.

Margaret was not in the main hall, but her bag of sewing sat on a low table beside her chair. Scissors! Arrah reached for them, but pulled back her hand because Margaret entered just then with a tall, slender, gray-haired man and a younger man. Margaret wore a purple gown of flowing silk embroidered on the bodice with pure gold thread. The visitor had to be a man of importance.

From the posture of the older man, she could see that Margaret had charmed him. From the time that she was very young, Arrah had seen this effect that her mother had on men. With her hazelnut eyes Margaret seemed to enchant men, regardless of who they were or where they came from.

The older man's hair was gray, and his long beard was gray as well. His rich mantle and the gold brooch that pinned it marked him as a chieftain. The younger man had pale white hair and an arrogant, self-important bearing. He was a short man, shorter than Arrah, and he kept his right hand constantly on his sword handle.

"Arrah!" said her mother. "This gentleman wishes to be talking about you."

Arrah gave the stranger a sullen, dismissive look. What was her father going to do? Sell her off like a ewe at sheep fair to the highest bidder?

Her mother and the men came closer. "Arrah, child. This is Cormac, chieftain of the Joyce, and his nephew, Glundel, the tanaist."

Cormac reached for both of Arrah's hands in an effusive gesture of happiness. "Ah, Arrah, you look more lovely each time I lay eyes on you."

Arrah drew back and sent him a smoldering glance. So this was the old fool her father wanted her to marry. He looked like a limp horse to her—an unctuous one at that. And Glundel—a name which meant white knee—all he could do was hold his sword handle, as if an enemy were going to materialize in the air.

The Joyce cleared his throat lightly, and an uncomfortable, mildly bewildered look swept his face, but he regained his composure and turned to Margaret. "Your own good heart must swell with joy and pride each time your lovely eyes will be laying sight of her. But it'll be easy to see where she gets her beauty from. One has only to set eyes on the mother."

Margaret blushed deeply. The visitor bent close to her. "Oh, I haven't seen the likes of such a blush since I was a boy and teasing the girls when I came out of fosterage."

"And I'll wager you've had your share of teasing girls, from what I've been hearing."

"I've been blessed, yes, with good women. All of them. I've twelve of the loveliest daughters a man can want to call his. Lovely as the months of the year. Each one of them." He looked down for a moment. "Unfortunately, my wives . . . have not been strong of constitution. I lost my beloved Cathleen."

Margaret crossed herself. "May the Lord have mercy on her soul."

Arrah looked at him. "Perhaps if you'd spent less time putting babies in their bellies, they'd have been stronger."

"Arrah! I'll not be tolerating such rudeness. The Joyce didn't journey far to suffer insults!"

But the Joyce pressed his hand against Margaret's. "Now, sweet and gentle lady. Don't be reprimanding her. She's young and high-spirited as the young are wont to be. There'll be plenty of time for gentling."

Reevnarg entered the main hall, his voice booming his greeting. "Cormac, friend. Welcome! Welcome to my roof." He handed his bird to a servant with orders, "Feed him well. He's been worked today."

"My old friend!"

"Aye, if I could count some of the Irish clans as my friends the same as I do with you, Cormac, then I'd be a happy man," Reevnarg said. The two men clasped each other's forearms in the formal greeting of chieftains. Then they grasped each other's shoulders and stood smiling, facing each other.

Arrah was glad to see that the black-bearded Seaghan MacNamara had not come in with her father. With any luck he had fallen off the cliffs and was being eaten by sharks.

"Aye, Glundel, but there are lines of worry marking your uncle's face," said Reevnarg.

"Not lines of worry, but lines of sadness. My Cathleen is no longer of this world," Cormac answered for himself.

Reevnarg pulled him close and the two men hugged each other for a moment.

Cormac wiped at a tear that rolled down his cheek. "Aye! Heaven 'tis a more gracious place now that she's there. There wasn't a woman with a sweeter disposition in all of Ireland. When she was well 'twas she who woke the sun and the very birds each morning with her singing and greeting the day."

"Aye. A good woman can make the very hair on a man's head sing. Me own Maggie's no different, although two spoons in a wooden cup can be singing better'n she. Her mother. Now there was a woman with a voice. And the servant, Debrogail, she sings like an angel. But me Maggie. She can sing no better than a rook!" And he grabbed his wife's rump and slapped it then pinched it.

Margaret pushed his hand away.

Cormac continued. "Aye, 'tis her sweet voice that I miss the most. But her end was a relief to her. She had such terrible hurts in her stomach. We carried her to the place where there are the healing stones. Close to the well of Saint Patrick. We kept her there for three days, the warm stones pressing against her belly. They seemed to be bringing her some relief. But when we returned home, there was more pain again. She couldn't stand the rattling of a cart journey a second time and no amount of meadowsweet or syrup of the mallow plant could be taking away her suffering. Aye! Death, when it comes slow and wrought with pain, is a terrible thing. She was crying all the time from it, and the worst part of it being I couldn't be helping her at all. Just holding her hand, watching her beautiful face so wracked with anguish. Better to die quickly at the point of a foe's sword, than to die the way my Cathleen died. Her end when it came was a relief. The good Lord be forgiving me. . . . But she didn't deserve such suffering." And the Joyce crossed himself as did Reevnarg, Margaret, and Arrah.

Arrah watched the Joyce with a vague change of heart. She no longer hated the man, for he showed great feeling for his wife. She'd overheard sailors' conversations about women often enough. Their coarse slang.

"Mutton chop. Piece of bush." Never had she heard a woman spoken of in such endearing terms. She looked at him more carefully, and saw from his clean features that once he must have been a handsome young man. There was dignity and grace in his bearing.

Her father spoke again. "Well, man. She's not suffering where she is now!"

"Aye. They say 'tis ill luck to be grieving too much. Keeps the soul from passing to heaven. I know. And I sent Cathleen off with a goodly wake, much singing and dancing. But when a man's been with a woman for such a time, he can't help but be feeling a sting of melancholy."

"Well, then, 'tis another wife you'll have need of."

Arrah bit her lower lip. But this was not the time for anger. She knew what she had to do.

"Aye. 'Twould be nice if I could get me a son. I love my daughters. But a woman can't follow her father's steps as a chieftain." The Joyce put his arm around his nephew's shoulders. "Glundel has been named as tanaist and will follow me as chieftain. But if I were to have a son, then he in turn might follow Glundel."

It was Glundel who spoke now. "With Arrah's eventual inheritance of lands passed to her by her mother," Glundel smiled at Margaret, "the Joyce and O'Donnell lineage would prosper."

" 'Tis time my Arrah learns to accept a man too. She's unruly as a spring colt. It's not fitting for a woman to be so high-spirited. A good strong man, firm but gentle, covering them is what women need to keep their dispositions sweet. Maggie, have a chamber readied for Arrah and Cormac, and do with it what you do to ensure the coupling is successful. I would hate to give back a single one of Cormac's ships or his fine black cows because my daughter is barren."

But Margaret refused. " 'Tis Friday. And the Good Lord would be forbidding such a coupling on Friday."

"Cod's eyes, woman. Enough of your forbidding. I have a longing for a grandson. Aye, this news will be calling for a feasting. And in a few months when her belly swells, we'll have a wedding." He reached into his game bag and pulled out two doves. "Will you be seeing to it that the kitchen will be roasting this for my supper tonight? I've a tooth for pigeon."

"Surely you jest. Have you forgotten and even after my telling you? 'Tis Friday and the Father, the Son, the Holy Ghost, the Holy Virgin, and all the saints will be turning a deaf ear to your prayers if you'll be taking a bite of fowl this day."

"Arrch, woman. Will you be leaving off with your talking like Father Thomas. Surely, the Lord won't be begrudging a man a bit of wing when he'll be living on fish and oatcakes for a month at sea!"

"Husband, you're a heathen, and you'll roast in hell for your ways."

"After the sea, hell can't be such a terrible place."

Margaret crossed herself. "Bite your tongue, O'Donnell, before the good Lord hears you and strikes you dead from this earth."

"And tell the cook we'll have a mutton too. We'll not serve fish when Cormac comes to visit."

"No, friend. I won't be touching neither fowl nor flesh on Friday, Saturday, or Wednesday," said the Joyce.

"Since when did you grow frighted of the devil?"

"A man gets older . . . he begins to think. He sees the horrors of battle. He'd rather not pass to hell. Passing an eternity on a battlefield, fire and spears piercing his flesh for all time. I've enough of that. I'll leave hell to the young men. I'd like a chair in heaven for myself. Providing, of course, it's as lovely as Ireland. And they say it is."

"Of course it is. 'Tis exactly the same. Heaven 'tis nothing but the part of Ireland that didn't fall to earth!"

While her father and Joyce talked, Arrah took the scissors from her mother's sewing basket without anyone noticing. Then she smiled and knelt in front of her father and kissed his hand. "In the name of the Virgin and all the saints will you be forgiving me, Father, for my show of temper?"

He raised his thick eyebrows in surprise, then spoke. "Rise, Daughter, rise. Of course I'll be forgiving you." He reached his hand out to her and helped her to her feet, then put his arm around her. She nestled her head against his shoulder. "Daughter. But you're lovely when you're dutiful and gentle as a daughter should be. I tell you, Cormac, but you've cheated me. There's many a man who would be paying double the bride price for her."

"Aye. There are men who'll pay more for a wife, but then they'll be beating her worse than the beasts in a field. I'll treat her gentle," and he smiled at Arrah.

Arrah smiled back at him, and for the first time saw a warm friendliness in his brown eyes. Now she saw that one eye drooped more than the other. He had a scar above his right eye. It looked like a slice from a dagger or a sword. The old man was lucky to have kept his eye at all, for there were many who wore a patch over a hollow socket. There were other scars, too, on his face. He'd seen his share of battles.

"My father, I know I was mean-spirited and disobedient earlier on the hills. But I was angry not to be able to choose mine own husband. But now I've seen and spoken with Cormac, the Joyce, and see him to be handsome and honorable. Any woman would be pleased to be looked upon as his wife."

Arrah saw that her words had had their intended effect, for Cormac lifted his chin and stood taller. A large smile brightened her father's dark face. Arrah continued. "I accept and rejoice at the will of my father and my future husband." She bowed her head. "I beg forgiveness for my rude remarks earlier. They stem from anger at my father, and"—here she paused—"and because I'm a woman, and am given to fluctuations of temperament. Nothing would give me greater happiness than to share your bed this night, and allow your manhood to guide me on the journey from maiden to woman. But alas, I cannot, for I am with the moon. But with a few days wait, I assure you, I will accept you with much eagerness." She bowed her head again.

"Arrch, women and their courses. Whenever a man will be needing one, they're always in flux. 'Tis for that reason the ancients had more than one wife."

Glundel handled his sword.

"And 'tis the same reason some still choose to do so," said the Joyce.

"Aye, but the church won't be liking it. Go now, Daughter, and get you rest so that you're well for the desires of your future husband. Cormac, I sail tomorrow for the coasts of Spain and Africa, but when Arrah is able, take your desire with her. And may the angels and the saints be blessing your coupling. She'll have strong sons for you! I feel it in my bones. You'll be seeing for yourself, my friend, the curses of fishergirls are nonsense. Nothing but old wives' ramblings."

"Come then, Reevnarg," said Glundel smiling, but handling his sword again. "Since my uncle's thoughts are occupied with other things, let us again discuss the finer points of the bride price."

Arrah bowed and left the hall. She had what she needed.

CHAPTER 4

All the sounds of wakefulness, the harping, the singing, the dancing, the laughter had stopped at the Castle of the Eagles, but Glundel, lying beside his uncle, couldn't sleep. Because they were honored guests, both Cormac and Glundel had been bedded down in a private chamber with linen on the bed instead of just sleeping on the floor in the feast hall like the common sailors. The bed was comfortable enough, but his uncle snored like a roaring bear. Twice Glundel shoved his elbow roughly into Cormac's side; the old man had turned onto his side and the snoring subsided for a time, but since had started again. Old fool! He could crack him over the head now and be done with it, except it was better to wait until they were alone in some secluded area, and he could attribute Cormac's death to an accident. Glundel as tanaist would take over the chieftainship of the Joyce as soon as his uncle died. In the meantime, he would put on the face of devotion and loyalty.

Glundel had been plotting for months how to win the strategically located Eagle Island. Whoever controlled Eagle Island controlled the shipping up and down the west coast, and hence became wealthy. It was Glundel himself who had suggested to his uncle that he betroth himself to Arrah. The old man was a fool and he kept saying he was too old for Reevnarg's daughter. Only persistent flattery of the stupidest kind had made Glundel able to convince Cormac to ask for Arrah's hand in marriage.

In his mind Glundel reviewed yet again the terms of his uncle's betrothal to Arrah.

It had been a particularly complicated inheritance agreement, because Reevnarg had called upon his judges to reinstate an ancient ruling of Brehon Law. Brehon Law existed in Ireland in its fullness before the ninth century but became somewhat disturbed by intermarriage of the Irish with Norse and Anglo-Norman invaders.

In ancient times, under Brehon Law women were viewed as equals and had the same property rights as men. Over the years the laws had been modified. Women could own cattle and their own personal articles such as looms and cloth but not land, which was considered to belong to the chieftainship.

But Reevnarg had given Eagle Island to Margaret because of a bet.

She had some secret power to see into the future, and she foretold Reevnarg's bloody victory for the chieftainship of the O'Donnell. But the conditions of his leadership were that he had to attack during a full moon. Reevnarg said that only fools and madmen attacked during full moon in lit view of the enemy. In addition he didn't believe in predictions, curses, future-seeing, or auguring, all of which he called "scared wives' tales."

But Margaret was so certain of Reevnarg's winning the chieftainship that she made a bet with him. If her prediction turned out to be false, she was willing to divorce Reevnarg so he could marry someone else and try to have a son. However, if her prediction turned true, then he was to give her control of Eagle Island.

Her prediction came true; Margaret became Mistress of the Eagles, with Eagle Island passing in perpetuity to female offspring.

Originally Margaret had planned to bequeath the island to Naira, her eldest daughter. But when Arrah returned with Reevnarg's eagle, and the talon wounds on her arm, Margaret took it as a sign that Eagle Island should be willed to Arrah upon her death.

Arrah in turn would pass Eagle Island to her daughter.

However, if Arrah died without female children, the island would be transferred to the control of her husband's family. Those were the terms of the betrothal.

But Glundel did not have the slightest intention of abiding by them. The law stated that a woman had no right to a chieftain's property. As soon as Cormac died, Glundel had every intention of claiming Eagle Island in the name of the chieftainship of the Joyce. He had no intention of seeing Eagle Island slip from him because of some old law. Furthermore, he had every intention to see that Arrah O'Donnell died without children.

But he would have to be careful. He could not act openly; he would have to rely on secret means. Reevnarg had not been given the name "red circle" without reason. His ruthlessness was legendary.

The men of the O'Donnell clan were furious to be bypassed by a woman in their inheritance of the strategically located Eagle Island and made their obvious displeasure known to Reevnarg at an assembly. But Reevnarg stayed steadfast in his commitment to Margaret, and promised the O'Don-nell that if any man wanted to take Eagle Island from Margaret he would first have to face "the sword of Reevnarg."

One man protested, and Reevnarg threw him to the floor and cut his throat there. After that no one else dared protest Reevnarg's giving a woman control of Eagle Island.

And his uncle Cormac had agreed to every term of the betrothal, nodding his head like a drunken ewe.

The chieftainship! His uncle was nothing but a useless bit of wind. A duck fart. Weeping over a woman. Christ, how he hated women! The way they looked at him always, as if he were a piece of dog jank. He would show them. It was a stupid thing allowing a woman to hold property. When he became chieftain he would put Arrah O'Donnell in her proper place. Again he shoved his elbow viciously into his uncle's ribs.

Arrah slowly slipped from her bed. She wished there was some way she could quiet her heart. She was certain that its pounding could be heard throughout the castle as she felt her way down the narrow stone steps from the sleeping quarters on the third floor, down to the main feast hall. As her eyes grew accustomed to the darkness, she saw the shadowed bodies lying about asleep.

She was suffocatingly hot one moment, as though the pressure of her beating heart in her chest was keeping out the air. The next moment she felt cold as though a poker of ice had been jabbed in her spine.

She went out through the kitchen. She saw the faint embers still in the hearth. Bridgett was supposed to cover them with ashes each night to prevent the fire from burning out, but Bridgett obviously had other things on her mind: she slept with a man on some straw close to the fire.

Oatcakes lay strewn about the floor, and a bowl of sausages had been dumped off the counter. A rat nibbled at these, and when he saw Arrah, he hunched his back before scurrying away. Arrah bent down and picked up a couple of sausages and went out.

Remembering the woman buried in the castle foundations, Arrah hesi-tated. Previously her heart had beat with the fear of being discovered by one of the sleeping, snoring sailors or servants who would alert her father. Now a coldness went through her and she couldn't stop shivering. She felt as though she'd been touched by a small, stone-cold hand, as though the ghost-woman had reached out and touched her on the back, pleading not to be buried in mortar. She thought of what lay behind her, the certainty of marriage to the Joyce, and what lay in front of her, the uncertainty of a ghost in a courtyard. Better to avoid the danger that was certain rather than worry about the danger that was uncertain. Arrah continued.

She saw the full moon. It was a splendid moon, luminescent and silver, so full it looked as though it would burst.

She whistled so softly that she herself could barely hear. The two great wolfhounds, Bran and Cuch, let loose for the night, bounded up. Cuch pressed his wet nose into her hand as did Bran, each of them smelling the sausage and trying to eat it, but she grabbed it back from them and put it in her pocket.

Keeping close to the wall she scurried behind the bawn, where the animals were closed, the smell of cows and sheep rising into the night. She glanced up and from habit her eyes sought to make out forms among the thousands of stars. The Great Bear, with its two pointer stars showing Polaris, the star of the north, and the other constellations that Legless Paddy had pointed out to her night after night.

As Arrah approached the gate, she heard the voices of the guards coming from their small house.

She crept to the main gate, and touching it in the dark, felt her way along the rough, slivery timbers. They smelled of flaxseed oil. Carefully, she lifted the wooden bar. It moved ever so slightly without making any noise and she was hopeful she could simply lift it and leave. She held her breath and lifted again. A loud scrape of wood on wood broke the silence of the night. Arrah froze. The voices in the guard house were suddenly quiet. She heard a scuffle, saw the flicker of light as the guards picked up a torch and prepared to come outside.

She held the meat close to the muzzles of the dogs. Then waiting until she saw the form of the two guards come out, she threw the sausages as far as she could. The dogs scurried after them.

The guards were nearly knocked off their feet as the two enormous hounds bolted past them. The dazed watchmen followed the dogs to see what they were pursuing. Arrah lifted the bar and made her escape out the gate.

She headed south along the shore of Eagle Island, where the cliff face gave way to a beach. She could feel the day's heat on the stones under her bare feet.

To Arrah's left, the sea shimmered silver and black. The summer tide lifted, waves rose moon-silvered to the sky, then fell back, ebony, only to rise again, silvered by the moon. To the east, the black coast of western Ireland lay in the distance like a sleeping cat. Silver and black. It's what she loved best about the night—its extremes. God, how beautiful the sea was at night!

Like a thief she crept to the beach. In her pack, she carried a pair of trews, and the wide-sleeved tunic that men and boys wore. The night was a black cloak dressed with crystal stars. She touched the scissors in her pocket, and looked at the moon. Arrah had told her mother that she was suffering discomfort and was going to her bed. Margaret wouldn't bother to look for her until late morning.

Arrah looked back at the Castle of the Eagles, standing rectangular and severe, luminescent and silver. The full moon turned the gray ramparts of the castle into mysterious, wonderful structures, as though they had been carved from magic, silver stone brought from the moon itself.

Father Thomas visited Arrah each day to teach her Latin letters and the parables of Christ and the lives of the saints. He told her the story of the Roman martyr, Eugenia, who had cut her hair, put on male dress, and become abbot of a monastery in Egypt. It was the remembrance of this story, along with seeing her mother's scissors, that had given Arrah her idea.

Her father was sailing with three ships. She could see them moored some distance out in the bay, the silhouettes of their masts like branchless trees reaching to the moon. Her father's largest ship, the *Maeve*, was the lead ship. It was two-masted, with both a mainmast and a foremast, and carried the O'Donnell coat of arms. It was the same coat of arms that hung on the wall over her father's chair in the castle: an eagle turned full face, with wings, talons, and tail feathers all outstretched and the head looking over the bird's right shoulder. The eagle covered the entire shield, his talons gripping the O'Donnell motto: *In Hoc Signo Vinces:* In this sign conquer.

Arrah took the scissors from her pocket, put down the pack of men's clothes on the beach, then began peeling off her woman's clothes: the linen overdress, with its snug lace bodice, and the long smock underneath. She dug a hole in the sand, and buried her clothes, then covered them with a boulder. Now she stood straight and naked. The moon streaming down on her turned her clean strong shoulders to ivory. Her breasts rose like alabaster hills. She had a bold, moon-touched beauty. She stretched long, taut legs and dug her toes in the sand. Her hair fell in a thick mass of curl midway along her thighs. She felt its silk brush the bare skin of her back and her buttocks. During the day her chestnut hair was highlighted with red and gold. But now in the moonlight, the hair seemed deep and black as the night itself. The moon was shining lustrously on the water, and as Arrah stood there naked beside the sea, she felt as though she, the moon, and the sea were one being. If she married she would be kept from this.

She sat down in the cool surf, felt the exploring, powerful thrust of the sea between her thighs reaching higher and higher with every forward surge. What was it like to be loved by a man? To feel his movements between her thighs? To feel his weight pressing on her breasts? What made her mother cry out when her father was home? What had made Bridgett's face glow the way it did?

Indecision is the worst enemy of a chieftain, her father always said. *While you're taking time to flip your mind back and forth, your enemies will cut your throat.* She would not suffer a change of heart. She had made her mind up and would stay with her decision.

Arrah slid the scissors into her thick hair and began to cut. The side of her neck and her shoulder felt suddenly cool and vulnerable. She stopped cutting and touched her neck, feeling an inexplicable sense of doom, a kind of tightening around her neck as though some terrible fate awaited her. She recalled the curse against the O'Donnell family: there would be no male heirs until a woman was hanged by her lover. Her father didn't believe in curses: neither would she. The dark hair had fallen into the alternately dark and moon-silvered sea.

The sea surged and carried her cut tresses away.

She couldn't take a currach to the ship, because the noise from the paddles might alert one of the watches posted on board. She would have to swim out to either the *Mary* or the *Skatha*, for her father was captain on the *Maeve*. On board, he was merciless. She knew the stories of what he did with disobedient sailors. She would smear her face with tar and disguise herself amongst the crew of one of the other ships.

From the pack of men's clothes she pulled a long, thin piece of torn bed linen. This she began to wrap tightly over her breasts to flatten them. Around and around she wrapped it. Then she pulled on the *léine* and the leggings and attached a dagger at her waist and plunged into the sea.

Often, as Margaret sat sewing, her needle moving like a flash of silver light in her fingers, she used to tell Arrah stories. Margaret's people were said to be descendants of the mer people. Her great-grandmother had lived in the O'Sullivan castle, but then later took to spending more and more time in the caves of Kerry that echoed like the belly of the sea. Some said that she was mad. Others said that she was a witch.

When Arrah was small she used to pretend that she was a mermaid swimming under the water with both her legs together as though they were a tail. Once, Arrah thought she'd seen a mermaid under the waves. It was just a gray, bleary form she felt more than saw passing. She'd surfaced and shouted to Naira and Debrogail that she'd seen a mermaid, but Naira called her a liar. Naira had never joined her in any play and called her games a stupid waste of time. Debrogail swam out with Arrah and together they had looked for the mermaid, but they had never found it.

It was wonderful underwater. There was no sound at all except her own breath as she expelled air a little at a time.

But now something made Arrah surface. It wasn't that she'd run out of breath as much as felt something. She began treading water and looked out over the black and silver sea. She listened. She saw the dark outlines of her father's ship bobbing in the near distance. And then she saw something else. The unmistakable silver fin of a shark gliding between her and the *Skatha*. For a moment she tread water silently.

Sharks couldn't see very well, but they had keen ears and could smell better than dogs. They could smell blood in the water up to five hundred arm lengths, and they could hear the splash of a swimmer even farther. What bit of luck had made her swim underwater tonight instead of on top. She would know in a moment if the shark had heard her when she surfaced.

She was a long way from the shore. There was time to reach her father's ship. But if he discovered her there, what would he do? Tie her to the mainmast, whip her, and keelhaul her? Tie her to the top of the mast with the goat carcass and leave her without water to die of thirst? He'd done these things to others.

The shark turned and began to glide toward her. Arrah dove.

Terror served her well. She'd never swum so fast; but speed took its toll. She couldn't sustain her breath and had to surface. As she did so a small wave caught her in the mouth and she coughed. She saw the fin gliding closer in the water. And beyond it another one. And close to it, a third, now coming at her, swimming in a straight, deliberate line.

Father or no father, she had no choice now. The *Maeve* loomed large in front of her, its mast spearing the moon. She reached the starboard. She could feel the sharks. Couldn't hear them or see them, but knew they were there. If she could reach the anchor cable, she could pull herself up. Faster now, but the sea seemed to pull at her arms like glue. She felt movement in the water behind her, knew that the shark was close, his fin like a sword in the water. It came at her, a flash of moonlight. She kicked at it with all her strength. Water slowed her legs. She connected with the shark's side, heavy but not solid, skin rough like a huge cat's tongue. She was thrust forward with the effort. Felt the anchor cable in the water. Grabbing it, she pulled herself up. Beneath her the silver shark fin circled, turning in the water, looking for prey. One hand over the other, the hemp cutting her hands, she pulled herself closer to the top.

Her breath came in sharp bursts and her knuckles burned as she slid over the gunwhale and slumped down limp on the deck. She blew her breath out and breathed in the tar smell of the ship. Her breath was loud: she felt the steps coming along the deck before she heard them.

Scurrying about she looked for a place to hide. Earlier she'd been thankful for the full moon, for it allowed her to see clearly her way down to the beach, but now she regretted it for all the deck lay exposed. On the fo'c's'le, hemp rope coiled like sleeping snakes; barrels of fresh water stood guard like lazy, fat sentinels, and currachs lay overturned. Quickly she slid down on her belly, hiding between a barrel and the hull. The steps came closer. Pulling the rope up over her face so as not to let the moon reflect, she tucked her chin down into her chest. The steps were close now, the easy pad of bare feet on wood. Her breath was too loud.

The footsteps moved away. Arrah felt her shoulders and the small of her back sink with relief against the deck.

Sailors would be coming aboard at the first redness of dawn to prepare for sailing.

Quietly she moved from the stern toward the center of the ship, found the hatch leading to the hold and peered into the profound blackness. Her eyes would grow accustomed to it in a moment, and feeling her way she climbed down the ladder. She pulled the hatch cover silently over her.

Up on deck the air had been fresh with the sea. Here in the hold there was nothing but the close, stale stink of wet wood, of blackness and compression, of moist salt and tar and dead cockroaches. She waited for her eyes to grow accustomed to the darkness, but it was so dark, there was no seeing. Like a blind man, she touched her way along the rough, stacked barrels of salt fish. Against her palms she felt the metal bands that held them together and the seams in the wood where individual boards joined. Then the barrels gave way to another feel, to the smooth, tanned hides of cattle. These in turn gave way to the bundles of rough woolen frieze. But as she touched the taut ropes of bundling, she was overcome with a heavy feeling of sleepiness, as though her head weighed too much for her body, as though her legs were going to collapse. During the encounter with the sharks, every nerve in her body had been alert. Now in the quiet, warm stink of the ship's hold she relaxed. She crawled up onto a bundle of frieze. The smell of the scratchy wool covered her, comforted her like a blanket. She laid her head down and slept.

In her dream a rope was being tightened about her neck. She tried to scream but there was no sound. She tried to fight the ropes that tied her hands behind her body, and flung herself awake. She realized where she was, and then the wool smell drew her again into sleep.

Dawn came unnoticed to Arrah. She didn't hear the trudging of feet across the deck above her. But in her dream, sailors were dancing a hornpipe. A dark, bearded stranger came and pulled her close, and spun her around and around in a dizzying whirl, and wouldn't allow her to stop dancing. In her dream he pulled her away to an alcove and there he pressed her against the wall. She could hear his breath coming closer and closer.

A sharper noise, a quick, opening slam of wood, jarred Arrah from sleep as someone opened the hatch. In a moment she was awake and blinking against the stream of light. She saw the hairy shins of a sailor come down the rungs of the ladder. The sailor was whistling.

CHAPTER
5

Glundel Joyce fingered the handle of his sword as he looked out on the drizzling sky from the window of the O'Donnell castle. A gray moth crawled along the edge of the sill. Wings damp with moisture, it couldn't fly. Glundel picked it up, tearing one wing from the moth. At that moment Margaret entered the main hall. Smiling at her, Glundel dropped the moth to the ground, then rubbed the dust from his fingers.

Despite the shadows beneath Margaret's eyes, her imperial bearing had not changed. God, he hated that superior attitude in women. Nonetheless, he knew well the words women liked to hear.

"Ah. Dear lady. How very lovely you look. If I were to be the husband of such a beautiful lady, I doubt that I would ever leave her side to sail the ocean."

"You flatter me too much, Glundel."

"If you were my wife, then I would do nothing all day but bestow compliments on you."

Margaret said nothing. She had never liked Glundel. She didn't know exactly why. Outwardly he seemed pleasant enough. But she had her feelings even though the secret dream pool in the chamber where she dyed her cloth had failed to tell her anything. She'd seen dangerous men in her husband's employ, men who fought and killed because of a wrong glance. But there was something in their ferocity that was forthright, whereas Glundel seemed calculating and devious. He had a slinking, insolent pride.

"Tell me, dear lady, has there been any word of Arrah?"

At the mention of her daughter's name, the shadows under Margaret's eyes seemed to deepen.

"This morning one of the fishermen dragging his currach along the beach dug up her skirt and these." Margaret showed him the scissors. "She always was a *cailin*, a tomboy. I've naught to believe except that she's sailed off with her father."

"A woman at sea!"

"You won't be knowing my daughter." Margaret sighed. "The Lord have mercy on them." It was considered bad luck to have a woman on ship. Margaret had gazed in the dream pool and later she had dreamed of a bark, a vessel of such splendor never to have sailed the west coast of Ireland. Its polished wood was inlaid with gold, and a hundred men oared each side. A woman was at the helm, robed in purple gold and silver. But when the woman turned around, her face was a skull. "I've already told your uncle," Margaret continued.

The door opened again and the Joyce entered. "Come along, Glundel. It's time for a silly old man to be returning to his castle."

"You'll not leave without proper provisions for your journey," Margaret said. "I'll be seeing that the cook readies you something."

"Thank you, dear lady," and Cormac bowed his head as Margaret left the hall.

"Return!" said Glundel with disbelief. "Surely you jest, Uncle." He rubbed the handle of his sword.

"Nay, son of my sister. 'Tis no jest. But the better wisdom of a foolish old man. Aye, when I was looking on Arrah and the fire that burns within her, I was desirous of her youth. When a man gets old, he comes to thinking that a young woman is like a fountain of youth, where he'll be dipping and coming out rejuvenated like a young buck." The Joyce gazed out the narrow window to the sea beyond. "Let the young go with the young. A new sail on an old ship still makes for an old ship. New canvas, but the timbers'll be rotting. No, come, Glundel. We'll off this day. I've twelve daughters and a fine nephew. And the good Lord be forgiving me for thinking that I needed another young wife to assist me in my dotage. I regret letting you talk me into asking for her hand."

"Dotage. Uncle, surely the honor of the Joyce demands that the terms of your agreement with the O'Donnell be met."

"The marriage was drawn between two foolish old men. Men who had forgotten the determination of the young. Aye, 'tis the old that think with their heads, but they'll be forgetting that the young think with their limbs."

"I refuse to see the clan honor of the Joyce so ridiculed by a . . . self-important hogminny."

"Choose your words better, Glundel. She's the daughter of my friend."

"Friend! Old man. You call the O'Donnell friend. He takes your cows and then takes his daughter."

"Reevnarg is a man of honor. He'll return the cows."

"I'll wager he's plotted against you. He'll have your cows *and* his daughter, and you'll be left to look like an old fool."

The Joyce put his arm around Glundel's shoulder. "Aye, Nephew, but you're young and impatient."

Glundel shook off the arm. "Impatient! Bah! As you get older, you forget what honor is. This isn't your honor alone. 'Tis mine as well. Mine as tanaist of the Joyce, soon to be chieftain."

"What ridicule is it for a man to grow wise?"

"Wise! Allowing your betrothed to slip from your grasp is wisdom? Then God grant. I'll willingly play the fool in your stead."

"Glundel. You're blood of my blood. You're the son of my sister and yet sometimes I wish it were not so, for you are rash. Affairs of the heart can never be satisfied with a sword."

"My uncle, chieftain of the Joyce, is a coward, and speaks with a coward's tongue."

"Glundel, listen," and he put his arm around the younger man's shoulders again.

"I'll not listen!" He threw the arm off. "You're a chieftain. And you'll continue to act so or someone else will act it in your stead," and drawing his broadsword, he flashed it in front of his uncle.

In a swift movement that took the young man completely by surprise, the Joyce drew his sword and held its point to Glundel's throat. "Do not be pressed to draw against me, Nephew. This body has not survived many battles without learning the ways of the sword. You'll listen—"

"I've ordered provisions—" Margaret drew open the door to the chamber, but when she saw the altercation, she closed it quickly.

"You'll listen," the Joyce continued. "You're not chieftain yet, and if you won't hear me as your uncle, you'll hear me as your chieftain."

Glundel felt the bitter taste of humiliation rise sour in the back of his throat. The old man had humbled him. Worse, he had done it in front of a woman. His hand closed more tightly against the cold metal of his sword.

"Drop the sword," the Joyce said.

Glundel lowered his arm, and the Joyce nodded in approval. "It's youth that makes you rash. I was exactly the same. Isn't it lovely to be young and have so much spirit?" Sheathing his weapon, he called out loudly, "My dear Margaret, come in. What fools men are to chase women from a room with their tedious haranguing of swords." He sheathed his weapon.

Margaret looked askance at Glundel. "I would my daughter have less of spirit, and more of common sense."

"Have no fear. She'll return to you. A daughter always returns to her mother. I'm to blame. 'Twas I who chased her away with my eagerness. 'Tis strange. I have no sense of being older. I leave my bed a little slower now in the morning, but my arm is still good with a sword. And yet when I see the young"—he looked at Glundel—"when I see them next to me, I'm forced to admit that I grow old. And though I condemn it as rashness"—he touched his nephew's arm—"it's their fire that I envy. An old man is like an ember. His fire is steady. But youth is like the first fire. Sparking and flaring."

"But is it not more comfortable close to an ember fire than to a crackling one, where one is always having to brush away the flying sparks from one's mantle?"

"Perhaps you're right, dear lady. And I'll take comfort for my old bones against the solid rump of a concubine."

Glundel listened with outward calm to the old fool. Inside he seethed.

"But enough of talk," said the Joyce. "I want to look upon Reevnarg's eagles one more time if you'll allow me to do so. And then we'll be off."

Glundel bowed his head. This time he would wait. But he would not forgive the old man for humiliating him.

"Surely. Reevnarg would be honored to know you're so appreciative of his birds. The cook is preparing a fare for you. It'll be ready as soon as you are," said Margaret.

"I'll wait here for you, Uncle."

Margaret walked about the room checking the amount of fish oil in the lanterns. Lately Bridgett had been neglectful of household duties and yesterday one of the torches had burned out.

Glundel watched Margaret from the back, and came so close behind her that her gown dragged across his toes.

Margaret turned around suddenly. "Glundel, you startled me!"

She tried to step back from him, but the wall prevented her. With one hand she reached back, feeling the tapestry that hung there.

"Let me pass, Glundel. I've no time for games with young men who have no respect for their own chieftains."

So, this cow's bitch had heard the old fart upbraid him. "You'll have time for me soon enough when I'm chieftain, dear lady." He lifted his hand to touch her cheek, but she turned away from him.

"You'll not be fondling me as you would a common kitchen wench, or I'll call for the guard. Remember you're under the roof of the O'Donnell."

"Aye, and the O'Donnell is gone now and left his woman alone. Do you wait for the O'Donnell's return?"

"Let me pass!"

"Do you not have need of a man while he's away?"

"Surely, Glundel, you're not suggesting what my ears are telling me you're suggesting."

"Suggesting! Dear lady, of course I'm not suggesting. 'Tis merely inquiring I am, as to whether or not a woman such as yourself would be feeling the need of a man. Perhaps you could be caring for a little intimate company before my uncle and I leave. I know that my uncle would be more than—"

"You're making a mockery of the chieftainship of the Joyce, and you're making a mockery of the laws of hospitality."

Glundel turned away from her irritably. "I don't understand why my uncle favored your Arrah. I'm not fond of women with brown skin."

"Then I trust you'll marry someone whose skin is as white as your desire."

"But I *am* married, dear lady. Do you not know my wife? She is called Branwen. Branwen O'Donnell. The youngest daughter of one of your own husband's kinsmen."

Margaret hesitated as though recalling something and then frowned. "Branwen . . . Her mother must be mad, her father, too, to allow such a thing."

"She has a cleft palate. I asked for her hand. Her parents knew full well if I didn't marry her, no one else would. It's bad luck to have an unmarried daughter."

"She's just a child!" said Margaret.

"A woman is like an ozier twig used for baskets. If the twig is too old then it can't be bent to the proper use."

Margaret was angry. "Yes, but when one weaves a basket one uses properly seasoned twigs and not the first buds themselves."

"But a bud is not a woman. And a woman has to learn her purpose early. A girl is easier than a woman, as my uncle has sadly discovered. I didn't wait for the bird to find its wings, but possessed it before it had a chance to fly from me."

"You're detestable!"

"I lack the patience or the foolishness of my old uncle. I would that my women were suppliant."

"Nay, Glundel. 'Tis not a woman that you'll be wishing for, poor child that she is. Poor donkey, humping her back to your lust."

"She's old enough to know what's expected of her. Unlike your daughter who, it seems, is of a disposition to take liberties of which she has no right."

"Arrah is her father's daughter. If you know my husband, then you know how she came to her headstrongness."

"I know nothing of your daughter except that she has failed to meet her obligations to my uncle as his wife. I will not sit by idly and watch as my uncle is made to be an object of ridicule. His mind grows addled in his dotage and he becomes oblivious to what the other clansmen will say."

"Your uncle is wise and far from his dotage. I council you to mind his words."

"And I council you to tell your daughter when she returns that she is betrothed to my uncle. The laws of betrothal are as binding as those of marriage. I leave you now, dear lady." Bowing, he departed abruptly.

Margaret suddenly felt a sense of frustration and helplessness, which left her even angrier. She remembered the empty light sconces and feeling her color rise, called Bridgett.

Glundel, hearing the tone of Margaret's voice, stopped outside of the main hall. Bridgett had earlier given him a sulky, despising look. If she had been his servant he would have beaten her. But now he realized there were possible gains to be made in this strife between mistress and servant. Glundel slunked back into the main hall, hid behind the wall and peeked into the kitchen where Margaret was standing.

"Debrogail, where's Bridgett?" Margaret asked.

"I don't know." Debrogail shook her head, but her eyes inadvertently went to the stairway leading upstairs to the chambers.

Margaret noticed a pale-gold silk kercher lying on the floor. She picked it up and put it in her pocket. Her voice was like the ice that formed on small pools in the winter. "Was Bridgett wearing my kercher?"

"I don't know." Debrogail shrugged. "I don't—"

Margaret picked up her skirts and ran up the stairs to her chambers. Glundel snuck behind her.

Wearing a gold silk dress that obviously belonged to her mistress, Bridgett stood looking in the mirror in front of her. The bondswoman saw her mistress's reflection in the mirror and turned. Glundel caught a glimpse of the servant. In the fine clothes she had a young, hesitant attractiveness.

"Filthy doxy!" screamed Margaret, ripping the gown down the front.

"You'd copulate with the dogs if they could but ask! You dare put my robes next to your wretched skin."

Glundel saw that Bridgett had almost nonexistent breasts, the kind he liked.

"And my gold bracelets too. Take them off this moment!"

"Yes, mistress," said Bridgett, but her voice was flat.

"Minx! For the next fortnight, you'll sleep in the bawn with the sheep and cattle."

"Yes, mistress!" Bridgett's servile words were sibilant with resentment.

Glundel stopped listening and quickly and silently left the corridor. The Brehon Laws of hospitality were such that Margaret couldn't refuse him lodging if he wished it. He searched out his uncle. After a repentent display of deference and politeness Glundel told the Joyce that he was going to stay a few more days at Eagle Castle to see if Arrah would have a change of heart. Glundel grasped his uncle to him and kissed his cheek and wished him good journey home.

The bawn was moist, warm, and shady and filled with the smell of hay and animals. Wooden mangers lined the walls. In one section a pile of hay was fenced off by rough boards.

Bridgett sat on the hay, a rough shawl wrapped around her. A rust-colored chicken pecked at the ground a short distance from her feet. Bridgett kicked it and sent it flying.

"Bridgett," Glundel spoke softly.

Bridgett lifted her sulky, wolfish eyes.

"What do you want?" she said.

"I've been looking for you."

"Everybody's always looking for me," she said caustically.

"Have you been crying?" He touched her cheek.

She pulled away. "No!"

"It was despicable of your mistress to treat you so. My servants have lovely clothes."

"Mistress has hundreds of dresses. She has so many she wouldn't even notice if I were to take one."

"I can give you beautiful dresses," he said.

"What sort?" she asked.

"Sort? Any sort. Any color. Silk. Satin. If you do something for me, I'll bring you dresses."

"The sailors always promise me dresses and nice things when they come home. But they never bring anything but common trinkets and tatters!"

"I'm not a common sailor," he said, "but tanaist to the Joyce. A tanaist's word is sacred. If he gives it, he must keep it."

"You can put your hand here," and she opened her rough shirt to expose her breasts for him. Before he could do anything, she'd taken his hand and brought it to her small dark nipple.

He hated dark nipples and couldn't look at them. He kept his eyes on her face. "Do you like it when men touch you?" he asked.

"I let men touch me if they promise to give me something."

"You're a friendly sort, aren't you?"

"How many dresses will you bring me?"

He pulled his hand away from her. "I'll bring you one to start."

"Two!"

"And if you do as I ask, I'll bring you more. I promise."

She eyed him. "And you won't go back on your word."

"No."

"I'll do it."

"That's my little chicken," he said, pinching her cheek.

She grabbed his hand and pulled it up between her thighs. He was revolted, but he didn't draw away his hand. She opened her legs for him. He couldn't stand to look there, so instead he looked at her eyes. She had a face like a sulking child who had just scored a victory. She lay down in the hay spreading herself, but he grabbed her hips sharply and turned her over. He closed his eyes and felt his way with his fingers before he plunged in.

CHAPTER
6

When Arrah saw the sailor coming down to the hold, she clambered back on the pile of frieze as quickly as she could, but her foot hit against a barrel, knocking it to the deck floor with a resounding crash.

"What the devil!" came the sailor's voice.

Arrah slid down into the space at the back between the hull and the load of frieze. She landed with a thud on the deck floor.

The sailor cursed. " 'Od's blood. Soon we'll be sailing with rats the size of calves."

A glimmer of light traveled across the ceiling of the hold. The sailor was carrying a lantern.

The light came closer and Arrah pulled herself in. The inside of her foot began to itch, but there wasn't room for her to bend down to scratch it. The itching intensified under her arch as though a nettle were being pressed under the skin. The sailor continued shuffling and cursing on the other side of the frieze. She rubbed one foot silently against the other, but her foot slipped and hit the bulwark.

The sailor stopped. She heard the clink of a sword blade pulled from its sheath. The lantern flicker came closer. The sailor was going to climb the pile of frieze. Arrah's stomach growled. She held her breath and pressed her fingers into her gut to stop the noise.

"Who's there?"

Arrah imagined herself becoming smaller and smaller, almost being sucked invisibly into the frieze, becoming part of the cargo herself. The ship rolled easily, the sound of the sea washing against the hull, and she saw the cast of lantern light turn away. She leaned against the bulwark in silent, breathless relief.

"Cursed, filthy beasts!" Arrah heard the thud of a sword against a timber as the sailor tried to spear a rat and missed.

The rat leaped up onto the hides, then across Arrah's head, its four feet clawing at her hair before it ran down her body and scurried away on the deck floor. Arrah shrieked.

This time the lantern approached much faster. Arrah tried to pull her skin inside herself. She could feel the lantern throw its strong glare over her body. She felt cold metal come down, thrusting at her. Enough was enough.

"Carbri O'Connor," she said angrily, "I didn't come to sea to be stabbed to death the first day out."

There was utter and complete silence from Carbri, but the sword was withdrawn instantly. Arrah heard the ship creak.

"Carbri, are you going to help me up?"

Carbri O'Connor was certain he'd heard a ghost. He was betrothed to Agneis de Burgo. His stepsister, Finola, had arranged the marriage, but he'd been thinking of Arrah, in fact had been thinking of nothing else for days, the way her eyes had smiled at him during the feast. When he'd danced with her, he'd felt her trim waist, her breasts against him, and he wanted to touch them. At night he tossed in his berth as his groin ached for her. Spirits knew what was on a man's mind. Now they were using Arrah's voice to trick him.

Arrah tried to grab the cords to pull herself up but there was no space between the frieze and the bulwark to bend her arms and get leverage.

"Carbri!"

Carbri pretended not to hear anything. He was not going to allow the spirits to trick him.

"Carbri, you're a mean-minded sailor. Are you going to leave me here to starve to death and be food for the rats, or will you help me up?"

The voice didn't sound like a spirit. Spirits didn't concern themselves with starving. Cautiously Carbri lifted the lantern and peered down into the space. "Arrah!" he whispered.

"Don't gawk like a fool! Help me up!"

"How was it you came to be down there?"

"The rats packed me down here so as to nibble on me when they tired of the wood. Now give a hand!" she ordered rather than asked.

"Can't you be climbing up?"

"If I was able to climb up, do you think I'd be asking a dumbstruck sailor to help me?"

He reached down and she grasped his hand. She stood on the tips of her toes and tried to climb up, making little sideways-upward reaches with her feet. But there were no toe holds. "I can't get up. Give me your other hand. Now pull!"

Carbri pulled. When she was halfway out, he grasped her buttocks to help her the rest of the way.

When she turned over, he stared at her incredulously. Her hair was cropped short. In the glow of the lantern the wide cheekbones seemed more sculpted than ever, the sultry eyes more dark in their determination. God's eyes, even with an androgynous kind of beauty she was a devil of a woman.

"Arrah, what is it you've done to your hair?" He reached out to touch it, but she drew away.

"What does it look like I was doing to it? Haven't you got eyes in your head to see with? I cut it off. I want to be a sailor."

"A sailor! God's blood, Arrah! And what is it Reevnarg'll be saying when he sees you?"

"How's he going to see me if you don't tell him?"

"He'll see you. He'll find you. You can't stay. We'll get a small boat and row back to Eagle Island."

"I didn't come out to go back!"

"You can't be staying here!"

"Why not?"

"Someone'll be finding you."

"You wouldn't have found me if I hadn't taken a fright from the rat. It scared me half to death."

"Pshaw! 'Tis a fine sailor you'll be making, scared half to death of a rat."

"I didn't know what it was," she defended. "You'd be scared too!"

Carbri's hazel eyes glowed in the light of the lantern. A halo of light circled gold around him almost like illustrations Arrah had seen of the saints. Except that Carbri's eyes hadn't the look of a saint.

He kept looking at her breasts. "And what was it you've done to yourself? The other night at the feasting you weren't flat. Have you cut them off too?"

"Fool! Of course not!" Her stomach growled unceremoniously.

"God's blood. Your belly creaks like a gate."

"Your belly would creak, too, if you were hungry!"

"I'll be bringing you some oatcakes. . . . Arrah! Your beautiful hair. Do you know that after I danced with you I dreamt that night I saw you running naked through a field of clover, your hair streaming about you. And then you came flying into my arms."

She ignored his words. "Will you have anything to drink on this ship?"

The swim and the frenzied effort of escaping from the sharks had left her throat parched.

" 'Twas a foolish thing you've done."

" 'Twas an easy thing, Carbri. Cut my hair or spend the rest of my days locked in with embroidery and threads."

"Will this be more freedom for you? The dark hold of a ship?"

"I'd a thousand times rather be in the hold of a ship than in bed with the Joyce."

His fine eyebrows lowered in a frown. "Your father wished you to be marrying the Joyce?"

Arrah nodded.

Carbri looked down. "And here you make your bed with rats."

"The Joyce has rats at his castle too. Now be bringing me something to eat and drink. How can I be spending time at the oars if my stomach is empty?"

"You can't be going up on deck. You'll have to be staying down here. I'll bring you your food and drink, and then when we reach France, I'll buy you proper passage home. The Joyce is a wise man. He won't be forcing a woman to stay with him against her will."

"But I can't smell the air or see the sun from down here."

"You can't be seeing the sun from the bottom of the ocean either, which is where the sailors'll be throwing you when they find you."

"I'll smear my face with tar, and wear a hat when I'm at the oars."

"Look at you." He grabbed her hands and turned them over. "These won't be the hands of a sailor. They're a woman's hands!"

She felt a surge of something deep within her, a feeling she'd never had before, as though here in the closed darkness of the ship, she wanted him to do more than just touch her hands. She didn't pull away. He sat cross-legged in front of her, and she saw the outline of his manhood pressed against the tight knit of his trews. He stroked her palms with an easy regular motion.

"Do you remember, Carbri, how when we were children, we oared currachs in the bay? How we used to pretend we were sailors? Remember how we jumped, you and I, naked into the sea?"

"Arrah, we were children then." He stopped stroking her palm and reached up to touch her chin. He looked at her breasts. "We're not children anymore. We can't be playing childish games." He wanted to touch her, he wanted to touch her skin, her breasts, all of her. During the past days, when he'd been close to her, it had been all he'd thought about: the way her head was thrown back when she laughed; the high tilt of her chin when she talked; the sultry eyes, always with a hint of challenge. He'd seen how a woman's eyes softened after lovemaking. He wanted to soften her eyes with love. "You could be blackening your face with a dozen barrels of tar, and still 'twould show that you're a woman."

"I'll not be called a weakling. You know well enough from when we were children, you couldn't throw me to the ground. You had an easier time defeating the other boys than me."

"I've done my turn at the oars. I wouldn't be finding it hard now to be pressing your shoulders to the ground and holding them there for as long as I wished."

She looked at him and knew he was right. She had sensed his strength the nights past when they'd danced together, the way he kept pulling her against him. Here in the hold of the ship she wondered what it would be like to be kissed by Carbri O'Connor. But she forced the thought from her mind.

"A turn at the oars will help chase away the girl in me."

"There's only one thing to chase away the girl in you, and it won't be the oars."

"Stop looking at me like a stag in rut!"

"How else will you be expecting a man to look at you?" He reached to touch her cheek.

She cast his hand away. "Bring me some food and drink. I'm hungry."

Carbri noticed the dried blood on her leg and reached out to touch it. "You injured yourself coming on board."

"A shark," Arrah said. "He tried to eat me."

Carbri looked at her with fascination. "Arrah, what a girl you are!"

Reevnarg's voice shouted down through the hatch. "O'Connor. Have you fallen to sleep?"

Arrah leapt to the bulwark and flattened against it. Carbri jumped off the frieze. "Aye, Captain. I was just on my leave up, sir." He whispered to Arrah. "I'll be coming back." He lifted the lantern to see her better. "You'll be leading a life of dangerous choices, Arrah, girl. Sharks and Reevnarg!"

"O'Connor!"

Carbri scurried up the ladder.

"What the devil was keeping you?" Reevnarg bellowed.

"Rats."

"Rats, was it?" Reevnarg looked at Carbri's trews. "A bit of bone like that in your bodkin. I'll be wondering but you weren't jigging the timbers. And us not gone even a morning's sail!"

The hatch slammed down suddenly, and Arrah was again left in complete darkness.

She reasoned that with at least forty men on board, she would not be detected as long as she kept from her father's sight. She ran her fingers along the hull of the ship and smeared her face with tar, then climbed the ladder up to the deck and daylight.

Carbri blanched when he saw her. "Take yourself back to the hold," he whispered. "I'll be bringing you what you need."

"You can be bringing me food and drink, Carbri, but you can't bring me the wind nor the sun!" She stood against the bulwark, her face turned to the wind so that it would blow the smell of the hold from her.

Carbri stared at her, at the splendid profile, at the high head, the straight back. Here with the wind and spray full in her face, she had a disarming look, as though she'd always been at sea, as though she were in some strange way a part of it.

"If anybody'll be asking you, you're my clansman and I brought you aboard. You're Padraic, the swab boy. And if you're to be a swab boy, then to work. Back to the hold. I'll be wanting to see a pail of rats killed and thrown overboard, and then I'll be wanting you to clean after the cats and rats down there."

Arrah's eyes were the same color as the spray on the sea. "I didn't come to sea to be locked in the hold."

"I'm the ship's second. If you won't be following my orders, I'll tell Reevnarg you're on board."

She sent him a smoldering look, but did as she was told. After she filled a pail with dead rats she carried the pail up on deck to throw its contents overboard.

Her father's voice boomed behind her like a cannon. "Take up the slack in the sail, you fool. She's wagging loose as your grandfather's tongue."

"Aye, sir," shouted a seaman.

Pulling her mantle up over her head, Arrah shrunk under the gunwhale. "You, lad, what the devil you doing?"

"Reevnarg!" It was Carbri's voice. "Ship off starboard."

"You, lad, look smart, or I'll heave you overboard. We'll have no hirples."

Arrah nodded silently and pulled her mantle higher on her face as her father moved to the other side of the deck to get a look at the approaching vessel.

"You with younger eyes, can you tell what she is?"

All the ship's crew stopped what they were doing. Even the men at oars stopped and stood in their benches and looked to see if they could make out anything that would identify the ship. But only the uppermost part of its mast showed.

"Not yet!" "She's too far," members of the crew yelled back.

If it was a pirate ship, they'd have to outdistance it, otherwise there would be a fight. All the sailors crossed themselves and rubbed and kissed their talismans.

"Back to work, slime buckets!" shouted the oar leader, and the whip cracked about the men's heads.

A square-rigged vessel was limited in the direction of wind it could use for forward movement. Since the wind was a so'wester and the ship was heading southeast, the rowers had to work with extra effort. A bodhran player beat out a steady rhythm on a goat-skin drum. The distant shape remained an ominous presence on the horizon, more and more of its mast showing as the day wore on.

The cooking was done on an open fire placed in a sand box. The crew ate fish, sea biscuits, soup made with chunks of salt pork, dried beans, onions, salt, and cabbage and drank tea-like infusions of mint and vervain. Carbri showed Arrah how to break off a piece of the meat, put it in her mouth, then take a swallow of tea and hold them both in her mouth till the meat softened.

The ship that was following had gained on them, so that her entire mast was visible on the horizon. As yet she had given no indication of who she was, a fact which worried Reevnarg's crew. If the ship was friendly, she had no reason to hide her identity.

One of the oarsmen took ill. It started with a howling and a rubbing of his belly. And even the worst threats from the oar leader couldn't make him take up his oars again. At midday he was laid in the fo'c's'le, sweat streaming from his face, clutching at his belly as though a fire burned through the lining of his stomach. Next morning he was dead.

The sailors dumped him into the sea then continued their duties.

Carbri took a measure of the speed at which the ship was traveling by dropping a brightly painted red chip of wood into the water at the bow of the boat. Using a minute glass, he paced the length to the stern of the ship and keeping in mind how long the walk took him, calculated the ship's speed. The ship that followed them was now completely visible on the horizon. The bodhran player was ordered to beat the drum more quickly.

Arrah overheard a conversation between Reevnarg and Carbri. It was her father who spoke first. "That lad. Your clansman. We've a vacant bench at the oars. Show him a turn. Show him what it is to be a seaman."

"He's a weakling, Reevnarg. He won't be capable of lifting an oar, much less rowing."

"Who's captain here? Carbri O'Connor or Reevnarg O'Donnell!"

Arrah knew that tone of voice. Without waiting she hid her face and went to the bench.

Before long the wooden oar ate at her hands. Her palms blistered. The blisters broke, then bled. Arrah ripped pieces from her cloak and wrapped these around her oars, but the oars soon felt too thick for her to hold them comfortably. She wrapped cloth around her hand, but the oar leader, who walked back and forth along the benches, shouted at her. "Stroke, damn you!"

"I was just—"

But the lash whizzed down around her head and she had to duck to avoid it. She hastily took up the oar again.

She couldn't remember where the pain had started. Was it in the back of her neck or in her shoulders or in her arms? Or even her legs? All of her ached, every joint, her fingers, her knees. If she stopped, the whip cracked around her head.

She thought of the strong arms of the oarsmen about her. They'd all started like her, spending first one day and then a second day and a third day and so on at the oars. Even her father had started at the oars. They'd all started with aching backs and bellies and shoulders and bleeding hands. Yet they'd grown strong with the effort. She gazed at the row of men, their shoulders broad as bulls, bent, then pulling against the oar. How many men had died, like that sailor, at the oars? But most went on to grow strong. Now as she rowed, the beat of the bodhran seemed to take on words. "Makes me . . . stronger . . . makes me . . . stronger." Over and over again.

The sun fell. The sea turned from blue, to green, to gold as though the sun itself had melted and been poured into it. Then the colors changed to shrimp pink, to oyster gray, to black. The sea was a black mirror. The moon shone back at itself from the water. No longer full, the moon looked as though someone had bitten a piece of it.

The oarsmen were fed, but Arrah was too tired to eat and fell asleep in her bench, her body huddled in her mantle. Carbri watched her, his heart aching with the beauty of her moonlit face.

During the night he took his bearings from the stars. He held a knotted string in his teeth and held it to a star above the horizon and measured the angle from the horizon. He saw the hunched figure sleeping there on the rower's bench. He looked about. No one was watching. He touched her cheek and pulled her mantle up close under her chin, then kissed her lightly on the cheek. "Arrah," he whispered, "I love you!"

During the night the other ship had gained on them again. Only a pirate ship would follow them. The next day the oar leader was merciless in his demands to "stroke, stroke, stroke!"

The hours passed in a relentless agony of aching joints. The ship behind them was gaining on them. The watch from the crow's-nest shouted down that he saw a red flag raised from its mast. Pirates dipped their flags in the blood of their victims to warn others not to resist their attacks.

The oar leader cursed violently. "Aye, lads, you'll have to row to save your arses now. They'll cut your plums out, lads, and make you eat them!"

The breeze calmed.

"Heave to, you lazy land-loving snokes. Put them oars in! Heave to! Heave to! Faster!" shouted the oar leader. The bodhran player beat faster.

Now it was the ash oars solely that pulled the ship through the water for what seemed an endless day. Arrah settled into a sense-deadened existence. The only thing she saw, the only thing she felt, the only thing she thought about was the oar in her hands. "Makes me . . . stronger . . . makes me . . . stronger."

The oarsmen rowed all night, the bodhran player beating with an even greater urgency, and yet the pirate ship was coming closer, her sail looming large and huge in front of the silver moon.

Carbri surveyed the calm night sea. It was a worrisome thing, for too much calm was often followed by storm. He looked for clouds, but there were none.

The watch, in his crow's-nest atop the mainmast, saw the first fragments of dawn, and still no wind. The second ship had gained again, so that as dawn broke Arrah saw the pirates poised with halberds and other weapons. She saw the red dawn reflected like blood in the sharp edges of their weapons.

"Prepare to be boarded," came the shout from the pirate ship.

Reevnarg shouted back, "Prepare for me to shove my sword up your arse so far I'll slice your tongue out!"

Reevnarg ordered the weapons broken out and sailors and fighting men alike had taken pikes and halberds to hand. The two ships were nearly touching before Carbri had a chance to come and try to take Arrah down to the hold, but was prevented from doing so when a pike flying through the air almost hit him in the head. He shoved Arrah under the rowing bench.

Suddenly pirates, throwing over ladders, landed on board the ship. Carbri stayed close to Arrah, protecting her the best he could. But the pirates fought fiercely and Carbri was hard-pressed to save his own life as he dodged swords and axes and pikes.

A pirate flew across from his ship on a swinging rope, and hit Carbri square in the belly with his feet, knocking him sliding across the deck on his back.

Arrah leaped after him to make certain he wasn't wounded. A pirate came at her, his knife drawn. He lunged. The blade of the knife passed in front of her face, so close that she saw the silvery dryness of fish scales on the blade. She snapped her head back, tried to slide her body back but the bulwark stopped her and she heard the unmistakable sound of ripping fabric. The face of the man in front of her changed, and she knew that he had seen her breasts.

She tried to grab up an oar, but it was too cumbersome to remove.

The pirate rushed at her, grabbing her around the waist; she struck at his shoulders and face, but to no avail. She grabbed her dagger, but he twisted her wrist and the weapon fell uselessly to the deck. She elbowed him in the belly; he doubled over and momentarily she escaped him. A pistol fell to the deck from somewhere and she grabbed it up and aimed it at him, but it was empty. He came at her, laughing hideously, and pulled his own pistol from his waist. He grabbed her hair roughly and pushed his pistol at her ear.

"So you think, you want to shoot me, eh. Bitch! I'll shoot you the only place a woman should be shot—right between the legs!"

He pushed Arrah roughly toward her father's deck house. The pirate kicked open the door, then kicked it shut and shoved her down on her father's bunk. "No one will be botherin' us in here. I'll do you myself first, and then let each of the others have a go! We'll see how much fight is left in you!" He grabbed her jerkin and ripped it completely open. Arrah screamed, but no one heard her.

"Turn over," he ordered. "No tricks or I'll shoot your cunt hole!"

She felt the linen of her father's bedcover against her face, but it was rough like gravel. A heavy wooden chest stood on the floor. The brass fittings on the chest were highly polished and she could see a perverse image of herself mirrored there. She closed her eyes.

He ripped down her trews. Outside she heard steel thudding the deck, and the shouts of men killing and being killed. There was the gruesome feeling of his filthy hands on her buttocks. "Aye. You'll get a taste of what it means to be had by a pirate."

Arrah felt the cold pistol slide between her legs and up between her buttocks, then the pirate pulled her back toward him. An enormous shriek of wood came from outside, sounding as though the wall of the deck house were being ripped off. Her father's chieftain brooch lay on the small table beside his berth. She grabbed the brooch, and turning, ripped the pin on the brooch down the pirate's face, putting out his eye as she did so. He grabbed at his face, and leaped back screaming. Arrah seized his pistol and shot the pirate in the groin. He fell to the floor and lay there writhing like a worm on a fishing hook. There was no more shot in the pistol; still she continued pulling the trigger.

The door to the cabin was kicked open again. A sword flashed behind her. Arrah saw nothing but the writhing pirate on the floor. The sword plunged into the pirate's heart and a spasm went through him and then he was still. A hand came and closed gently over Arrah's hand and pulled the pistol from it and threw it on the bed. Carbri reached down and pulled up Arrah's trews.

"Carbri," she cried. "Hold me! Dear God, hold me!" and he pulled her to him. He touched her wet cheek and his being ached with an intense longing to protect her forever.

A sailor moved into the doorway, announcing, "That's it! We've defeated the pir—" The speaker stopped in midword, as he saw the ripped bodice and Arrah's breasts peeking out from beneath the shield of Carbri's arms. "A woman!" shouted the sailor.

More sailors came to stand in the doorway. "A woman!" "Throw her overboard." "Now!"

Arrah grasped at the torn edges of fabric and tried to close them with her fingers, but to no avail.

Carbri grabbed up the bedcover from Reevnarg's bed and threw it over Arrah's shoulders.

She was aware of a hulking shadow coming into the midst of the men. She heard her father's voice. "Tie the pirates to the anchor rope. Drown them all. Every last one of them!"

"She's the fault," a sailor called. "Drown her as well!"

The sailors parted. A dark imposing figure came out of their midst.

From somewhere within herself, Arrah drew up her strength and confronted her father's eyes.

"Arrah!" His voice clapped out like thunder across the ship's deck. His eyes were blue-black like the belly of a storm.

Arrah would not allow herself to be weak. She felt the sailors' eyes on her. She felt hatred in their gaze, and fear and lust. "I told you I wouldn't marry the Joyce."

A wind had started whipping the sails.

"So, you've come to sea, have you? Well then, 'tis time you know what it means to be a sailor. Spread-eagle them both and flog them. Daughter or no daughter, I'll not tolerate disobedience on my ship."

CHAPTER
7

Debrogail was out in the hills picking white milfoil flowers which were effective in treating wounds, particularly wounds caused by metal weapons. But her mind wasn't on her work. She was waiting for evening to come so she could be with Bres. Now that his wound was healing well, she rarely had a chance to spend time with him, for Naira was always about, her cold eyes like an eagle's, always watching. Bres and Debrogail had to content themselves with moments stolen in snippets, secret kisses behind the darkness of an alcove, silent brushes of hands as they passed each other in a corridor.

But tonight they would be together. Debrogail planned to put a sleeping potion in Naira's wine, something that would keep her in deep slumber until the morning. Finally she and Bres would have their night of love.

She thought of how very soft and tender his lips had been when he had kissed her. He was not the first to have kissed her. When one was a servant, one had little choice in determining who took pleasure with her at night.

Debrogail's mother had died when Debrogail was but a child. Her mother had been sick for a long time, coughing and coughing. Her mother had shown Debrogail what plants to gather for various ailments. But even the treatments of the common speedwell plant failed to cure her when she began to spit blood.

One night Debrogail had woken to realize that her mother wasn't coughing and in that sleepy haze of childhood, she had thought that the herbs and infusions had finally brought her peace. Still some inner sense had made Debrogail get up and go to her.

"Mother," Debrogail had called, "Mother," but her mother didn't reply.

The glow from the fire's embers lit her mother's still face. She had a strange red birthmark, the color of raspberries, staining almost her entire right cheek. Debrogail had no such mark, and had been told that birthmarks often skipped a generation.

Debrogail touched her mother's cheek. It was cold as stone.

After her mother died, Mistress Margaret took Debrogail to sleep on a straw pallet in her own room. "The soldiers are brutes," she said to Debrogail. "They'll not leave a girl be a child for long." For several months Debrogail had slept in that chamber.

One night Mistress and Reevnarg left Eagle Island to travel to one of their many castles on the mainland. Debrogail was left behind, and that night she bedded herself down in the kitchen next to the embers. One of the soldiers came the same night. He grabbed away the blanket from her. She felt the cold air cover her, and then she felt his rough hands. She tried to cry out, but he covered her mouth with his mouth. She bit his lip. He punched her then pulled his knife.

"You see this," he growled, his voice hoarse with ale and want. "You cry out anymore and I'll cut your pretty little throat." He forced her legs apart abruptly and grunting and groaning brutally entered, hurting her and hurting her.

He began to shudder uncontrollably. In the midst of shuddering, the soldier dropped his dagger. Debrogail grabbed it up and stabbed him deeply in the throat. She kept his dagger as a remembrance of that night, and thereafter never went to sleep without keeping it beside her.

Reevnarg's soldiers and sailors all knew well enough to stay away unless she invited them at night. But Debrogail was not allowed to refuse visitors, chieftains, and ship captains, and they took their pleasure as they wished.

One time a chieftain pinched her nipples with his fingernails and she screamed. He hit her. Debrogail drew her dagger to defend herself. He came at her with his sword, threatening to kill her, but Mistress Arrah stepped in front of him. She grabbed the dagger from Debrogail's hand and confronted him. "Get you to your rest, or I'll call my father," she said. Mistress Arrah was often given to wandering in the middle of the night and had appeared from nowhere. The chieftain took his anger and walked away.

The next day, Reevnarg himself spoke with the man. "You're welcome to use the servants for pleasure, but you're not to abuse them." That chieftain had never returned.

Mistress Naira, on the other hand, never cared what happened to any of the servants. She always remained aloof. She preferred instead to play at being the great lady. Mistress Naira was always brilliantly dressed in rustling robes of green and blue silk encrusted with pearls and gold embroidery. But Mistress Naira's beauty was a kind of calculated beauty. Whereas Arrah always seemed to be rushing about, Naira never hurried, but always walked with the slow grace of a woman who held the world and most of the people in it in contempt. She held the soldiers and the sailors in disdain but most of all she held Arrah in disdain because of her wild, unladylike behavior.

Life became much easier about the castle of the Eagles for Debrogail and the other servants after Naira had married and moved to the mainland. But then her husband had died. He had been hunting when his horse stumbled. He bit through his tongue in the fall and developed a poisoning in his blood and died. Naira had returned to Eagle Island because of the many chieftains who visited her father there.

She planned to leave Eagle Island and return to her castle at Glen Head as soon as she found a second husband. Debrogail knew she and Bres would have to be careful to avoid detection by Naira.

"I hate her," Debrogail had confided to Bres. "She reminds me of a spider who wants to capture everything in her web. And most of all she wants you."

"Aye," said Bres. "She knows I've a longing for you." He touched Debrogail's cheek.

"She's beaten me twice as much since you've come."

Bres leaped up, his usually teasing eyes flashing with anger. "I'll make her stop. How dare she—"

But Debrogail touched his lips in a gesture of silence. "She'll hear. You mustn't say anything. If you tell her anything she'll send you away from me."

"My darling Debrogail," said Bres, "if I could take every stroke of the whip upon my skin, I surely would to save you the blows."

Debrogail said, "She's not much strength. They land, but don't cause me no suffering."

"I've caused you nothing but pain," said Bres.

"No, my love, you've brought me joy. I think of only you."

After an interminable day, evening came for Debrogail. The far distant hills of the mainland turned blue, then purple, then black in the sunset. The torches were lit and the bards began to sing the old songs. Sometimes the bards allowed Debrogail to sing, but not too often for they were jealous of her splendid voice.

This night Margaret asked her to sing. There were no words to describe Debrogail's voice as she sang the tragic, beautiful song of how a prince and princess of warring clans were turned into whelks, because their love was courageous enough to brave death.

When she finished singing, everyone clapped. Bres clapped especially loud and asked Debrogail to sing another song, but Naira, seeing that Bres enjoyed Debrogail's singing, said, "No! I've heard enough of those whining sad songs. Play, bards! Play something rollicking and good spirited." The bards were only too happy to comply.

When Naira asked Bres to dance he complained that he'd twisted his ankle that afternoon. "Very well," she said. "We'll play at cards instead."

During the evening, Debrogail kept her attention on Bres, only glancing away when Naira looked at her. Bres reached across the table, took Naira's hand, and kissed it. It was the signal that Naira was preparing to retire. Bres distracted Naira, showing her a trick with cards, and while he did so, Debrogail, from behind, slipped a sleeping potion into Naira's wine, then returned to the kitchen to wait.

Bres lifted his goblet in a toast to Naira. "To the loveliness of the O'Donnell women," he said.

Naira smiled at him. She had beguiling eyes when she smiled, and the lights from the torches were reflected in them like small bright needle points. But they were hard, unlike Debrogail's eyes. Soon he would be in her soft, welcoming arms. Naira lifted her cup to her lips.

But at that moment there was a commotion from the other end of the hall. An arm-wrestling match that began as a test of strength erupted into a full-blown brawl. Bres, with the reflexes of a fighting man, stood abruptly and moved toward the disturbance.

Margaret passed by and spoke to Naira about a new dress of red Italian silk her dressmaker had just completed. Naira set down her unfinished goblet of wine and rose and left with her mother. Sullen Bridgett, still sulking from having been banished to the bawn, noticed the nearly full tankard of wine. Servants weren't allowed to drink the expensive wines of France and Italy, but had to content themselves with the heath beer and ale. Bridgett took up the tankard and when she saw no one looking, drank it down with hostile satisfaction.

A blast of wind hit the sails of Reevnarg's ship just as Carbri and Arrah were being tied to the mainmast. All on board had sensed the storm, had felt it in their bones. What surprised them was the speed at which it traveled. The long black bitch of cloud and wind leaped off the horizon like a predator.

"Batten down!" shouted Reevnarg.

For a moment everyone seemed to forget about Arrah and Carbri. The wind shrieked, then mysteriously calmed, then hit like a fist. The carcass of the he-goat, which was hung to the mast to assure favorable winds, crashed to the deck. It was an evil omen of the worst kind.

Reevnarg bellowed. "To the sails!"

"It's a devil wind," shouted one of the sailors. "It's the woman. Throw the woman off!"

"The woman!" shouted the rest of the sailors. They stared at Arrah with eyes made ugly by fear.

"Leave her! Furl up, damn you," shouted Reevnarg, grabbing the whip from the oar leader. "I'll not lose my ship to cowards!" He lashed at the sailors.

But they were more terrified of the woman witch on board than the sting of the whip. They'd had their sign—the devil wind, and they would mutiny to get her off the ship.

They came at Arrah like a herd, twenty-five or thirty of them, ignoring Reevnarg's lash and his orders, all of them thinking of nothing except ridding the ship of the she-witch who was the cause of the storm. Foam and salt sprayed the craft.

Carbri flung away his ropes and drew his sword, standing in front of Arrah. "Free the currach!" he yelled to her. The mob of sailors would have grabbed him and dispensed with him, too, but a single wave lifted the ship. When it crashed down, several sailors pitched headlong into the lashing sea. Arrah was flung against the bulwark. Only desperate clutching kept her from being thrown overboard.

Carbri toppled, too, losing his sword. "Untie the currach!" he shouted, grabbing a weapon from another fallen sailor. "Throw it overboard." The waves grew larger, leaping at the sky. The sea was trying to escape itself; a wave swamped the deck. Arrah clung to the bulwark. She felt as though she were being sucked into the sea. The wave passed.

"Hurry!" Carbri shouted.

Arrah pushed the currach over into the sea.

The crack of Reevnarg's whip split the air again. "Fish jank, the lot of you! The woman's going, can't you see! Filthy land-lubbing dogs! I lose this ship . . . my ghost'll follow the lot of you to hell. I'll torture every one of you!" The whip cracked. "Tie in, damn you!"

Arrah lifted one leg over the side; Carbri was beside her. She looked down at the gray-white sea and then back at Reevnarg.

Their eyes locked for a moment and she saw the expression she had seen there on his face when she had brought back the eagle to him, a mixture of pride and regret. And he momentarily lowered his whip, as if he was about to say something, but the sailors advanced, and his words remained unfinished as he cracked his whip again. "Jump, Daughter. Damn you, jump before these swills get you!" he shouted.

She took Carbri's hand. Together clutching the currach's rope, they jumped in.

The water closed over their heads. Arrah kicked to the surface. She held one side of the small boat, while Carbri crawled in from the other side. He helped her in. Two oars were tied inside the currach.

Another high wave came, and lifted her father's ship. The small currach was in the trough, and so, for a moment, the large ship looked as though it were suspended in mid-air above them, absolutely motionless, as though frozen. Arrah screamed for she thought that the *Maeve* was going to come crashing down on them.

But the wind snatched all sound from her lips; the wave crashed down. Now Arrah and Carbri were at the peak of a wave, and the *Maeve* below them.

There was no land to be seen anywhere. It was impossible to see where sea ended and sky began. Wind and water raged, yet Arrah and Carbri in their fierce, blind concentration grew oblivious to all the elements, grew oblivious to everything except keeping the boat bailed and holding on to avoid being hurled out.

Arrah had no idea how long the rain beat, how many times waves crashed at them. Time simply passed.

A day? Darkness came early. Was it night? She didn't know. She only knew that somehow they had to keep the boat from capsizing.

They didn't even see the rock that ripped the bottom from the currach. Suddenly Arrah and Carbri both tumbled into the churning gray water. Arrah was picked up, then hurled down by the sea.

Bres was locked in a passionate embrace with Debrogail. The night was chilled. Lightning struck, the illumination showing both the man and woman uncovered, their bodies slippery like seals from the sweat of their exertions. Bres thrust himself deeply into Debrogail. She lifted her feet high onto his shoulders to take him better into herself. Thunder rolled and they didn't hear the door to the chamber open.

As the couple collapsed into each other, a figure stood silently in the dark shadows by the doorway.

"Oh, my love! My love!" Bres's voice was broken by the breathlessness that comes after love.

"My darling," said Debrogail. "I thank God for the sword wound you received that day." She lay back on the bed, twisting her fingers into Bres's hair.

"I thank him, too, for giving me such a pretty nurse."

"How was it," asked Debrogail, "that Reevnarg learned of the attack of your uncle?"

"I sent word to Seaghan."

"You're a traitor then," said Debrogail, half-joking, half-serious. "Will you be a traitor to love some day as well?"

"No," said Bres. "I'm no traitor. Seaghan is my cousin. I love him like a brother. I warned him of his father's attack!"

"You, too, then are an outcast, like he is."

"It's far better to cast out with those you love, than to be included as friends among those whose ideas you do not share. Brion MacNamara allows his hatred of Seaghan to rule. I could no longer swear allegiance to Brion."

"My darling Bres! What are we going to do? If Naira finds out she'll order me killed."

"We'll go to Seaghan in France. We'll leave as soon as the storm passes."

"I could dress up in Mistress Margaret's fine dresses the way that Bridgett does and pretend I'm not a servant," laughed Debrogail.

"You'll have dresses plenty in France. Seaghan's a rich devil. He'll pay me well. You won't need to wear Margaret's."

"There's no denying I'm a servant. Only Bridgett pretends she's not! How long will you love a servant?"

"I love you!" Bres said seriously. He raised himself on his elbow. "I love you." Even in the shadows she was impish and impossibly pretty.

"Perhaps that's true! You love me because I healed your wounds. But you're a chieftain's nephew."

"I'm no longer anyone's nephew. I made my choice when I came to Seaghan. I, too, am disowned."

"You can't marry a servant," said Debrogail.

"When a man breaks even one of his country's laws, he becomes free of all of them. Freedom is a wonderful thing. I can marry whomever I wish."

"You'll have to marry an important lady."

"Important ladies! Do you think important ladies would do such tricks with their tongue the way that you do. Important ladies are too busy being important to worry about a man's pleasure."

"Then I'll be your concubine."

"Charming Debrogail. Do you think that any wife would tolerate your attentions to me?" He gave her a long kiss on the lips again.

"All the chieftains have concubines."

"Later, yes, when wives tire of husbands. But not when they're first wed. Any wife I chose would grow green as the shamrocks with jealousy of your loveliness! You would have no peace!"

"Truly spoken," came the voice from the doorway.

Debrogail and Bres jumped with fright.

Lightning struck, illuminating the room again, and they saw Naira standing there. "Guards!" she shouted imperiously.

Bres and Debrogail leaped out of bed. Bres grabbed for his sword, but the guards were there ahead of him.

"Get back to bed," ordered Naira. "Not you, strumpet! Just Bres."

"Naira!" shouted Bres. "Don't harm the girl. It was my doing!"

Naira sat down on the edge of the bed and smiled superbly. In the light of the guard's torch, she looked like a cat that was going to eat a mouse. She looked appreciatively at Bres sitting in the bed.

"Bres," cried Debrogail. "My life is nothing without you!" She saw the guards looking at her and tried to cover her nakedness the best she could with her hands.

"For Christ's sake, man," shouted Bres at the guard. "Let her have her clothes."

The guards remained motionless. Naira nodded and one of the guards grabbed a blanket and threw it at Debrogail.

Naira continued. "I'll permit Debrogail to go unharmed. I'll send her to one of my other castles where she can cavort with others of her type. I'll release her"—Naira hesitated—"if you agree to marry me!"

Bres pulled the sheets up closer to his chest. A thousand thoughts raced through his mind. He didn't love Naira. Would never love her. He loved Debrogail. Loved her. He would not betray. "I will n—"

"If you don't agree, I'll order her killed. Here, now, in front of you, the guard will cut her throat."

The guard lifted his sword up to Debrogail's throat.

"Don't do it," Debrogail screamed to Bres. "I'm not afraid to die."

Bres leaped to help her. Immediately three guards subdued him. Debrogail tried to rush to him, the blanket slipping from her. The two lovers were both naked, their desperate vulnerability making them sadly beautiful as they unsuccessfully tried to reach for each other's hand.

The guard's sword came up again, ready for the down thrust—

"I'll marry you!" shouted Bres.

"No!" cried Debrogail.

"I'll marry you! I'll do anything you want, but don't harm her!" he pleaded.

Naira nodded and the guard pulled Debrogail kicking and screaming from the chamber.

"A wise choice, my darling," said Naira. "Tomorrow I'll begin planning our wedding," and she kissed him fully on the lips. Then speaking to the guard, she said, "Watch him, that he doesn't escape."

She left the chamber, and calling another guard, spoke to him. "When the storm stops, you're to take her to the castle at Glen Head on the mainland. You are to give orders to the chief mason that Debrogail is to be bound and buried alive beneath the castle. No one else is to know. Do you understand?"

"Yes, mistress!"

"Do as I order, and I'll pay you handsomely upon your return."

"Yes, mistress!"

PART II

CHAPTER 8

There was just sensation, no thought yet—the sensation of being impossibly thirsty. A parchedness in her throat, so dry and so rough. She was buried alive. She was the child buried beneath the Castle of the Eagles. There was dirt up her nose and in her mouth, and she was gasping for air, and yet no air came. There was sound: a distant gull, the high, ethereal quaver far, far against the sky. Something firm, solid, yet giving, beneath her. Warmth on her back, and the sound of the surf, quiet and regular.

Now she realized what the dryness in her mouth was—sand—between her teeth and crusting her tongue.

A hand on her shoulder, and someone shaking it gently. She lifted her head slowly. She saw bare feet, large splayed toes. She sat up slowly, Carbri helping her, his hands lifting her shoulders. He smiled at her.

Arrah tried to speak, but her mouth was too dry, and her voice came too guttural to be understood. They had washed up on a sandy beach and the weather had cleared. The sky was that pale, hazy blue of hot summer. She felt the sun's heat on her face and breast, found herself squinting her eyes against it. Carbri knelt down directly in front of her.

He helped her up and they went looking for water. Off the beach area in a small ravine they found a spot where the rain had pooled.

"Where are we?" Arrah asked.

Carbri turned his head. "See that rock there?"

Arrah saw a huge sloping, hulking rock jutting off a few hundred paces in the distance.

"There's a fishing village called Biarritz. The people here speak neither French nor Spanish, but a strange tongue called Basque. We'll have to journey northward to Paris. There's an Irishman there by the name of O'Reilly. Your father knows him. He'll be able to give us information of ships traveling back to Ireland."

"How long have we been here?"

"Through the night," Carbri answered.

She felt a bruise on her cheek and reached up to it. Carbri reached out his hand and gently touched her chin, slowly lifting it so that he could eye it better.

"Arrah, but what a girl you are." His clear hazel eyes held hers in sunlit admiration, and then she felt his eyes fall to her breasts.

"I'm hungry!" she said.

"God's blood! Is that all you can be thinking about! Always your belly."

"What else is there to think about when a body's hungry? Give me your dagger."

Like all sailors, Carbri kept a length of rope attached from his dagger to his belt so he wouldn't lose it when the weather grew fierce.

They went back to the beach and began to dig down for clams, gathering a sizable pile. With his flint Carbri started a small fire. The clams popped open before long and Arrah and Carbri devoured them hungrily.

"I wish we'd gotten more," Arrah said, looking about.

"You were saying we had enough!"

"I was too hungry to wait any longer!"

"We'll go on to Biarritz tomorrow. There'll be food there a-plenty. Enough even for you, my glutton!" He looked at her. "Arrah, you look to be thriving on this life." And so she did. Despite the bruise on her face, despite her sea-tangled, sandy hair, there was an intense vigorousness about her. Her face was flushed with excitement. He reached his hand to her cheek.

She liked the feel of his hand there, and felt that curious wonder rise in her once more.

Carbri ran his thumb along her jaw. She didn't pull away. He let his thumb slip to the root of her throat. She'd never had a man touch her there before and she closed her eyes to the sensation of his fingers. Her breath quickened. She felt the soft brush of his lips against her neck, against her chin, and she turned her lips to his. There was a gentleness to his lips, almost nothing more than an exchange of breath. She wanted more and kissed him. Carbri's weight pressed her back against the sand. It was a good weight, lean, not as passionate as she would have liked, but she welcomed it. She felt his calloused fingers push away her torn shirt. Gently, he cupped her breast, lightly rolling her nipple between his thumb and forefinger. He lowered his mouth, and when his breath warmed her breast, she shivered as though cold. Then Carbri lifted his mouth to hers, and kissed her, intensely this time, and she felt something deep inside her respond to him.

She felt him rise over her, felt his hands at her trews. She wanted him. The summer air brushed her nether lips with a breeze. That first touching of his flesh found her with gentleness. It was then that hurt came and instinctively she recoiled. Carbri drew back, but was unable to stop, and before she realized what had happened, he ran through the barrier of her maidenhood and spilled into her.

Carbri lay panting against her neck. "I'm sorry," he said. "You were raising so much want in me." He kissed her once more, her forehead, her cheeks and eyes.

Arrah was disillusioned. Was this all there was to love? Was this the reason the bards sang song after song? Was this why women whined beneath their men? If this was love, then it was the biggest disappointment of her life.

But then she felt a throb of pleasure in that place Carbri had just entered. He began to move again, a steady rhythm like a drum at a dance, and as he continued to move, her girl's pain flowed from her. A woman's pleasure replaced it, and when he spilled the second time, she answered him with a woman's feral cry of joy.

Disguised as a vendor of trinkets and charms, Glundel Joyce sailed to Eagle Island. His face was blackened with the brine of walnuts. Even his pale beard had been dyed. He wore a rough, ragged cloak and he had put pitch on his teeth to make them appear rotten.

Glundel had taken care of his uncle. It was easy enough to do. The old man was a gull, trusting as a ninny. They had set out hunting together, but even before they reached the wild forested regions where hunting was best, Glundel had complained of being enormously thirsty and had sent the rest of the party ahead stalking. Cormac, too, complained of thirst. The pig brains fried with fat and onions which was the old man's favorite food, and on which they had supped the evening before, had been salty. Not surprising, since Glundel had sprinkled his plate with a substantial amount of sea salt when Cormac wasn't looking.

Glundel and Cormac went to the well together. Glundel sent down the pail for water and then lifted it. "Drink, Uncle," he had offered generously.

The old man lifted the pail to his mouth. Glundel gave a swift punch to the center of the old man's belly where it was tenderest. Cormac doubled over. Glundel grabbed up a rock and slammed it into his uncle's head, then dumped him into the well below.

Glundel began shouting, "Help! Help!" The rest of the hunting party came running. A rope was lowered and one of the servants was sent down to bring up the old man. Glundel Joyce, the new chieftain, had wept inconsolably over the body of his dead uncle.

Up to now Glundel's scheme to take Eagle Island had gone as he had planned. Slowly he had poisoned Cormac's wife, all the while putting into the old fool's head the notion of asking for Arrah in marriage. Regardless of what the old man said the laws of betrothal were as binding as marriage. Cormac was dead. Glundel had no intention of seeing Eagle Island slip from him now.

Disguised with his rough cloak and rotten teeth, Glundel Joyce entered the kitchen of Eagle Castle. He carried a large leather bag filled with his wares. Bridgett was bent over a table, her haunch curving beneath the rough cut of her skirts. No one else was in the kitchen. Glundel went quietly to her, and slid his hand down her hip. He was going to take her from behind so that he wouldn't have to look at her. Bridgett started.

"Shh," Glundel whispered, "don't turn around."

But Bridgett, compliant as she was, had no intention of doing things with someone she didn't know. There were favors to be gained, however small they might be, and she had no intention of letting one pass by her.

"Master Glundel, sir," she squealed with delight when she saw who it was.

"Shh! Little fool. Do you want to tell the world I'm here?"

"You can be fooling Mistress Margaret with the way you look, but not Bridgett," she said more quietly. "I was thinking you was forgetting all about Bridgett. But now that you're back . . ." She knelt down in front of him.

The very act of her doing so made a thickness rise in Glundel's trews. It was a woman's place to be subservient to a man's pleasure.

With expert hands she reached up to that swelling and began to rub. Then she reached in to the opening there and pulled out his erect manthing. It was a miserable thing, very small and thin like a little boy's. If he'd been a servant she would have laughed and jeered, but since he was a tanaist, she knew better. "Look at the yard you got on you!" she lied. It was a game she played with men. "Oh, you make me feel so good." And they believed her. Every one. Men were all so stupid! No matter if their things were wee and useless. Take their cocks in your mouth and you could do anything with them. She took his flesh into her mouth and began to suck. She took him all in, and moved her lips expertly up and down his throbbing shaft. She was supremely disdainful of men. It took ridiculously little time for the frantic pulsing to begin. He grabbed her head and pulled her farther forward in a spasmodic motion, and she laughed to herself as he climaxed.

She pushed his hands away and stood.

"Did you bring me my dress?" she asked.

Glundel's eyes were closed, and he nodded.

"What kind?"

He opened his eyes and took a breath, tucking himself back in his trews. "One like I promised you!"

"What color is it?"

"It's very lovely." From his bag he pulled out a sand-colored velvet dress. It was of a simple style with a high waist, without any of the embroidery that the wife of a chieftain would wear. Nonetheless, compared to Bridgett's rough sack, the dress was superb. Bridgett reached to touch it.

Glundel pulled it back. "First I want you to do something for me." He pulled a vial from his pocket. "In exchange for the dress!"

Bridgett looked at the vial. "I won't be able to wear that dress anyway," she said. "Mistress will think I stole it."

"Bridgett. You have special talents with your mouth." He tried to touch her cheek.

She drew back.

"I could take you away from these." He walked about the kitchen, flicking spoons and ladles dismissively. "You're a desirable wench. I saw you in the finery of Margaret's robes. You looked every bit as splendid as she! It's cloth and vestments that make a woman beautiful. Do you always want to be a servant in sack?"

Bridgett looked at him with scornful cynicism. "What do you want me to do?"

Glundel held up the vial. "There is poison in this. Oil of henbane, enough to kill your mistress," he whispered. "My uncle's dead. He fell into a well. I am now not just tanaist, but chieftain of the Joyce. According to Mistress Margaret's desires, if she dies, the island should pass to Arrah. But according to the laws, Eagle Island, as a chieftain's territory, cannot go to a woman, but must go to a man. If Mistress Margaret dies, the island should pass to me as chieftain since Arrah's betrothed husband is dead. Dear girl, I can take you from the kitchen into my bed."

"I hate Mistress Margaret!" whispered Bridgett.

"I'll free you from her. Wait until there is none of her family here on the island. Then pour this in the beverage that she drinks each night before retiring. After she dies, I promise, you'll sit at my side as Mistress of the Eagles."

The summer sun of France beat down on Arrah and Carbri as they traveled northward toward Paris. The two lovers were vagabonds, in love with each other and in love with the sun and the country and the way it smelled on each other's skin.

At first, Carbri and Arrah, traveling as the young Irish tanaist and his apprenticing clansman, slept in public houses. But unlike the Celts, the Continentals were less particular about washing, and the beds were infested with lice and dark beetles. It was a summer of gentle weather and often they took sleep wherever they could, in haystacks, in grassy fields, curled into each other, holding each other all night long, breathing each other's breath under the stars and moon.

In Navarre they fell to sleep under the pungent, sweet aroma of the mimosa trees. Arrah had never smelled anything so heady. In the mornings she woke first and watched as the sun lit the tops of the yellow blossoms, turning them to burnished gold. She looked down on Carbri's handsome young face, the fine hairs high on his cheeks, the lips quivering ever so lightly in his sleep. It was she who always kissed him awake, teasing him about slothfulness, and often they would make love before rising and traveling on. This life of travel, of changing her pillow each night, evoked a sense of adventure in her that she had dreamt about since she was a child.

The houses in Navarre were tiled bright red, a sharp contrast to the drab, weathered thatches of Irish roofs. The French houses were whitewashed, with brilliantly painted window boxes: sky-blues, reds like freshly drawn blood, and greens like the green of her own hills. The skies were immense and blue, a kind of blue that she'd never seen in Ireland, and the sun so hot and yellow it was almost white.

She tasted foods that she'd never eaten: a sweet cake made from yogurt, honey, and flour that delighted her. In another town she ate *piperade*, a vegetable stew. Its aroma made her mouth water as soon as she stepped inside the door of the tavern. The tavern keeper set a wooden bowl in front of her, filled with the tantalizing food. She was ravenous from walking and ate greedily. The stew was a mixture of bacon, onions, and peppers with eggs, and compared to the oatcakes and boiled beef and fish of Ireland, the food of Navarre was a feast from heaven.

"Arrah," Carbri teased. "You'll be eating like a starved urchin."

"If you'll be making me walk so far, then in the name of the saints, Carbri O'Connor, I have to eat!" She asked for more from the tavern keeper.

"Monsieur," said the tavern keeper. "It is not good to allow your bondsman to eat so much. He will get lazy, yes, and then not work for you."

Carbri winked at Arrah. Then answered the tavern keeper. "Lazy, yes. He is very, very lazy!"

"Then you should not feed him, sir. Unless he works."

"You'll be giving sound advice, good man, and tomorrow I won't be feeding him so well. But he's a moody boy. Given to all manner of sullenness if he won't be getting enough to eat. He's had a bit of a walk today so be a good man and be dishing him out a wee bit more."

"To what town are you going?"

"Paris."

"Paris! That is a long distance, yes. And there are many thieves between here and Paris. Thieves who will cut your throat even before they ask for your money."

"Well, be letting them come. Carbri O'Connor can be handling a sword and dagger with the best of them." Carbri kept his coinage in a leather bag made from cowhide on a strong string about his neck. It was the first thing he had checked after being washed ashore. Later in a market, he bought a sword made of Toledo steel from a dark-faced Spanish merchant. He bought one for Arrah as well.

Two men were playing dice at a back table. Somebody suddenly shouted, "Filthy, cheating slop!" A table crashed against the tile floor.

The tavern keeper, grabbing up a long stick, shouted, "Hey, you! Breaking up my tables?"

"I'll break up your tables *and* your head!" yelled one of the dice players. He picked up a chair and hurled it at the tavern keeper so he had to dive for safety.

"Grab him! Dog."

A shot exploded in the tavern. Carbri flew at Arrah, knocking her to the floor. A cacophony of breaking wood, of fist on bone, and steel on steel broke out. Carbri tried to take Arrah out of the tavern, but she had seen the pistol drop and slapped away Carbri's hands. She crawled toward the firearm. The entire tavern was now in an uproar with fighting. A body fell on Arrah, flattening her against the floor, but she held her pistol, and pushed the body off. Arrah stood. Someone threw a tankard. She ducked, and with Carbri behind her, ran out the door.

"Are you crazy?" Carbri shouted at her. "You could've been killed in there!"

Her face was flushed with excitement. "Look at what I found!"

"Useless things," he said, dismissing the pistol. "In the time it takes to load one, a man can be cutting your head off with a sword ten times."

"But it can kill a man at twenty paces, something you can't do with a sword." She thrust the pistol into the waist of her trews.

"I can throw a dagger just as easily and hit my mark."

They traveled from one walled town to another seeing much of the everyday life of France: cows being driven home from the pastures, children playing running games and kick the stone, men and women talking in doorways. Carbri and Arrah also saw criminals flogged in open squares with knotted chains.

Arrah preferred the countryside to the towns and villages. On the roads and in the country when no one else was about, Carbri acknowledged her as Arrah. He took her hand when he walked, or put his arm about her shoulder. In the towns and villages he treated her differently.

"I'm not your servant to be ordered about so," she complained.

He slapped her rump. "When you're through dressing like a man, then you can stop being treated like a man. In the meantime, you'll be my boy. Now, do as your tanaist'll be ordering. Fetch the tavernkeep to bring me more ale." Carbri had spoken French for some time. Two or three of the sailors on Reevnarg's ships had come from French ports, and Arrah, who had learned Latin from Father Thomas, was now beginning to understand a goodly portion of conversation.

As she and Carbri traveled north, the thick forests gave way to another kind of greenery: shrubs in straight lines, looking like files of men with very short, leafy bodies holding up huge, long arms above their heads.

"Look," said Carbri, pointing. "See how the grape vines'll be tied to make the picking easier."

"The land looks parched," said Arrah, all of a sudden missing the green glory of the west coast of Ireland.

"Aye, 'tisn't Ireland. But there's something else. Come." He looked about to make certain that no peasant was about, then clambered over a stone fence, motioning for her to follow. He went to the vines and lifted a bunch of grapes. "Eat," he said. The translucent green fruit burst like small sweet showers of rain in her throat. She had never eaten anything so succulent, so wonderful.

Carbri watched her plucking grape after grape from the bunch. She looked elfish and mischievous. She held a grape between her lips and kissed him, pushing the grape into his mouth. He took it from her, then touching his tongue between her lips, pushed her to the ground and made love to her in the shade of the vines. After he licked her eyebrows lightly and her nose, he reached up, grabbed down a bunch of grapes, and fed them to Arrah one by one.

"The French are fools," he said. "All a body needs do is to look at the likes of you to see you're not a man. But the likes of them. They're blind!"

Suddenly Arrah screamed.

Carbri jumped up, and she after him, and she began furiously brushing at her legs. They had lain down close to an ant hill and at least a dozen of the small black creatures were crawling on her bare skin.

"You're the biggest fool of all, Carbri O'Connor, laying me down on an anthill."

"Ants will be knowing," Carbri laughed, "that God gave you the sweetest arse this side of heaven. Now, can you be blaming them, for wanting to have a wee bite?" and he pretended to throw her to the ground again. She yelled, but instead of stopping he began to tickle her and she screamed more loudly.

A dog barked. Carbri grabbed Arrah and their clothes, and off they ran through the vineyard and over the fence like a couple of hares pursued by hounds.

When Arrah looked back she saw a small fat peasant, shouting and carrying a pitchfork, running far behind them. But the peasant's short legs were no match for Arrah's and Carbri's youth and he quickly abandoned his chase. Laughing and out of breath the two vagabonds put on their clothes and continued on their way to Paris, sleeping under trees and in haystacks, making love whenever the mood took them.

Despite the forlorn, desperate atmosphere of her prison and the dreary passing of days and nights, Debrogail was determined not to lose hope. She passed the hours remembering the brief happiness she'd spent with Bres.

Her only contact came from the cruel old prison keeper who had locked her in her cell.

"I'm cold," she told him.

"Well, is you now? If'n I was you I'd plan on getting used to that. Whar you're headed it'll be a lot colder for a lot longer," he said, laughing.

"What's to happen to me?" she asked.

"You'll find out soon enough," he snarled.

To try to keep up her spirits and to keep herself warm, Debrogail began to sing and to dance.

The prison keep came back and pounded on her cell door. "You stop that wailin' in there."

"If I'm going to be kept in this miserable place," she shouted back, "at least I'll sing. You can't keep me from that." The keeper opened the door and struck her with a staff, and she crumpled to the floor.

"Now you'll listen to what I say, or you'll get more of the same."

Although the prison was intolerably cold, and the food was inadequate and left her hungry all the time, Debrogail believed that somehow Bres would come and save her. But as she lay there, her head stinging with the blow from the staff, she began to lose hope. "Bres, Bres! Where are you?" she cried. "What have I done to deserve this?"

But no, she wouldn't cry. She determined she was not going to give up. She could sing quietly to herself, and she could dance in her cell to keep herself warm. She knew that if she gave up, she would die of cold, which is probably what Mistress Naira wanted. She would not let her win so easily. She began to whirl, her long lovely legs only a shadow in the dark cell.

In the meantime, the digging of Debrogail's grave was going on beneath the castle. But the chief stonemason was an old man, and not well. The heavy work of digging a hole in solid rock only worsened his condition and before long he struggled home to his bed.

Before he did so he instructed several of the guards to dig the hole. But the guards, seeing how ill the stonemason was, and knowing the terrain around Glen Head was the hardest and rockiest in all of God's creation, didn't see any need for urgency.

One night it was not the cruel old prison guard who brought Debrogail her daily serving of bread, but another guard, one she hadn't seen before, a thin man.

Debrogail had been dancing when he entered. She had grown weaker over time, and thinner with the bad food, and she no longer danced as often or as long as before. But as she danced she pretended she was dancing for Bres.

"Where's the other guard?" she asked.

"Sick" was all he answered before closing the door again.

She ran up to the door and screamed after him. "Come back! Come back! I'm cold! What is to happen to me?" but she heard the outer door of the prison close, and she was left alone once more.

With the cruel guard gone, she thought she might be able to sing again. She took a drink of the water the guard had given her, and began first to hum and then to sing, her clear, splendid voice echoing off the stones so it sounded like an angel had arrived in that hell-bound place.

After a time she sensed that dark eyes watched her from behind the grate of the prison door, but when she looked there, whoever was watching had disappeared. She continued her singing and this time when she looked up, there was no mistaking—someone was watching her. She saw the flicker of his shadow as he hid.

"Who are you?" she called after him. Nothing but the prison's silence answered her.

"Come back! Please," she said. "I won't stop singing if you want to listen."

She heard shuffling from the corridor and the man who had been watching her returned. She couldn't see his face but from the sounds of his movement she thought that he dragged his leg or something that served as a leg. "With a voice like that, you must have done some terrible thing for Mistress Naira to order you here," he said quietly.

"My only crime was to love a man whom my mistress and your mistress also fell in love with."

"Love should not be a crime," he said quietly. "Seeing you in here is like seeing a nightingale in a cage."

"At least a nightingale has her feathers to keep her warm. I have nothing."

"Wait," he said, and then pushed an old blanket through the bars of her door peephole. It was moth-eaten and ragged, but she grabbed it and wrapped it around her shoulders. It was the first time she had been close to feeling warm in days and days.

"How long have you been here?" he asked.

"I don't know," she said. "The prison keep. The old one. He doesn't tell me anything," said Debrogail.

"Rory. He hasn't a bit of kindness for anything except himself. Will you sing for me just a little more? You promised you wouldn't stop if I listened."

His voice sounded so sad she couldn't refuse him. This time she left off with the rousing songs with which she had accompanied her own dancing and sang instead the story of the prince and princess turned to whelks.

"Thank you, Debrogail," he said simply and quietly when she finished.

"You know my name, but I don't know yours," she said.

"Magnus," he replied.

"Do you know what is to happen to me?" she asked.

"I have to go now."

As he left she heard his clunking, hesitant step on the stone.

But the next night Magnus didn't come.

"Where's Magnus?" she asked the guard.

"They don't give me pay to answer questions," he said nastily, and closed the prison door behind him.

The next time a guard entered her cell it was a man whom she'd never seen before. Carrying a lantern, he hobbled with crutches made from a crotched tree branch. His right leg ended at his knee. Because he was bent, Debrogail assumed he was an old man, but as he approached and held up the lamp to see her face, she saw that he was younger than she'd first thought. His face and neck were badly scarred, giving him a sinister appearance.

"Debrogail," he said, "I brought you these." And from beneath his tunic he pulled a pair of woolen slippers, and she recognized the sad voice as that of Magnus, the man who'd spoken to her through her door two nights ago.

Debrogail, too cold to even thank him, grabbed the slippers.

"I'm sorry I wasn't able to come last night, but my wife took a turn for the worse. She is with child and I had to stay with her. I told her about you, about your voice, and she told me to bring you the slippers."

"Oh, Magnus. Thank you for making me believe there's still some kindness in this world."

"There isn't a creature in this world with more kindness than my Cathlin," Magnus answered. "She's like a saint."

Not knowing what to think, Debrogail looked at his crutches.

"My foot," he said ruefully, "I received a spear wound in battle, and the green rot set in. The surgeon had to cut it off. I nearly died. There are many women who would not look twice at a man like me. There's not much that I can be good for. But I met Cathlin, and she cared for me. She's not beautiful as you are, but she has the kindest eyes and warmest heart in all of Ireland. I wish I could take your song and carry it home to her in a jar. She's always loved to hear singing. Her family, when they were alive, all sang beautifully. I've asked the bard here to go to her, but he's the same as bards everywhere. They'll play when the lord and lady are about, but they hold the common folk in contempt."

"I know," said Debrogail. She'd seen enough of the jealousy of bards at Eagle Castle. They thought that only those who had gone through the years of training as they had should have the right to sing and play harps.

"Would you sing for her one night, if I brought her here?" Magnus asked.

If you can bring an ill woman down here, you could help me escape, Debrogail thought hopefully.

CHAPTER 9

Seaghan MacNamara was unable to sleep. At his house in Paris, he tossed and turned.

Arrah O'Donnell came back knocking against his mind, like a moth against a lantern glass. It wasn't simply her beauty that enticed him, for although she was beautiful, she wasn't pretty in the same way that dozens of other women were pretty, in the same way that Tiltiu, his father's wife, had been pretty.

Arrah had another quality. A kind of spirit that burned in her veins, a spirit that challenged everything. That day when Reevnarg had ripped up Arrah's sleeve and showed him the scars on her arm, Seaghan had felt desire shoot through him, sharp as a sword. He wanted then to tear her clothes from her shoulders and possess her there on the grass, completely and deeply, the way a stallion possessed a mare. He remembered how she had felt when he had danced with her, when she had been close against him, when he'd felt her womanliness against his thigh.

Once, when he'd been in Genoa, he'd visited the home of a nobleman there. The Genoan, for amusement, kept two tigers in individual cages in an enclosed section of his garden. The female was in heat, and the two animals growled at each other, their breaths hot and hissing like the breath of dragons. They bit the metal cage wires that kept them separated. Like imprisoned sunlight, their magnificent bodies paced their cages, their tiger eyes burning outward from between the wires. Finally the Genoan gave a signal. An attendant opened the cages, and the tigers mated fiercely and violently. The coupling had left him intensely aroused.

Arrah O'Donnell had the same effect on him, the rise and fall of her breasts, the way she had looked at him, her eyes smoldering when she had tried to pull away from him during the dance, the determination in her arm. He could have snapped it like a twig had he wished to, the way he'd done with enemies' arms. The full, bold gaze, the affrontery of her eyes, her moist lips, her nostrils flaring with the breathlessness of the dance. But she was betrothed to the Joyce. He had to put her out of his mind.

But as he lay in his bed, he felt an aching rising in his back. The memory of other women, the slow lift of rising above them, the arch, the pounding. He could feel the heat rise in his groin, and the pressure in his member grew taut against the tight skin. He turned on his belly. Outside he heard the wind.

Momentarily escaping the tyranny of clouds, the moon appeared, seductive and slender, and shined down naked on his firm, muscled haunches, the dark patterns of hair over his legs.

He ground himself into the mattress. But there was no relief, and naked he rose from his bed. He went down the corridor, grabbed the sleeping chamber wench and even before she woke, he'd penetrated her.

She screamed at his entrance, then quieted as she realized what was happening. She gazed up at him in the darkness, then closed her eyes and opened her mouth. She began to moan with his rutting and then to whine. He sought relief for his pain. She convulsed under him again and again, yet he would not stop. Finally the contractions began to rise in his back and to travel into him until his aching spilled and found relief.

He looked at the wench beneath him and she smiled at him. "Oh, monsieur," she said. "At first I thought I was dreaming and then . . . Oh, monsieur!" she said again, and she raised her arms to pull him closer, and the deep look of pleasure on her face gave way to concern. "Was I not giving you much *plaisir?*" she asked, noticing his brooding look.

"Yes." But he pushed her arm away. "Come to my room in the morning," he said, "and I'll—"

"Oh! With *plaisir!*" she said.

But the tone of her voice showed that she'd misunderstood him.

"I'll give you money," he said impatiently.

She was going to touch his dark-haired, powerful chest again, but stopped. "So many of scars, monsieur. You were getting so many scars, where? You are fighting too much, yes?" she asked.

"Yes." He stood over her now, she looking up at him in admiration.

"You are very beautiful, monsieur. I have seen much of men. But none like you. But why is monsieur fighting too much?"

He bent down and patted her thigh. "Go back to sleep and come to me in the morning."

*   *   *

Arrah had never imagined such a city as Paris. The noise of wooden carts traveling at breakneck speeds over the cobblestones nearly deafened her. The stench of human waste, poured into the street gutter along with dead dogs, animal offal, and rotting vegetable parings, nauseated her. Elbows of people in the streets jostled her. All she thought of was returning to the west coast of Ireland where the clean sea smell permeated everything, where as far out as she looked she saw the sweep of the surging sea, the lace peak of white caps rising to the clouds.

As Arrah and Carbri walked, a bucket of chicken entrails nearly hit her. She leaped back, and looking up to a third story window, saw a woman. Arrah shouted up at her. The woman shouted down, put her thumb behind her front teeth and flicked it at Arrah.

She hoped that they would soon find the house that they were looking for because Paris disgusted her. Eochan O'Reilly, the brother of the O'Reilly chieftain, had temporarily settled in France after his younger brother had wrested the chieftainship from him, and kept news of all the ships that sailed to and from Ireland. Arrah and Carbri were hoping to board one that would take them home.

As they walked along the Seine, Arrah noticed that they had arrived in a richer quarter of the city, where fewer people walked about in rags, and the houses were in a better state of repair. Ever since arriving in Paris, Arrah had been aware of a large stone edifice, its gray spire piercing the sky like a needle. Carbri had told her that it was a cathedral, Notre Dame de Paris; and it was in its direction that they headed. They crossed a bridge onto an island in the middle of the river. It was on this island that O'Reilly had his hotel.

Carbri stopped to ask directions and Arrah walked slowly ahead, attempting to get a glimpse of the enormous edifice. In the street a little farther along, she saw a beautiful two-wheeled carriage. Made of brightly polished golden oak pulled by two magnificent dapple-gray horses, it stopped. A footman in fine blue livery opened its door. A big man stepped out, dressed in a mantle of rough green cloth. His profile showed only briefly before he turned his back, but it was long enough for Arrah to recognize Seaghan MacNamara. Joyous to see someone she knew, she called out and ran ahead, but a cart went by in the street and her voice was drowned out.

Seaghan MacNamara reached into the door; a woman's foot emerged. Arrah stopped short. The small graceful foot was covered with leather so soft that Arrah thought it might have been satin. On the toe perched a stuffed bird, a small swallow that had been painted red to match the shoes.

The woman glided down the carriage steps into the arms of Mac-Namara. She moved in a rustle of fine satin, the like of which Arrah had never seen: a deep rich color like ripe cherries, with a design of silver quilting at the shoulder and silver slashes along the sleeve, and silver petals decorating the skirt. A strand of pearls adorned the woman's white neck, as did a large ruby encrusted in a gold ball about the size of a walnut which hung at the root of her throat.

Her hair hung long and fine and dark and was interwoven with pearls. Arrah touched her own shorn hair.

The woman and MacNamara moved toward a house, but a short line of fresh horse droppings barred her way. Some pigeons strutted about it. The woman made a move to walk around, but MacNamara, in a fluid, easy motion, reached down with an arm and picked her up as though she were as light as a child. As he did so, he glanced up; Arrah turned her head abruptly so he couldn't see her.

She looked down at her own garments. In her trews and shirt and muddy boots and rough cloak, she looked like a road-weary lad.

The woman smiled at Seaghan MacNamara, and he held her a moment before putting her down. At the door to the house he kissed her hand. Arrah turned away and walked back toward Carbri.

Carbri had asked her to marry him when they returned to Ireland. He said that as tanaist to the O'Connor clan, he could marry whomever he wished. He would not marry Agneis de Burgo, despite the arrangements his stepsister, Finola, had made for his betrothal. Arrah had agreed. She, too, could marry whomever she wished. As Carbri's wife, she would wear dresses as beautiful as any she'd seen in Paris. Her father always brought back fine fabrics with him. On Eagle Island she, Arrah, would tell the seamstresses exactly what she wanted: silver quilting and silver trim along the sleeves and a strand of pearls. Already her hair was growing. Before long she would have hair as lovely as before.

She walked back to Carbri and told him that she thought she'd seen MacNamara.

" 'Tis likely," Carbri answered. "O'Reilly lives in the quarter. He and MacNamara are friends."

Carbri found the house they were looking for and knocked. A servant ushered the two travellers through the house into a courtyard.

Nothing could have prepared Arrah for the sight that met her. It was a veritable garden of paradise: strange plants she'd never seen before, with huge, bright blossoms, bigger than a man's palms. The passing sunlight flitted from scarlet petals to azure petals. Perfumes rose thick with the approaching evening, hyacinth and rose, and exotic fragrances she couldn't identify.

In one corner three men stood talking. She recognized one figure immediately. From the powerful cast of the shoulders, the dark hair and the green mantle, she knew even from the back that it was Seaghan Mac-Namara.

A man with neatly trimmed, straw-colored hair and a short-cropped blond beard stood facing them. He was a medium-sized man with easy graceful manners. He greeted Carbri with an outstretched hand. "Carbri O'Connor. Welcome to my home. These are my friends."

Carbri and MacNamara merely nodded at each other. Carbri and the other men embraced by holding each other's forearms and shoulders. Arrah didn't attempt the formal greeting. It was used only by men of rank, chieftains and their tanaists. She gave a sideways glance at MacNamara, but looked away immediately when she saw his dark eyes on her.

Carbri now introduced Arrah as his young clansman, Padraic. Arrah nodded without looking up. She could feel MacNamara's eyes on her.

"Welcome, welcome, young Paddy!" said O'Reilly. "Any O'Connor clansman is welcome to be hosted under my roof. I'll order a bath prepared for both of you immediately." He shouted out some orders to the servants.

Arrah knew her face was spattered with road mud. Her hands and fingers were dirty. She pulled her cloak close about her and continued looking down.

"Somewhat timid, I'd say he is, for an O'Connor, is he not?" Arrah recognized MacNamara's voice. From the shadow that darkened the ground in front of her Arrah could tell that he had moved closer.

"A country lad that left roaming the hills with sheep to sail with Reevnarg. He's a good lad, a little timid albeit. But a fortnight in Paris and he'll be able to tell the difference between a woman and a sheep. Won't you, lad?"

A round of laughter followed. Damn Carbri O'Connor. When he was with others, he was always making jokes at her.

She moved away from the group and followed a short walkway in the garden. She looked back briefly, and as she did so, she caught Seaghan MacNamara watching her. She looked quickly away.

Her gaze was held by an orange tree, covered with perfect, miniature fruits. She reached out and touched one of the small perfect orange spheres.

"Your clansman seems to have taken an interest in our host's fruit trees."
Arrah recognized MacNamara's voice, the edge in it. She immediately
moved away from the orange tree.

"Aye," said O'Reilly. "It's one of my diversions here, grafting and experi-
menting with various plants. We could never be planting oranges in Ireland, could we now? And still, I'll be telling you by the piper that played
afore Moses, it's not the homeland. And a man will never be forgetting his
homeland."

"But you've clipped your beard short in the French style," Carbri noted.
In the group only MacNamara and Eochan wore their beards short and
squared off. The others wore theirs long the way Reevnarg wore his. "And
what fine cloths is it that you'll be wearing? You've traded the frieze mantles
of the O'Reilly for the silks of the French." Eochan O'Reilly was elaborately dressed in a cream satin shirt with delicate, blue stitching and
sleeves ruffled at the wrist. The front of his doublet was dark blue, ending in
a large codpiece. He wore tight cream stockings and knee-high blue boots.

"Aye. A man won't be getting a breath of notice at court if he's not stylish.
Except for this ruffian here, who gets more notice than all the men put
together. From princesses to servant girls. Isn't that right, MacNamara?"

Arrah glanced up. Beside the elaborate elegance of O'Reilly, who fit in
exactly with the measured formality of the garden, MacNamara looked out
of place. His squared chin and massive shoulders were too arrogant and
masculine, too primitive, too rough for the careful lines of this place. On
most men, a cloak simply hung limp from the shoulders. MacNamara's
cloak seemed pushed out by the width of his shoulders, as if by some
formidable and intense virility. There was something brutal and dangerous
in MacNamara. Damn his black eyes. He'd caught her looking at him
again. She glanced away but could still feel his gaze on her, could feel her
cheeks grow hot.

She turned her back to him. She didn't want him to compare her to the
woman he'd helped from the carriage. Had she been one of the ladies in
waiting that O'Reilly had spoken of? Arrah was determined not to look at
MacNamara again. Instead she watched an ant carrying a crumb of bread
along the sloped rough top of a stone.

"Will you not be taking a tankard of the grape," O'Reilly asked Carbri,
"and be telling us how is it, then, that you've put into Paris?"

"There was a storm in the Bay of Biscay. We were sailing with Reevnarg
O'Donnell."

"How's the old sea serpent?"

"Disagreeable. Cankered and huffish as ever. Heading for Portugal to be trading Irish hides and frieze for wine."

"The best wines are in France herself."

"Aye, but he claims that the French traders would be secretly punching holes in his hides, then be telling him that they're rat-eaten. 'Tis the Portuguese traders who'll be offering him the best price. Come upon by a storm, we were. The lot of us. Paddy and me, tying in the rigging when a wave swamped us. Washed overboard, with nothing but a herring's tail between us to hold on to. The good humor of the sea gods took us in."

"You'll stay this night then and take sup here. Your baths will soon be ready."

"We'll be thanking you for your hospitality," said Carbri, looking about him again. "Despite your heart's aching for Ireland, I see that life in France will be kind to you."

"Aye. But I've want of what is rightfully mine. I have a ship to take arms and mercenaries to assist clansmen who are loyal to me against my brother. But her captain was yesternight killed in a quarrel over a doxy in a bistro."

At the mention of the word *ship*, Arrah came back and stood beside Carbri. O'Reilly glanced at her and continued. "You know the ways of the sail, O'Connor. Will you be willing to take charge of her? Travel to Rathlin Island to pick up the galloglass mercenaries waiting there?"

Seaghan MacNamara intervened sardonically. "Surely you're not going to send a boy to command a man's mission?"

Arrah glared at him briefly, but not wanting to take the chance of being recognized, she looked away.

Carbri defended himself well. "Begging your pardon, MacNamara, but I've naught sailed with Reevnarg O'Donnell these last years without learning something."

"Aye," said O'Reilly. "If the lad knows enough to navigate for the O'Donnell, he knows enough to steer his own ship. You can go and look at her after you've bathed and taken the evening meal."

"Begging your hospitality, but we'd like to go now," Carbri said. His and Arrah's faces were bright with excitement.

"The zeal of youth!" O'Reilly smiled. "Go back then. The way of the bridge. Continue past the grain and bird merchant. She's docked there. Called the *Belle Étoile*. A weary bark, but seaworthy enough. Take your pick of sailors from those around the dock. They're a sorry lot. But with the wars . . ." He shrugged. "Here's a sack of gold to be paying with. But mind, you don't give a sovereign until you're on the open sea."

"I've naught sailed with the O'Donnell to be fooled by quay birds."

O'Reilly gave Carbri the rest of his instructions.

"Thank you, Eochan O'Reilly." Carbri and O'Reilly embraced once more, then Carbri and Arrah turned to leave, but MacNamara stepped in front of them. "Wait. This is an expedition for men, not boys," he said, looking directly at Arrah.

"Aye, he's young," said Carbri, "but his heart is brave. He's a good lad. Serves me well enough," and he put his arm around Arrah in a gesture of camaraderie.

"I don't like the looks of your kinsman, O'Connor. He has the look of a milksop and not a man."

"You forget, friends," said O'Reilly, "that we were young too. I held my sword as ably as a lad as I do now."

"Aye," said MacNamara, "but you never had the look of this pigeon-heart about you." And he shoved Arrah's shoulder roughly.

Arrah was too angry to avoid his gaze any longer. "Ruffian!" She shoved him back, but he was immovable as a boulder.

Carbri came between them. "MacNamara, choose your quarrels with someone who has your own skills!" said Carbri.

"O'Connor, you treat your kinsman like a mother treats her girl child! I just mean to test the metal of this *boy*. He's going about men. He'd best learn their ways." He gave Arrah a malevolent look, stared blatantly at the pistol thrust in the waist of her trews. "He carries a gun, yet he has not the look of one who could please a mistress when he holds her naked in his arms." He touched Arrah's chin. "He has not even the ghost of a beard."

She slapped away his hand. "And you, sirrah, have the beard and manners of a billy goat." And she used the same gesture she'd seen the woman in the street use earlier. She bit her thumb, then flicked it at MacNamara.

He smiled, his black eyes glinting dangerously. "Aye, now! The boy has spirit. Are you as good with your sword as you are with your tongue?"

"Leave off. He's not been schooled in weapons," said Carbri.

"Is this the way you teach your clansman, O'Connor, like a mother, that he knows not the sword? Is it not time he learned then? Come, lad. Give us a show!" MacNamara drew his weapon.

"Stop your sport with boys, MacNamara, and fight with a man. I'll give you a show," and Carbri pulled his sword, but MacNamara knocked it clanging to the cobblestones.

"Brute!" Arrah shouted at him.

"Boy or not," MacNamara said with ironic amusement. "You need to be schooled. It's easy to judge from the state of the hay whether the pitchfork is any good." He smiled maliciously, brushing his sword briefly against her groin. "Have you used your steel with a wench yet? I'll wager not."

"It's not of your concern."

He turned and looked at the others and joked with them. "We'll have to be finding him a codpiece with an extra bit of padding. The ladies look there to be judging the quality of the man's weapon. I'll wager you're a sore disappointment for a woman."

Arrah remembered the woman descending from the carriage. "And I'll wager you're a disappointment yourself."

She felt his sardonic gaze. "By Jove. Listen to the boy. No hair on his chin, nothing between his legs, and still he mouths impudence. Come, lad, on guard!"

Arrah drew.

"Don't! You're no match!" shouted Carbri. "Stop this! In the name of hospitality, O'Reilly. The quarrel is between a skilled swordsman and a boy."

"Rest easy, Mother O'Connor," said MacNamara. "I mean the lad no harm. But 'tis time he sworded. Come, lad, show us what sort of metal is in your sword." MacNamara's teeth sparkled. He waited for her, his smile mocking. "Come, lad. 'Tis time you learned the lessons of manhood."

Arrah struck with all her strength against MacNamara's weapon. Seaghan MacNamara took a step backward. A high stone wall stood several paces behind him. "Good hit, lad," and he stepped back once more. She was encouraged and hit harder, and once more he stepped back in the direction of the wall.

From the corner of her eye, she saw Carbri leap for his sword, but O'Reilly stopped him. MacNamara parried with her. She was able to block his thrusts easily, and growing more confident, she again took the offensive. A few more hits and she would back him against the wall. But he crossed her sword and held it with his, then suddenly leaped behind her. As he did so, his sword released hers and she spun and faced him again. His thrusts were harder and quicker now and she was on the retreat. MacNamara was smiling coldly.

She realized he was playing with her, like a cat played with a mouse. He was allowing her to strike, only to make her aware of how very much in control he was. He was advancing on her steadily, striking, pushing her back, trapping her to the wall behind. She tried to move sideways, but each time his sword was there with lightning speed, directing her relentlessly back. There was nothing she could do except to parry MacNamara's thrust. She felt the solidity of the wall at her back. Damn! She grasped the sword with both hands and struck with all her might. Her skull shook with the impact. He smiled. She lifted her arm again, tried to strike, but her sword never had a chance to connect, for MacNamara, with a quick upward movement of his arm, grabbed her elbow in his hand and pinned it above her head. The mound of her breast was thus readily visible despite the flattening garments she wore. She saw his eyes drop there. She heard her own quick breath, and that of MacNamara, and felt the hot brute force of his arm on hers.

His face was very close to hers. She could smell the hot overpowering maleness of him. His huge form pressed squarely against hers so that she felt the hard muscle of his thigh pushing its heat against hers. Her arm was still up and she tried to bring it down, not to protect herself from his sword, but to protect herself from his mouth, which came closer and closer. Warmth from his breath brushed her lips.

His eyes were so black, it was impossible to see where the iris began and the pupil ended, yet she saw herself mirrored there. She couldn't see around him or above him, or behind him. He filled her sight and moved in even closer against her. She felt as though he was going to draw her into him, that he was going to envelop her, possess her in his heat.

She heard Carbri call and O'Reilly's response telling Carbri to rest easy. But Carbri's voice and Eochan's voice were small and distant, as though they were voices in a dream, or an echo, or voices from another world, as though everything she knew had disappeared completely from the other side of this huge hot mountain that held himself in front of her.

Now he slammed her arm against the wall so her sword fell to the ground with a clatter. He ripped up the sleeve of her shirt exposing the scars about her wrist. His black eyes held hers.

"The devil take you, MacNamara! You've had your game. Now let me go." She pushed against him.

"Hold on, Arrah!" he said softly. Then he shouted to the men behind him. "Aye, the lad's got spirit. I'm going to show him a maneuver or two. Eochan, take Carbri and show him those new maps you had drawn."

Arrah wanted to call out to Carbri, but there was nothing but a dark, hot silence inside her.

The dizzying heat of MacNamara kept pressing on her and when he spoke she felt his warm breath against her lips. "You'll always lack the sword of a real man," he said quietly, reaching into the waist of her trews. She felt his calloused hands graze the skin of her stomach as he drew out her pistol. "Now I can feel you the way a man wants to feel a woman," and she felt the disarming hardness of his groin pressing on her.

She drew back, but there was no place else to go, and the pressure of him between her legs persisted, firm and solid and hot. He held her there and she felt the dizzying, overpowering heat of him. MacNamara clasped his hands under her arms and held her up against the wall.

"Why don't you want to be a woman, Arrah O'Donnell?"

She came from the world of dizziness to the reality of the moment. "What do you know about women?" She immediately regretted her words, for everything about the look of MacNamara, his swarthy arrogance, his overwhelming virility, all indicated that he knew a great deal about women. She remembered the easy way, too, that he had swept the woman in the street into his arms, the way the woman had lingered there looking at him. Arrah tried to grab her pistol from him. He snatched her wrist in his hand. The power of his fingers stunned her. She was accustomed to the strong hands of men. Years of work at oars and ropes, pulling and rigging sails, turned a man's fingers into powerful grips like a carpenter's vise. Her father and Carbri had strong hands. But never had she felt such strength as the fingers of MacNamara had.

"Why do you try to be a man? Try to act as though you have plums?"

"Give the pistol back!"

"Why do you try to put such hardness between your legs, when you're . . ." She felt his thumb stroking the top of her wristbone, felt his hand turn hers over so that his thumb caressed the underside of her wrist, where the skin was sensitive. "When you're soft . . ." His voice lingered on the word, his tongue, breath, and lips holding it as though it were a caress. Although he stood in front of her, she felt as though his breath and lips had brushed the back of her neck.

"Why don't you leave me alone!"

His voice was almost a whisper. "I want you. The day with the eagle, your spirit was soaring proud and fierce as a bird's. I wanted to possess you then, Arrah of the Eagles. But Reevnarg said you were betrothed." He glanced away briefly and his voice drifted off for a moment. "I've already come between one man and his wife. To do so again, and in the home of my host, would have gone against all laws of hospitality." He returned his dark eyes to hers. "And then you escaped like a bird escapes its keeper. You flew off with that boy. Now, with your hair cut, your beauty more severe and proud than ever . . . I—"

His arrogance enraged her. "Boy! Do you think that Carbri and I, all this time . . . Carbri's as much as you!"

"Carbri is a boy. You, Arrah, need a man to make love to you and possess you in ways that Carbri never dreamed of having you. He's a fine navigator, I admit, but he's a lad, and he drinks too much."

"Lies!" She grabbed her dagger and tried to slash him with it, but she'd grabbed it clumsily, and part of her hand was over the blade. MacNamara grasped over her fingers.

"Drop the dagger," he said.

"No!"

"Drop it, I said," and he squeezed her fingers around it.

She felt the sharp metal cut her palm. "No!"

"Damn you, Arrah O'Donnell. I'll make you drop it." And he took her arm and hit it backwards sharply against the wall so her hand flew open from the force and the dagger fell. There was a line of blood on her palm. "Damn your stubbornness." MacNamara reached into his shirt and pulled out a handkerchief. She tried to pull her hand away, but MacNamara pushed her back roughly against the wall.

"Don't fight me now!" His eyes were brilliant and black, and all the casual mirth that had been there earlier was gone from them. He tied the handkerchief about her hand. "Leave Carbri O'Connor and come with me."

"I love Carbri! I'm going to marry him."

She saw the expression on his face grow distant. He released his hold so that she thought he was going to let her go. Abruptly he pushed her back against the wall. "Marry him, then. Damn your stubborn heart! Marry him. But I tell you this." He grasped her tightly and his voice dropped suddenly so that it was like an intimate, quiet rumble. "When you realize your error, I'm going to come for you and make love to you the way you need to be made love to. I'm going to find that place in you that is soft and dark and secret . . . and you'll never want to play at being a man again." He handed back her pistol. He took her sword hand and raising it to his lips, kissed it. "I wish I'd met you before, Arrah of the Eagles, before your father betrothed you to the Joyce," he said quietly. He turned and left the garden just as the others returned.

CHAPTER
10

In a shadowed, narrow street in Paris, Seaghan MacNamara hunched his shoulders and lowered his face against the wind. The night, despite the afternoon's sun, had turned foul; he cursed heavily under his breath. He grabbed his mantle, trying to pull it close about him, but the wind was fierce and ripped the cloak from him, revealing broadly muscled shoulders. Already his shirt was plastered to his skin by the rain.

He reached a partially broken door set into a crumbling wall where the very stones seemed to be rotting. Forcefully he knocked on the door.

The square peephole opened and a lantern on the inside was raised to show the identity of the knocker. But the lamp showed more about its holder than the man who arrived. The face on the inside was mutilated, without ears, without lips. The defaced man couldn't smile, but nodded to the visitor, and opened the door to him.

Two other men sat at a long rough table in the room. On the table stood a candle burning low, the wax melted in a soft, limp, almost twisted-looking shape. Also on the table were three wooden cups; some sawed rib bones of pigs painted with black dots to make dice; a deck of cards, the top one showing the King of Swords; and a cylindrical-looking piece of wood about the length of a forearm with a steel hook projecting from one end. Of the two men sitting there, one of them had a stump of arm that ended at his elbow, the other had a patch on one eye.

The one-eyed man stood immediately when he saw MacNamara enter. When he smiled, his remaining good eye blinked shut to show a deep blue, red, and green tattoo on his lid. The tattoo was of an open eye.

The mouthless one proffered a cup of wine, but MacNamara declined. "I thank you, but no." Then the wind howled and caught up a loose shutter and slammed it open. The candle blew out and the room was in darkness.

"Close the cursed thing," ordered the voice of the man with the tattooed eye. There was the sound of the shuffling of feet, the wind howling, the slamming of the shutter.

MacNamara spoke again but the words were lost to the slamming of the shutter and the howl of the wind. The man with the tattooed eye bent close to the visitor to better hear what he said.

The word "woman" rose above the wind. Coins jangled. There was the vaguely muffled sound of a leather pouch filled with gold coins thrown onto a rough wooden table. In the shadows, the man with the stump arm turned toward the table, but he didn't reach for the bag.

"I'll do what I can," said the tattooed man.

"I go now," said MacNamara, and without another word he pulled open the door and went back to the storm.

Naira waited in bed for Bres. They had been married a fortnight. Soon they would return to her castle at Glen Head which she needed Bres's help in fortifying because it was rumored that her former husband's family would try to take it from her. And as soon as possible she wanted to inspect Debrogail's grave to make sure she was dead, even if it meant digging up her body.

At first Bres had been reluctant to make love to Naira, maintaining an annoying faithfulness to Debrogail. But Naira knew the secrets to make a man desire her. She had gone down to the old woman who lived in the cave at the edge of the sea, the old woman with the great raspberry birthmark on her neck and cheek. Naira asked her to mix together a potion to make Bres lust for her.

"Come, my precious," said the old woman.

The old woman kept her face wrapped up all the time. But as she was mixing her potion, the cloth fell away and Naira saw the birthmark. Naira knew that the old woman had become a midwife because no one would marry her with such a mark. The woman mixed a concoction, then had Naira say the words:

> Ground pits from cherries three
> milk of rook and honey bee
> bring the desire of my love to me.

"Grind this with nuts in a sweetcake," directed the old woman, "and he won't realize what he's eating. And use your own talents. You have muscles in your pleasure cave. Open and close them five hundred times each day to make them strong. Use them when you are with your man."

But as Naira was about to leave, the old woman had grabbed her arm and said, "There is something else you should know. Do you know the story of the curse against the O'Donnell family?"

Like everyone else, Naira had heard the story often enough. The story was part of the bloody O'Donnell legacy. As a young man, Reevnarg's brother had been washed overboard from a ship and saved by a poor fisherman's daughter. She was a powerful swimmer, but she had been rejected by all men because her beauty was marred by a reddish-purple birthmark that covered almost half her face. When Reevnarg's brother recovered sufficiently, he undressed her and loved her. There were no stains on her long pale limbs and he took his pleasure repeatedly, and she loved him. But when he prepared to leave, she pleaded with him to stay. He replied that because he was a chieftain's son, he couldn't marry anyone who had such a mark on her face.

In a fit of anger she drew her scaling knife and killed him, but Reevnarg's father sought revenge. He ordered that the fishergirl's hands be bound behind her back. He commanded that a huge stone be tied about her neck and that she be thrown from a cliff into the sea. But before she died, she cursed Reevnarg's family and said the family would have no male heirs until a woman of his family was hanged by her lover. Reevnarg's father died shortly after. He was on his ship, and when he climbed into the masts he slipped and hanged himself in the cords. That was the story of the curse.

But the old woman told her more, much more. For two days Naira had taken to her bed with the shock of the news.

Earlier in the night Naira had brushed her long hair until it shone gloriously. She touched rose scent to her shoulders, between her breasts and between her thighs.

When Bres came to bed, he saw Naira sitting there propped up against the pillows. Admittedly she looked lovely, if a snake could be lovely. She wore a white transparent gown of delicately embroidered silk, her hair flowing over her shoulders. The gown had slipped from one shoulder taking her hair back with it, and there he noticed a small raspberry-colored birthmark.

"Aren't you even going to touch me?" she asked.

He reached up and touched the birthmark. "The hangman's mark," he said quietly. "I've never seen it on a woman before."

"Oh, that," she said, shrugging with feigned nonchalance. But she drew up her robe again. "Mother told me I was born with it because she looked on the midwife's face before I was born. Now come, my darling. Your wife wants to make love with you!"

Bres had promised himself he would not forget Debrogail. He remembered her laughing, teasing eyes, the way her hands felt on his wounded body. First there had been her touches when she dressed the wound on his arm, later she had teased him, telling him she was looking for wounds on his thigh. He remembered her fingers on his manhood.

Naira was passionate. She kissed him. In his mind Naira became Debrogail, and he was kissing Debrogail and not Naira. He was looking down on her pale breasts; she had beautiful breasts. She had perfect nipples, not too large, not too small, but the perfect size, and that perfect russet hue, and fragrant skin. He felt a heat growing at his groin as he kissed Naira's nipple, making him hard. She readily parted her thighs. He wished somehow he could feel some sense of loyalty to Debrogail, but when he found himself in Naira he seemed to stop thinking of everything except her hot moistness clutching at him. She had somehow learned to tighten and loosen her portal of Venus around his shaft as though it were a mouth. When he was in her and she began to tighten about him, firm, clutching, rhythmic, it was as though he found himself with his phallus inserted in the keyhole of heaven. He had promised himself he would be loyal to Debrogail, at least in mind. But his phallus had no sense of loyalty, only of pleasure, selfish, indulgent pleasure. The ecstasy of Naira's rhythmic motions traveled down his cock, until he could contain his pleasure no more.

CHAPTER
11

The Place des Grèves, the square where sailors and dock workers collected looking for work, was a wild, rough section of Paris, filled with shouting and cursing and shrill, raucous laughter, an area of alehouses and enormous rats, of fish hawkers, and drunken men and red-lipped women leaning into each other for support as they stumbled down the street.

Carbri and Arrah began looking for a crew almost immediately. O'Reilly had been right. It was a sorry lot of sailors on the square. Arrah wondered if there was a man about who wasn't missing an ear or an eye, a finger, a hand, or a leg.

As Carbri talked with sailors, Arrah began to wonder how good a judge of seamen he was. He chose men her father never would have tolerated. He accepted one sailor who kept digging at himself as though the crabs in his groin were going to eat him alive. Arrah didn't agree with Carbri's choice. A man who was always at himself couldn't attend properly to the cords. After some argument, Carbri agreed. She refused yet another sailor who had gone blind from too many sun sightings. Arrah felt sorry for him, but one of the rules of the sea was that a sailor had to earn his keep.

A sailor with a black leather patch over his right eye approached Arrah and Carbri. "Begging your pardon, friends. But I hear word you're hiring on for the *Belle Étoile*. I go by the name of Patch, and these here will be me two mates."

Arrah looked at the speaker called Patch. He had an open eye tattooed on the lid of his good eye so that each time he blinked she saw a red and blue and green eye looking at her. Sailors often had tattoos on their eyelids since it was common belief among them that the tattoo kept watch while they slept. Patch was a wiry little man with a face that looked not bearded as much as unshaven. A few strands of red stuck out from the grayish brown hair on his face. He had intense, bright eyes that reminded Arrah of the blue of the lakes of Connacht. But she was puzzled by one thing: despite his weathered face, he had unnaturally white hands.

"Aye, now. So tell us where it is you've sailed."

"You name it, I've sailed it. Ain't a man on the sea knows more about a ship than me. I give good service. Me two mates as well. Mute, called so on account his tongue was trimmed, and this here is Hook."

Arrah glanced at the sailor called Mute, whose face was scarred and mutilated, but she couldn't look long since the face was without a lower lip or ears, and it disturbed her.

Hook had a swarthy, pockmarked face. He had no left arm, just a hook. "Aye. Don't let the looks of Angel darling be fooling you." He held up a sharp, devastating-looking hook that had been sharpened to look like the tip of a cutlass blade. "Filed off and sharpened her meself, I did. Won't be needing no other weapon aside from me Angel. Me and Angel. We've sent more devils to hell than you can count. Ain't that right, Angel, me darling?" and twice he kissed the wooden stump into which the hook was embedded.

"And what of the cords? You'll be cutting them when you take hold?" asked Carbri.

"I use me mouth and me other hand. Like a parrot. You ever seen a parrot climb his cage? With his beak he does it. Holding on like. Same as me." And he closed his two lips tight together to prove it. "I got callouses on me lips and tongue. Same as other men have on their hands."

Carbri was reluctant. He turned away and talked to Arrah. Carbri distrusted them. Normally sailors weren't so eager. And there hadn't been any discussion of money yet.

"You, Patch," he said, "you can sign on. But your friends . . . I have to be saying nay."

"But they're good mates, I tell ye. The best anywhere. They won't let ye down. I'd rather sail with these two than five others with two good hands and lips and ears, and the whole lot of it."

"Only you," said Carbri, "otherwise you don't come at all."

In a narrow street two doors down from the Place des Grèves, a man ran breathlessly into an alehouse. "Captain Whip!" he shouted.

The tavern was nearly black inside and it took a moment for the running man's eyes to readjust from the morning light. Men sat in shadows around rough tables.

The evening fire in the tavern hadn't been restoked, and all that remained in the hearth were some warm ashes from earlier; most of the tavern was dark. Shafts of light came streaming in from cracks about the shutters, slanted rays that showed dust hanging like pockets of mist in the air. Some partial walls near the back added to the dark atmosphere. It was to a table near the back that the runner delivered his news. A candle stood on the middle of the table, but it remained unlit. It was impossible to see the men's features clearly; however, it was obvious that one of them wore a broadbrimmed black hat with plumes. On the table beside him lay a coiled whip. It was because of the whip that the man had earned his nickname.

"What's her cargo?" asked Captain Whip.

"He don't say," said the breathless man. "But captain, he's carrying a bulge of gold in his pockets."

"How many of them?"

"Just two. A young captain and a lad with him."

Captain Whip gave orders to three men. "Camel and Christophe. And you, Sebastian. You offer yourselves. And mind you don't double me, or I'll cut off your flowers when I catch you and feed them to the Hirple here."

Three shadowed men stood. Then a fourth, the older man nicknamed Hirple, a sailor's term meaning limping and faltering, also stood. But he stooped awkwardly because of an old leg injury that had never healed properly.

"You, Hirple. Where the devil do you think you're going?" asked the captain, reaching for his whip.

"With them." He motioned to the three departing men.

"You'll stay with me!" He lifted the whip from the table.

"But more of us on board, we'll have a better chance at—"

Captain Whip struck at the speaker's face with the whip handle. "Blackhearted shark. One more word of your lies, I'll ram this handle up your arse end and pull it up your throat." He laughed. "Course, you'd think that was a bit of all right, wouldn't you?"

The man called Hirple said nothing.

"Wouldn't you?"

"No!"

"Missing the arsehole of your bitch birdie all ready?"

Hirple said nothing.

"Lying filth. I know you, Hirple. I know you better and in ways your own sweet mother didn't know you." And Captain Whip threw his head back and laughed. "You can't be five minutes, can you now, without seeing

Christophe. Jealous like a dog, you are. Zounds, Hirple! What ails, lad? Afraid your lambkin will find Camel with more pith than you? To me way of thinking, it'll be doing some good to the lad. Mark me words. Like new rigging on a ship." And he threw back his head and laughed.

Hirple said nothing, but his fists clenched.

Captain Whip noticed. "Angry now, are we? Ah, never mind, Hirple. It's good sport, is all. I like to be laughing. Drink up now! Or I'll piss in your tankard, lad, and make you drink it."

Outside on the square, Carbri agreed to hire on a sailor Arrah didn't like. The sailor's eyes kept wandering to the bulge in Carbri's pocket where he had put the sack of gold. Carbri insisted the man, who had many years' experience, be taken on.

When the would-be mariner discovered that he was only to be paid on board, he secretly pulled a knife from the crease of his back. Carbri, talking to another sailor, was oblivious to the gleam of steel, but Arrah saw the metal's glint, leaped at Carbri's knees and sent him sprawling safely to the ground. A blade flew through the air and stuck in the sailor's forearm. He screamed and dropped his own dagger as though his arm had been struck by lightning.

Carbri and Arrah were down, and desperate, rough sailors gathered about, coming in for the final kill like wolves around an injured deer.

But there was a shout, and Patch, along with his two colleagues, leaped into the group. Patch brandished a sword in one hand and another dagger in the other. Mute, too, had a sword.

Hook slashed out with the vicious point of his arm. "One step forward, mates, and Angel and me'll send you to visit the pearly gates."

There was grumbling, but no one moved forward. Hook reached out his good hand to Carbri to help him up. Carbri looked at it then grasped it. The circle of men broke up. Carbri brushed the mud and dirt from his garments. "I'll be owing you an apology, man. And your mate too. You can both hire on with Patch here." The two men smiled, Hook with two yellow teeth, and Mute with his bizarre, mutilated face.

"You're indebted to your lad," said Patch, motioning at Arrah. "If he hadn't pushed ye out of the way, ye'd been a dead man."

"Right you are," said Carbri, smiling at Arrah.

"Will you make me the bosun, then?" she asked.

"Bosun! You've no experience at all," said Carbri.

"I had no experience with saving your life either," she said spiritedly. "I can learn. You and Patch can teach me."

"The lad has a point," said Patch, winking at Arrah with his tattooed eye.

"It's a silly idea!" said Carbri.

"It isn't a silly idea. You learned about the sea from my father. You knew nothing when you started. I can learn too!"

"No!" said Carbri.

"Yes, or I won't sail with you!" Arrah's voice was edged with steel.

Carbri blew air out loudly through his lips. He had no intention of allowing her to become bosun but it was silly to argue here in front of a would-be crew. "All right," he said reluctantly, "but you'll do exactly as I tell you!"

Arrah noticed Patch resheathing his dagger in his boot. When they'd first spoken to him, she'd noticed only one dagger at his belt along with his sword. Yet he'd thrown one, held another in his hand, and still had the one in his belt. The sailor who'd attacked them had also pulled a hidden dagger. She saw Patch retrieve his dagger. He wiped the blood from it on his trousers, then reached behind his back. How many hidden daggers did sailors carry?

Carbri carried only one dagger: the one at his belt along with his sword. Carbri was honest and forthright and good-humored. Not given to stealth, he didn't expect it in others, and therefore he kept his weapons fully visible. Arrah came to a realization about Carbri: he'd learned certain things about sailing from her father, but there were many things about sailors he didn't know. Never again would she assume that a man was unarmed simply because he showed no weapon. She, too, would carry daggers inside her boots and hidden at her back. She was thankful to have Patch and Hook and Mute aboard, and now she felt shame for her earlier reluctance to take them on.

As she was thinking about daggers, Carbri was already hiring on more sailors: a pleasant-looking dark-complected Frenchman called Sebastian, who wore a red rag about his neck, and his companion, called Christophe. And another, Camel, a hump-backed sailor who had dark greasy hair like a tarred mop. Before long the *Belle Étoile* had a motley crew of thirty sailors.

The men set to work immediately fixing the ship and getting it ready for sailing. Some sailors scraped barnacles from her hull, others tarred the bulwark, while others rebuilt rotting shroud boards or mended sails.

Arrah asked questions constantly about everything and anything that the crew did, from the simplest to the most complicated. "How did you tie that rope so fast?" "When will you teach me how to use the astrolabe?" At first she asked questions of Carbri, but he always said, "You needn't be concerning yourself about it. Just be telling Patch that there's not enough pitch melted into the starboard floor. Tell him to be looking at things with his good eye instead of his patch."

When Carbri refused to answer her questions, she asked some of the crew members, but she found them sullen and resentful. "If you don't know, what the devil are you doing here?"

Only Patch was patient and willing to tell her whatever she wanted to know. One of the first things he told her was, "The first rule of sailing is this: If ye can't tie good knots, tie lots of them."

When she asked him about his white hands, he told her he had burned them in a ship's fire.

Arrah and Carbri went looking for ammunition for the two swivel guns on the poop deck, but found that all the powder and shot had been requisitioned by the army. The munitions dealer said he would have no more supplies for a week. They would have to sail without.

The ship was readied and the cargo of wine for transport to Rathlin Island was loaded. Carbri had instructions from O'Reilly to sell the wine there and use the money as an advance to pay the mercenaries.

The *Belle Étoile* sailed along the Seine and out to sea, the wake rising behind the ship.

Magnus brought his wife, Cathlin, down to Debrogail's cell. Because of his injury, he couldn't carry her, but Cathlin's kindness had touched most of the guards at some time or another, and four men carried her on a stretcher and laid her on the floor. Debrogail immediately kneeled to her, taking the woman's hands in hers.

"Cathlin," she said, "you and Magnus have been so kind to me."

"The world is filled with small kindnesses. God has granted me the gentlest, kindest man a woman could ask for, and if I can repay him by doing a small kindness for someone else, then I will." She smiled weakly.

Cathlin had almond-colored hair, similar to Debrogail's. In robust health, she would have been more handsome than pretty, but because of illness, her face and hands had an almost transparent, haunting quality. Despite her pregnancy, she was thin as a harp string. The guards helped prop her up, and she sat with her hands resting on her stomach.

Debrogail began by singing quiet odes and ballads, and when she glanced over at Cathlin, the woman seemed to have taken on an almost otherworldly quality. She seemed to hang on Debrogail's songs, and when Debrogail began to sing the song of the whelks, tears sprang to Cathlin's eyes and she joined in Debrogail's singing, her voice frail and quavering but pleasant. Afterwards, Cathlin said. "I remember as a small child, when my mother used to sing that."

Debrogail shifted to merrier tunes, and she began to dance and to swirl about, using the blanket in a most enticing way. The guards began to whoop and shout and clap in time to her steps. Some of them had already joined Magnus on previous days to watch and hear Debrogail, and on occasion they had brought her warm broth with a piece of meat in it. All were eager to hear her again. One guard called outside to others and before long the cell was filled with soldiers clapping. Some of the guards grabbed each other's hands and they began to leap about.

Cathlin, too, clapped briefly in time to the music, but then she tired and let her hands fall. Magnus, sitting devotedly beside her with his hand resting on her stomach, bent over and kissed her.

When Debrogail stopped singing, Cathlin said, "Oh, Debrogail. I've not been well, and it's been a long time since I've known such joy. My parents were both singers, not bards, just singers for the common people. We would sit around the fire at night, and they would sing to us. And then they all died in a plague when I was a child. I feel it's a good omen for the baby to be so close and for me to feel such joy. Will you sing more?"

Everyone hooted and yelled in agreement. Debrogail joked and flattered and the guards blushed like children as she chucked them under the chin.

But then the mortar-faced prison keep called Rory arrived, breaking up the feeling of joviality. "What's going on here? Is this a dungeon or a tavern!" he shouted.

"What are you going to do? Tell Mistress Naira that we've brought a spark of light to this hell-wrought place?"

"I might just do that."

"That's your way, isn't it, Rory? Jawing to her about everything. Hoping it'll give you advancement in her eyes."

"It's not by listenin' to that banshee wail you get ahead in this world, and you fools would be well to be larnin' that. A messenger just came. He would have been here earlier, but a squall blew his boat off course. Mistress Naira is arriving in three days' time to see if her orders was carried out. I'll have no more of this wailin' here."

Three days! And she was checking if her orders were carried out! Fear plunged into the cell like a stone. The hole wasn't dug. Since Mistress Naira was far away, and the stonemason sick, they had seen no reason to hurry, especially since some had heard Magnus talk of her and had come themselves to hear her beautiful voice.

Dread and urgency now filled them. They felt remorse for Debrogail, but they were men after all, and not fools, and who but the most foolish of men allowed themselves to be charmed by a servant girl? There were tavern girls if one wanted entertainment, and they did more than just sing.

They shuffled out of the cell quickly as possible, not looking at Debrogail. Four men bent to pick up Cathlin's stretcher.

"Are you all going to abandon me?" cried Debrogail.

But no one answered her. Even Magnus seemed afraid to meet her eyes as he turned toward his wife, pretending to be occupied with holding her hand.

"Wait," said Cathlin, and she reached out her hand to Debrogail. "You called me kind. Yet no one has been kinder to me than you, blessing me with your angel's voice." Tears sprang to Cathlin's eyes. "I wish I could take you out of here. I—"

"Take her away!" ordered Rory.

"God bless you, Debrogail," said Cathlin. "I'll send some sweet cakes with Magnus tomorrow."

"And if you ever bring her back I'll order you reported to Mistress Naira!"

Debrogail was in despair; Mistress Naira was arriving. The next night Magnus didn't come. Each time Debrogail heard the slightest noise she rushed to the door thinking he had come, but no one even entered the corridor adjacent to her cell. Even Rory didn't show to bring her her customary bread and water. Maybe Mistress Naira had ordered her starved to death.

She began to think that they had used her. They had used her voice to amuse themselves for a while, even Cathlin had used her to forget her own illness, and suddenly now that Mistress Naira was coming they had abandoned her. No one came near her.

And then she heard the rattling of keys and the unmistakable sound of Magnus's wooden crutches. "Magnus! Magnus!" she called.

When he opened the door, one look at Magnus's face told her that something terrible had gone wrong. "Oh, Magnus," she said. "I . . ." Her words sounded empty, hollow and inadequate, as if it wasn't she who had spoken them but some other person, a stranger. A few moments ago she had thought that perhaps Magnus, too, had used her.

"The baby was too large, and turned some way. There was nothing that could be done. The midwife couldn't even take the baby from her. They're both dead." And letting his crutches drop and falling to his knees, his shoulders began to quiver as he wept. "Oh, Debrogail, I loved her so."

She wished she could say something, anything to offer him comfort, yet from all appearances, she was soon to die herself.

"Debrogail," he said finally, wiping at his tears with his sleeve. "There's something you don't know. You're to be buried alive."

Buried alive! So that was the depth of Naira's jealousy. She thought of the terrible unfairness of it all. Her mother had been right. She was a servant girl, and it was her duty in life to serve. She should have been more like Bridgett, sullen and morose, and doing the minimum required of her, instead of being a fool working with generosity of spirit and good humor. Most of the time she hadn't allowed herself to feel jealousy, but there were times when she saw Arrah and Naira in all their finery, their gold chains and brooches on their dresses, when she, too, had wanted those. And when she looked on Naira's hands or even Arrah's hands, they were soft compared to her own, which were soap-reddened and rough. But despite these differences, she had kept her cheer. She had kept such good cheer that Bres had fallen in love with her. And now she was going to serve Mistress Naira's jealousy with her own life.

And for a while she had even been naive enough to believe that Bres would come for her.

Debrogail turned on Magnus and screamed at him. "All the time you knew and yet you asked me to sing for you, to try and make you and your wife happy! Happy! Where's my happiness!"

"Please! Rory's off guard, but he's not far off, sleeping in a corner. He'll hear you!"

"If he's sleeping, then please, Magnus! Help me escape! Pretend I hit you! Took your crutches away. Anything, I beg you!"

"Mistress Naira is coming tomorrow. She's sent word she's going to check the hole to make certain you're in it."

"I won't!" and Debrogail made a rush for the door, but Magnus grabbed her leg and held it.

"Let me go! Let me go! Magnus!" She began to strike at the top of his head.

"You have to listen!" said Magnus, struggling with Debrogail. "Cathlin is dead. Before she died she said it was a sin to bury someone with a voice like yours. She said it would be like killing a nightingale," choked Magnus.

"Like seeing her own mother killed. Listen, please! I don't have the strength to struggle with you."

Debrogail stopped and listened. Magnus continued. "She told me I was to take her body and bring it here, and bury it instead of you. One of my friends is bringing her now. But we must hurry, before one of the others makes his rounds. Everyone here fears Mistress Naira. They'll give us away.

"The stonemason has never seen you or Cathlin. We'll tell him we gave you lots of ale to drink to calm you and that you drank so much you passed out. He's still under the weather and won't protest. It's pure stone where they've been digging. They just finished the hole a little while ago. He's scared to death, and just wants it done quickly. Rory's sick. He coughed up blood this morning. We'll put your clothes on Cathlin."

"Magnus, please just tell me the way out of here."

"If Mistress Naira doesn't find someone in that hole, she'll order us drawn and quartered. It's dark where they dug the hole. A body changes with death. She thinks you've been dead a month. We'll turn Cathlin's body so that only the back of her head shows. Most women don't like to look at death. I imagine Mistress Naira is no different. From the back, your hair is similar to hers, almond-colored."

At that moment one of the other guards arrived, carrying Cathlin's inert body over his shoulder. He was one of the guards who had listened to her that night when Cathlin had come to the cell.

Debrogail was shivering so badly that she couldn't move. Her teeth chattered.

"Debrogail, please hurry."

She'd been given an old shift to wear by the soldier who'd taken her from Eagle Castle that night. Now she tried to slip it off her head but she was shaking so that she couldn't manage it. Magnus helped her, but when he went to undress his wife, he began to cry again. He took his dead wife's hand in his hands and brought it to his lips, his tears streaming down on her swollen fingers.

And then he seemed to take some strength from the dead woman's hand, and slowly began to remove her clothes, showing the full belly that had once been the source of his joy.

He handed Cathlin's nightgown to Debrogail and although she was still shivering she managed to put it on. The other guard gave her Cathlin's cloak.

"Debrogail, he'll take you to my house. Wait for me there. I'll help bury Cathlin, and meet you there."

Debrogail was still too stunned to move. The other guard took her by the shoulders and led her toward the door. She paused for a moment to look back at Magnus.

His head was on his wife's stomach. She heard him whisper, "Good-bye, my child," and then he covered her with Debrogail's blanket. He kissed his dead wife's eyes and lips. "Good-bye, my Cathlin. May God grant you peace in heaven."

And then he was still, kneeling quietly beside his wife, the lamp lighting both their faces.

"You were wrong, Cathlin," Debrogail whispered. "The world is filled with great kindness. God bless you both!" Hurrying, she followed the guard down the corridor.

Patch kept his tattooed eye on the trim of the sails. Arrah asked him how he knew where to direction the canvas. As always he answered her cheerfully. "Well, ye see them there red-colored ribbon-like things on the sails? That one there to the windward is called the grandmother's tongue, and if she begins to wagging like a scolding lady, then ye knows, lad, your ship is pinched, which means she's sailing too close to the wind. You got to be either heading your ship downwind a bit or bring in sail. When them is flowing smooth-like, straight in line with each other, it'll be meaning that the trim of the sail is good."

Arrah absorbed every bit of knowledge about the wind, the sea, and the ship. She had limitless curiosity and limitless energy as she moved about the deck or climbed the shrouds to the sails. She had a natural ability, was as lithe and sinewy as a feline, and was as comfortable in the sails as a cat in a tree.

The sea wind freshened her face so that it glowed. She asked questions constantly. "Why aren't you crowding sail? Why are you coming about instead of jibing?" and so on, in a never-ending stream of "why . . . why . . . why?" When she thought no one was looking, she would blow Carbri a kiss. Sometimes she caught Patch watching her, his small, wizened, squirrellike face and good eye squinting against the sun. Sometimes, too, she caught Sebastian and Camel looking at her, but she would shoot them a dismissive look.

She asked Carbri to show her how to use the astrolabe.

"Arrah," he said, "you won't be needing to learn that."

"I want to know how," she said. "If you don't show me, someone else will."

Reluctantly he showed her how to hold the instrument to the sky in the proper way, then showed her the constellations on a sky map and how to plot the ship's position from them. She held up the astrolabe until her arms ached, and gazed at the marks on the circle and measured the angle of the sun during the day, and made calculations. At night, she did the same with the stars, so that Patch remarked to her one day, "You'll get moonstruck if you look at the sky too much."

She scoured the land map, memorizing its outlines and coastlines and landmarks. At night she would lie in the narrow bunk beside Carbri and holding the lamp close, would study the map. Carbri would begin to stroke her thighs and take the map from her and let it fall to the floor. He would kiss her lips and her breasts. Temporarily she forgot the maps, but after a time she would take up the parchments and begin studying them again. "Arrah, you're more interested in that map than you are in me," he told her one night.

She looked at Carbri and saw the fine gold hairs on his arm, and kissed his shoulder. "No, I'm not," she said, but inevitably, she returned to her scrutiny of the maps. Carbri turned onto his side and looked at her and began to brush his hand gently over her haunches and doing so, he fell asleep.

She was so enthusiastic about learning about the ship that she slept little and wandered the deck at all hours. The sailors whispered about her, called her "the catamite."

Arrah knew what they whispered, but she cared little for the prattle. She'd seen enough on the ship to know that the sailors were often at each other.

One quiet afternoon when it was a warm day with a brisk breeze blowing that sped the ship along, the sailors were left with little to do. Carbri sat tying a small bundle of knotted rope.

"What is it you're doing?" she asked.

"For the love of Christ, you won't be needing to know what every knot is for!" he scolded sharply.

"It's my work to know."

He saw the crew members listening. He took her aside and spoke quietly. " 'Od's blood! I was saying you could be bosun, but I was never meaning for it to happen." He sighed. "A woman can't be bosun, any more than she can be a captain."

"Damn you, Carbri O'Connor. I will be bosun!" and she spun on the deck and walked to the prow.

Mute, who was sitting eating a dish of lentils and hard bread, heard the exchange. He got up stiffly, dipped his bowl into a pail of salt water to rinse it, then hung it into a mesh bag to allow it to dry. He went over to where Arrah stood staring out at the sea. He made a series of gesticulations and hand motions and throwing motions and grunts and guttural sounds with his tongue, none of which she could understand.

Patch came over. "He's trying to tell ye about the monkey fist. Sailors tie them if they've nothing else to occupy them. Or, if they need to be thinking about something. Or, if they're being pushed along nice and easy in a fresh breeze and they won't have much to be worrying them. They'll be bringing a man good luck. It's an old sailor's tale that if you tie ten thousand monkey fists, you'll live to a ripe old age and die in your sleep.

"But a monkey fist'll be having a use as well. You use a monkey fist if you have a heavy bit of rope to throw. Come, I'll show you." He took a light length of rope and then a heavy one. "A sailor ties a monkey fist in one end of a light line. The other end he ties to the heavier rope. Watch up there. Hook!" he shouted up to the yardarm. "Grab hold!" He threw the lighter rope up, and Hook pulled it up, dragging up the heavier rope at the other end along with it.

Arrah was furious with Carbri. She didn't speak to him, and didn't sleep with him, and took small amounts of rest on the deck if the weather was nice, or in the hold on the cargo the way that the rest of the sailors did. Now she asked Patch all her questions.

She asked him what happened to Mute.

"Pirates," explained Patch, "by the name of Captain Whip. Pirates, when they'll be attacking, will attack ships smaller than themselves usually. They can't for the most part be taking on great merchants, 'cause they've too many guards and soldiers. But small ones like us they can be taking without much trouble. They trimmed Mute's ears and made him eat them. The same with his tongue."

Arrah felt nausea rise in her.

"What's the matter, lad? You've not much stomach for a sailor. There are worse things done on ships and I've seen the lot."

The other sailors called Arrah a parchment fart, and ridiculed her enthusiasm. Only Patch welcomed her questions. He talked freely about the ocean, the way other men would talk about a woman, alternatively cursing her and extolling her virtues.

Arrah missed the pleasure of Carbri's manhood, and often caught herself longing for it. But she refused to yield, and to push him from her mind she threw herself into learning with even greater fervor.

One afternoon as she was going down the steps into the cargo hold she encountered Carbri coming up. He caught her, and pressing her against the railing, kissed her. Arrah felt desire rise in her and kissed him back passionately. But remembering their quarrel, she pulled away. "Keep your kisses, until you decide that I am bosun, and not just in name."

"Aye, but you're a stubborn lass, Arrah O'Donnell. Stop this foolishness now and be coming up to the master's berth, and I'll be showing you a captain's desire that's poking up stiff as a mainmast."

"No!"

"Arrah! Come along! I'll be loving you more than the stars above."

"I want to be bosun."

"Arrah, for the love of—"

"I won't love you again until you agree!"

"It's ill luck!"

"I don't give a damn for your ill luck. I'll not sleep with you until you agree to let me be bosun."

"Arrah!" he sighed.

"Not until you swear."

"All right, for the love of Christ. You can be having the job of bosun. But why for the love of God, would a creature with a splendid arse the likes of yours be concerning herself about anchors and ropes is beyond my thinking."

She kissed him lightly, but he pulled her to him forcefully. "Now, come and be giving us a kiss like a good girl." She responded not like a girl but like a woman in heat, the fire in her ignited now. They went immediately to the cabin. She was in a frenzy of want and tore at his clothes and bit his shoulder, and implored him to take her, and when he didn't move quickly enough, she wriggled on top and impaled herself on that point of pleasure, her white shoulders shaking like a sail in the wind.

Again she began spending her nights with Carbri.

One day as she stood looking out over the bulwark, she felt someone thrust himself against her buttocks. She turned about immediately, thinking it was Carbri, but was confronted with foul breath, from a mouthful of rotting teeth. The unsavory-looking mariner called Camel had rubbed himself against her.

"Get away!" she ordered.

Camel didn't move. He licked his mouth with a big yellow tongue. "I'll give you a farthing if you do with me what you do with the captain!"

"Find a knothole, filthy pig!" She tried to step past him.

He blocked her way with his arm. "You're an uppity lad, for a catamite that's masquerading for bosun!"

She thrust her pistol under his nose. "Get out of my way or I'll shoot."

He stepped aside and sneered after her. "Your time will come, pretty boy! Mark me words!" and laughing, he walked away.

At midnight a fresh breeze began to blow up. The waves pitched higher and higher and edges of the crests frothed like the high-tossed manes of war horses. Carbri had gone to his berth, for Patch had the first watch. Arrah stood out on the deck and looked up at the sky, which was absolutely clear, so clear that it seemed she could hear the crystal sound of the stars. It was her grandmother who always said that on clear nights there was a moment in which the stars were so brilliant that they turned blue.

The wind was rising. The sails cracked noisily, as though chattering in the wind to each other. Sailors told tales of speaking ships, of sails talking to each other of their voyages, the strange and bizarre things they'd seen. Arrah saw a star fall, its tail drawing behind it like a curved sword. And then a second and a third.

She looked back at the high crucifix of the mast and the stars blazing behind it. What a glorious sight it was, that dazzle of sail and stars.

Carbri, woken from his sleep, came on deck and cast a glance at the sky. The wind was rising. The sea heaped up, foam crests blew in streaks. Carbri shouted at Arrah to go inside, but she didn't respond to him. He went closer to her. As he spoke in her ear he felt the wind whip her hair at his face so it stung his lips and chin like small, sharp grains of sand.

"I want to stay outside," she yelled back.

It was pointless to argue with her and he scurried about the deck shouting at the deck hands as they furled in the sails.

Arrah walked along the starboard, where the wind was so strong that she could lean into it without falling over. The wind seemed to touch something primeval, something elemental and raw inside her. It blew into her nostrils and mouth with such force it carried away her breath. The wind put into her a newness—a violent, raw spirit. She took strength from it and lifted her head to it, opened her mouth to it.

This was what she had dreamed of when her father had told her tales of the sea. All her life she had dreamed of being at sea, of sharing its power, of being the kind of sailor her father was, strong, powerful, free. But when she'd been a child, she, Carbri, and Debrogail had built a small boat and sailed it around the bay. Even Naira, after much coaxing, had come with them. When her father had seen them, he had grinned broadly, and said,

"So you want to be sailors, do you?" And then he had walked out into the water and grabbed both her and Naira and plunged their heads deep into the water, and held them so they came up sputtering. "That's what it means to be a sailor," he said, "to drink so much water you think you'll drown. Now, go back to the castle and help your mother with her embroidery."

She remembered the song her grandmother had sung to her.

> Arrah of the distant eyes.
> The wind sings in your mind.
> Arrah of the distant eyes,
> You'll always choose the path
>   that's wild.

The sea was the path she had chosen now, and by God, she would follow its course.

CHAPTER 12

As the *Belle Étoile* sailed north toward Rathlin Island the weather changed. The ship entered a fog-haunted region where the mist wafted thick and dense as a witch's brew over the sea. There was no wind. The ship was calmed and the sea became like a dream place, so quiet that the members of the crew grew afraid, as though ghosts hovered at their shoulders. Sometimes the fog dipped in so thick that sailors couldn't see from one end of the ship to the other, or even to the top of the mast. No one had seen a thing: no land, no ship, not even a jumping fish for three days.

The watch was tripled. Everybody had to keep a steady lookout, and Arrah spent hours and hours staring into the thick gray mist. She remembered how the bards at Eagle Castle would sing of the first mists of Ireland, how when the ancient people, the Tuatha de Danaans, first arrived, they caused a mist to gather for three days so they could land unseen. Arrah's eyes made shapes in the gray swirl. Feathered ghosts and silent amorphous beings swirled about. The ship rang its bell constantly to warn other ships of its presence, but the sea and mist answered with silence.

The crew took soundings to try to get some indication of how far the ship was from land. Patch dropped a lead pipe into the water. The pipe was attached to a rope which was marked with colored rags at various depths, so that he could determine whether or not there was any rapid shelving off in the ocean bottom. The pipe was filled with tallow so the depths could be checked to see if the ocean floor was covered with sand, clay, or pebbles, but wherever the ship was in the ocean, it seemed bottomless, for the tallow always came back clean.

Arrah caught her breath. Out in the fog, she thought she saw movement. It seemed like a swirl of cloud, like a shape, but her mind had been making shapes for hours. She blinked and the shape disappeared and only the great gray mist swirled like a beast yawning and stretching, and then the fog returned to its dense and impenetrable presence. She had been staring into the grayness for hours and hours: there was nothing there. But, no! There was something, the gray-white behind the grayness, a large, square-shaped . . . The fog seemed to be lifting, and behind it . . . a sail. She squeezed her eyes shut briefly. When she opened them the thing was still there, the whiteness in the white like the sails of a ship coming toward them. Forgetting decorum, she ran down the deck, shouting, "Carbri!" Twice more she shouted his name.

Camel, who was standing beside her, gave her a mean leer. "Oh, it's Carbri, now, is it?"

Immediately she realized her mistake. "What of it? He has a name. He was my friend before he was my captain. Now mind to your own affairs. Sail off starboard!" she yelled.

Almost the entire crew of the *Belle Étoile* came running.

"What flag will she be flying?" someone asked.

"I could barely make out her sails," said Arrah.

Carbri cupped hands to his mouth and shouted, "Ahoy! Ahoy!"

A voice from the other ship shouted the same words.

"What ship are you?" shouted Carbri.

"The *Twilight Moon*. A merchant under direction of Captain Jean LeGrand. And you?"

Information continued to be shouted back and forth.

Patch looked out into the mist. It wafted and billowed about, sometimes allowing the crew to see vague outlines of the ship, sometimes completely obscuring it as if shrouded by thick, impenetrable canvas. "Listen," he said. "I can tell by earshot. She's advancing on us."

"But how can she be advancing? We've no wind," said a tall, thin sailor.

"No wind! Me hearties," yelled Hook, "with a belly of cook's biscuits? If we was all to fart, there'd be enough wind to send us to Chiney and home again!"

"Stop your foolery and listen!" said Patch. The sound of oar strokes came through the fog. "There's your answer. She's a galleon. Not dependent on the wind."

Arrah glanced up at the *Belle Étoile*'s own sails. They hung slack like the skin on an old woman's cheeks.

"She's a pirate, I'll wager. Any other ship would be holding her distance," said Patch.

"Break out the pikes, me hearties!" shouted Hook. "Are ye ready, Angel darling? We've battle to do," and he lightly kissed the sharp point of his hook.

"There she is! For the love of Christ. Headed right for us."

"You'll be taking yourself to the hold and hiding," said Carbri to Arrah.

"I'll not."

"You can't be staying up here!"

"I'll fight with you."

The pirate ship was approaching closer and closer. Arrah saw why it had been able to come so fast. Although the pirate ship had three masts, it also had twelve oars on each side. The *Belle Étoile*, meanwhile, crimped along like a crab with two broken legs, with only the current to move her.

A voice came from across the *Twilight Moon*. "If ye won't be fighting, we'll let ye keep your plums. Otherwise off with them. Right, me hearties? Stand by to be boarded by Captain Whip."

Mute gargled loudly in his throat, trying to say something. Patch shouted back across the water. "We've one here who knows your promises, black dog! You made him eat his tongue and ears."

"I'll take yours in good time."

"You're welcome here, dog! Angel and I'll pluck your heart out and feed it to the sharks!"

The pirate ship moved relentlessly toward them. Arrah could see ladders stretching out like long arms from the ship.

Little by little she began to see the pirate crew more clearly. The crew members had swords, pikes, knives, and similar weapons. Only the captain carried a firearm, a heavy pistol, which he brandished in one hand. He swung a sword in the other. Around his neck coiled a long black whip.

In moments pirates would be boarding. Already some of them were hanging like monkeys waiting to swing over on the mast cords.

"Hand over your booty, mates!"

"We've no booty."

"Then you'll walk the plank after I skins you alive!"

Arrah was filled with an intense sense of possession. She'd helped scrub the *Belle Étoile*, had helped nail new planks into place. She wasn't giving up without a fight. "We'll see who walks the plank. Filthy blackguard!" shouted Arrah, drawing her sword.

The captain menaced with his whip. "I've want of a birdie, and your loins look tender, lad! I'll teach you a pirate's manners when I get hold of you!"

"Shove it up a fish's arse!" shouted Carbri.

A single shot sounded. At first Arrah thought the pirate had fired in some sort of signal, but Carbri, beside her, fell into a slump on the floor.

Naira and Bres had arrived at the castle at Glen Head, and she was eager to see that Debrogail had been buried according to her instructions. She stood with her men in the lower reaches of the castle as they dug up the floor to expose the body to her.

Bres was up in her chambers, sleeping. When they arrived she had noticed that his eyes were never at rest, that they seemed to roam everywhere, looking for Debrogail. She had told him that she made inquiries amongst the other servants and they told her that Debrogail had gone out to the hills with one of the male servants. They seemed to be very much in love, laughing and teasing each other, and holding hands and exchanging kisses as they set off looking for her plants for various infusions and healing teas.

Naira had cajoled Bres into making love to her, and he had fallen asleep as he always did. As she left him he lay quietly snoring, his handsome blond head at peace on her pillow. It was a good sound—the sound of a man snoring—a comforting sound, and she had kissed him softly before she left.

At Eagle Castle, Bres had sat around, passive as a bag of sand.

But at Glen Head some of Bres's former spirit seemed to return, as he busied himself with instructions for fortifying the castle. He was a man after all, and men were trained for fighting. Despite himself, the discipline of years exerted itself once more, and he shouted orders for weapons to be broken out and food supplies to be stocked. Naira knew that the forces of the family of her former husband were not strong. When the attack came they would be ready. Later she would tell him Debrogail was dead.

The digging up of the floor under which Debrogail was buried was taking an impossibly long time. Rory, the prison keep, was coughing and hacking like a sick horse. The stonemason claimed he was still suffering from ague and burning with fever, and had no strength to tear at the rocks and the dirt.

And that useless Magnus, hobbling about on crutches, seemed to be adding to the unendurably long process by his constant mutterings of how it was bad luck to disturb the dead, and how a body buried for a month would be repulsive to his lady's eyes.

"Shut up, with your crippled excuses," she finally shouted at him, "or I'll order you entombed as well." Magnus had been one of her husband's favored soldiers because he had saved his life. Her former husband had left instructions for Magnus to be well cared-for after his death, but she was in charge now.

The pounding and breaking and digging with picks and shovels continued until a corner of a woman's cloak became visible. The smell of death seeped from the tomb.

Rory coughed.

Magnus pretended to gag. He had smelled death often enough to know its stink and no longer be troubled by it, but he hoped that his retching would induce Mistress Naira to do the same. The previous night the stonemason had been too ill to complete the work himself. Magnus had offered to supervise the burial. He'd ordered a friend to search out the carcasses of a couple of dead dogs, stinking and putrid.

The dead dogs had been dropped in beneath Cathlin's body. If Mistress Naira discovered his deed, she would order him killed as well. He would take full responsibility. He was not afraid of death for it would take him to Cathlin.

He fully expected Mistress Naira to succumb to the stink, but she didn't. She only grimaced and held a scented handkerchief to her nose and told the diggers to hurry.

Then the back of Cathlin's almond-colored head became visible. Magnus had not been prepared to see her again. Tears sprang to his eyes. His arms ached as they had never ached with a desire to hold Cathlin, to see her face one final time. Debrogail seemed far, far away. Naira ceased to exist. He would give himself freely to the tomb; his life without Cathlin was totally without light or happiness. "What have I done to you, my darling?" he whispered. He took a halting step toward the grave.

"Get out of the way, you fool," ordered Naira. "How can I see with you there in front?"

Magnus took another step closer to the grave.

And then from somewhere Cathlin's voice seemed to call to him, to whisper to him from below. *Magnus, Magnus, stop. You'll come to me, and we'll be together again. But not now! I love you! Will always love you, and if you love me, then stop. Stop!*

And then somewhere a light flickered. A voice called. "Naira! Naira!"

A figure came down the corridor, and Magnus, stunned from his trance-like state, turned to see a young man carrying a torch. Magnus knew immediately that the young man was Bres.

Naira blanched. "Stand up all of you, in front of the grave! If any of you breathes a word of this, you'll all end up there," she said, pointing at the hole. Then she turned and ran down the corridor to Bres. "My darling! What brings you here?"

This was the first time he had ever called to her for anything, and she was eager to know why he had done so, but if he caught even a glimpse of Debrogail's body, all would be lost to her.

"Your former husband's family has attacked the castle! I had a dream . . ." He had dreamt that a gaunt but ethereal-looking woman was calling to him, and she had shown him the way to the dungeon. She was expecting a child. He had woken almost in a trance, and followed the directions of the dream to the dungeon below. But he couldn't tell Naira that. "I had a dream about a child," he said absentmindedly. Now that he was fully awake, the particulars of the dream evaded him, and he wasn't even certain what had brought him down here.

"My darling," Naira breathed, taking his arm and leading him away. "Sometimes dreams foretell the future. Let's hope your dream foretells of a strong child for you and me! Now let's leave this dismal place, and make sure that we defend the castle well for our child. I was checking the mortar for rot. There are places where it's crumbling down here, and I don't want the enemy to penetrate."

The stonemason, feeling wretched and miserable as if he were burning up with the fires of hell, sat down.

Coughing and spitting, Rory took over the orders for closing up the wall. The damp was clogging his lungs like moss, and he wanted to be out of this place as soon as possible. Despite his threats he had said nothing about what had gone on with Debrogail's singing. Coward that he was, he was afraid for his skin. It wasn't his fault the stonemason had taken ill, and the digging had been delayed. As far as Rory knew, the singing banshee had been buried according to Mistress Naira's satisfaction, and that was all that mattered.

Magnus turned and hobbled away.

"Oh, leave the hard work for the rest of us, will ye?" Rory jeered after him.

"She brought a brief moment of light into a dismal world," Magnus said sadly. "I'll leave the dismal job to dismal men!"

CHAPTER
13

From the very beginning of her journey, Arrah had been careful to speak in the measured, low tones of a young man, but she screamed when Carbri fell. From her cry of panic it was obvious what her sex was. Stunned, everyone stood looking at her as though she were an apparition.

Arrah was concerned for Carbri, but she knew that if she bent to him all would be lost. She began to fire the words of her father's command. "Stand to!" She no longer spoke in the low tones of a timorous boy, but now in the voice of a woman, and she spoke with authority. In that split second of silence after Carbri was shot, a memory jogged her mind. *Power is nine parts grabbed, one part given*, Reevnarg often said. She'd grown up with the tumult of his orders bellowed at soldiers and sailors. He told the story frequently enough of how he had taken over from an ailing captain. He had been no more than a lad. In the same breath that he had announced that the captain was dead, he had started giving the orders for burial. Because the orders were sound, the rest of the crew obeyed him. Giving orders was like losing your virginity. The first time was the hardest. "Pick him up and take him out of the way! There behind the barrels," she commanded, pointing at Carbri.

A group of men did as she ordered.

An evil look swept over the captain's face. "Kill her, me hearties, and I'll cut your plums out. She's mine. You hear! Mine!"

"Don't drag him, carry him. And be quick about it," Arrah ordered.

But there was dissension from Camel. "I'll not take orders from a woman."

Arrah pulled her pistol and aimed for Camel's head. "Do as I say, or I shoot. The rest of you too!" She pointed her weapon back and forth along their ranks.

Camel sneered so his foul mouth looked even uglier. He stepped quickly behind another crew member and spoke from there. "You got one shot in that. Kill one, the rest'll be left."

Patch moved silently behind Camel, and grabbing his head, pressed his dagger point at Camel's jugular. "Do as she says or die."

"Listen to the hen crow!" yelled Captain Whip. The pirate ship was close enough to grapple onto the *Belle Étoile*. A ladder from the pirate ship came crashing down. "Aye," continued Captain Whip. "I'll teach you a taste of a pirate's cock!"

Fighting was swift, with the clash and thunk of metal and wood, as pikes and trident-pointed glaives and more ladders were struck out in an attempt to board the *Belle Étoile*. A sharp splatter of light flared as lit rags soaked in fish oil were heaved across. Torches fell on the deck. Sailors rushed to tie in the sails before they caught fire. Others raced to smother the flames.

At the stern, pirates were roping the two ships together.

A young pirate leaped across and dropped to his feet directly in front of Arrah, his dagger between his teeth.

Her sword in full back swing, Arrah was ready for him. For a moment she and the young man looked at each other. He had beautiful eyes. They were dark blue, framed by dark lashes, the kind of eyes a girl might wish for. She stopped in mid-swing. In another time he might have been her lover. She might have held hands with him, kissed him and lain under the moon the way she had with Carbri.

The young man removed the dagger from his teeth and smiled brightly. If she didn't kill him, he would turn her over to his captain. Her sword fell against his neck. She felt the impact of the terrible softness all the way to her palm, and nearly dropped her sword with horror. She had expected its blow to be different, more resistant, harder. He looked at her with mild surprise, and opened his mouth as if to speak. He dropped his dagger to the deck, lifted one hand to his neck, then collapsed. She was temporarily immobilized, staring at him as his blood pulsed out from the side of his neck and then collected in a pool beneath his head. If only his eyes would close so they wouldn't look at her.

Something touched her shoulder and she lifted her sword to protect herself, but didn't use it. Patch stood beside her. He motioned upward, grabbed a coil of light rope and began climbing the mast. When he saw that she wasn't following he looked back.

"I won't leave Carbri lying there," she shouted.

"If he's dead, there's not a thing you can do. If you stay, you'll take the lust of Captain Whip."

She followed, and as she did so, she came nose to nose with a musket. It was one of the *Belle Étoile's* own crew who was holding it—Christophe. He motioned with the musket for her to move in the direction of the pirate ship.

"Captain Whip'll reward me nicely for your buttocks. Drop your sword."

"Foul traitor," she said.

"I ain't no traitor. He ordered us to hire on with you in Paris. I rang that bell the whole time long to keep him awares of our position. Now, move!"

She did as she was told, moving slowly. How many others had Captain Whip told to hire on? She tried to think back to the square in Paris. Who had come with Christophe? The whole crew could have been sent by Captain Whip.

Arrah wasn't certain exactly when she realized she was no longer being prodded by Christophe's musket. She turned about. Hook was behind her smiling broadly and kissing Angel. "That's me darling Angel. Sweet chuck." He slashed at another pirate's throat with his lethal hook.

Patch was beside her again, taking her arm, trying to push her up the mast. "Hurry!" he said, then scooted past her up into the stays.

Patch with his small feet leaped the cords with squirrellike speed. Arrah followed him with an instinctive agility and crawled up to the crow's-nest.

Arrah looked down. Below her was a turmoil of bloodied fighting men, all of them on the deck of the *Belle Étoile*. It was impossible to determine who was fighting for what. Many bodies lay inert on the deck. The pirate ship was deserted. Even Captain Whip was standing on the deck of the *Belle Étoile*, whipping indiscriminately at whoever was closest to him. Sailors and pirates alike were so occupied with battle that no one looked up.

"There," said Patch. "You have one shot."

Arrah saw Captain Whip, whipping with one hand and slashing his sword with the other. She had a clear shot. If she missed, it was the end. She drew her pistol, aimed for his face, exhaled, and fired.

Captain Whip looked up at her and she saw his evil smile. He took a step forward, coming for her. He reached out with his sword, then dropped it. He took a step forward again, then faltered. The whip fell from his hands. It was then she noticed the widening red stain on the front of his tunic. She'd shot him in the heart.

Captain Whip fell forward into the arms of one of his own men. The man pushed the dying captain away and he fell flat on his back on the deck.

The other man spun about quickly and saw Arrah with the pistol in her hand. He was a compactly built man with a balding crown and a pointed, sharklike face. He looked at Arrah with wide, surprised eyes, then down at the captain. The shark-faced man smiled.

He threw his arms up and began to shout and to leap about in an off-balance way as though he had a favored leg. He began hacking his sword at the dead captain. At first the fighting around him continued, but little by little waves of realization, like the waves about a pebble tossed into a pool, spread out. Other pirates stopped fighting as well, but instead of drawing up their swords, they followed the suit of the first man, moved in around the captain and began hacking at his body. The words shouted by the first man began to be taken up like a chorus. "He's dead! He's dead." Completely oblivious now to the crew of the *Belle Étoile*, the pirates whooped and slapped each other on the back and danced and hacked at their leader's corpse in a kind of diabolic frenzy. So violent was their excitement that at any moment Arrah expected them to pick up the pieces of their captain and begin to devour his flesh.

Stop it, she wanted to shout. Stop it. But she was afraid that if she interrupted them, they would leave off with their captain and start on her. She hadn't been afraid up till now. She'd been too preoccupied to feel fear, but it filled her now, made her cold, as though a great chunk of ice had been pressed against her heart. When her father had first taught her how to ride a horse, the horse had thrown her off. Reevnarg had leaped off his animal, picked her up and in the same motion, set her up on its back again. Then he had handed her the riding whip. She had hesitated. *Don't ever let them know you're afraid. Control the beast, or it will control you. Remember the O'Donnell motto: In this sign conquer. Pick up the whip, Daughter.*

Her pistol was no longer loaded, but she had to bluff. She held it threateningly in one hand, her sword in the other. Standing taller than she felt, she yelled, "Stop it! Stop it!" Temporarily stunned, the pirates stood still.

She grabbed a loose rope and literally flew down to the deck. She landed sturdily, pistol in hand. To the side, Arrah glanced at what was left of Captain Whip, none of it recognizable, but rather like pieces of meat on a butcher's table. She had to find Carbri.

"Move away," she said, pointing her pistol. "Slowly." She saw suspicious, blood-smeared faces staring at her, gold earrings and toothless gums. She saw the whip close to the mutilated corpse. She felt nausea rise, but fought it down. Keeping her empty pistol aimed at the pirates, she bent to the bloody pool and lifted the captain's whip.

She pulled one of the captain's pistols from his body.

The shark-faced man who had begun the frenzy suddenly called out, "She killed him. Who are you? Have you a name? And might Neptune smile on you wherever you sail. Hip for she! She's killed the evil dog. The saints bless you!"

The suspicious, sea-weathered faces remained silent.

"You've killed the cruelest, blackest night-soil ordure what ever sailed a ship on any sea. Give us a look-see." The shark-faced man grabbed the hand of a simple-looking lad close by. He had no nails, only rough nail beds. "These he lost as a cabin boy, for taking a bit of orange peel from the captain's quarters when we was a sailing from Araby. And looky here. You, Whale. Show the Captain Girl your hand. Fingers he lost for stealing bread because he was hungry. He killed us and maimed us."

The shark-faced man, who seemed to have taken the lead amongst the pirates, continued. "We're free of this black dog. Thanks be to God and to you girl. Have you a name?"

"Arrah O'Donnell."

"Captain Girl, I'll be laying down me sword." He threw it to the deck with a clatter. "I'll take up, wherever you'll be wishing to sail. Hip for Captain Girl!" he shouted. "Hip for she! Hip for she! Now lay down your arms. If any of you dogs so much as holds back a dagger, I'll cut your throats meself. I go by the name of Hirple. Hirple on account of this limp. On account of that no-good dog lying there, who shot me leg 'cause he was wanting to watch me dance."

"Filthy, double-talking dog!" shouted Hook. "I know the name of Hirple. We spent time together, you and me, on a bark the name of the *Christian*!" He leaped at the man called Hirple, but some of the crew pulled him off.

"It'll be your way, ain't it, Hook? Killing unarmed men?" countered Hirple.

"You're a cutthroat who'd sell your mother for a farthing. Spying for the captain. Lying and thieving. Angel and me'll slice your throat now, before you go scheming of ways to get ours."

"Don't you go believing him, Captain Girl." Hirple knelt in front of her, and pressing his palms together lifted them to her in a gesture of pleading. "The captain made me do his spying!"

"Silence!" Arrah shouted. All these accusations. Hook had been hired on at the same time as Christophe and Christophe had turned on her, while Hook had saved her life. She'd heard enough stories from her father's sailors to know of secret alliances between crew members on ships. They would support one captain, then withdraw their support when a more powerful man showed himself, then give him their support, then withdraw it in turn. One thing was certain: she couldn't afford to antagonize the pirate crew. For the moment, anyway, they seemed to be with her. If they turned on her, there were enough of them to hack her and her whole crew to pieces the way they had done with Captain Whip. "Patch. Let them keep daggers. Lock weapons in the armory. The rest of you, clean up this deck." As for double-talk and secret dealing, she couldn't think of them now. She had to go to Carbri.

Camel came forward, his sword drawn. He'd seen Hirple give a subtle raise of his eyebrows. Camel knew that Hirple wanted to take control of the ship from the woman, and get himself named captain. But he, Camel, deserved to be captain. The men would follow him before they followed Hirple or some woman. "Captain Girl!" he sneered. "I ain't takin' no orders from no Captain Girl!" Camel spit onto the deck beside Arrah. "I say we throw this bitch now—"

But Camel never had a chance to finish. Arrah shot him square in the face with Captain Whip's pistol.

Arrah was surprised at how easy it had been to kill him. The habit of death had indeed come quickly to her.

"A captain should never act like his own quartermaster," said Patch.

"A captain can do whatever *she* well pleases," countered Hirple. And shouting again before Patch had a chance to respond, he yelled at the pirates. "Heave to, slime buckets. You heard Captain Girl. Throw the carcasses to the sharks. Swab down this deck!"

Arrah ran to the longboat under which Carbri lay and lifted it. She took Carbri's hand and called his name softly. Dirt or powder or tar lined the areas under his eyes and the cleft of his chin. A large bloody area had formed on his chest. She glanced up. About her, sailors were bending to the ears of dead men and ripping gold earrings from them.

Arrah remembered her grandmother's words: *I feel the wind in your mind, a restless yearning.* Arrah had dreamed of the sea from the time she was small. But the sea had been a fantasy to her, some wondrous place with its mirrored surface and exotic stories of mermaids and wind and sails.

This was the reality of the sea. A ship deck greasy with blood. Carbri shot, others wounded. Handless men. Eyeless men and men without ears. Not a whole man among them. Rats that contented themselves not only with eating the food supplies, but also the cords and the wood itself. Cockroaches and worms and stale water.

She remembered the clean fresh linen of her own bed at Eagle Island, the smell of it the day it was washed and hung out on the castle ramparts to dry and then brought to her bed. The smell of sunshine on her pillow. She thought of the sound of the sheep bells quietly tinkling in the hills of Eagle Island, of the fragrance of the meadow flowers. And of her mother, who wanted her to be a lady. What would her mother think of her now? Oh, Mother! Mother! The pistol's weight was enormous in her hands and she wanted to drop it, but couldn't. The strain of holding the pistol so tightly had seemed to paralyze her fingers around the barrel. *Control or be controlled.*

CHAPTER
14

Carbri's eyes flickered as he saw Arrah and he managed a thin smile. "Aye, Arrah. She's a mean old bitch, the sea."

"It wasn't the sea that shot you. It was Captain Whip."

"Let me lay my eyes on him," said Patch. He ripped away at Carbri's shirt. "The shot's missed his heart, but he's bled dreadful."

Carbri gritted his teeth as Patch touched his dagger point to the chest flesh above the bone. Arrah watched carefully. She tried not to flinch as Patch probed and began to dig out the shot. Carbri, holding her hand, squeezed her fingers until they ached. Finally the lead was out, a bloody ball in the palm of Patch's hand. Carbri's face was soaked with sweat, and taking a rag, Arrah rinsed it in brine and wiped his forehead. The whites of his eyes were red with pain. Then Patch used hot grease from the galley to sear the flesh so that it didn't bleed further. Carbri screamed when it was poured on the wound, then passed out again.

Arrah had a decision to make now. She had two ships at her command. It was obvious that she couldn't have Hirple and Hook on the same ship. She would have to put Hook in charge of the crew of the *Belle Étoile*. She herself would take the pirate ship and half the sailors. She had no way of knowing how many pirates would stay with her, or how long they would remain loyal to her. She would simply have to gamble.

She ordered Carbri carried onto the *Twilight Moon*.

The captain's quarters, when she entered them, were an overwhelming surprise. Captain Whip hadn't much concern for the rest of the ship, but he deprived himself of no luxury in his cabin. His bed was spread with a red velvet cover and red velvet drapes hung on the lead glass windows. His table was edged with gold leaf and covered with a fine leather pad of pine green. A twelve-armed candelabra of pure silver graced the corner of the table. A silver hand mirror and brush lay on a shelf. The floor shone like an amber-colored mirror.

The cabin was filled with trunks, and Arrah opened them and gasped at the richness therein: gold and red brocades, green satin fabric like the hills of Ireland, and blue that glimmered like ice on a moonlit night. Arrah remembered the beauty of the woman she'd seen step out of the carriage in Paris. She wanted to hold the bolts of fabric up in front of her and look at herself in the mirror, but Hirple and Sebastian, who had carried Carbri in, stood watching her.

"You can go now," she said, and turning back to the trunk, removed one bolt of fabric and then another. From a second trunk, she pulled out a dozen dresses, each a different hue like colors in a rainbow.

Sebastian and Hirple were still there when she looked up. Sebastian was quiet, almost sullen. She was aware of his dark French eyes watching her.

Hirple was beside her, freely offering information in an uninterrupted stream, more information than Arrah cared to hear. "He stole it all, he did. From a Spanish merchant what was traveling to England. The ambassador and his young daughter. To be married, she was. It was easy enough for us. We followed them out of port. Same as what we did with you and waited for the fog. The ambassador was afraid for his daughter's honor and he gave us everything. Even his gold-rimmed spectacles. Didn't fight like what you did. Trunks we got down in the hold. Linens the likes of which I ain't never seen. And more cloth than a body could wear in two lifetimes. We ransomed off the daughter and the old Spaniard. Captain Whip, he was like a goat in horny time with that girl on board. But you can't ransom them back if they've been spoiled. Spaniards is partic'lar about that. Might as well cut their throats if you've deflowered them. She had a nun traveling with her. Old and ugly she was."

"That's enough," ordered Sebastian. "I think that Captain Arrah has heard—"

But Hirple continued talking. "Face like a dead seal. She wasn't no nun when we finished with her."

Sebastian drew his knife. "One more word and I'll cut your throat."

Arrah looked briefly at Sebastian. There was some quality about him. She couldn't quite ascertain what it was, but he seemed different from the rest of the sailors, more reserved, more reined in.

"I was just telling Captain Girl a story. Ain't nothing wrong with that. Her being captain, she'll want to be knowing where it's all come from."

"Leave me. Both of you," Arrah said again.

"Her dowry stuff. We sold some of it off. But the soldiers get to being suspicious. We was waiting to rid ourselves of it a little later. Then we split the profits like."

"Go!" she said imperiously.

Sebastian pushed Hirple out the door. The Frenchman hesitated and she saw his eyes travel down her body to the tightly knit trews, over to the captain's bed where Carbri lay, then back to her. "If you need something, I'll put myself outside."

The dresses lying over the trunks caught her eye again. Arrah peeled off her rough woolen mantle, trews, and tunic and dropped them to the deck floor. She loosed the binding that had held her breasts flattened. It had been such a long time that they had been bound down. She felt the cool air touch her skin, felt the sense of freedom. She inhaled deeply and felt her breasts rise, free and full. Her nipples grew erect from the chill and she rubbed the tightness away from them. She was captain of her own ship and no longer had to pass herself off as a boy. Never again would she bind her breasts.

As she looked among the various garments, she noticed a small crack in the panel behind the trunks, and pushing and shoving at the trunk with all her might, she managed to move it away. She was breathing hard when she jiggled the panel and felt it give in her hand. Inside the panel was another trunk, a deeply marred black chest. Although it was smaller than the other chests, it was much heavier. The metal handles dug into her palms as she pulled. With great effort, she finally managed to get the chest from the wall.

The chest was locked and she found no key in the cabin. She remembered Sebastian outside the cabin and quickly stepped into the blue dress.

She was too impatient to do up all ten buttons on the dress, and fastened it only half way. When she went to the door, and asked for an axe, she saw Sebastian's eyes fall to her breasts, but made no move to cover them. She'd hidden them long enough. "You heard me," she said. "An axe."

He came back with a halberd almost immediately and she closed and locked the door behind her. The lock fell away in the first blow, and kneeling, she opened the trunk to find it filled with gold, more gold than she'd ever seen even among her father's treasures. Crowns and sovereigns. A whole case of them. Did the rest of the pirates know about the gold? Was that why Hirple and the others were being so cooperative? She pushed the gold back into the hiding place in the wall, and shoved the trunk up against it.

A Venetian mirror hung on one wall. It had been a long time since she had seen herself in a mirror and she was pleased with what she saw. Her hair was longer than her shoulders. Her skin glowed. The dress turned her eyes to a pure blue. Her breasts were luminous.

When she had run away from Eagle Island, she had been a girl, vulnerable to the whims of a father who could think of nothing except to marry her off to one of his old friends. Never again would her father order her about. She was Captain Arrah O'Donnell now. She took her sword and tied it to her waist and put two pistols into the belt. Her bearing was splendid as she left the captain's quarters. Not one of her sailors would doubt her command, even for a moment.

Out on deck, the dress's silver thread shimmered like streams of crystal. Her unbound breasts rose like moons. She heard Sebastian suck in his breath as she walked by. The others too. Patch looked at her. "I've only one good eye," he said, "but I ain't never seen a woman so lovely. Ye have the look about ye like one of them goddesses that old sailors will be telling stories about."

In the beauty of mist and lantern light she walked the deck of her own ship. She looked up at the masts reaching skyward in the mist. She rubbed her hand along the bulwark. In the mist, the ship looked magical. She touched its wood as though it were carved in ivory. She picked up a belaying pin and rolled it lightly against her palm. Hers. Every cord. Every square of canvas. Every dowel. She was captain of it all.

She ordered the ale broken out and a celebration began almost immediately. Sailors began to leap back and forth joyfully between the *Twilight Moon* and the *Belle Étoile*. The sailors cheered her name.

Sebastian, taking her in with his dark eyes, lifted his ale cup to her in a toast. "To Captain Arrah. The most beautiful captain on the sea."

The rest of the crew took up the cheer and she smiled at them.

"It is bad luck, Captain, if you do not take a drink of ale with your crew."

Sebastian handed her his cup, and she took a swallow of the bitter ale, and then another.

"Dance with me, Captain Arrah." Sebastian held his arms out to her, and she stepped into them. Someone pulled out a fife, and someone else began to beat a belaying pin on an empty barrel like a drum.

They began to dance, and he swirled her on the tilting deck of the ship. Then Patch took his turn with her, and then Hook, and she felt the sharp metal of Angel grab the palm of her hand. Then Mute, with his strange mutilated face, grasped her and whirled her about in a dizzying jig. Hirple took her in his arms, and began to fling her about with his strange, disconcerting step. "Stop!" she shouted, and Hirple let her loose.

But he noticed something about her. "Our Captain Girl ain't wearing no earrings."

"No earrings!" came the disbelieving cry from the sailors and pirates.

"Aye, Captain Girl. Any pirate worth a thimble o' salt will be wearing gold earrings."

"I'm not a pirate," she said.

"Earrings help a body to hear better. The more earrings a sailor has the better he can hear the whisperings of the wind," insisted Hirple.

"Aye, aye, 'tis true," came the rumbling from her crew.

Arrah looked at Patch. He nodded in agreement.

"Now, sitty down on this here barrel and old Hirple'll share with you his earrings."

Hook pushed to the front of the crew. "Don't let that dog lay a hand on you. He'll slit your throat while he's notching you an ear hole."

"Filthy slime bucket. I'll slice you're throat yet, Hook."

"I'll pierce your ears," said Patch. "Come, lass, I'll fix you up. Sit down here, now. I've a needle for mending the sails." She saw a quick light of silver like an insect flash through the darkness.

"Sit! Sit!" came the bizarre refrain from the sailors around her. In the mist and lantern light their faces looked nightmarish. Was this a trick by all of them to overcome her? Just an opportunity which they would take to cut her throat? Had Patch merely won her confidence so that he could kill her? Patch's dagger blade glistened sinisterly at his belt.

"Sit, sit!" they shouted again, the force of their many wills weighing on her heavy as the ocean itself. Sometimes a captain had to submit to the will of his men if he wanted to remain as captain. It was one of the rules of sailing—there were always more sailors than captains. But one had to know when to yield and when not to.

She sat down. Patch grabbed a piece of cork and came and stood beside her, pulling her head against his chest. Arrah heard the beating of his heart against her ear, a strong heart.

He pressed the piece of cork against the back of her ear. Arrah didn't know how much pain to expect and involuntarily she grimaced. She felt a slight sting in her earlobe, and then some fumbling, and before she realized what happened she had a gold earring. She reached up and felt it dangling against her neck, and she smiled.

All the men cheered.

Sebastian came up to her again. "One more dance, Captain."

But she refused. "I've work that needs attention." She looked skyward.

"Tomorrow, the weather willing, we'll be sailing again." The sailors seemed suddenly subdued. She left them and returned to her cabin.

She kissed Carbri's feverish cheek lightly, then returned to study the charts. A ferocious dragon was drawn on the map in the channel between the Antrim coast and Rathlin Island. It showed the Dragon's Mouth, a great whirlpool.

Her grandmother would sometimes sing a song about a mermaid who was accidentally captured in the nets of fishermen. She vowed that if they promised to set her free, she would show them how to navigate the whirlpool, for the fishing was the best there of any place in the sea. The fishermen agreed and she took them across the whirlpool which was not whirling then, but calm as a mirror. They let their nets down and lifted them back nearly bursting from the weight of fish.

The fishermen were overwhelmed but instead of setting the mermaid free, they kept her so that the next time they came out to sea, they could again cast their nets down. Only one fisherman insisted that they had made a promise to set the mermaid free. But his companions jeered him. Secretly, when the moon was darkened by a cloud, he cut the mermaid's ropes and lifted her back into the sea. The others, furious with him for spoiling their good luck, chopped him into small pieces and tossed him to the fishes. The mermaid went to the dragon in the whirlpool and caused him to open his jaws wider than he'd ever done and the ship was pulled down, never to be seen again.

The mermaid, feeling sorry for the old man's family—for he had ten children, all of them girls—came to his eldest daughter in a dream and told her how to sail the whirlpool. There were certain times it could be navigated, and the girl caught enough fish that she was able to feed her family.

As Arrah stared at the charts and maps her eyes grew tired from the uneven shadows thrown by the lamp. The strain of the afternoon's fighting began to sink into her back and up into her shoulders. She lowered her head to her desk to rest her eyes, but was pulled into the vortex of a deep and dark, dream-filled sleep.

She was sailing across a crystal sea. She stood alone in a boat and a voice spoke to her, a voice that seemed to come from some place before memory. It was a woman's voice, but the voice seemed wordless; it was just sound. In Arrah's dream a woman, crowned in purple and silver shells, rose from the water.

Harp music floated on the air. The woman was beautiful, with hair so long that it brushed the waves of the ocean as she stood there. She was

Arrah's mother as a young woman. But she was dressed in the clothes of antiquity, in a dress of chain mail, which, in one turn of her body, looked like pure precious silver and at the same time like the scales of thousands of fishes, but gold and crimson and purple. In the dress, her young mother looked like a warrior queen of the sea. She was splendid beyond anything that Arrah had ever seen. Her hair was the same color as Arrah's.

Her mother sang with her grandmother's voice, but with a different quality, as though enchanted. It was a pure crystal sound. "Arrah . . . When the tide turns, Arrah . . . when the moon and sun align, the tides turn . . ." Her mother reached out her hands and her dress rose to either side of her. "And the Dragon will be stilled! I leave you now."

Her splendid silver dress flowed out around her like clouds, the color of the moon, and then she raised her arms and turned, and her arms became the sails of a ship, and her head the top of the mast, and for a moment she hung there on the crystal sea, and then Arrah watched as she brought her arms together and began to spin around like a whirlpool. The water about her turned white with skulls.

Arrah opened her eyes but didn't yet lift her head. In a brief moment of sleep, she seemed to have traveled through a different world. Some of the island people said that her mother had been a witch before she married her father, and that when she married, she had lost her power.

"Arrah!" A voice called.

Carbri was awake. She touched his flushed face.

"I was watching you sleep," he said. "It's been so long since I've seen you dressed as a woman. You are so beautiful." She bent to him. He touched the line of her forehead. "You come from the place of dreams. In that dress you look otherworldly. Like a mermaid. Like a sea witch."

"What does it mean, when the moon and sun align?"

"Won't you be forgetting about navigation sometimes?" But when he saw from the firm line of her mouth that she was determined, he explained impatiently. "At certain times of the year, the moon rises in exactly the same place that the sun sets. It's then that the tides are highest. Why will you be wanting to know?"

"A dream I had," and she reached down to pull the covers up over him, for there was a chill in the night.

"For the love of Christ. Can't you see I'm being roasted alive?" He threw off the covers with a violence and irritation that she'd never seen in him before. But the quick action sent a lance of pain through his body that flattened him weak on the bed.

The sudden movement had ripped open the seared flesh and now she saw the fresh blood beginning to seep through the dressing again and she yelled for Patch.

The days passed. The weather was uncooperative. For five days the fog continued, hanging like a shroud over the sea. Nonetheless, the ship dog-legged forward on tides and currents that weren't supposed to be there. Patch said Arrah had some innate sense, some sort of internal lodestone that told her more than just the direction of north. The *Twilight Moon* with its oars towed the *Belle Étoile* silently behind it.

When Arrah wasn't on deck, she was beside Carbri in her cabin. His condition worsened. A dark lump had begun to appear in the area just under his left arm. He slid in and out of delirium, sometimes losing all sense of where he was, and who he was, and tossing so violently that Arrah had to order him tied to his bed. He ripped at the ropes and tried to shred them with his fingers and so his arms had to be tied down as well.

She kept wet cloths pressed against his forehead, but the fever seemed to be burning him up.

Patch came and looked at him and spoke in a low voice. "Arrah . . . I was doing me best, but sometimes the poison will be getting in anyhow. That lump here. That'll be the beginning of green rot setting in. He'll be needing a leech healer. Otherwise it'll be getting worse and we'll have to hack his arm off. There's only one man who can be properly treating the green rot and that's Dr. MacDougall on Rathlin Island."

"But that's where we're going. If this cursed fog would lift, we'd be there in two days."

"Aye, lass, to An Rubha, and coming in from due east. But MacDougall is at Church Quarter on the south side." He went to her table and pointed a finger at her chart, near the bottom of the belly of the skin where the Dragon's Mouth was etched in fierce black ink. "A whirlpool the likes of which there ain't anywhere else. We can't be sailing to Church Quarter directly. It'll be taking us two, maybe three extra days afore we come back to the south side to Church Quarter. That there arm of his'll be black like sailor's pitch by then, and stinking so bad you won't be able to sit in the same room with him."

"Patch, listen. One of my father's men, when I was small, used to tell me he knew someone who sailed the Dragon's Mouth."

"Aye. There's enough that tell the story. But fancy talk, all of them. I've yet to lay this here eye on one what made it."

"I'm going to navigate the Dragon's Mouth."

Carbri, who had momentarily regained consciousness, rasped her name. His voice was thick with pain. "Arrah. You can't—"

"I will—"

He tried to fight the ropes. "Loose me, for the love of Christ."

Arrah went to him. His face felt hot as though he'd been sitting close to a fire.

"You'll be killed. Like dozens of fools." Carbri's voice came in gasps, as though every intake of breath pained him. "Patch, don't let her!"

"I have my own ship now, and I'll navigate her. Legless Paddy told me how someone he knew had sailed the Dragon's Mouth."

"Nobody believes him. He makes up stories, just so people will be stopping and talking to him. It's madness," said Carbri.

"It can be done."

Carbri swallowed as though trying to wet his tongue so he could talk again. "Arrah. The sea. She's a terrible mother. You challenge her and she'll destroy you the way she destroys everything." He took a great gasping breath and continued. "You think because you are brave you can outwit her. She eats bravery. The rocks . . . she eats rocks. The hulls of ships. The bodies of men. Millions of dead crab. All the rotting filth. She sucks it in and lives on it. She'll eat you up."

Carbri's eyes bulged and his face streamed with sweat from the effort of talking. Arrah took a cloth, dipped it in a bucket of water, and wiped his face.

"She won't eat me up."

"Arrah, if you do this, you'll die."

"And if I don't—you'll die."

Someone shouted from the deck. "There's a wind coming. The fog's lifting."

"Arrah, I beg you," Carbri pleaded. "Don't do this. I love you."

"If you love me, then be brave with me."

CHAPTER 15

"C aptain Girl," said Hirple, "you've not saved us from Captain Whip so as to send us to death in the Dragon's Mouth!"

"There'll be no death. The line of the moon and the sun is such that the tide won't run so fast. The currents will be manageable."

Arrah had studied the maps of the shoreline and the arrows that foretold the direction of the wind and currents. Spring tides occurred twice a month near the times of the full moon and new moon. She remembered the wild, wide whites of Paddy's eyes as he spoke of the "howling, shrieking black vortex." But later, when she told Paddy's story to Reevnarg, he dismissed it as Paddy's wild fancy.

Patch spoke, "Captain Girl. There's no arguing with him what thinks the devil's at the bottom of the sea. Ye've two ships. So take your own now. I'll sail with ye. Leave the rest of these lubbers to sail on the *Belle Étoile*. We'll meet them in Church Quarter after they've sailed around Rathlin Island."

Carbri was completely lost to a fever. He vacillated between periods of unconsciousness, during which he slept as though dead, and periods of frenetic, wild language and movement during which he looked at her with terror-stricken, unknowing eyes, as though she were a stranger ready to do him evil.

"It's foolishness to sacrifice a whole ship for one man what's half dead already," said Hirple.

"I'm captain here. I'll decide what's foolish and what's not."

"There's the question of looty, Captain Girl." Hirple continued. "We always divided the income from it even-like. Captain Whip taking two parts and the rest of us getting one part. But I won't be seeing the sense in taking his share to the bottom of the sea with you."

"I'm captain now. His treasure belongs to me!"

"We keep the looty on the other ship."

"Hirple, you scoundrel's dog," countered Hook. "You think of nothing but your pockets."

"And you, coward's cunt, think only of your own neck. I'll see your throat cut yet, dog!"

They went at each other.

Arrah pulled both pistols from her waist and fired one in the air. The next one she pointed at Hirple. "There's not enough crew on these ships. But two hands less won't make the difference. Any more bickering, any more mention of loot, I'll silence you myself."

Hirple straightened his tunic.

Speaking to her crew, she asked, "Will you sail with me?"

One by one they shook their heads. "I've a wife and the little ones at home."

"Aye. So has I," came the refrain. "And me!" "And me!"

Sebastian came forward. He stood, legs akimbo, his hands on his hips. "I'll sail with you." But his eyes were dark and sullen when he spoke.

And Hirple came forward.

"Let's hurry then!" Already the tops of the sails had caught the dawn sun and were burning red with reflection. The sea was red, as though a stream of blood were running into it. Elsewhere, too, where the crest of sun had not yet touched, the sea was still a dark and smooth mirror.

She gave orders for the ropes between the two ships to be untied. Sailors left the *Twilight Moon* for the *Belle Étoile*, but before they did they crossed themselves and pressed talismans into Arrah's hand: swallows' wings and herring tails, and cauls from newborn children, all of which were supposed to keep sailors from drowning.

She accepted their tokens. She had learned with Paddy how disappointed a man became when his gifts were refused. Also, over the last few days as captain of her own ship, she'd gained insight into the feelings of men. She realized that if she failed to navigate the whirlpool, then not a single sailor would blame himself. To them, she would become nothing but the memory of a foolish woman who'd neglected all warnings. If she was successful, then every sailor who had pressed even the smallest feather into her hand would think himself personally responsible for her safe journey across the maelstrom.

The ropes were thrown over and she waved at Hook and Mute and the rest of the crew left behind. She signalled to Patch and he nodded his head in acknowledgement and began tightening the running rigging to lift the sails. Sebastian climbed to the crow's-nest. Hirple skulked about.

She took the helm, felt the satisfying solidness of the oak wheel in her hand. The *Twilight Moon* skipped along the waves as though dancing on them. The sun had risen above the horizon. The sea was an endless grace of green and soon the other ship was nothing, not even a speck on the sea behind them.

Arrah heard the lapping of the waves against the hull. The corner of a sail flapped. A brisk wind, seemingly filled with its own music, had risen. She lifted her face to it, loving the feel of breeze in her hair and against her cheeks.

The telltales flowed smoothly and in parallel, indicating that the trim of her sails was good. Patch smiled at her and blinked his one eye frequently, the way he did when he was pleased with something. "It's rare to see a man make a ship so weatherly, never mind a woman. It's either God or the devil hisself that's guarding ye, lass."

Dark, low edges of land grew visible on the horizon. Arrah was in her cabin with Carbri when she heard Sebastian shout.

"Captain Arrah! To the starboard!"

Arrah saw a great circle of blue in a sea of green. She felt the breeze go still.

She left her cabin, heard the slamming of the door behind her and then silence: still, utter, complete silence. The sails fell quiet. Even the sea seemed to stop lapping against the side of the ship. Arrah felt swept away in a dream, in one of those silent, dreadful nightmares of childhood when she opened her mouth to scream and nothing came out except silence. It was as though the sea had swallowed all sound down into its own depths. The sun looked as though it had stopped and was impaled on the mast. Birds flew overhead, their wings like black scars on the sun. The ship wasn't far from shore. Less than half a league to the south was the gray, dark desolation of the cliffs along the coast of Antrim. To the north were the dark rocks of Rathlin Island. In her mind spoke a silent voice: Carbri saying that sailors could tell when land was close because of flocks of birds overhead. But these birds were silent, too, as though the sea had sucked their cries from their throats.

She grew aware of the beating of her heart, as though it were the only sound she could hear, and then she heard a deep distant roar like a rumble of thunder.

In the north over Rathlin Island she saw a dark cloud moving across the sky. She tried to remember Paddy's words: *Whirlpools. Tides. Winds. Currents.* They were a meaningless swirl in her mind. She pressed her fingers hard against her eyes, pressing out everything except the words she needed. Yesterday she had known what she had to do. The directions seemed precise, clear, and guiding, the way a compass pointed to polar north. Now everything was an abyss of confusion, like a language that she had never heard. But bit by bit the words in her memory began to float to the surface, like salvage from a ship after a wreck.

Finally Paddy's words came clear: *Tides overlap in narrow sea passages. One current fights the other current, like two warriors in battle each grabbing for a sword, and they fall to the ground and roll and roll and roll. That's what a whirlpool is.*

As she looked out on the sea, she could see its rippling grow more and more choppy with the ridges rising into peaked caps. The sea seemed to be undergoing some enormous transformation as though it were turning itself inside out. The noise, low at first, began to grow from a sound like the roll of thunder into something huge and terrifying and hideous, as though the very bottoms of the sea would be heaved up in a moment. Where the rocks narrowed, she could see the currents rising and moving toward the east like a long silver dragon swimming close to the surface of the sea, like a hundred sea dragons.

When she and Debrogail played as children, they would each take the end of a long length of hemp and shake it in a game to see who could get the highest waves on the rope. But those times had been innocent moments in a child's game. This huge and powerful movement of water went beyond anything she'd ever seen or imagined. The terrible dragon currents arched their backs and plunged and heaved with a monstrous speed, a monstrous noise that made the inside of her ears ache. Even her hands over them couldn't keep out the painful roar.

The character of the sea was changing again. The currents began to break as they arched and began to spin in small pockets, and the sea looked as though it were beginning to boil. It re-formed and rose and broke again, heaving and hissing, flinging itself skyward. Small swirls began to form where the sea broke, and one small swirl joined with another, and then another, until the entire area was a huge dark spiral, a swirling ebony wall of water, smooth and shining and dark and dangerous, and going down endlessly.

She watched the dark swirl with a fascinated, mesmerized horror, watched the swaying spin swirl round and round and round. She saw Patch and Sebastian open their mouths as though shouting at her, but their words were soundless. The roar of water had captured and transformed her senses so that she heard only a single sound, a woman's voice, singing, so distant, so beautiful, a crystal sound, like the single string of a harp plucked. The voice guided her to Paddy's words: *At certain moons when the tide runs, it's in perfect balance like a good ship. And then there's no maelstrom.* All she had to do was wait for the ebb to begin and she would be able to sail the whirlpool.

She had been so intent on Paddy's words that she hadn't noticed the dark swoop of cloud coming closer and closer, like a huge predatory bird over the sea. The wind attacked the sails like an enraged eagle, striking with talons of air, ripping out the clews so the mainsail flapped useless as a rag. She saw Patch bent by the wind, hunched like an old woman trying to furl in the canvas before it succumbed completely to the violence of wind. The cords appeared to be in league with the wind, wrapping themselves about Patch's legs like snakes.

The wind in a fury attacked the mizzen mast and snapped it off as easily as a twig and sent it to the deck with an ear-shattering splinter. If the wind pushed them to the swirl of water, the ship would be destroyed.

The wind shrieked. Arrah screamed back at it. "You bitch! You whore! You bloody whore. You won't take me!" The ship plunged. Arrah grabbed for the yardarm, but loose, it swung away from her. The ship pitched and the arm flew back, lethal and heavy, aimed at her. Arrah threw herself flat against the deck, smashing her elbow on the wood. The shock traveled through her entire body, jolting her as though she'd been hit by lightning. She felt strong arms around her, felt herself lifted. Sebastian was beside her.

"Bare your breasts!" he shouted at her.

"What?"

"Bare your breasts. Calm Neptune's anger."

She hesitated.

"Do it," he said. "Look there!"

Arrah looked out and all she could see was an enormous wall of water coming at them—immensely tall like a mountain, as though all the solidness of the land she knew had been transformed into a high, terrible black wave. She froze. Sebastian grabbed at her bodice and ripped it away. She heard nothing, but felt the violence of spraying water and wind attack her breasts. Sebastian grabbed her and began pushing her toward the bulwark. She screamed and struggled against him and the wind and storm, and suddenly Patch was there beside her, grabbing her too. Had they both turned against her? Were they going to throw her to the sea to quiet it? But Patch pushed her against one of the bitts, two carved posts on either side of the main mast, and grabbing a coil of rope, wrapped it around her and himself as fast as he could. Close to the bulwark, she saw Sebastian lashing himself to the stairway that led to the fo'c's'le.

She saw the wave coming toward the ship. Earlier she had felt that the sea had sucked all sound from the air, now she could feel the wave sucking breath from her lungs even before it had arrived.

She tried to ready herself for its impact, but there could be no way of readying herself for that wall of water as it rolled down. She felt the ship plunge sickeningly. She closed her eyes.

The wall of water crashed over her, knocking her head against the mast, stunning her, sending the ship deep down into the blackness, down into a swirling sphere of black. Arrah was whirled into the deep and deeper belly of the sea that spun around her, inescapable, heavy and suffocating as stone.

CHAPTER
16

The wind had spent itself and a beautiful luminous moon, so full it looked as though it would burst, filled with a clarity beyond what Arrah had ever seen, emerged from the clouds. Blazing down it turned the sea into a glory of silver light. The deck was a mass of wriggling, dying fish.

Patch stood beside Arrah. "Ye see that, lass? Ye know what us old salts will be saying. The sea, she cleans herself at the full moon. I would be wagering she did a damned thorough job this time."

Arrah's dress was in shreds. She felt as though her body, too, had been ripped and hacked and clawed by the sea.

Sebastian, who had been busy untying his ropes, came slipping and sliding across the deck to her. He looked at her, then said, "I'm sorry, Captain Arrah, for treating you roughly. I was"—he shrugged—"afraid that you would be washed overboard. I had to attach you before the wave came. Your lovely breasts . . . they saved us from the wrath of the sea."

She looked at him but didn't say anything. His actions had totally stunned her. She rubbed her hands down her breasts and thighs to see if she were actually there and living. Then she grabbed a piece of sail and draped it over her shoulders and breasts.

Patch grinned at her and blinked his tattooed eye. "You made it, Arrah, lass. You navigated the Dragon's Mouth."

"Patch. Am I dreaming? Are we alive, or dead and living somewhere else?"

"Alive. Alive. The sails are shredded," said Patch. Arrah looked up at the main sail that hung limp like a wet rag. "Nothing that a bit of time and a needle can't be repairing," continued Patch.

"I feel like I've sailed a thousand leagues through a graveyard."

"Ye've done that lassie and done it well! This old salt has sailed many a ship, but there ain't a captain alive that can compare with ye, Captain Arrah. I'd sail to hell and back with ye."

"Carbri! I have to see if Carbri is all right!"

Sebastian watched her go, watched the seductive movement of her hips as she ran up the stairs, taking them two at a time. He *had* intended to throw her overboard. Now he was glad that he had not succeeded.

From the first he had found the young bosun different, not like the other catamites he saw shipboard. Most of them were pitiable, slinking and defeated, looking like dogs that were whipped. There was nothing defeated about Captain Arrah, even when she had been bosun.

Sebastian knew that Captain Whip had an enormous quantity of gold hidden in his cabin. There were two manners in which he, Sebastian, could get some of it from Captain Arrah. One was to kill her, but it would be a pity to kill one who was so beautiful. Hirple also knew about the gold. Hirple would have no hesitation at killing her. He, Sebastian, would have to keep guard of Hirple. The other manner to get her gold was to have her share it with him. Captain Carbri had the heart of a pigeon, not of a man. He would die soon. Taking a fever and nearly dying from a simple gunshot wound. He, Sebastian, had had dozens of wounds, and had gone on fighting.

She was beautiful. Her breasts, they were splendid. But when he had seen the great whirlpool, he had become terrified, and was willing to sacrifice her beautiful breasts to save himself. He had seen it done before— a bare-breasted woman passenger thrown into the sea to calm it. But the sea had calmed without Arrah being thrown in, and now he was glad.

He had seen nearly all her breasts the other night, and would have taken her, had she not had the pistols and the sword. She used her weapons skillfully.

He would make Captain Arrah take notice of him by helping her in any way he could. Women in the ports liked him. He never had any problems getting girls. Arrah would fall in love with him. It was simply a question of time. He had learned patience.

He had no family. He once had a mother, but when she remarried, the new husband woke him early one morning. His stepfather blindfolded him and tied his hands behind his back and carried him out of the house. From the smell, Sebastian knew he was at the docks. There was the sound of money and Sebastian was picked up and thrown over someone's shoulders.

He heard the sound of bare feet on wooden stairs and when the blindfold was taken off he found himself in the hold of a ship, face to face to a man with a red scarf around his neck and two gold earrings in either ear.

He was out in the middle of the ocean. He began crying when he saw nothing but water about him. The quartermaster showed his whip. "You don't stop crying like a baby, I'll give you reason to cry."

Sebastian had been at sea ever since, passing from one ship to another like a rat. His last ship, an old bark called the *Formidable*, had been hijacked by Captain Whip. The others had fought and had been killed, most of them, but when Sebastian had heard the name Captain Whip, he'd had enough sense to jump ship and swim to the *Twilight Moon* and swear his allegiance to Captain Whip before the captain took the other ship. It was one thing Sebastian had learned from his years at sea—how to survive.

But at the time he had jumped ship, he had no idea how painful it would be serving under Captain Whip. There were many times that Sebastian had wished himself dead. But now Whip was dead, and just a woman was in charge.

There were means by which a woman could be persuaded to share her money.

Rathlin Island was a desolate, barren-looking place with low, twisted, arthritic-looking shrubs that clung desperately to the rocks.

As soon as the ship docked, Arrah sent Sebastian to find the leech healer. He came immediately, bringing with him on his garments the biting smell of camphor, so bitter that Arrah could almost taste it. He wore a tightly fitting cap of red leather and a loose white sleeveless knee-length gown over his shirt and stockings. He lit incense as soon as he entered the captain's quarters, even before he had looked at Carbri.

The leech healer carried with him a rolled parchment and a medicine bag called a *les* containing clay jars. Crinkling his nose, the surgeon lifted one of Carbri's eyelids, then looked down at Carbri's wound. He unrolled his astrological chart, a circular disc consisting of various layers of parchment, all joined at the center with a silk thread, and painted with bright figures of animals: an orange bear, a golden lion, a dun-colored centaur, a red crab, and a blue fish, among others.

The leech healer asked when the wound had been inflicted, then turned the various layers, aligning the signs of the zodiac with numbers and drawings of various body parts. When he had finished computing the astrological correspondences of the wound, the healer dipped into one of the jars with a wooden stick and pulled out slimy black leeches. He pulled back the rag dressing from Carbri's wound and brought the leeches to it. While the leeches began to swell up with blood, the surgeon mixed a poultice from the contents of his clay jars. From the smell Arrah could tell that one of the ingredients was sulphur. The others were ground sorrel and apple juice. While he was mixing he gave instructions to Arrah. "Go out on the rocks and pick some lovage. You'll see it. Small white flowers growing in clusters. Large dark-green leaves. Boil the plant down and mash it and make him eat it. I'll lance the wound, and cup it after the leeches have taken out the bad blood, but without the lovage he won't heal. It's a particular problem for sailors: wounds not healing and gangrene setting in. You should take care that all your crew eats it frequently. It'll keep their gums from bleeding and their teeth from falling out."

Arrah left immediately to look for the healing plant. She enjoyed the walk to the rocks. It seemed to her that she'd spent an eternity with nothing but the pitching deck of a ship beneath her feet, and now she enjoyed the satisfying strain of climbing across the solidness of rock.

Kittiwake gulls, uttering their lovely plaintive cry, flew in graceful circles overhead. She disturbed a flock of sea pies, which took flight with a piercing noise.

Below the birds was the sea. Even now as she looked out she thought she could see the dark circle of the whirlpool and the dark currents flowing like monsters into it.

Patch and Sebastian had called her courageous. She'd heard her father and his sailors and chieftains speak of men of courage. But she'd never really known what courage was until now. Courage was nothing more than not allowing fear to paralyze you. If you didn't stop moving, you didn't have time to think about being afraid.

Hirple was on deck assisting the carpenters in remasting and otherwise repairing the damaged ship. But when he saw that the doctor had left, he came to the captain's quarters.

Patch was there. "Well, what are ye waiting for, lad? There's the ship what needs tending to," said Patch.

Hirple looked about him. "Captain Whip. He was the greediest dog this side of Africa. More gold he had than any other pirate. Most, they spend what they get. Not him. He was hoarding it."

Patch looked at Hirple and his tattooed eye blinked a couple of times. He scratched his chin. "Gold? How much gold?"

"Plenty! Enough to keep me and you like kings for the rest of our lives. Just me and you. We'll rid ourselves of the she-gusset—"

Before the shark-faced man could say another word, Patch had a dagger at his throat. "Another breath about Captain Arrah, whoreson, and I'll slice your gullet."

They both heard Arrah's quick footsteps at the same time and turned toward the door. Patch released Hirple, who swallowed and brushed his hand down the front of his chest.

"By the saints, it'll be doing me heart good to know that Captain Carbri is tended to," said Hirple.

"I was ordering ye to scrape off them barnacles. Now, move to it," ordered Patch.

"Aye, aye." Hirple threw Arrah a sideways glance, then scuffled out.

For three days Arrah sat constantly by Carbri, forcing a mash of lovage into his mouth and rinsing the wound. The leech healer had inserted a hollow piece of cattle horn and two tubes that looked like pieces from a sheep heart to Carbri's arm. The tubes drained the poison and pus to a basin on the floor.

The fever dropped and the swelling began to go down. On the fourth day after the treatment, Carbri sat up and smiled at her weakly. "Arrah, what a good woman you are. A man couldn't be asking for anything more." That night Carbri ate the first solid food he'd taken in days. Arrah sent Sebastian out to the public house and he came back with a boiled chicken and boiled nettles.

The ship needed a larger crew to sail her, but Church Quarter had only a small group of fishermen and their families. The next morning the *Twilight Moon*, her repairs made, sailed for An Rubha, on the south point of the island, where it would meet the *Belle Étoile* and take on crew and more supplies.

At the ship's arrival at the southern village, a crowd was already waiting for Arrah. News had traveled fast on the small island and everyone wanted to see the woman who had navigated the Dragon's Mouth.

"The devil's queen. A witch."

"An enchantress!"

"Sea witch!"

Carbri was finally beginning to recover. Nonetheless, he remained too frail to take on the hiring of the galloglass, for which O'Reilly had hired him. Arrah and Patch took it upon themselves to recruit them.

The galloglass were heavily armed fighting mercenaries who were originally of Scottish descent. They were interested in hard coinage and not vague fears of witchcraft. In the taverns amongst themselves, they maintained a steady ribaldry about sailing with a ship commanded by a woman.

"It's a bloody queer thing, I tell you. A woman at the helm."

"'Tisnt the she what's sailing the ship, 'tis O'Connor."

"O'Connor! That cunt-whipped gelding! 'Twas the she who sailed the Dragon, not the he. 'Tis the she who'll take command."

"I'd like it well enough! If 'twas she sailing under me."

"Bleating horny goat. There's only one thing you'll be thinking of."

"God's eyes, man! What else is there to be thinking of? Good battle! Good drink! The bush of a wench!"

While mercenaries were willing to sail with Arrah, the sailors at the dock stubbornly refused to sign on as crew for the *Twilight Moon*. They were a superstitious lot who, while they held the captain who had sailed the Mouth in awe, were terrified of the woman herself. A woman such as that! Only God or maybe the devil himself knew the spells she could be casting on a man.

Patch had a plan. They would try and hire in the alehouses. Arrah should come to the tavern so the sailors could see for themselves that she wasn't a witch, but the hiring on would be best left to him. If hiring, done with the pleasantries of a few tankards of ale and promise of good wages, wasn't enough of an enticement for the sailors, then they would be "pressed" into service by himself, Hook, and Mute.

Carbri was impatient with the notion. "I'm nearly well now," he said. "Keep your man warm in his berth at night, and leave this silliness of sailing your own ship." But Arrah remained adamant. She insisted on accompanying Carbri to the tavern.

The Centaur was a roughly thatched stone building, the gray thatch weighted down with rocks hung from ropes thrown over the pitch of the roof.

Patch, Hook, and Mute were already at a table with a group of sailors when Arrah and Carbri arrived. They sat down at a table in a corner of the room where a small cooking fire burned.

When Arrah had pulled into the dock she was dressed in the robes of a woman. Now, in an attempt to recruit men, she had reverted to her man's dress, but her dark jerkin, which was cut in a long slash down from her throat, showed her lush, white breasts. The dark trews accentuated the shape of her hips. The sailors grew even more fearful of her. She exuded both power and a raw sensuality in every movement. Beside her sat Carbri O'Connor, his wan face thin and weak. That's what happened to men when they sailed with a sea witch.

A persistent and brazen billy goat, with long ears that flopped with each step, walked about the tavern. He stopped here and there to nibble on a sleeve, or on the hair of a seated drinker. The billy goat had a great liking for ale, and would try to lick at the tankards whenever he could. Sailors and soldiers pulled his ears or beard playfully. Sometimes if he became too brazen, they gave him a sharp cuff to the head. The goat would then shake his ears and walk off to find more genial patrons.

A woman server by the name of Mary MacDonal brought ale to Arrah and Carbri. Even in the dim light of the tavern, the woman's bright blue eyes and florid skin were evident. She was a comely creature, round, yet solid, with a voluptuous body, a robust appetite for food, drink, and life, all of which showed handsomely in her face. She'd had four husbands and would talk freely of them to whoever cared to listen and kept up a steady stream of obscenity with her patrons all within earshot of her current husband, a dour Scot.

She set down a jug of ale so vigorously on the wooden table, Arrah thought the pottery bottom would split. "So you're the one who sailed the Devil's Mouth," said the florid-faced woman.

"Yes," said Arrah, looking at Mary, who was about Arrah's mother's age, but freer than Margaret with both her smile and her bearing.

"Hey there, Mary! Be bringing us another jug now, will you, lass," came the shout from another corner of the tavern.

"Patience, man!"

"Patience, is it? How much patience is a man supposed to be having? He could be dying of thirst before he was getting served in this place. And will you be taking this damned stinking goat out of here afore he eats all of me hair off me head? What do you say, Mary? Shall we be trimming out his plums?"

Ruffled as a hen, Mary rushed in the direction of the table. Soldiers and sailors grabbed at her haunches, but she slapped away their hands, broke a jug over one of their heads. "Lay a knife to one of his plums, I'll cut *yours* off!"

"Rest easy, lass. I wasn't meaning no harm here to Finn. Was I, Finn? Stinking old goat," he said, putting away his dagger and scratching the goat's chin. "But I needed to be getting Mary's attentions. Otherwise, she'll be doing nothing but prattling and not tending to her customers. Come now, lass, and fill us a tankard or we'll be taking ourselves to a place what will."

At the taps, Mary's husband cleared his throat loudly. Finn eyed Arrah from across the room, lifted his head and began to walk toward her, but became distracted by some spilled ale. He began to lick at it.

The air was thick with the smell of men, the smolder of the turf fire, and rumor. Arrah felt the eyes of the men on her and heard snatches of their conversation from different corners of the room.

"Be damned," said one, loud enough so that he knew she could hear. "It's ill luck. Neptune will have his own. A woman at sea."

"If Neptune would've wanted her, he would've taken her. Enchantress, I say. Casting a spell on the sea."

"You're just jealous, 'cause you wouldn't sail the Dragon."

"I wouldn't sail with the likes of she," breathed another. "I'll be wagering she was saying a black mass on the deck. Blood and all."

"Lily heart. You see blood every time you take a piss."

The other sailor crossed himself. "By the cross of the Bloody Jesus. There ain't a sea in this world I'll be fearing. But for the likes of her, I'm afraid to look on her."

"You. You're afraid to look at your own bunions."

"She frightens me, I tell you, that sea witch."

Carbri sat sullenly, not speaking to Arrah. He had been against her sailing from the start. Now he sat listening to the whispering, but because of his wound, felt powerless to do anything about it. He drank too quickly, emptying two tankards of ale almost immediately. Then he asked for a jug of the stronger, distilled usquebaugh. He ordered his tankard filled a third time, and then a fourth. Suddenly, after barely speaking, he began to shout, "A toast, I say. A toast to Arrah O'Donnell. Navigated the Dragon's Mouth." His voice was heavy with sarcasm, and Arrah saw an ugly expression on his face she'd never seen before. The tavern quieted at the mock toast. Everybody looked at Carbri and Arrah, waiting for him to say something else. When he didn't, the tavern conversation resumed to its previous level.

Carbri reached for the jug again, but Arrah grabbed it quickly and pulled it back toward her. He took hold of it. "Hand it back, Arrah."

"You've had enough!"

"Aye, Arrah, but what a woman you're turning out to be. Navigated the Dragon, she did," he said to no one in particular.

"You've a ship to sail," said Arrah firmly.

"You won't be denying a man who's in pain a little bit of solace, now will you?" He gave a sharp tug, but Arrah retained her grasp. "Me arm will be hurting me powerfully." He was slurring his words.

"Will you leave it to the four winds to steer it to the mouth of the Shannon?"

"I ashk you. Has Carbri O'Connor ever shirked his duties because of a tankard of ale?"

"No."

"Well, then! 'Tis Arrah O'Donnell who's telling the man who saved her life what to be drinking and what not to be drinking."

"I saved your life too," she shot back angrily. "If not for me you'd be dead with gangrene now."

He seemed to think about what she said for a moment, then said, "A toast to saving lives!" He smiled irresistibly—that wonderful, charming smile that could soften stone.

He continued. The drink had made him feel stronger, almost invincible, and he forgot his earlier dejection. "If not for me, your father's sailors would have tossed you to the sharks, you wouldn't be talking about saving my life." All trace of the earlier sullenness was gone and he smiled again, that wonderful, endearing smile, and Arrah smiled, too, for she loved him intensely at this moment.

He lifted his hand from the jug and patted hers. Then stuck out his chin. "Now give me a kiss, Arrah. I love you!" This was the old Carbri she knew—smiling and good-humored. His recent bad mood was the result of his wound. She released the jug and kissed him. His mouth had the strong distilled taste of malt.

He went to pour himself more whiskey, but the jug was empty. "Hey, Mary!" he shouted, but Mary was sitting in the lap of some sailor, her back turned to Carbri. He looked at Arrah and shrugged. "What the devil. I have to water the ocean. Will you ashk the lass to bring us another when she turns about?"

Arrah sighed and nodded. He touched her shoulder as he passed her.

She felt something wet nudging her hand. The goat had come up and was licking at her fingertips.

"He's taken a shine to you, me Finn has," said Mary, a smile lighting her face. "He won't be failing when he comes to telling character. When Finn takes a liking to a body, I take a liking to the body too."

Arrah wished that the goat hadn't taken a liking to her. A pungent, dank smell, a smell like wet dog but very much stronger, arose from the animal's coat. "He's friendly enough," she said, sliding away on her bench.

"Friendly! Friendly! By the name of the saints, lass, he's the friendliest of God's creatures to be put on this earth. Suckled him meself. Didn't I, Finn?" She bent down and scratched the goat under his chin and kissed the top of his nose. "Me own jugs was raising him up. I'd lost me wee wain. A girl and but two weeks. Poor babe she was. And me jugs near to bursting. So full of milk I was.

"And this wee thing. His ma ripped to shreds by a pack of madded dogs, she was. And him not two days old, bleating his heart out. So I picked him in me lap and right away he was knowing what to do. And he was takin' me titoons so easy like. But when he got teeth, I had to stop. Lord alive! Just like a son he is to me now.

"Aye, I'm glad he likes you. 'Cause I likes you. I likes you the moment I saw you set foot in here. Me father a sailor too. But he threatened to drown me if I was to so much as put a toe on a ship. And he would've done it too. He beat me mother so she was dead. I watched him do it. Me clinging to his knees shouting 'Pap. Pap.' And when he was finished with her he started in on me, but I was smaller than me ma, and hid under the hen board, and him being drunk, he fell over trying to get me out. And so he didn't kill me. But he burned off me brother's ear for sassing him back. Held a candle to it, he did. Aye. He warn't an easy man, me pap." Mary smacked her lips, shook her head, then continued.

"I'm of a mind to be asking you to take me on your ship. What's a woman to do? She needs a pillow. And he's got one," she said, nodding in the direction of her dour-faced husband. "And in exchange for me pillow I let him climb on me at night. And so it is. We've all a master of sorts to serve. But he's not a fun man to be living with. He don't beat me the way that me pap did. But I've lived most all me life here. And I've wanted to see other places besides these cursed rocks all the time. Would you take me on?"

Mary had talked at such length and without interruption that the question left Arrah momentarily surprised. "Take you on?"

"Yes. But mind, I couldn't come without old Finn here. But he don't cause much trouble, and he won't be fussy for food. And you with all those men. You'll need a servant of sorts. I could be that. I ain't never seen a woman captaining a ship before. And it makes me thinking you're special. And I'd like to be spending time in your company."

Arrah looked at Mary and liked the forthright honesty about her. "You're welcome on my ship," she said.

"Mary!" came a voice from across the tavern. "Bring us a bit, will ya?"
"No, lad," shouted Mary. "Get it yourself. I'm through serving."

Patch had a particular way of pressing men into service. He would
swagger into an alehouse in an affected way, for Patch was not a man given
naturally to swaggering. Along with Mute and Hook, he had approached a
group of men. "Aye now, me hearties. Can I be sitting down with you to be
chewing the hardtack of a seaman's life?"

They had talked about ships and women, and Patch had bought several
jugs of ale. One of the sailors commented on Patch's generosity.

"What's a man in this world when he's without good company? A
tankard of usquebaugh, the Irish water of life, and the solid hip of a wench
in me pallet at night. What more is it that a man can be asking for?" said
Patch.

"Aye." Hook was talking now. "The Frenchies is always chortling about
their wine. Wine's not spirits. It's baby's milk."

"Aye. Not like usquebaugh. Now, have another snort."

"You're too kind is what you are. Gladly, I'll take another mouthful."

The sailor noticed Patch's white hands. "What was it what scarred your
hands the likes o' that?"

"Burned, they was, in a magician's trick when I was a boy. But enough of
this prattle. Drink up. Ye won't be insulting a man's hospitality by stopping
at a mere mouthful, will ye? And what is it they call ye, man?"

"Well, if that's how you say it. I can't refuse your goodness. Thank you. I
go by the name of Oscar. And this boy is called Gerrard."

"Coxblood, Oscar. But you insult me mortally. You've naught the thirst
of a sparrow. Drink up, for the love of the saints. These spirits was given to
man by God to be enjoyed. You'll be insulting the good Lord hisself by not
drinking, man." Patch bent low and whispered, "And after now, I'll be
taking you to a widow!"

They talked and drank amply, and then Patch's tattooed eye winked twice
at Hook, and Hook got up. "I've some matters that need tending. Angel and
me. We'll look back at you on ship deck."

Patch turned again to the sailor. "Coxbones, man. You'll be insulting me
own hospitality. Drink up. And let's off to softer climes. The bow of a
woman's belly."

Patch and Mute stood, Patch grasping his hands at the table's edge,
pretending to stagger into it. Patch wobbled forward through the tables.

Mute pretended to fall against a pillar, then he seemed to take bearings with his belly and headed for the door.

Outside, Patch hesitated. He hiccuped loudly, then put his arm around the unsuspecting sailor's shoulders as though he were holding himself up.

"A moment. Old Blue feels like he was drinking all the water in the seven seas." Patch saw Hook's shadow beside the tavern. "Feels like a month since I last"—he hiccuped again—"pissed." He staggered once more.

"Aye!"

As Oscar and Gerrard were relieving themselves, Patch turned and looked at them. "In the name of the saints," he said to Oscar. "That's a damned sorry stream for a sailor. Ye see that rock there. I'll wager I can be hitting it."

"Not at this distance. What the devil do you think I am?"

"Well, come closer then. I'll wager I can hit it from here."

Hook was behind, his wooden arm raised over Oscar's head. Mute lifted a bully stick above Gerrard's head. Down came the wooden arm. Down came the bully stick, and the two sailors seemed to melt to the ground.

"Aye, there's nothing like the kiss of Angel to put a body to sleep. Ain't that right, darling?" said Hook.

Mute picked up Oscar, who was the larger of the two sailors, and threw him over his shoulder as though the drunk were a sack of grain. Patch picked up the other in the same way, and whistling and singing, their voices rising in bawdy sounds to the night, they returned to the *Twilight Moon*.

Later Patch and his two mates would try another tavern, until they had a full, if not willing, crew of seamen.

The seamen were chained to the hold and let loose when the ship was far enough at sea that escape would be unlikely.

CHAPTER 17

Debrogail and Magnus traveled to Galway, the Royal English town where they planned to seek indenture at the castle of Geralde de Burgo. He had a reputation as a lover of fine music and had the best bards in Ireland to entertain him. On the way there, Debrogail, desperate for revenge against Naira, asked Magnus to take her to a witch.

The crone had pure white skin without any color whatsoever and pale pink eyes like those of a rabbit. She pulled a mandrake root, one of the roots that looked like the human body, from among her plants, then pierced it with a needle. "She will die in first childbirth," said the witch, "if you exchange something of yours for her life."

"What do you want?" asked Debrogail.

"In return for her life I ask for your tongue."

"My tongue!"

"Your song is a gift of God, as is life. When God takes something away, he wants something of equal value in return," said the crone.

Debrogail shook her head.

The witch looked at her with amusement. "You're a clever girl. The cost of revenge is often greater than the prize. For your wisdom let me tell you something:

"False is fair and fair is false.
You'll find what you've lost in the hangman's cell."

Debrogail looked at the old crone as though she were an apparition. "Bres and I will find each other in the hangman's cell. Magnus saved me so I could be hanged!" cried Debrogail in disbelief. "Has God turned his back on me?"

"I can tell you no more," said the old witch. At de Burgo's castle

Debrogail and Magnus told everyone they were brother and sister, that they had been servants at the O'Reilly castle and were escaping the devastating fighting that was taking place between the troops of the two brothers. Because Debrogail was pretty, the guard at the gate had allowed her to pass, but refused Magnus entry, saying that Master de Burgo had no use of a one-legged man. But Debrogail pleaded with the guard, telling him that her brother had lost his leg saving her life, and that she would work doubly hard, triply hard if he could stay with her. Since de Burgo was away and not there to hear her sing, Debrogail was taken into the kitchen.

News of the enchantress sea captain, Arrah O'Donnell, spread quickly from Rathlin Island down the west coast of Ireland. Among those who heard it was Agneis de Burgo, the betrothed of Carbri O'Connor. Agneis was a young, innocent girl with thick red hair and a smattering of freckles across her nose.

When de Burgo returned to the castle with more news of Arrah O'Donnell, Debrogail watched as Agneis, brokenhearted and weeping, threw herself on her father's knees, bewailing the fact that her beloved Carbri with the laughing eyes had become enchanted by a sea witch.

Agneis's father, Geralde de Burgo, was not brokenhearted. He was furious. Debrogail filled his tankard of wine. He immediately crashed it against a wall and railed about the treachery of Carbri O'Connor. The marriage to Carbri O'Connor would have meant the acquisition of a large territory around Lough Mask.

Phillipc de Burgo, Geralde's eldest but illegitimate son, approached his father. He volunteered to go and search out Arrah O'Donnell and kill her. Then Carbri O'Connor would get hold of his senses and marry Agneis. Geralde de Burgo agreed. He ordered one hundred of his best archers and one hundred of his best swordsmen on board two ships to go and search out the sea witch. De Burgo's eldest legitimate son volunteered to take charge of the second ship.

Debrogail was frightened and confused. She had a great sense of loyalty in her heart for Arrah. She wanted to warn her of the impending attack, but was afraid if she breathed even a word outside the castle walls, Mistress Naira would find her again and order her entombed. And then there had been the riddle of the old witch—she would find what she'd lost in the hangman's cell. Debrogail's mind was a jumble. Her thoughts whirled like a dance. Would they ever stop turning? She put fish oil in the tankard, and wine in the torch sconces. When Agneis took a sip from her tankard, she got instead a mouth of fish oil, and spit out the revolting stuff.

Geralde de Burgo had heard from one of his guards that a new servant had been taken into indenture who had the voice of an angel, but he had been too occupied with Carbri O'Connor's renouncement of his daughter to concern himself with anything but the upcoming battle against Arrah O'Donnell.

But with his two sons heading the expedition to destroy her, de Burgo was confident victory would be his. He turned his attentions once more to his other passions—women, magic, and music.

De Burgo had high color in his cheeks, and although he had a substantial girth, as was expected of a man of his age, he still exuded an aura of manly power. The women of the castle whispered and giggled whenever he passed them. When Debrogail asked why, a comely little chamber wench just giggled some more. "You'll find out soon enough."

The overseer of the servants had a small child who frequently had colic. Night after night the child screamed in pain. Infusions of all sorts were given to him. Nothing seemed to help. One night Debrogail picked him up and she began to sing to him. The child quieted immediately.

De Burgo himself was about that night. To keep his manly powers at their highest levels, he practiced black magic in the cellars of secret apartments that were below the waters of the sea at Galway. He was returning from those secret chambers when he heard the song of Debrogail, her voice lilting and more beautiful than any he'd heard.

He followed the voice to the kitchen, where he saw her holding the child, rocking it, her hair falling like wings over her shoulder. He couldn't see her face for a moment and then she turned, and he was swept away by the fineness of her features, the fine curve of her cheekbones, the doelike eyes. He didn't lust for her as much as long to look at her and listen to her, the way he might with a splendid jewelled music box, for she was truly beautiful, and her voice was enchanting. He was afraid to move for fear that she might stop singing.

When she did stop, there were tears in his eyes. He took her from the kitchen the same night and called her to his chamber.

In his studies of magic, Geralde de Burgo had learned that the Easterns would pleasure their women without allowing themselves the release of the lust shudder, for they believed that each spilling of seed shortened the life of a man. He had embraced this philosophy and had, through various experimentations in his subterranean chambers, perfected a powder which when rubbed on his manhood kept him from coming to the lust shudder for an extended period of time.

De Burgo had a great wart on the end of his penis. The powder that he took in his secret chambers, coupled with the wart on the end of his member, made him a most unusual love partner. The women in the castle were delighted when he called them to his bed and afterward giggled amongst themselves.

His own wife was a timid thing. Pretty, but with the brain of a clam. De Burgo made no secret to his other women that his wife had grown increasingly reluctant in bed. He had been forced to make love to her to beget children, but each coupling had given him as much pleasure as trying to force open an oyster with an old root.

For several nights, Geralde de Burgo resisted the urge to make love to Debrogail. Each night she would sing to him in his chamber to ease away the worries of the world. He was afraid that if he used her body, she would stop singing. At the same time he desired her beauty. Finally one night he succumbed.

He looked at her in the candlelight. "By the gods, but you're beautiful. Get undressed," he commanded.

Debrogail undressed slowly, first untying the kercher from her hair so that it fell in russet tresses about her shoulders. She shook her head. Her hair was a fragrant almond wave. She never stopped singing as she undressed, and as she removed her laine, the over-robe, she began to dance.

De Burgo had never seen her dance. Her long limbs were like malleable gold in the candlelight. Her hair was long, falling over her breasts, covering the faint golden rose of her nipples, and then lifting from them, exposing them momentarily as she twirled. Her head back, her back arched, her arms reaching, her dance was a mesmerizing whirl, enchanting him, enticing him.

When she stopped he stood behind her and ran his finger down her shoulder blades, down to the small of her back and along the outline of her buttocks. Then he turned her around and pulled a string of pearls from his pocket and clasped them about her neck, so she stood there naked, her only adornment her hair and pearls. Her breasts rose full, firm, and golden. Her doe eyes watched his hand as he reached to himself and pulled his member from his trews. It was swollen hard and erect.

"It's a great honor," she said, "to be desired by my lord."

"Is that what the servants say?" he asked.

"Yes!" And then she asked quickly, "Did I please my lord?"

"Christ, dear girl." He grabbed her hand and pulled it to his swollen organ. "Can't you feel how much you pleased me."

She lied now, for in truth she found the wart on the end of de Burgo's penis to be revolting. "What a handsome man you are between your legs."

"It pleases my women," de Burgo said confidently. "I'll show you just how much," and he directed her to his bed.

"I'm certain they love you," she said. "And I wish that I could know it for myself . . . and once I would have gone with you gladly. But I love a young man, and love changes a woman. If I permit you to love me, I feel that I would betray him. If my song pleases my lord, it is because I'm in love. Betrayal would take the joy from my song, and I would please you less."

"You don't sing from there," he said in a matter-of-fact voice that covered his own disappointment.

Debrogail noticed that de Burgo's manhood was looking a little less manly. She smiled her most charming smile. "Allow me to please you in a way that no other can—allow me to please you with my songs."

De Burgo sighed and nodded, then shouted to his chamber attendant. "Bring me another wench."

As a servant's daughter she had always been vulnerable to the desires of men of power. This was the first time she was able to refuse the lust of a man of rank. "Thank you, my lord," she said, bending to her knees and kissing his hand.

"If only you weren't so beautiful," he said. "Or if only your voice wasn't such a pleasure to me! Ah, Debrogail." He stroked his beard. "Perhaps a man is always destined to want for something. Oh, Debrogail," he said, lifting her so she stood. "Come sit here and sing to me then."

The *Belle Étoile* and the *Twilight Moon* had left Rathlin Island together, sailing west-northwest, following the Antrim coastline. Carbri had resumed command of the *Belle Étoile* while Arrah, despite Carbri's protestations, captained the *Twilight Moon.*

The feelings of the sailors who had been pressed into service began to change. At first Patch's threats of whippings kept them at their posts, but as the good conditions continued and they began to see for themselves Arrah's capabilities as a captain they became enthusiastic. Never had they known even a man to have so much vitality and drive, much less a woman. In some uncanny way she'd mastered the skills of the sea and knew them better than most men they'd served under. After a few days Patch no longer had to threaten any of them with the whip. They looked upon their captain with awe and wonderment.

Since they were sailing within sight of land, Arrah became obsessed with fixing the land in her mind. Her father had often said that the greatest danger to a seaman was not the sea, but the land. Far more ships were crashed up on rocks than swamped on the open sea. On the deck she stood as though in a trance, staring at the coastline, fixing every ridge, every hill, every small protrusion in her mind. She took the compass needle, rubbed it with a lodestone, and set the needle on a straw floating in a bowl of water and measured the distances: twenty degrees, thirteen degrees, sixty degrees. She never put anything to pen, but went over the forms and figures again and again, until a map began to form in her mind. The position of rocks and shoals, and tidal speeds and currents, she measured all and put them to memory, for the future safety of her ship and crew would depend on her.

Patch watched her and joked with her. "Arrah. It won't be necessary for you to be remembering every stone that a seagull's spit out."

Her men watched her. One admitted, "I tell you one thing. I'd much rather take my orders from she than the damn scourge I sailed with last."

Sebastian watched her too. He watched the curving of her breast lift under her tunic as she lifted her arm to hold the astrolabe to the stars. He saw the flash of white breast lit by starlight as the cloth gaped open. He watched the curve of her buttock as she leaned over the bulwark or bent to pick a coil of rope from the deck. He watched her walk about the ship, her carriage magnificent as though the deck was an empire. The few times he had looked at her boldly, she had met his gaze with chilling dismissal. Never mind. He had patience. Captain Carbri had recovered. But a woman like Arrah, eventually she would lose interest in him.

Hirple, too, watched her, looking for a chance to overcome her. But that damned Frenchy Sebastian was hanging about her like a cunt-struck fool. And if it wasn't Frenchy, then it was that bloody one-eyed bucket, Patch. He'd looked for an ally amongst the pirates, but they all held the she-bitch in some sort of stupid wonder. None of them would raise a hand against her. There were those who were pressed into service, and he had found the buttocks of a young chicken to his liking. But the boy was spineless as a jellyfish and couldn't be counted on to raise so much as an eyebrow against the bitch.

Whenever Hirple walked past Arrah's cabin, he would stop momentarily and glance in the window to see if he could see her. If she wasn't in her cabin, he would lay his hand on the door and try it, but it was always locked.

As her ship approached Bloody Foreland, Arrah saw the red granite coastline from which it took its name. She continued sailing southward past the steep, towering cliffs of Aran Island that rose in an impenetrable, unscalable gray wall of several hundred feet on the windward side.

It was at this point that the two ships had planned to leave the shoreline. Instead of coasting Donegal Bay, they would sail directly to Erris Head and Eagle Island, thereby crossing the open Atlantic. Since the ships were traveling at a speed of about seven knots, the open sailing would spare them a full afternoon of time.

Carbri was happy. A moderate nor'easter was blowing, with about half the waves showing whitecaps. A sailor couldn't ask for better conditions. The *Belle Étoile* was running the wind. They would reach Eagle Island by late afternoon. The two ships would moor and he would sleep with Arrah this night.

He thought of the firm curve of her haunches beneath his hands and he ached to hold her now. He recalled with longing the way she responded to him, the way she pressed her hips against his, the way she was wet and ready for him. She was a wanton. He would be happy when he was back at Eagle Island with her. All those men on the *Twilight Moon*. He'd seen the way they looked at her.

His arm was hurting, but not unbearably. The leech healer at Rathlin Island had given him some meadowsweet plants and told him to steep a handful of the dried plant in a half jug of water and to take that for pain. Carbri had taken the infusion and followed it with a few solid swallows of spirits. His head was cloaked in a comfortable cloud of softness.

The watch shouting down from the crow's-nest interrupted his thoughts. "She's turning, sir. The *Twilight Moon*, she's heading for shore."

To the port, Carbri saw that the *Twilight Moon* had come about, was close reaching the wind and heading toward the coast. What was Arrah doing? Had she run into some trouble? Her ship gone awry? "Come about," Carbri shouted. "Come about."

The helmsman picked up the command. "Ready about!" He warned the crew to be ready to turn the sail. Then came the words from the helmsman. "Hard-a-lee." The ship seemed to groan, then take in her breath, as it butted headlong against the waves with the effort of changing direction. Now the ship's speed slowed as it reacted to the wind and tide.

Carbri felt a low surge of anger rise in him. Somehow he already knew that there was nothing wrong with Arrah's ship. He had orders to sail up the

Shannon as quickly as possible, but she, she had no orders at all except her own desires. She was with all those men on board and her wanton nature. Damn her and her notions of seamanship. He would make her follow him. He would take her back to Eagle Island. As soon as he returned from Clonmacnoise, he would marry her. That would put an end to her sailing.

He checked the sails' trim to see if there was any way he could increase his speed. But there wasn't. The *Twilight Moon* had a greater sail area, and as long she had no wish to be caught, she wouldn't be.

The *Twilight Moon* disappeared behind Duck Island. Was she mad? A wind could spring up at any time. She could be driven up on any of the numerous rocks. Strong tidal currents ran swift in the channel. He looked at the sun. Damn, but he wouldn't make Eagle Island by this afternoon either.

When he caught up to her, her sails were reefed and she was dropping the lead pipe and taking a sounding on the south side of Duck Island. It was a high, rocky island, windswept and bare on the west, with off-lying dangers. She was closer in than she should have been. Sailor's Island lay less than a half-cable's length to her starboard.

Carbri tied in his sails and dropped anchor. He cupped his hands against the breeze and shouted to her, but she made no sign that she had heard him.

He felt it was foolhardy to take a large vessel in so close, and so he ordered the longboat dropped over the side. He rowed to the *Twilight Moon*.

"Why did you stop following me?" he shouted at Arrah even before she had a chance to greet him.

"I can't learn the coastline if I don't come in close."

"I know the coastline, I'll get you home."

"I don't want *you* to *take* me home. I want to learn how to get myself home."

"Arrah, this is nonsense."

"My father always said that a good sailor knows his coastlines better than he knows the warts on his hand. The only way a sailor can know the coastline is by traveling it and sounding it." Although she was talking to him, she continued with the lead pipe, throwing it and drawing it back in.

Carbri saw the sailors standing around listening to them, their mouths pulled loosely open in toothless smiles. They knew what Carbri wanted. "Slime buckets," he yelled at them.

As a group, they shuffled and lifted their feet, pretending that they were going to move, but as soon as Carbri had his back turned, they listened intently again.

"I miss you. I miss you in my berth at night," Carbri said.

The sailors grimaced and made obscene gestures with their fingers behind Carbri's back.

"I miss you too. But I want to sound this coastline."

"You can be avoiding the whole thing."

"I don't want to avoid it. I want to know it. Every inlet. Every rock!"

"Nobody will be knowing the coastline like that. Not even your father. Surely, he knows the shore about Eagle Island. But not . . ." He allowed his words to trail off and held out his hands in futility. Already her face was set in that determined look, the full lips in a tight line, the eyes meeting his directly and stubbornly. Those damn seductive haunches. Their full curves shown off in the turn of her trews.

He pulled her gently toward him, loosened the rope of the lead pipe from her fingers. Her fingers were wet from the rope, and he kissed them lightly. God, how he wanted her.

Arrah, whose passions flowed hot and close to the surface, had missed making love with Carbri and eagerly met his advances. Her own lust was the only thing that could distract her from the sea.

"Come," said Carbri, and led her to the captain's quarters.

In the cabin she sought his mouth and body hungrily.

Still favoring his arm, he pulled his trews off and opened his jerkin. The wound on his shoulder had scabbed over. Arrah pulled her own garments off. Because Carbri still couldn't support himself on his hurt arm, she told him to sit on her chair. His member poked out stiff as an attentive soldier from between his legs. Completely naked she stood in front of him. "God, but you're beautiful," he said, and slowly ran his hand down her breast, then stretched his chin to lift his tongue to her nipple. He followed the smooth curves of her body down to her navel. She touched his hair, tilted his face upward and kissed him, then lowered herself onto his erect phallus, straddling him as though she were riding a horse. She was wet and hungry for him, welcomed the hard penetration, the solid impalement, and threw her head back with pleasure and rode him, perspiration beading like small pearls on her breasts, until Carbri shuddered and grew limp from his spasm of pleasure.

Outside on the deck the goat chewed contentedly on the ridge of a barrel. The sailors jeered each other and catcalled and made obscene remarks to themselves and to Mary.

"Well, that's a bit of all right."

"I'd give me best teeth to have what the O'Connor has now."

"Dreamer!" said Mary. "Yea best teeth ain't but one in yea mouth. And even it's loose. Finn here has got better chompers than yea does."

"Aye, but she's a woman, ain't she, our Arrah?"

"Not me. I like me women to be acting like women, and not like men."

"Pshaw. Now, there ain't a woman what is more like a woman than our captain. You seen her bend to the bulwark. Now there's a pair of legs I'd like to feel around me."

Because the door to the master's cabin was low, Carbri had to bend if he didn't want to bump his head when he came out. The sailors didn't see his face and began to whistle and hoot. But he looked up and his fallen expression made them realize that something was the matter. They would have jeered him except that Arrah came out too. "I've come this far, and I can go the rest of the way myself," she said.

"Patch," said Carbri. "Tell her to be sensible."

Patch looked at Arrah. "No, sir. I can't be telling a body who's sailed the Dragon nothing."

"That's right, Patch," exploded Carbri with an uncharacteristic anger. "Play the fool. Don't you know, both of you? It was chance. The Fates turning a blind eye to you."

"Begging your pardon, Carbri, sir," said Patch, "but I think that Captain Arrah is quite able to bring the ship by herself."

"Zounds! You one-eyed bucket. You're the reason she's on this ship! Always explaining to her one thing and then another. Arrah, I insist that you come back."

"No. This is my ship. And if you order me about, you can leave!"

Carbri blanched, and seeing him thus, Arrah regretted her anger. Her voice softened. "You can't order me about! I won't let you." She grasped his hand. He pulled it away, but she grasped it back. "I love you! But I have to do what I have to do. You take the mercenaries that I'm carrying, then sail on to Clonmacnoise. I'll wait for you at Eagle Island. When you return, we'll be married."

"You give your word?" he asked.

She nodded.

"A captain can't go back on his word. Isn't that right, Patch?" asked Carbri.

"No, sir! Only the blackest of men go back on their word."

Carbri frowned, put his arm around Arrah's shoulder and kissed her forehead. "God's blood. I miss holding you at night." He grasped her to him one more time. "By thunder! What are all you gawking at? Like dead fish, the lot of you."

The sailors grumbled and shuffled their feet.

Carbri prepared to leave as well but hesitated. Evening was settling. A shroud of fog was coming off the sea, and the base of the islands was ragged in mist so that only the tops of a few spindly trees were visible. Shaped by the wind, they looked like monks bowed in prayer. He gave Arrah a sideways glance, then gave her some directions. "In these bays it's best to be mooring with one anchor in toward the beach and the other well out to northeast in case you'll be having a shift of wind." He gave Arrah one last hug and looked at her. "I love you. Godspeed." He kissed her again, descended to his longboat, looked back at her one more time, and gave orders to be rowed back to his ship.

For nearly a week the *Twilight Moon* had sailed along the coast of Ireland, sounding in and out among the islands, inlets, and cliffs. Like all individuals of intense passions, Arrah became obsessed. She slept little and ate only when Mary insisted she do so.

It was a sharp day, with wind gusts that sent the clouds hurly-burly across the sky.

Mary brought food on a tray to the deck.

"You have to eat, Arrah. You have to sleep."

"I don't have time to sleep."

"Yea've taken charge of a ship. But yea can't be larning ever'thing there's to be larning in one night, now can yea?"

"I can't do it in one night. But I will learn it."

"Yea won't be larning nothing if'n yea won't be keeping up your strength, girl—"

A shout from Hook, who was keeping the crow's-nest, interrupted Mary's admonitions. "Sail to the starboard!"

The object was barely recognizable, barely a white speck on the blue horizon, like a thread of cloud hanging from heaven onto the ocean.

It wasn't the first ship they had seen. There had been merchants that passed at far distances. The crew watched the ship silently, to ascertain its movements. "What flag's she flying?" Arrah shouted up to Hook.

"Can't tell yet," came back the answer.

The white thing grew larger and larger until the unmistakable triangular shape of a topsail became visible.

The information came down from the crow's-nest. "There's two ships. Both flying the St. George's of England, and a mast with . . . an ermine."

Arrah knew it as de Burgo's insignia. Obviously he had heard that Carbri no longer planned to marry Agneis. By destroying her ship, she surmised, de Burgo hoped Carbri would change his mind and again agree to marry Agneis. "Prepare for battle!" Arrah shouted.

De Burgo's son, Phillipe, was fighting for his patrimony. He was the eldest son of Geralde de Burgo, but he had been born illegitimately.

Illegitimacy had posed no problem for Phillipe to follow as heir to his father, because under Brehon Laws, titles were passed to the strongest young nobleman. Strength was determined by fighting, a fact which kept much of Ireland in a kind of perpetual violence as brother fought brother and kinsman fought kinsman to determine who would take the title of chieftain. Pure determination and bullying force of will had gained Phillipe de Burgo an awesome reputation as a victorious land tactician. He was readily recognized to follow his father as heir.

Unfortunately, when Phillipe's father swore allegiance to the English king, he swore to abide by England's law of primogeniture, which gave all property to the eldest legitimate son. Under English laws Phillipe was to be left virtually impoverished, without land, without property.

Coupled with Phillipe's illegitimacy was his reputation as a hotspur. He seemed to have inherited at least some of his mother's volatile personality. When she was younger, she was sudden and quick in quarrel, and was known as a "pepper head." Unfortunately, as she grew older, the severity of her temper increased. People called her crazy, possessed. Some people said that one of Geralde de Burgo's black-magic spells had gone awry and turned her into a madwoman. Whatever the reason, Phillipe's mother, in various furies, tried to murder two of the servants, as well as her own son and his father. Finally she hurled herself to her death from the highest tower of Galway Castle to the stones below.

There was only one way for Phillipe to lay claim to his patrimony. His half-sister, Agneis, was his father's favored child. If he, Phillipe, won the battle, destroyed Arrah O'Donnell, and brought Carbri home for Agneis, then she would persuade his father to officially recognize Phillipe as legitimate and rename him as heir to the de Burgo lands.

It was for that reason he had so readily volunteered to defeat Arrah O'Donnell.

*   *   *

Arrah shouted orders to jibe. The *Twilight Moon* veered forty-five degrees from the course she was drawing. The other ship did the same.

"She's coming closer, Captain," Hook shouted down.

"Damn you, Hook!" Patch stretched his neck upward so that the deep brown line of his chin was readily visible. "Even with one eye, we can see she's coming closer. Tell us something we can't see!"

"She's carrying artillery too."

"Artillery? How much?"

"How much! How much! How do I know how much? She's not broadside, so how can I be seeing? I canna' be taking me eyes out of me head and twisting them about and checking."

Patch, agile as a squirrel, scooted up the stays. "In the name of the piper that piped afore Moses. She's got ten guns to a side."

"We'll outsail her."

Patch landed with a soft quick thud of his bare feet on the deck floor. "With every stitch out we don't have half the sail as she does."

"We'll break out the oars and row!"

"Two hundred oars would be needed for the current around here."

Hook landed down on the deck now too. "They have big guns, Captain. They'll blow us right out of the water."

The *Twilight Moon's* sails suddenly cracked noisily, like the snap of a whip. The wind was gusting.

"They can't blow us out of the water if we put something between us and them. That island . . ."

Finn, who sensed the excitement, was running about the boat ramming the bulwark with his horns. "That's it!" shouted Arrah. "We'll pass through the sound, turn around, and ram them. We're smaller and more maneuverable than they are and our beak is strong enough."

"Arrah girl, you've got the gods and saints on your side, lass. Or the devil. I don'na know which."

"But we'll crash up on the rocks," came the dissension from Hirple this time.

"We have no choice," Arrah said. "It's the rocks or cannon fire!"

"I do not like the cast of that sky, Captain. It is a storm sky. We will break up on the rocks," said Sebastian.

The waves were moving in a series of three or four high, steep waves, then a series of short rollers.

"Captain," said Patch. "The wind and waves are too strong for a jibe. Better to come about in a big broad loop."

"We don't have time."

She felt the *Twilight Moon* buck in the water. This would be her first real battle. The battle with the pirates had happened too quickly for her to ponder over its events. She had simply acted. But now the feeling of waiting for battle brought a kind of quivering in her stomach as though it were being lifted and dropped with the motion of the waves. She had felt exactly the same way when she knew that Carbri was going to make love to her that first time. Was that how men felt when they went into battle, like a virgin before deflowering? It was a feeling, half excitement, half fear. Each wave seemed to bring de Burgo's ship closer and closer behind them, the huge white sails bearing down on them like a bird of prey.

"Unfurl all sheets."

"Captain! The power of this wind'll snap the mast if we crowd sail."

"If we don't, their cannons will burst our hull. Now do as I say. And break out the oars."

"Oars!"

"Just do as I say! Hook, watch for rocks."

They moved westward past the northern point of the island. If the bottom was shallow here or if there were unseen rocks, the devil would take the *Twilight Moon.*

The English ship was advancing steadily. Arrah could see the bowsprit with the elongated face of a snarling beast painted orange with deep-red carnivorous fangs. After a while, Arrah could make out the men's features. She saw a thin-faced man wearing a dark flat hat with a feather, and recognized him as Geralde de Burgo's son, Phillipe de Burgo, who had once asked for her hand in matrimony.

Although Phillipe had been pleasant enough to look upon, she had found his personality erratic, and declined him. He had screamed at her during a walk for no other reason than she had wanted to descend the three hundred steps of Eagle Island to the sea below. He had demanded that she was his hostess and her obligation was to stay with him and entertain him. When she had descended the steps regardless of his yelling, he had picked up stones and hurled them down at her. Finally even Reevnarg had been relieved to be rid of him. Eventually Arrah heard that Phillipe had married someone else.

"Look at his face now," said Mary. "All pinched up like his codpiece is too tight. Oh, I won't be liking the looks of him. He's not a man to be crossing."

On the bow of de Burgo's ship, above the water line, Arrah saw a gun port open and the black, brutal muzzle of a gun come forward. A projection of the island was just ahead. They had to move.

"All hands to the oars. Everybody! Mary, you too."

"Me! I ain't—"

"Everybody! Damn you, everybody! Down to the oar deck." The enemy ship volleyed a cannon ball at the *Twilight Moon.* Arrah felt her breath stop. There was a puff of smoke and an explosion and she saw the ball erupt from the cannon, its trajectory low and short of the *Twilight Moon.*

From the nether regions of her mind came a comment of her father's from some past conversation. *Cannons on ships, they're near to useless. They take ten minutes to reload. Their range is short. And the ship has to be full broadside for a captain to use all his fire.* De Burgo's ship was chasing them headlong. To fire the rest of her guns at the *Twilight Moon,* the ship would have to turn broadside.

She shouted at Patch, who was at the helm. "Take us round the point. Then turn her about so she's facing the way we came. Make certain her beak doesn't stick out."

She gave a quick look to the shoreline: rocky with low cliffs and some sandy patches. "Hook, can you swim?"

"Swim!" Hook grimaced horribly, as though he'd just eaten something very sour.

"Yes, swim!"

"Swim! It's a bad-luck thing—a sailor knowing how to swim. The sea takes a man when she wants him. No point in fighting her."

Mute made an explosive sound in his throat.

"You can swim?" Arrah asked him.

Patch spoke now. "Mute! He's part fish. That's why he's so ugly. His mother was a she-bass. His old man, desperate for a poke, dragged a fish out of the sea. Threw it back when he was satisfied. Mute here, before they trimmed his tongue, he was washed overboard in the Biscay. Three days he was in the sea. When they pulled him out his eyes were swollen shut from the salt and he couldn't see. But he was still swimming."

Mute was nodding his head, his ugly mouth gaping in a smile indicating that he could swim.

"When we turn the point, swim up there to the shore. See that hill? Climb it as fast as you can. Faster than you can. Take care they don't see you." She motioned behind her toward de Burgo's ship. "When you get to the top, watch them, and just as they come past the point"—she grabbed his scarf from about his neck—"wave this. Then we'll row out and ram them."

Overjoyed, Mute grabbed the scarf.

"Wait!" Arrah shouted. She had wanted to tell him of the importance of timing. If Mute waited too long to wave, the other ship would be full broadside and would open all guns. If he waited too long, then the enemy would ram the *Twilight Moon*. But Mute had already dived into the water and surfaced. He tossed his head to shake his wet hair back from his eyes and began to swim in long, even strokes. She would have to depend on the Fates and luck that he gave the signal at the right time.

Arrah didn't run down the seven steps to the oar deck so much as she flew down them. Jumping from the top railing, her hands outstretched, she looked as though she was in flight. Mary sat on the bench, holding an oar as though it were covered with excrement.

Arrah grabbed an oar and began to shout, "Pull hard! Pull! Stroke!"

No one rowed harder than Arrah herself. Pulling with all her might, she pushed herself to the limits of pain and endurance. There was a terrifying beauty in her supreme exertion, something frightening yet exquisite, something unearthly. All the while, she yelled, "Stroke . . . Stroke . . . Stroke . . ." Words rendered as half prayer, half curse. The others took up the chant, bent lower and faster to the oars. Within minutes, men were soaked with perspiration as though they'd run a great, interminable distance and they were enveloped in an ammoniac smell, the sweat stink of overexertion. All of them, Arrah, her sailors, even Mary, rowed like a crew possessed and heading for hell. "Stroke! Stroke!" The sails combined with the oars pushed the *Twilight Moon* around the point of the island.

On deck, Patch turned the ship about.

The rowers were panting and gasping for breath. Half of them coughed and hacked, and many spit.

"Stay here!" ordered Arrah. "Hold the ship against the current. Hold on until I tell you to row. Then pull! Your lives depend on it."

Grabbing the rope handrail, she leaped the steps up to the main deck. She watched Mute crouched on top of the hill. Hidden to the English ship by a gray rise of rock, he stretched his neck over the edge like a pigeon peering down to the sea below. The wind caught the scarf, made it flap in his hands. Here behind the rocks, the ship was wind-sheltered. Nonetheless, a strong gust could whip around the point at any moment. "Hold on," she whispered to the wind. She felt the ship moving with the current; felt the strain of the rowers holding it steady. "Hold on!" she whispered. A cormorant swam about on top of the waves. Sea gulls cried plaintively. Seaweed floated near the rocks. The coastal people said that this seaweed was the souls of babies that had died before they were baptized.

She could feel de Burgo's ship coming closer. The sky was overcast. The water was beginning to turn gray, the way it always did before the wind picked up. The cormorant spread its wings and lifted its cumbersome, ugly body in flight back up to the rocks. There was a break in the clouds. The sun peeked through for a moment. She saw the glint of Mute's earring, then it faded as the sun disappeared. "Hold on," she whispered.

Mute waved the handkerchief.

"Now," shouted Arrah. "Stroke! Stroke!" She felt like a blind woman. When she was small, she, Carbri, and Debrogail would play a game. Pretending to be blind, each of them would close his or her eyes and hold on to the other person's hand and have them lead them across the fields and rocks. "Watch," Debrogail or Carbri would say. "There's a stone." And Arrah would reach out tentatively with her foot, feel the outline of the stone with her toe, and then step over it. Now she was like that again, completely trusting, vulnerable, relying solely on the judgment of another being to guide. "Stroke!" she yelled. "Stroke!" She could not see the other ship at all, could only rely on the skill of Mute to judge distances, and the power of her oarsmen to row. She saw the waves moving out in half-circles in front of her as the wake from the English ship came closer.

Patch, his one eye never wavering from his course, held the helm with both hands. "Aye, Arrah Girl. I tell you. There's nothing more satisfying than the sound of one ship ramming another. Except for the sound of a sword stuck true in a man's guts."

"Stroke! Stroke!" she yelled. The inside of her lungs burned as though she were holding her breath. "Stroke!" she yelled again. Still it seemed that she was holding her breath.

On shore, the rocks moved past, the dark stratifications of rocks, gray and less gray and darker gray. A long diagonal line of stone shot up like a lance on the island side. Then a patch of brown-looking lichen flowers. She had a feeling that the ship was moving too slow, and then that it was moving too fast. Two slanted lines crossed each other in the dark rock like two black swords crossing each other and for a moment she thought of Seaghan MacNamara, the way his sword had crossed hers, how easily he had pushed her against the garden wall. Would de Burgo's son defeat her just as easily?

Some inner sense told Arrah that if they were to collide, they should have done so by now. Another patch of brown moss went by, and a sharp outcrop of rock like a crow's wing. The goat bleated forlornly as though calling for Mary, who was still on the oar deck.

The *Twilight Moon* had moved into the sound, out past the protecting finger of the island. To the starboard, the de Burgo ship was turning broadside.

Phillipe de Burgo had outguessed her, outmaneuvered her. She saw the volley of fire. Smelled the fire and sulphur and iron. The shot fell in the water no farther than an arm's length away. Water splashed up. Arrows whizzed past her; the air was a lethal place.

"Helm!" she shouted. "Row. Row!" She grabbed the whip from Patch, and leaping down onto the oar deck, began to lash the backs of the rowers. "Stroke! Stroke! The devil's in your wake!" De Burgo's men were not going to take her ship. She'd taken it from pirates and sailed across the Dragon's Mouth and they were not going to take it from her.

Back up the steps. She took them three at a time and in two leaps was on deck again. Hirple, moving more slowly, had followed her.

"Captain Arrah," he shouted. "Look there!"

The dark outlines of more mastheads showed behind the English ships. More sails to the windward.

"Captain Arrah," continued Hirple, holding his chest as though his heart were going to stop. "We'll be surrounded. There's nothing we can do. Jump ship and head for the islands and hope they don't follows." The rest of the crew stood behind him, their faces dark and tense.

Arrah cracked the whip at her gawking crew, sending them scurrying like rats. "Damn you! Get back and row!" If she could get her ship behind one of the other islands some cable's length to the north, then perhaps she could get out of the sound before the other English ships came. "Mary! You're useless at oars. Bring embers and coals from the galley and be quick about it!"

Before anyone could move, a cannon ball landed square on the helm, shattering it, sending wood flying, and knocking back both Patch and Finn, so they tumbled together and ended up in a heap on the floor. De Burgo's ship was nearly fully broadside. Without a helm, the *Twilight Moon* sat like a wingless duck on the water, waiting for the fatal shot.

"Finn, Finn!" cried Mary, rushing to the bewildered, bleating goat, disentangling his legs from those of Patch.

"Mary! Get the embers! The rest of you, tie in. Then back to the oars!" Out of the shelter of the island, the wind was rising. Without a helm, the ship would be at the mercy of the wind, blown back up against the rocks, crashing like an eggshell against them.

De Burgo's ship, knowing the *Twilight Moon* was crippled, was shifting its position in the water, turning again, preparing to draw forward so that it could close with the full broadside force of its guns on the *Twilight Moon*.

The sails were tied in. The men were rowing again.

Mary, puffing and panting, came up the stairs with a pail of hot coals. She ducked against the arrows whizzing past on the deck. "Finn!" she called. "Come here, lad."

"Powder up the cannon. Be quick about it," shouted Arrah.

"We've no cannon balls."

"Do as I say! Mary, bring up more coals. And tell them to keep rowing. Their guns haven't a range beyond one hundred and fifty yards. You there, help me turn the gun."

Pushing and panting and shoving, they wheeled the cannon to the starboard.

"By the saints. This thing weighs more than the Lord's arse end. If she slips, she'll run us clear through to Chiney."

"Put in the fuse!"

De Burgo's ship would be full broadside in a minute. Arrah shovelled the hot coals into the front of her single cannon. She shovelled in the second pail.

"Cod's eyes, Arrah," said Patch, running up. "Ye should have been an admiral. But for the love of the Lord, lassie, point your muzzle high. Crank it up. It's de Burgo you want to be shooting. Not the fishes."

"Fire!" came Arrah's order. There was the smell of sulphur and hot metal. Arrah saw the coals catch flame as they shot like small comets across the sky and hit squarely in the sails of the enemy ship. She saw the small flames flare into larger ones. "Now wind, blow," she whispered, and the wind gusted and suddenly the main mast and the aft sail flared like two huge, flaming torches.

Pandemonium broke out on de Burgo's ship. The assistant gunner's task was to watch the rise and fall of the sea so that the gunner could shoot while the ship was on the crest of a wave instead of in the trough. This action gave farther range to the guns. The assistant panicked when he saw the sheets flare and shouted when the ship was in the trough. The cannon volley fell short. The sea, splashing up, looked as though it were boiling.

De Burgo planted a fist in the gunner's face. The top of his knuckles stung from the gunner's teeth. Half the ship's artillery was on the wrong side. One couldn't move artillery from one side to front or back without balancing by moving other artillery to the other side, otherwise the ship would sink. God, he hated the sea! He hated ships. He hated his father! If he didn't sink that bloody woman's ship, all would be lost. A rage flowed in Phillipe de Burgo. He had to sink her at all cost. The angrier de Burgo became, the more frustrated he became, and the more unreasonable.

Fire was about him. Let the God-forsaken ship burn! He had to destroy that whore who had stolen his sister's husband. He'd caught a glimpse of Arrah O'Donnell on deck, her hands outstretched like she was communicating with the spirits. His own brother was coming up behind in the second ship. If Phillipe was to be successful in getting his father to name him as legitimate heir, then he had to act now, while the glory could still be called his, before he had to share it with his brother.

His ship's sails were blazing, and even the archers had been ordered by the ship's captain to take to buckets and put out the fire. De Burgo ordered the archers to stand to and aim for anything that moved on the *Twilight Moon*.

"But, sir," said the ship's captain. "We need all hands on bucket brigade if we're not to burn."

"If you don't give the order to shoot, damn you, I'll throw you into the fire! Now, tell them to shoot. And what the devil? Why are the gunports closed? You there, gunner! Open the ports and keep firing."

"We're off target."

"Shoot, damn you! Shoot. I want that ship blown to the blackest depths of hell."

"Sir, the sea's rising. The water'll come in the gunports. We'll sink."

Phillipe de Burgo struck the gunner across the face again. "Damned mutinous dog. Open the gunports and fire. And keep firing until I tell you to stop or I'll shoot you myself."

To avoid the flurry of arrows shot at her ship, Arrah had ducked behind the master's cabin. The second de Burgo ship had now entered the narrow sound behind the first. It was turning, but its gunports were still closed. And then, as one of three ships began to move ahead, she saw the crest of the O'Donnell flying from the masthead: the rampant eagle. They were her father's ships. That was the *Skatha* approaching. Without thinking, Arrah stepped out from behind the cabin and into full target on the deck. It was at that moment that the arrow hit her.

CHAPTER
18

When Arrah was a child, she had caught brimstone butterflies with Carbri and Debrogail, and they had spread the wings and pinned them with embroidery needles onto pieces of leather. With the arrow piercing her right breast, she felt like a pinned butterfly.

The arrow had come with such force and speed that it had sunk itself into the frame of the master's cabin, thereby holding her to the wood. She wanted to collapse on the deck floor and felt her legs grow weak, but the upward ripping of the arrow under her collarbone made her stand straighter.

She forced herself not to think of the pain. There were gradations of color from brown to tan to white on the feathers of the arrow: eagle feathers, or a falcon's maybe. Pain was like fear. It was a matter of simply forcing it from her mind.

All about her she saw chaos. The first de Burgo ship was burning and three longboats were lowered from it, carrying armored soldiers. The *Twilight Moon* had no hot coals left. Patch had taken a barrel of powder and plunged a fuse into the bunghole, lit it and thrown it at one of the approaching boats. A shower of wood and water had erupted like a sore from the sea. It became a mass of floating wood and, for a moment, bodies, but because de Burgo's soldiers wore armor, they sank in the water.

Two other longboats came on either side of her ship. At least two dozen de Burgo archers shot up at her crew. One after another, she saw her men fall.

De Burgo's men began to board her ship.

Arrah tried to pull away from the cabin wall, but the pain of the arrow sliding through her flesh was excruciating. De Burgo's men were all armored. She wore nothing but her jerkin and trews.

Slowly, Phillipe de Burgo himself approached her, his face twisted grotesquely with anger. He brandished his sword and aimed it for her heart.

Patch came behind. A quick sword slash against the back of de Burgo's unarmored leg sent him to his knees, howling like an injured hound. In one solid swing Patch hacked into his neck.

Patch's eye cover was pushed up to the side. As he came close, Arrah saw that the place where his right eye once had been was now a gray, dry socket something like a dried prune, but not as dark. She had to look away from him.

She felt him grasp the arrow, closed her eyes against what she knew was coming. He snapped off the arrow shaft. The vibration of the breaking shaft pained her whole body. He threw the feathered wood to the deck floor. He came very close to her. For a moment, she had a vision of him with his single eye, as a macabre agent of death. He embraced her, putting his hands squarely behind her back. His clothes smelled of gunpowder. His breath smelled like death. His tattooed eye blinked a myriad of colors: red, blue, and black. His other eyehole descended backward into nothingness.

He pulled her sharply toward him. She screamed as the arrow shaft moved in her shoulder. She was no longer pinned to the wall. Behind Patch she saw the tarnished armor of another soldier. She pulled Patch to the deck with her and they rolled behind a barrel.

She rose slowly to one knee and then another. She tried to hold a sword in her left hand, but because she was right-handed, the sword was a foreign, clumsy thing. She had no choice but to grasp the sword with her right. Each time she tried to move her arm, a knife seemed to cut away a piece of her chest. She wouldn't give in to the pain. She wouldn't. She began to cry, then cursed herself. Her father once fought for three days with an arrow sticking into his neck. If she wanted to be a captain, then she had to fight like one. Pain was the enemy to overcome. If her father could do it, she could do it. She got to her feet. She wouldn't let it hurt her. She struck out with her sword.

The rest of the battle was a blur of color and pain and sound: wood shrieking, metal clanging, and bloodied men screaming.

Patch glanced at her fighting and realized that she was completely untutored in swording, that she had no grace with the weapon at all, that she handled the sword not like a swordsman, but like a wild, erect animal. She lunged and swung without any attention to form. She appeared to have no fear of death and didn't believe in holding back, only in attacking.

Somehow she managed to bring her sword home into the knees, thighs, and necks of the enemy soldiers. He'd seen men like that sometimes, men who had that uncanny kind of luck. Men who did everything wrong, yet for whom things turned out all right.

Fighting so wildly gave Arrah a strange advantage. Immediately it was obvious to de Burgo's soldiers that she was a woman. They had never seen a female with such fury. Afraid of her, many held back, thinking she was in some way bewitched. Her own men, seeing her fight with such passion despite the bleeding wound, were inspired by her courage and spirit. Her remaining crew of twenty-five fought like fifty men.

But not all the enemy was afraid of her. A blond brute of an Englishman, who showed a Norse ancestry in his face, attacked her. He wore a dull, steel-gray helmet. There was the pleasure of knowing he was going to kill on his face. He knocked her sword from her hand, kicked her in the stomach, and stood above her with his weapon aimed for her face.

Even the arrow in her shoulder hadn't hurt as much as his foot in her belly. A blackness rose from her belly into her head. Somewhere behind the darkness, a larger darkness loomed and leaped. She tried to open her eyes, but couldn't.

Arrah awoke to a trimmed dark beard and dark eyes. Seaghan Mac-Namara was looking over her. She was in her own berth in the cabin of her ship. She turned slightly, felt the slide of the linen along her naked limbs. Someone had undressed her.

His arm was above her head and he stroked her forehead. "You'd fainted just as I came on board. That was a vicious wound you took."

Her right breast throbbed. The sheets in her berth were bloody. She reached up to touch her face; her hands were covered with bloody dressings.

She tried to sit up, but MacNamara gently held her down. "Don't try to move," he said. "Phillipe de Burgo's ship sank."

"What happened?" she asked.

"Carbri told us what you were doing. Your father, from his spies, heard that Geralde de Burgo was planning an attack on you! We found you in the midst of battle with them."

"My father?" She glanced at the door.

"The *Maeve* will be alongside soon."

"My crew?"

"Patch is outside. A dozen are dead. Mary is scared out of her wits. The rest are nursing wounds."

She remembered the arrow, and Patch's pulling it through. She had continued fighting, but then a darkness closed over her. Everything else was a blank.

Seaghan's face was very close to hers and she tried to sit up.

"It'll hurt if you move."

"I want to."

He put his arm under her and lifted her to a sitting position. A white pain stabbed through her torso into her head. The covers fell away from her breast and she saw streaks of dried blood on her skin. A satin dressing like a torn shirt was on her shoulder and across one breast. She pulled the covers up protectively against her. MacNamara helped her.

She shivered.

MacNamara took off his mantle, pulled her forward gently. It was the same garment he'd worn the first time she'd met him, a rough, dark-green frieze lined with green satin. As he draped the cloak over her bare shoulders and back, she could feel the warm satin against her skin, the heat of MacNamara's body still in the cloak. The heavy warmth enveloped her: a smell of salt and satin and wool, and the close sandalwood smell of a man.

She noticed the fine wide sweep of his forehead, and then the rest of him. Seaghan MacNamara had a brace of pistols stuck into his belt. He had two daggers and a cutlass. His torso was bare except for a leather vest. She had never seen him with bare arms, and now saw just how powerful the arms were, thick and hard with a matting of dark hair. The muscles of his chest looked as though they had been sculpted from copper-colored steel. All of his skin had a glistening swarthiness, except that his shoulders and upper arms were covered with dozens of small scars that looked almost like whip scars. On the index finger of his right hand he wore a large gold ring that looked like a seal ring. Although she didn't recognize the motif, with its rearing unicorn and fleur-de-lis, she knew it immediately not to be Irish. He wore green silk hose embroidered with what looked like pure gold thread. He wore knee-length black leather boots. The green emphasized his black beard and dark eyes, making them appear darker. She realized now that the dressing on her chest was of satin. He had ripped his shirt to wrap her wound.

His presence had a disconcerting effect on her that was almost frightening. She hadn't really been afraid during the battle, but now she was frightened of MacNamara, because he seemed to awake in her a duality of feeling. She wanted to cast off his cloak, and yet its heat warmed her. The last time he had been this close to her, he had so unnerved her that she thought of little else except the feel of his thigh between her legs for days. Only with obsessive work, and then later with Carbri's illness, had she been able to rid herself of the intense feelings. Now she felt those feelings beginning to awaken again. They were disquieting, but not disquieting enough for her to pull her hand away when he took it. He had protected her, and in some strange way, she welcomed his protection.

A curious, bewildered look lit his dark eyes. She saw his tongue touch the back of his teeth. "Rumor has it that you've sold your soul to the devil. That you're a sea witch or the devil's mistress. That you used magic to overcome Captain Whip and to sail the Dragon's—"

"I'm no witch," she said quietly. "I've not used witchcraft. Ever. Any one of Captain Whip's men—Hirple, Sebastian, the others—could have attacked him and killed him. But they were afraid. That's the only difference between me and the others. They were afraid. I didn't have time to think about being afraid. The same with the Devil's Mouth."

His voice was soft and close. "But you weren't afraid. And by not being afraid, you've made others afraid of you. And so they call you a witch." His mouth was very close to hers. She tried to draw back, but his power was such that she couldn't move away from him. She felt his breath brush her lips as he spoke. "They say you enchant men, yet destroy them like the sirens or mermaids of old!"

Despite the pain, she leaped out of bed sharply. Just as quickly he stood towering above her. He grabbed her and pulled her close to him. Whereas it was just his face that was close to her before, now his entire mass was pressed against hers. She felt the incredible hardness of his body pressing her. She felt the roughness of his chest hair against her breast skin. With one hand he held her shoulder, with the other he pressed the back of her waist, pulling her closer to him. She wanted to throw off his cloak, wanted to throw off all remembrance, all feel of him, yet couldn't. She braced her hands on his chest, trying to push him away. She felt the steel hardness of his muscles beneath her palms. The more she pushed him away, the closer he pulled her.

"Passionate Arrah. When I see you, it's like I see the sea itself. You're fierce and soft. Your body leaves its mark on a man. Like when the grass is long on the summer meadow, and you lie down in it, and your body leaves its imprint."

Arrah bristled. "And the woman in the carriage? And Carbri's sister? Did they leave their mark on you as well?"

He picked her up abruptly and carried her back to the berth. "You're wounded and you'll rest."

"I'm not a weakling who needs to be coddled."

"You'll stay here until I say you can get up. I'm not Mother O'Connor or one of your crew that you can order about."

She struggled against him.

"Stop it, Arrah!" He grasped her shoulders hard and pinned her to the berth. "You're strong but you'll never be as strong as I am."

"You're hurting me!"

"Then stop struggling!"

"I won't!"

"Damn you, Arrah O'Donnell. You'll listen to me." And grabbing both her wrists he pinned her hands above her head. "You fight like a hellcat. Even with your wound. Your sailors are in awe of you. Patch told me how you fought. That you are uncompletely untutored in swording, but that you handle the sword like a wild animal. That you have no fear of death and hold back nothing. That you attack and attack and attack until you collapse. But I'm not afraid of you!" He looked at her intensely.

She saw herself, small and bright, in the pupils of his dark eyes. He looked at her wrists where dressings covered her hands. Then he lifted her hand, turned her wrist over and kissed her where there was no dressing underneath. She felt the soft warmth of his lips on her skin. The quiet gentleness from such a powerful, enormous man took her aback.

"Do you know why the sea rages, Arrah?"

She didn't answer him.

"It rages against its barriers, like you. If you're not a witch, Arrah O'Donnell, who are you that you rage with such courage?"

"I had no choice."

"Who are you, Arrah O'Donnell, that you know no fear? That you usurp a ship from its pirate captain? That you sail the Dragon's Mouth?"

"And who are you, Seaghan MacNamara? That you don't live with your clansmen? That you wander Ireland and France like a vagabond sailor? That you dress like a king or a chieftain, or a ploughman?"

His visage grew almost sad for a moment. "It's too long a story to tell you now, but what's important is that I was a young lad, and foolish, and I was cast out." He poured an infusion of mint tea and handed it to her. "Mary made this for you." She allowed him to help her lift the cup to her mouth.

He put his hands gently on her shoulders. "Now, listen to me. I know that you're planning to marry Carbri. Geralde de Burgo wants the lands that were promised to him by the O'Connor in exchange for his daughter. He has already convinced the O'Connor clans to name someone other than Carbri as tanaist. If Carbri doesn't marry de Burgo's daughter, Carbri will never take the title of the O'Connor."

"He can't do that! Carbri was chosen as the most capable leader from the O'Connor."

"You shouldn't narrow your eyes like that, because it gives the impression that you're closing some of the world out. And a sea captain should always look on as much of the world as she can."

"And you," she asked. "Why do you narrow your eyes?"

"I've seen much of the world, and it doesn't please me. You're headed for danger. There are terrible things in the hearts of men. De Burgo's son was killed today, and he won't rest until he sees you hanged." He reached up and touched her neck.

The heat from his fingers seemed to travel down her spine and made her shiver. Words were gone from her. There was only the protecting warmth of his fingers against her neck.

He spoke again. "The gods grant wishes to those whom they destroy. If you sell your soul to the devil, he always collects."

She pulled away from his touch. "I haven't sold my soul to anyone."

His face grew tense; his brow knitted together keen and hard like iron. "You've sold your soul to Mōrrīgan. To the ancient Irish, she was the goddess of war and love, and is the cruelest mistress of all. Once you've lain with her, all other mistresses are dull and dispirited. She gives no peace. You wait for the rush and excitement, and for the fear, which itself is pleasure giving. I saw it in your eyes the night I saw you dance. You didn't dance like a woman, but like a warrior."

A knock on the door sounded and Seaghan MacNamara in a fluid motion rose to answer it. His back was as massive as a ship's timbers. No one entered, but Arrah heard an exchange of voices. When Seaghan turned, he was carrying something in his arms. She saw yellow, burning eyes, dark ears, and tawny, orange, and cream fur. It was a tiger cub.

Seaghan sat on her berth once again. His voice grew strangely soft and smooth, but his eyes were dark and swift. "I brought you this, from an acquaintance in Venice. Because under your soft breast skin, Arrah, burns the heart of a tiger."

She saw Seaghan's nostrils flare. She saw his mouth open. She saw his fine dark eyes, and the roughness of his large hands. The tiger turned its yellow eyes on her.

"His name is Kian," continued Seaghan, "which was the sun god of the ancient peoples."

She took the tiger from him and held it against her breast. The silky tiger fur brushed against her nipples.

Seaghan saw the late afternoon sun going down. The sun slanted across the rich black-and-tawny fur of the tiger and the flesh of Arrah's breast, so that the upper globes of her were in daylight, but the under parts were in shadow. She stirred an intense desire in him, an almost uncontrollable ache that settled at the bottom of his spine. She was fascinating and enchanting, luminously beautiful and dark at the same time.

Arrah stroked the luxurious fur of the beast, and then buried her face in the silky, thick white fur of the tiger's chest. She could hear the animal's heart beat and beat, and felt like she never wanted to leave the warm shelter of fur and heartbeat.

"Do you know, Arrah, to the ancients of the east, the tiger represented strength and valor. Beneath this velvet paw you find these." He took the tiger's paws and spread apart the toes, exposing the fierce claws.

MacNamara's thick fingers and muscled, sun-browned forearms corded with veins looked sinister, brutal, and overpowering, and yet there was enormous gentleness in him. Arrah felt a dark desire seeping in her blood.

"You are in a most dangerous position because winning comes so easily to you. You've captivated and enchanted the crews of two ships. Patch told me what kind of woman you are. He said that when he showed you something even once, you could do it better than he could even though he'd been doing it all his life. That's the kind of woman you are. And you know no fear. And despite the odds, you continue to set your will to a task.

"But even tigers can be defeated. In Genoa I saw one of these magnificent beasts destroyed because it did not know when its keeper was stronger than it was. I don't want to see you defeated."

Something told her she should draw away from him, get up this moment, otherwise she wouldn't be able to. There was a dangerous power to him, huge and overwhelming; his power frightened her, and yet she felt herself being drawn to it. She wanted to reach out and touch him.

"I want you to come with me to France. I have lands there. I'll give you anything you want." He touched her face and lowered his fingers to the root of her throat. "Rubies, emeralds, the finest clothes. Whatever you want is

yours. But first you must come to me of your own accord and without
secret. Renounce Carbri, let him go to Agneis."

"Carbri loves me," she said, drawing back from him.

"Carbri has courage, but he doesn't have your daring. Don't make a
mistake that you'll both regret. Let me love you! Your courage, your
daring, your boldness, they flame my senses. Carbri will want to take them
away from you. Is that not right?"

Arrah didn't answer him, but what Seaghan said was true. Carbri always
wanted to change her, to stop her from asking questions about the sea, to
stop her from sailing her ship, to stop her from taking control.

Seaghan continued. "Carbri needs a woman who's dependent on him,
and you are independent. Love consists of this—in two solitudes coming
together, in protecting and touching each other." He lifted her wrist to his
lips and turned it over and pressed his lips to her skin. She didn't feel his lips
just on the skin of her wrist, but everywhere, on the back of her neck,
against her ears, against her eyes, closing them.

She shivered involuntarily. With powerful fingers he lifted her chin and
brought her lips to his. It was a tender kiss, a kiss offering protection more
than lust, and it seemed to fill her with strength, and she felt her blood
rising to it, but he drew away. "I want you, Arrah, I want to make love to
you, but I want to make love to you when you are strong, not when you're
vulnerable. If you love Carbri, send him back to Agneis and let me love
you!"

She found herself wondering what it would be like to make love to
Seaghan, Seaghan who kissed her with such intense tenderness. She
wanted Seaghan to take her into his arms once more and kiss her as he had
just kissed her, and then maybe she would know what to do.

"Seaghan—" she started to say.

But they were interrupted by the great boom of her father's voice. "Where
is my daughter!" Seaghan pulled away from Arrah and stood just as the
door to the cabin was flung open.

CHAPTER
19

Arrah pulled MacNamara's cloak about her and met her father's gray eyes boldly and directly. Momentarily they were both motionless, looking across the short distance that was the master's cabin. She sat a little higher in the bed. She would not allow him to take her ship from her.

Reevnarg nodded to MacNamara. "It was a battle well fought. We've pulled a dozen prisoners off the hills. Will you go, MacNamara, and see that they're left in one piece? Battle is one thing, mutilation another."

MacNamara nodded. He glanced briefly at Arrah and then left her quarters, the light catching his enormous shoulders and showing the small white scars as he left.

Reevnarg approached. There was something else about him that was different. Arrah wasn't sure what it was.

He stopped a short distance from her bed. She saw the gold chieftain's brooch on his chest rise and fall as he took a deep breath and then exhaled it in a sigh. "Well, Daughter, you've made quite a name for yourself."

"You too, Father, have quite a name."

"I'm a man!" He hacked through her words like an axe. He came close and stood right next to her bed. She saw his eyes were moist. "Look at you! My beautiful daughter. Blood on your hands. Blood on your face. What sort of life have you chosen for yourself? Oh, Arrah!" He looked at the floor.

She'd never seen her father with his head lowered like this. All the time she remembered him, he'd stood tall and erect as an oak.

"Your mother's dead."

"Mother! My mother!" Suddenly Arrah realized the meaning of the dream she had had before she sailed the Dragon, the water turning to skulls. Arrah felt now as though she were dreaming again, as though she tried to grasp at her father's words, but the effort was like trying to grasp water in her hands.

"One morning Bridgett took her breakfast in. She found her dead."

Arrah tried to remember all she could of her mother: quiet, gently determined, the way she had wanted Arrah to be. "But mother was never sick."

"No. 'Tis true she was never sickly. Not that you can remember anyway. She was ill for a time after you were born. But when she recovered, she was . . ." His voice trailed off. He walked slowly to the window and lifting the curtain peered out. "I've seen men bed down healthy at night and be dead the next day. Aye, there's no telling when the grim reaper will come. She was a good woman, your mother. If you make as good a wife to someone, then I will have raised you well."

"I'll never be that kind of wife to anyone."

He looked at her. "It wasn't the right way for her to have died—alone."

Her father was right. It was wrong for her mother to have died alone. But was death ever right? Was there ever a right time to die? That night on the ship, her mother had tried to tell her something, but she had only listened to half of her mother's message. She had been too busy navigating to realize that her mother had died. Arrah realized that she had never really known her mother, that she knew nothing about her mother's passions, her fears.

"It must have been a lonely death," Reevnarg said. "Her husband off. But that's the lot of a sailor's wife." His voice trailed off as he looked about her cabin. "But her daughters . . . Naira off at Glen Head with Bres. And you—"

"I did what I had to," said Arrah.

"You should have been there."

"You can't blame me for my mother's passing." Arrah's voice was insistent and defensive.

He looked at her again. There was a pained expression on his face as though he were suffering from an intolerable headache. "No, Daughter. She was a good woman, I tell you. And I miss her dearly. When I blame someone it takes some of the hurt away." His shoulders buckled and he turned away.

Arrah had never seen her father cry. And then the full realization of his words came to her. Her mother was dead. Her mother. And Arrah was overcome by weeping that shook her body in the same way that her father's body was shaking. She wanted to go to him, to put her arm around his shoulder, to comfort him and in turn be comforted, but something prevented her, so she cried and he cried, both of them alone in their grief.

After a time, he turned. His eyes were red-rimmed, but he had regained his composure. "Your men call you the sea witch. My guess is it's futile to try to sway you from this life of sailing. And who am I to tell you? You've outdone your father. You've sailed the Dragon's Mouth. If you'd been a son, you would have made me prouder than any father could be." Some of her father's old vigor came back as he talked.

"You can still be proud of me, Father."

He looked at her with an expression that she'd never seen before. In any contact that Arrah had with her father, his expression had always been one of stern reproof or paternal amusement. In the past, he had always criticized her for not behaving like a good daughter, or praised her for doing exactly as he expected. His face now showed none of these qualities.

"It's good to lay eyes on you again, Daughter." He came to her and their eyes met, and then he clasped her to him. She felt his tears brush against her cheek. "Jove has taken my wife, but he's returned my daughter. Christ, I thank him for that. I *am* proud of you, Daughter. I am proud. Damn."

He quickly wiped his face on his sleeve. "Enough of this now. If you're going to be captain, then you'd best learn the sailing directions for Eagle Sound. I'll say them to you only once, and never again, so make sure that you remember them. A captain that can't remember the currents and compass marks cannot be hoping to bring his crew home to safety.

"The tidal stream in the entrance runs three knots at spring increasing to four or five knots in the narrows off the point. The flood stream sweeping round the south bend forms eddies in the pool and sets strongly across the shallows. Do not be attempting to enter when the flood is running unless you've a commanding wind at your back. Anchor or heave to the outside and wait the slack. Enter with your needle bearing the pier at three hundred and twenty-nine degrees. Keep your eye on the shoreline and you'll be making it without difficulty."

He hesitated, then spoke again. "I know my words will fall on deaf ears, but I'm your father, and so I'll be having to say them anyway. Captaining is a different way of life than navigating. Any man with a bit of common sense and a good eye and a good feel for the sea can be making his way along it. But captaining and commanding'll be different. You'll be needing more than a feel for the sea. You'll be needing a feel for the hearts of men. And Lord knows, as there are different kinds of men, so there are different feelings. You'll not only have to smell the sea, you'll have to smell danger. Aye, Arrah, danger has a smell. A smell like fish jank, horse stink, and gunpowder. You can smell it when men are scared. And you'll have to be able to see into their hearts. They run deeper and blacker than any sea on earth. And . . . you'll need a strong weapon."

He pulled a sword from his scabbard. It was the same sword that hung above his chair back in the main hall of Eagle Castle. It was a magnificent weapon, with a handle of pure silver emblazoned with an emerald half the size of a man's thumb encircled with small rubies.

"I've no son to pass this to. And if the truth be known, Daughter, no son could have honored me more than you have. The weapon is yours."

She reached for it, and he glanced at the scars on her arm.

"I should have known then," he said. "You've wild blood in your veins. The same my sister had. Your mother was always against my naming you for her. Said it would bring ill luck down on you because of her violent end. But I loved her, and I love you. Your sister, Naira, thought you were dead. She asked me to give Eagle Island to her, since she was the eldest daughter. But I refused. Even as you jumped into the sea with Carbri, I knew somehow you'd come back. Aye, maybe it's just as well your mother passed to heaven. She wouldn't be pleased with me giving you a sword."

"Poor Mother. She was never pleased with me."

"Nay, Daughter. If you knew what a headstrong woman she was when I married her. She was the likes of you. Running across the cliffs like a goat. And damn goat-headed. But she fell. She nearly didn't have you. And then, after that, she . . . I couldn't have borne losing her. She was more precious to me than more children. So I told her to talk to the old woman. She gave her something. After that she was quieter and gentled." His voice trailed off and he stared into space.

Arrah looked at him. When he thought of Margaret he changed. It was that change which Arrah had detected in him: part of him had gone with the death of his wife.

He seemed to shake himself from that other world. "Take it now," he said, his voice filled with the old tone of command.

The sword was heavier than the one Carbri had bought for her, but at the same time, it had a certain suppleness. The handle itself was embossed with a series of concentric circles so that the metal wouldn't slip in battle. She could feel the roughness of the design like a fine rasp against her palm.

"It looks as though it was forged for your arm, lass. But mind now, a man who carries a sword like that will be having to frequently defend it. As a woman, if you take to this life, it'll be no different for you. And also, I've decided to give you the *Skatha*. She's served me well enough. If you'd been a boy, she'd have already been yours to command."

"Father," she said. "I'm not as courageous as you think. I was afraid. I was afraid just before I killed the pirate."

"Only the stupidest of men are not afraid. There can be no courage without fear. And damn, but you have courage, Daughter." A look of regret crossed his eyes, which then gave way to lighter feelings. "You would've had an easier life with the Joyce. And speaking of marriage. Young Carbri harbored at Eagle Island on his way up the Shannon. He told me that he and you were planning to be wed. Carbri's a good lad. There'll be more bloodshed with de Burgo. But you've made your choice, and I've learned enough these past weeks to know the folly of trying to dissuade you."

"Father, I'm not so sure now I want to marry Carbri."

"Don't worry, Daughter. We're stronger than de Burgo. We can keep him at bay." Reevnarg bit his lip and continued. "I've spoken to Father Thomas. He made a scowl on his face like he'd swallowed a cup of shark piss. Called it fornication—you and Carbri jumping over the broom the way you did. Aye, I don't know what this land will be coming to when 'tis called a sin for a young man and woman to do what comes to them naturally. Your mother and I. There was no priest. Just flowers and music and dance." His voice trailed off again momentarily, but he stopped his remembrance with a click of his tongue.

"Aye, the Lord must've been suffering from a bout of belly gas when He called Father Thomas into his service. Ah, well! Sin or no sin. He's agreed to wed you. Sword or no sword, Daughter, I'm willing to wager Carbri has enough spunk in him to want his conjugal rights. I'll have grandsons at my knee yet."

Marriage! Seaghan had just kissed her the way that Carbri had never kissed her. Her father didn't understand. He assumed she didn't want to marry Carbri because of more battles with de Burgo.

"I—" she started to say, but her father interrupted.

"Aye, lass. It's good to look on the likes of you again. I'm off now. I've to sail down to Killary Harbour. There's a bit of turmoil with the MacDayats of Bun Dorcha, next to the Joyce's territory. Refusing to pay our tribute of hides and dried fish. They attacked my men. MacNamara is going with me. I'll be home soon enough.

"Mind now, Daughter, that you keep your eyes ope'd for de Burgo. His son's dead, and the old man won't be liking it, the man he thought would be his son-in-law marrying my daughter, and O'Connor lands coming to us." Reevnarg walked toward the door.

"Father," she called after him.

He turned and looked at her.

"Why is Seaghan MacNamara always about?"

"He warned me of Brion MacNamara's attack on Eagle Island. He knows much of what passes here and elsewhere. Some call him a traitor, but a man like that has useful information."

"If he's a traitor, why do you allow him to sail with you? How do you know he won't turn on you?"

"I don't, but he's the best swordsman in Ireland. A man doesn't turn down a good sword when it's offered to him. And he has good connections with merchants."

"Why is he never with his clan? Always elsewhere?"

"His father remarried. But the wife, instead of loving her husband, cared more for Seaghan. The MacNamara killed her and cast out Seaghan. He's been a wanderer ever since. He has huge lands in France. He was adopted by a monster."

"A monster?"

"Yes, but I don't know the details, and I've no time to discuss it now. Mary will look after you!" He shouted for the woman.

She came bustling in, her wide skirts ruffled about her like a mother hen's feathers. "Aye, so the lass has regained her senses, has she?"

"Aye, she has," said Reevnarg. "And I've lingered too long now with tales. I'm pressed for my affairs. Mary! Tend well to my daughter." He turned and left.

Arrah pulled the linens back from her bed and began to get up.

"Well, will yea be looking at that. Mortally wounded she is and already she's chippering about."

"I wasn't mortally wounded."

"I seen yea fighting. In the name of the Lord and all the sainteys, but I hates pain. A little pain that comes in the morning when I've indulged a wee bit in spirits is all right. But Lord, that sort of pain!" She looked at Arrah's wound. "He did a fine enough job of dressing it, I'd say. Didn't leave much for Mary to do. He's a handsome devil, ain't he, that MacNamara."

Arrah didn't say anything, but Mary's eyes caught the subtle change in Arrah's expression. Mary glanced at the bed and saw MacNamara's satin-lined cloak. Arrah tried to get up, but Mary stopped her.

"Yea've experience with a ship, the kind that Mary, if she lived to be a hundred years, won't be having. Heaven forbid. Yea've experience with a ship, but not much with men. Listen to Mary. Stay away from Mac-Namara. It's like falling in love with the devil hisself. Remember, Lucifer was the brightest star in heaven before he was cast to hell. He'll be taking yea farther and faster and higher than yea've ever been. And I don't care what seas yea'll be sailing or what winds yea'll be feeling on yer face. Or how many masts yea'll be climbing. He'll do more. He'll take yea to Paradise and back. But he'll want yer soul. Yea can't be living with a man like that. And he'll leave. And after, yea'll never be able to forget him. Never. He'll always be on yer mind. Not a day will yea pass without thinking of him. Never. He'll be causing yea nothing but hurt. Like the arrow that was in yer shoulder. Except that it'll be worse. He'll be like a thorn in yer soul. And yea'll never find a body who can pull it out. Never!"

CHAPTER
20

The sight of Eagle Bay, as Arrah returned home, was a miracle of beauty: the distant mainland sweeping down to the sea, with its small islands, and the three hundred steps in the cliffside, gold and purple and crimson in the setting sun, and on the leeward side of the island, the nets of the fishermen tacked to the sides of their houses to dry and the salted fish laid out on the beach to dry. The high outline of Eagle Castle rose like a sentinel behind the beach.

Arrah moored her ship, then took a currach to shore. It was a strange entourage that stepped out onto the sand: Arrah holding the tiger cub in her arms and an emerald-handled sword tied at her waist; Finn following her, bleating and trying to chew on the tiger's tail; and Mary slapping Finn's nose and trying to smooth her voluminous skirts as though they were feathers. Behind them came Hook carrying on a dialogue with Angel and Patch; Patch taking in the shores and hills with his tattooed eye, and Mute grunting and moaning his pleasure. Behind them came Sebastian and Hirple.

Arrah felt the joy of homecoming, but as her feet touched the shore, she remembered that her mother was dead. The remembrance brought a burst of sadness, like biting into a small bitter apple. There was no one for her at the castle.

Some of the fisherfolk were on the beach to greet her, including the midwife with the large birthmark. She grabbed Arrah's hands in hers and whispered to her in a kind of breathless secrecy. "Come and see me in the cave where I live immediately. It's a matter of utmost urgency." But before Arrah could ask her what was of the utmost secrecy, the old woman was gone.

The rest of the fisherfolk held their hands close to their bodies and looked at her only when her face was turned from them. It was many of these same fishermen who had told her stories when she was a child, yet now they seemed afraid of her. The women gathered their children close to them. A boy was looking for eggs in the thatched roof of a house, and when he saw her, he hid low against the straw.

The dogs set up a furious barking when she entered the castle gate. They showed their fangs and pulled at their chains so that they reared in the air and struck out their front legs like rearing horses. But when Cuch saw Arrah, he immediately began to whine and whimper with joy.

From the other side of the castle Arrah heard the great terrible whine of Bran and she knew that she would have to greet him as well.

Of the servants only Paddy seemed to be unguarded in his greeting of her. He smiled so broadly at Arrah that his eyes squinted shut and he reached up to Arrah with his gnarled hands. She bent down and grasped them in hers, felt his fingers, lifeless and cold, brittle as twigs in the fall, marred by one scar after another.

"Arrah. I told you, lass, it could be done. They all thinks that I was a-telling 'em crazy stories. That I lost me mind as well as me legs. But 'tis true, lass, you can be sailing the Devil's Mouth. I was always knowing you to be special, something that the others weren't."

She bent and hugged him, and then went to the back of the castle where Bran was tied. He whined and shook with the excitement of seeing Arrah.

As she petted him, his great pink tongue licking her hand, she remembered how he had grabbed a magpie out of the air one afternoon, and how Seaghan MacNamara had spoken the prophecy of Englishmen being in Ireland as long as the magpies remained. He was never far from her mind these days. She loved Carbri and felt a tremendous loyalty to the young man who had risked his own life and jumped into the sea to be with her. And yet MacNamara held her with binding fascination. She found herself dreaming of him at night. He would be making love to her, and when she woke her sheets were damp with perspiration.

Bridgett worked in the kitchen. She greeted Arrah then went to a counter where the large carcass of half a bullock lay ready to be put on the spit. Singing and humming, Bridgett pretended to put all her attention to the meat. Arrah had never once remembered Bridgett singing or humming, and looked at her with suspicion.

"Bridgett, what have you been up to?"

"Up to! Nothing, mistress, nothing. I was praying to God that he would make your journey a safe one," she said, "and he answered my prayers. You're home, safe."

Arrah eyed her. She knew Bridgett well enough to know she was lying. Bridgett would never pray for the safe arrival home of anyone. Rather, she was the kind who gloated in the misfortune of others. But perhaps Bridgett had found a servant or a sailor who had paid her particular attention. The attention of men was the only thing that put Bridgett in a cheery mood.

When Arrah didn't say anything, Bridgett said, "The old midwife with the birthmark was here asking for you. She told me to tell you she should see you."

"I saw her down by the beach. Did she say what she wanted?" Arrah asked.

"Only she was telling me that she was going to be giving you the woman knowledge . . . the same as what she was doing for your . . . ah . . . mother . . . for Mistress Margaret. Also, the old woman was saying that Mistress Margaret had a vision about your father's death."

Her father's death. She had never once thought of her father's death. He was so powerful, so seemingly invincible.

"I'll go and see her right away," said Arrah.

"Yes, mistress," said Bridgett. She was relieved to see Arrah leave the kitchen. Ever since Mistress Margaret had died, Bridgett had worried that someone would discover her part in her death. But no one had. She had done as Glundel told her—waited until none of Mistress Margaret's family was on Eagle Island, then given the poison to her in her warm, honeyed nighttime drink. The next morning Mistress Margaret was dead. No one had suspected Bridgett's part. Now all she had to do was wait for Glundel to return and take her away as he had promised.

The old midwife with the birthmark lived in a cave on the shore. A small, low peat fire burned with a blue flame in the mouth of the cave on Eagle Island.

Eagle Castle had been built by a MacNamara ancestor. He had an extremely beautiful wife, so beautiful that he brought her to Eagle Island along with only his ugliest bondsmen so there was no hope of her falling in love with anyone else. He built a secret stairway from a lower room in the castle up to her chambers from where he could spy on her.

But unknown to him there was a hidden watery passage that led from the sea to the castle floor.

A ship wrecked off the island and a handsome young sailor was washed into the secret passage, and up into the lower chamber where the woman kept the whelks she used for dyeing cloth. She hid the young man from her husband and brought him food in secret. One day the husband, hidden in the stairway, discovered the lovers in their embrace. He ordered them put into the underwater passage and both entrances filled with stones.

The woman pleaded with her husband to spare her, since she was with child. He disregarded her and she cursed him, saying that the MacNamara would lose Eagle Island and that the sons of the MacNamara would be destined to betray their fathers.

The curse of the young woman had held prophetic power. The legacy of the MacNamara had been one of lost territory and betrayed affections.

When Margaret was still carrying Arrah in her womb, she had discovered the dyeing chamber entrance to the pool. She'd been taking purple dye from the whelks when she saw steam rising from beneath the floor of the dyeing room. At first she had been afraid, but the steam seemed to have a dreamlike effect on her, and she began to lift the flagstones that formed the floor of the castle.

Beneath the floor she discovered a small, warm pool of water filled to waist height with small round boulders the size of a man's head. In her expectant state she should not have lifted stones and boulders, and yet she continued to do so, lifting and lifting as if entranced by the steam and warm water.

As she lifted, she saw a vision. She saw the birth of her daughter, and then she saw Arrah as a child with her arm bloodied and ripped by the talons of an eagle.

Margaret was stunned and frightened and she had told the midwife with the birthmark of her vision.

The midwife had continued to question Margaret about the visions, which had come sporadically over the years. Occasionally hot water seemed to enter the passage, rising from beneath the ocean floor, circulating with the cold water, causing steam to spiral and swirl through the stones. When Margaret saw the steam rising, she would excitedly lift the flagstones, eager to see what visions the swirling, steamy pool mist held for her. She would sit for a long time watching the spiral turn and turn, curve and twist, and in that trancelike state that overtook her, she could see sometimes the future, sometimes the past.

Except for the vision of Arrah's torn arm, Margaret had never shared with the midwife any of her other visions, but the midwife suspected that it was in the dream pool that Margaret had seen the vision of Reevnarg's taking over the chieftainship of the O'Donnell.

Once Margaret had tried to swim down into the dream pool to see where it led. At the bottom it turned sharply and there Margaret discovered a skull and had been afraid to go farther.

Now, the midwife had decided, it was time for the dream pool to serve another function.

The midwife was hunched over her fire. When she saw Arrah, she straightened and pulled her scarf across her face, but not before Arrah saw her disfiguring birthmark.

Arrah remembered the old woman coming to see her mother, but she had forgotten how large and unsightly the dark discoloration had been.

"Now that you're about to be married," said the old woman, "it's time you learned the woman knowledge."

"Yes," said Arrah. "My mother spoke to me of it, before I was betrothed to the Joyce." As her eyes grew accustomed to the dimness of the cave, she saw an abundance of lobster pots tossed in a careless pile on the floor. There were plants hung everywhere on the cave wall.

"I will give it to you. A captain cannot always be full-bellied with child. Being with child makes a woman clumsy and awkward. There are ways of preventing childbirth. Come with me."

She took a torch from the wall and led Arrah into a back cavity of the cave. "There's a plant called the gromwell. It grows on wood edges and scrub, producing gray-white nutlets that prevent conception."

She took a small clay jar from the top of a stone shelf. "This will put an end to your condition if you get yourself with child. Your mother took this powder. But you must take care not to use it too often, for each ingestion makes a woman ill and leaves her weakened.

"Your mother did not learn all of the woman knowledge, for she was afraid of the moon. She said Father Thomas told her that the moon at crescent was the devil's horns. Nonetheless, she had a certain power that came to her from her mother's mother, who was of the sea people. You're very beautiful. Your skin blooms with the vigors of the sea because you are one of them. The older you get the more beautiful you will become. You are not a witch, and your mother was not a witch, although some said that she was. Rather, she was a mystic. A magician or witch tries to control what is about her. A mystic simply tries to understand. And she understood much. She saw things in visions in a dream pool. You, too, have her power of visions, but before you come to know that power you must swim a secret passageway.

"From your mother's chamber, behind the fireplace, a hidden stairwell leads to the dyeing room, where she kept the whelks. As you know, Eagle Castle was built by a MacNamara ancestor. He ordered the stairs built so that he could secretly spy on his wife."

Arrah had heard the stories of MacNamara's insane jealousy of his wife, and his vicious treatment of her and her lover. It was the ghost of the young expectant wife who supposedly walked at Eagle Castle. But this was the first she had heard of a secret stairway.

The old woman went on. "Take the stairs down and you will find that they lead to a panel behind the door to the dyeing room.

"As you open the hidden panel in the dyeing room you will see that the panel casts a purple shadow on one slab. Lift that slab and you will find the pool and watery passageway that leads down under the castle to the three hundred steps. You must swim the entire passageway, come out under the three hundred steps for air, and then swim back. When you resurface through the dream pool, you, too, will have the power of visions. Your mother discovered the passage one day when she was swimming beneath the sea. She swam right up into the dyeing room where she kept her whelks, and she would swim regularly in the passage. She said the water had magic powers."

"My mother. Swimming beneath the sea!" Arrah remembered her father's words. *Running across the cliffs like a goat.*

"The water in the passage will give you the power of visions, the same as it did with your mother. Your mother told me before she died that she had forseen the death of your father, which is soon to come. She said that she wished you to see the vision so that you could prevent his death."

Arrah had been able to do nothing to help her mother avoid death. If she could do something to prevent her father's death, then she would do it.

She went to the chimney in her mother's chamber. All was as the old woman said, and she carefully went down the steps. She took a torch with her, but it flickered wildly in that dark, steep stairway. All these years she had lived in Eagle Castle, and never known about this passage.

The stair ended abruptly at a stone wall. Arrah pushed on a low panel, and it swung open, perfectly balanced into the dyeing room. How many times had Arrah been in this room as a child with her mother? She and Debrogail had even spent an entire afternoon in this room, and not once had they noticed the secret door.

The panel threw its shadow on a flagstone, on the very flagstone where she and Debrogail had played with the dried peas years ago when Margaret had punished them for carrying the precious whelks back to the sea.

That afternoon Arrah had wanted to see then where the mist was coming from, but silly Debrogail began to scream.

In her child's mind, Arrah had thought that the steam had something to do with the dyeing process. She thought of Debrogail. She hadn't been among the servants to greet her, and made her mind up to ask one of the servants where she was.

Arrah lifted the large flat flagstone. The dark pool opened in front of her, about a foot beneath the stones, and then a strange thing began to happen, just as it had happened that afternoon with Debrogail—steam began to rise from the pool.

This time Arrah realized that it had nothing to do with the dyeing process. She watched as the warm mist began to curl and swirl.

The level of the water in the pool itself began to rise, and it began to make a breathing, hissing sound. She turned and saw the chamber begin to fill with the spiraling haze. The light from her lamp turned the steam into red and yellow smoke, and for a moment she imagined that hell must be like this chamber, or rather heaven, for the warm steam was truly pleasant and seductive. The steam rose up on her face and neck and hands and she sucked it into her lungs. She watched the red and gold and black water for some time, and for a moment she felt as though the world had turned upside down and she was watching a sunrise at her feet, for the colors reflected from her torch in the bubbling water were like the colors of the sunrise.

As the water rose, she saw images in the steam. She saw her own face, and at first thought it was a reflection in the water, and so it seemed to be, but then she saw a dark figure behind her face: a very tall, immense, black-hooded figure. He was standing on the top of a wooden structure . . . was it gallows? But then the steam swirled and the image disappeared. Had she imagined what she saw, like seeing shapes in clouds? She blinked her eyes, trying to get the image back, but it was gone, and once again there was nothing but the sun-yellow steam and blood-red steam boiling and hissing and rising up from the rocks below. Was this how her mother saw her visions? No. The old woman had told her she had to swim the passage first.

She pulled off her clothes and went headfirst into the pool, looking for the passage that the old woman had told her about. Near the bottom the pool turned into a sharp elbow. She followed the current. As she swam farther out the water grew colder, the passageway narrower. There was stone all about her. The passageway was only barely larger than a man's shoulders. Her feet and arms kept striking stone as she swam. She was running out of breath, and a panic of constriction was setting in. She would have to turn around and go back, and she stopped swimming and realized that there wasn't enough room to turn around. Her lungs were bursting. She had no more air. She gulped in salt water; it burned her throat, her lungs. Just then the passageway opened into a breathing space above her. She came up abruptly, cracking her head on the stone above. She went down again, fought the blackness inside her skull, forced herself to surface.

For some time—she had no idea how long—she did nothing but breathe. Then her senses tried to take awareness of her surroundings. She turned about, looking for something, but it was completely dark. Her eyes were useless. The only sound was the still-quick breath from her exertions.

Why had the old woman lied to her about the passage? There was nothing here. She was lucky to have found the air pocket at all. She would go back and talk to the old woman.

Arrah felt the way back into the narrow channel, but suddenly realized that in her panic she had lost her sense of direction. She was lost. There were only two directions to go, but she didn't know which one to take. She shouted. In the low pocket, the stone caught her voice and threw it back with an intensity that nearly deafened her. Then there was just a liquid silence, a small lap of water against a small shelf of stone. She tried to remember with her hands, but there was no way she could. "Mother," she said, "help me!" and then taking a deep breath Arrah plunged back into the passageway and began to swim.

She was running out of air when a jut of rock told her that she had gone the wrong way. Arrah panicked. A quick feel of the passage told her there was no room for her to move forward; the passage was completely blocked. She couldn't turn around to go backward. She had to half swim, half crawl backward. She was on the verge of passing out when she hit the airhole again. This time she didn't lose her way, but as she came to the surface in the dyeing room, she came face to face with two skulls bobbing on top of the water.

Arrah screamed and in that dark, frightened moment, lucidity came to her. The skulls were the remains of the lovers who had been buried there. Her frantic swimming must have dislodged them from the bottom. There was no way her mother could have swum this passageway. Even Arrah had barely made it back safely. The old woman had wanted her to die in the passageway. She had won Arrah's confidence by flattery and by mentioning her mother, then tricked her into swimming into the passageway by lying about Reevnarg's death. Arrah was determined to find out why.

But when she returned to the old woman's cave she found it empty. It was as though she had never been there. Even the lobster pots had gone. When Arrah questioned the fisherfolk, they told her that there had been an old woman who lived there, but that she had left some time ago and none knew her whereabouts.

The days passed slowly without giving up to Arrah any further information as to why the old woman had wanted her dead. Arrah asked after Debrogail, and was told by Bridgett that she had run off with one of the guards one night because Bres had married Mistress Naira.

The news surprised Arrah. It was unlike Debrogail, and normally Arrah's curious nature would have made her ask further questions about the servant girl, but Arrah was too taken up by thoughts of the old midwife and why she had wanted her to drown in the passageway.

She asked all the fisherfolk again and again what they knew of the old woman's whereabouts or who she was. Anything that might give Arrah a clue. But the fisherfolk knew nothing or if they knew something they refused to speak.

She visited her mother's grave, looking for some explanation of the things that had happened. She and her mother had agreed on few things, and yet Arrah had loved her.

There was a game that Arrah remembered playing with her mother when she was very small and it was the hour for bed at night. Margaret would pull the down comforter up under Arrah's chin. Then her mother would spread her hands in front of her about the width of her shoulders. "I don't love you this much," Margaret would say, and spread her arms farther. "I don't love you this much." And each time, she would spread her arms farther until they were stretched out to their maximum width on either side of her. "How much do I love you? I love you high as the sky and wide as the ocean."

Then Margaret would softly kiss the lids of Arrah's eyes. "God bless. And may the angels keep you and bring you pleasant dreams," she would say, and touch Arrah's cheek with her smooth, cool fingertips. Her mother's fingertips were always cool, white, smooth as candles.

Arrah hoped to find some of her mother's presence there, but the graveyard was chilled and lonely, as an impenetrable haze rose from the ocean. The world was gray, damp, void of answers. Only a lonely eagle soared, before it spread its wings and flew off in the misty air.

She was tormented with a sense of futility, of bewilderment and frustration. Time didn't seem to move forward, but seemed to have stopped so that one day was the same as the one before it, and the one before it.

Arrah grew increasingly frustrated, and one day as Paddy stopped her to talk, she answered him shortly that she didn't have time to talk.

"Oh, so now that you've sailed the Dragon's Mouth, you've no time for Legless Paddy, is that it, lass?"

Arrah was filled with shame. It was Legless who after all had given her instructions to sail the Dragon's Mouth. Arrah knelt down beside him and explained what had happened with the midwife and the underground passage.

Paddy frowned. "The midwife was the sister of the fishergirl that cursed your family. I was tellin' your father the same thing, a long time ago. But your father's not one to be believing much that Legless Paddy tells him. He said that only the fishergirl herself had the birthmark. That she had no sisters. He thinks I'm nothing but a teller of wild tales."

"How do you know she had sisters?" asked Arrah.

"Because before I was Legless Paddy, I was Paddy and I loved the girls, the same as any other sailor. You know that wee Debrogail, who played with you when you were small. Before she was born, I slept with her mother a few nights, as I slept with other women. I saw her one night down by the sea cave where the midwife lived. Your father had sent me out to gather eaglets on the cliff side to be training them for hunting. I was spry then, before the sharks got me, and could leap like a goat.

"Now, being a man, I was never paying much attention to the midwife. She came and went for the women in the castle, and I saw that her face was always covered, but I wasn't making much notice of it. But this day out on the cliffs, that midwife and Debrogail's mother, their faces were both uncovered. They didn't know there was anyone else about. I was seeing from the purple on their cheeks that Debrogail's mother and that midwife were sisters. I was shouting to them. I liked Debrogail's mother better than any of the other women I'd been with. Birthmark and all, I didn't care. There's more to a woman than the color of her cheek. But they weren't hearing me. I was up high in the cliffs, and you know how the surf thunders down there.

"I wasn't thinking much of it. And then one night, I was laying with Debrogail's mother. A sailor, if he's any kind of a sailor, always has one ear open. She was saying something about revenging her sister for the birthmark. I was going to tell Reevnarg, but then I thought if I was saying something to him, he would be sending Debrogail's mother away from the castle. And I cared for her, and didn't want to see her sent away. So I kept my tongue hushed.

"And then I lost my legs to that accursed shark. And I had other things to be worrying my mind than midwives and servants with birthmarks. But then Debrogail's mother died with that coughing and spitting up of blood that she did, and when I was grieving her, I was drinking a lot, I admit. I was saying to Reevnarg that I thought maybe she was a sister to the fishergirl that killed his brother. 'No,' he said, 'she had no sisters.' But he wasn't there when his father ordered that poor girl bound and thrown into the sea. I'll wager the father of those girls hid them somewhere. Reevnarg's father—the state he was in after the death of his son, he was ready to kill anything with purple on her face. Hanged he was in his own masts on the same trip. Aye. Revenge. It's a terrible thing! Often it'll cost the avenger more than the avenged."

Arrah listened with disbelief. If what Legless Paddy said was true, then it was Debrogail's aunt who had tricked her into swimming the passage, and Debrogail in all likelihood was party to what had happened. No wonder Debrogail was nowhere around. No wonder she had been so friendly to Arrah as a child. It was all part of the revenge plan.

Yet there was one thing about Paddy's story that troubled Arrah. "Are you Debrogail's father?" she asked.

"There's no telling with the servant women," Paddy said. "I was a sailor and often gone, and the women—they'll take their pleasure where they can. But there weren't many men who were with her. They thought her birthmark a mark of evil. She didn't have any children when I lay with her. And the time of Debrogail's birth was right for me to sire her, and when I saw her, I was always hoping she was mine," Paddy said ruefully.

"Why didn't you ever tell Debrogail you could have been her father?" asked Arrah.

"A pretty waif like that. And an ugly old sailor like me, the butt of everyone's jokes. Better for the child to think her father was some handsome man, not just Legless Paddy, who everybody thinks is full of crazy talk and an old fool."

"Paddy, you're not an old fool," Arrah said.

"Thank you, lass. Debrogail would never hurt you. You know that, don't you, lass?"

Arrah looked at the ground. The old woman had tricked Arrah into near death by drowning, and Debrogail had disappeared. And if they wanted revenge they would want it on Naira as well.

Arrah had never been close to Naira, who had always been contemptuous and distant. But regardless of that, Naira was her sister, and Arrah was determined to protect her in any way she could.

She ordered her ship readied and sailed for Glen Head.

Arrah carried the tiger cub to shore with her. Naira looked splendid in a high-necked dress that picked up the blue of her eyes so they glimmered like a winter sky. The comely Bres stood beside her. The last time Arrah had seen him, he'd been laughing with Debrogail. Men were so fickle. Arrah had seen it with her father's sailors and the servant girls. One moment they told one woman they loved her, and the next moment they lay in the arms of another. Arrah noticed that Bres's face was serious.

"My sister! Where did you get that fabulous creature?" asked Naira, pointing to the tiger.

"Seaghan MacNamara gave him to me."

"As always you were the one that men gave wonderful things to. No man has ever given me such a fabulous creature," and she looked at Bres.

Naira lifted the tiger from Arrah, and buried her face in its soft fur and listened to the beat of its tiger heart, and then Arrah saw tears form on Naira's cheek.

Arrah had never seen Naira cry. "Is something the matter, Naira?" Arrah asked.

"Arrah. I was spiteful to you." Naira looked at Bres. "I admit, I was jealous of you. Father . . . He always . . ." Naira struggled with her words. "Whatever you did, you always seemed to please him more than I pleased him. No matter what sort of mischief you got into, it seemed to turn out for the better for you. But now with our mother dead, you and father are all I have left." And she threw her arm around Arrah. The two sisters stood there, the tiger between them.

Arrah was stunned at Naira's welcome. As long as Arrah had known Naira, she was always cold and aloof. Arrah remained stiff and uncomfortable with this show of affection from her sister.

"I'm tired of being a stranger in my own family," cried Naira. "Hug me, my sister!"

All these years, they had been like strangers to each other. It was good to hold Naira. Her skin carried the mild aroma of rosewater, the same scent Margaret had worn. Maybe now with the tragedy of their mother's death, they could truly be like sisters. Arrah clutched Naira tightly, swept up in a wave of feeling she'd never had for her.

"Come," said Naira, wiping at her own tears and taking Arrah's arm. "All along the coast they speak of you! You were always the wild one. No wonder Father gave you the Island of the Eagles."

"Don't believe everything they say. Every time a story is told it becomes exaggerated. It's like the men who fish for herring, but come home saying they caught a whale in their net," said Arrah.

"You sailed the Dragon's Mouth."

"So did Legless Paddy many years ago."

"He tells so many lies no one believes him."

"Naira, there's something I must tell you."

"Your expression is grave, my sister, and bears the look of ill news. Wait until after we've eaten. It's so long since I've seen you and I want to relish my joy. I thought you were dead. We'd all thought you were dead. Even Mother. And you returned, captain of your own ship. It must be satisfying, getting what you always dreamed of." Naira's sentence had more the tone of a question than a statement.

"Yes," said Arrah.

"Do you think any man will marry a woman who's a captain of ships? All those men around you. A man is bound to get jealous. I know Bres would, wouldn't you, Bres?" asked Naira, her voice honeyed and soft.

"Yes, Naira, I would," he answered flatly.

Naira was particularly pleased with the fact that Bres had come with her today. She had been concerned that Bres wouldn't believe her story of what happened to Debrogail. First of all, Naira had made excuses to Bres that Debrogail had gone out to woods looking for her various plants, and that that was the reason the servant girl wasn't at Glen Head. Then she had used the excuse of the battle with her former husband's forces to say that Debrogail had not been able to get back to the castle.

When she had realized that Bres was getting impatient, she had concocted a story that she was especially pleased with. She had told Bres that some soldiers had found Debrogail's body. She apparently had had a liaison with a bog cutter. They had been making love under a tree when lightning struck the tree and fell on them both, crushing them to their death together. She had even taken Bres out to the grave site—it had been easy enough sending out a guard to dig a hole and refill it.

Bres had been devastated and had fallen on the grave site, weeping. Naira had comforted him in her most sympathetic way. "Now you see how much good I did you," she said softly. "Imagine if you'd been married to her, she would have cuckolded you with every man she set her eyes on. I grew up with Debrogail. I saw what she did with one man after another. Now, weep no more, my darling. I love you."

She played on his sense of position. "Bres, you're a chieftain's nephew. It's unbecoming of you to weep for a servant girl, especially such an indiscriminate one."

But he continued to weep, and so again she played on his sense of loyalty. "This is your home now. If you return to MacNamara lands you will be cast out as surely as your kinsman Seaghan." She chose her words carefully. She did not want Bres to know that she knew that he had tipped Seaghan MacNamara about the attack. To do so would put him on the defensive and send him farther from her. What she wanted was to draw him closer, so she gave sympathy and understanding. "I've seen my father after a battle is lost. He blames everyone and suspects betrayal even where there is none. I'm certain your uncle Brion is no different. He will think you betrayed him. You're loyal, Bres. You're not a traitor. Now, show your loyalty to the O'Donnell and stay and protect his daughter, and your wife."

At the mention of the word *loyalty*, Bres had stopped crying. And although he agreed with her verbally, he had remained sad and passive, somewhat distant, so she had another idea. She called Rory, her prison keeper, to her. He was the ugliest man a woman could set her eyes on, a repulsive, constantly coughing man. She said she would pay him and another guard as well a gold sovereign each to say that they had been with Debrogail.

She had set up the ploy carefully, secretly prearranging a time with Rory when she and Bres would take a walk through the castle courtyard.

Her plan had worked flawlessly. She and Bres heard the drunken laughter of men. Rory's voice had been unmistakable with its phlegmy, interrupting cough. "Aye, that lusty little bitch, Debrogail. I'll miss her I will. Wet she was for whatever I could give her, and whenever I wanted, there she laid down for me. On the floor, wanting it like no other woman I've seen." "Aye," came the voice of the other guard. "She was the same, wet and hungry for every man."

Calling them filthy liars, Bres stormed the two men, his dagger drawn, and killed them both before they could answer him.

"Bres," she questioned, "are you going to kill all my guards because of a servant girl?" Secretly she was glad Bres had killed them, for dead men did not talk of gold sovereigns.

Bres had fled her, running through the courtyard, howling his pain, and she thought she had lost him. But despite his denial of the guards' words,

Bres had believed them. Later that night he came to her and made love to her, made love to her with passion, like a man possessed, and she knew she had won him.

Now she planned on getting with child as soon as possible. She was certain that Bres, with his sense of honor and duty, would remain with her once she was with child.

When Naira mentioned Bres's jealousy, Arrah became momentarily distracted by the possibilities of marriage to Seaghan. She and Naira would be two sisters wedded to two kinsmen. There was a kind of closeness to the four-part relationship that her mother would have approved of.

Despite everything that had happened, she found her thoughts being drawn back to Seaghan, and when she had seen the two skulls she had wished that his strong arms could have been there to comfort her.

But she also loved Carbri. Loved his good humor and his laugh, and his bright hazel eyes.

Under different circumstances Arrah could have talked to Naira about such feelings. Naira had been married once, was married now, and perhaps these were the kinds of confidences that sisters shared. But maybe she and Naira had been strangers too long for them to share confidences of the heart so quickly. And besides, there were other things, more urgent things to talk about.

"Naira, remember the old midwife with the birthmark?"

"What of her?"

"She tried to kill me. I'm afraid she'll try to kill you."

"Kill you! Why would she want to kill you?" Naira looked aghast at the suggestion.

As Arrah explained what Legless Paddy had told her about Reevnarg's brother and the fishergirl, and the revenge of the sisters against Reevnarg's family, Naira listened intently.

"But surely, Sister. Father was right. The fishergirl's sister wouldn't dare to come to Eagle Island. Besides, the way I heard tell the curse, only the fishergirl herself had the birthmark. She didn't have any sisters. Father himself says so," said Naira.

"Paddy says Father's wrong."

"Was Paddy there with Father's brother?" Naira asked.

"No. But he heard others talking who were there," replied Arrah.

"Well, then. You said yourself stories are exaggerated."

"And Debrogail has disappeared from Eagle Castle," Arrah added.

Arrah saw a look of pain darken Bres's eyes. It was the same expression she had seen in Seaghan on occasion. In that expression there could be no denial that the two were kinsmen.

Bres spoke for the first time. He spoke with a vehemence and anger that surprised Arrah, considering how once he had laughed with the servant girl. "Debrogail's dead."

"Debrogail?" Naira's voice was colored with amused curiosity. She glanced at Bres. "I sent her here. But when Bres and I arrived after our marriage, she had run off with some bog cutter. That's just like the servants, isn't it? They'll copulate like dogs. Whoever pays them attention, and the women spread their legs."

Debrogail dead. The news stunned Arrah as the news of her mother's death had earlier stunned her. *Copulate like dogs.* It was an expression her mother would have used. So it was Naira's doing that Debrogail had left Eagle Island, and had nothing to do with the midwife. But everything she had heard confused Arrah. It was unlike Debrogail to behave like Bridgett or the others, opening her legs to every sailor. Yet perhaps it wasn't unlike Debrogail. After Debrogail had been forced by Margaret to call Arrah "Mistress," things had changed between them. They had giggled as girls, but never as women. Debrogail had become an even greater stranger to her than Naira, and now she was dead.

Naira continued. "She died under a tree struck by lightning. She was coupled to the young man who was her diversion at the time."

Arrah barely heard her. She would have to tell Legless Paddy of Debrogail's death. Legless Paddy, who had hoped she was his daughter. The Fates were not kind to some men. First he had lost his legs, then the woman he loved, and now his daughter.

"Enough talk now of midwives with birthmarks. I'll alert my guards to keep watch for the midwife. You must be tired from all your adventures. You'll sleep safe in my castle tonight."

"I'm sorry, Naira. I planned to spend the night, but I must return. I'll have to tell Legless Paddy of Debrogail's death."

"But why on earth for?" asked Naira.

"Because he's her father," replied Arrah.

"Father! But what sort of inconceivable . . ." Naira felt as if her legs were giving out from under her. "But what sort of nonsense"—somehow she mustered a smile—"for you to return tonight." But Naira couldn't hold her smile and the former harshness returned to her voice. "All because of some stupid fishergirl."

"Father's returning as well," said Arrah. "I'll sail back for Eagle Island tonight. I'm all alone there, Naira. Won't you return with me? Now that Mother's gone, it's a lonely place."

"We'll come Arrah, Bres and I. But we must stay here a while longer. Bres helped defeat my former husband's family when they attacked us, but in all likelihood, they'll regroup again. It's a poor warrior who admits total defeat just because he's lost the battle."

Although Naira spoke of her former husband's troops, she was thinking of herself. Resentment and rancor pumped like bile inside her heart. Naira was determined to become Mistress of Eagle Island.

"I must go now, Naira," Arrah said.

"My sister." Naira smiled superbly as she hugged Arrah to her. "I'm delighted. We . . . Bres and I were both delighted to see you."

"I'm glad to have a sister, Naira," Arrah said, hugging Naira one more time.

"So am I," said Naira. "We've been strangers too long."

When Arrah returned to Eagle Island she noticed that the purple color had gone from the heath so it looked gray-silver, almost dead.

At the castle the dogs barked and whined, but she didn't pet them this time. She saw Legless Paddy's wizened face grinning up at her, calling her name. She bent down and took his hands in hers.

"Debrogail's dead," she said simply.

"I was makin' some ducks for when she returned." And two enormous tears trickled down his face.

"I'm sorry," Arrah said, and then because she couldn't say anything else, she got up and went inside.

She was saddened and confused by all she'd heard from Paddy and Naira about Debrogail, and yet there seemed to be no answers for her on Eagle Island. There were so many questions she wanted to ask Debrogail, to ask her mother. Neither was alive to answer them. Perhaps death did that to people, left survivors asking more questions about the dead than they had ever asked them when they were alive. Perhaps, ultimately, that was what death was all about—unanswered questions.

To overcome her sense of aimlessness, she ordered that all preparations be readied for a great festivity. Her father liked feasts when he returned.

Bulls and boars were slaughtered, and the carcasses readied for the spits by basting them with garlic, salt, and goose fat. Scullions returned from the garden, their baskets laden with parsnips, leeks, garlic, and cabbages cut from stalks. Walnuts soaked in brine, and rows of pastry shells filled with mincemeat lined the cupboard.

Arrah ordered that her finest linens be put on her bed, sheets of rennes. Each morning they were freshly changed and dried petals of roses and woodruff were sprinkled on them. At night she lay in the bed alone, thinking of her near death. The tiger cub lay at her feet, watching her with yellow eyes and licking at his paws. Dreams of death haunted her, and she would wake thrashing, trying to swim out of the constriction of the watery passageway. And there were other dreams—dreams of Seaghan Mac-Namara, his hand in her back as he lifted her up, the taste of his breath warm against her lips—Seaghan MacNamara, kissing her breasts, making love to her, but always his head turned into two skulls, and the bed where they loved turned to a grave.

Arrah went through the trunkloads of clothes that she had brought from the pirate ship. She'd already locked the gold in the treasury room.

She tried on a white satin dress, and then a blue one that made her eyes burn like the blue flame in a turf fire, and then a magenta one, colored like a sunset, that turned her eyes to slate-gray–silver, like whitecaps on the sea.

"Yea'll be looking so lovely," said Mary. "Carbri will be happy as fleas on a dog when he'll be laying eyes on you. I've never laid eyes on yea looking more beautiful."

But Arrah found the leather and metal basquines suffocatingly uncomfortable. The tightly laced partlets flattened her breasts. She hadn't unbound them to have them flattened now.

Arrah decided she would send the gowns to Naira, who always loved the finery of beautiful clothes and jewels. Arrah had felt a certain warmth after leaving Glen Head. *When God closes a door, he opens a window.* That's what her mother would have said. Through her death, Arrah had gained a sister, and yet something left her feeling dissatisfied and uncertain and she didn't know why.

She thought of Seaghan, and put some of the dresses back on again. Her arms in the thickly quilted sleeves couldn't hang by their sides naturally, but stuck out at an angle, like sausages. Yet if Seaghan had been in the courts of Europe, then these were the kinds of dresses he was accustomed to seeing on women, not jerkins and trews. The woman in the red dress in Paris had worn a similar wide-skirted dress with wide, slashed sleeves.

And then Arrah noticed a silver-green dress hanging in her wardrobe, a dress that she'd never seen before. Her mother must have ordered it hung in her wardrobe after she had run away. In some ways it looked like a wedding dress, yet it wasn't a wedding dress for it contained none of the traditional lace.

It was a dress made of silk and pearls. There was a hardness to it, yet a floating softness as though the essence of pearls had been spun into thread and woven into some magical silk cloth. The pearls sewn onto the cloth gave the dress an almost armorlike quality, like mail, but at the same time there was a lightness to it, like sea foam. It was impossible to give it a color, for as Arrah ran her hand over the wonderful garment, it seemed to change. It was the white of pearl, but sometimes it was silver as a moonbeam, or green as the sea, or gray as steel. The dress was stark and glorious as the moon.

Without saying a word, she slipped into the gown. In it Arrah was temptress and warrior.

The servants were speechless, their mouths gaping, as they looked at her. Arrah took her sword and buckled it to her waist. There was no huge bulky skirt or fat sleeves. The dress simply was, like air, like moon, like water.

Then the cry came from the watch. "Ship ahoy."

Arrah ran to the window. The masts were there. She saw the flags from her father's ships. The pearl dress would be for later, for the feast. She slipped it off and put on a simple dress of green velvet with an ermine collar.

As she looked out again she saw a huge, unmistakable form getting into a currach and preparing to row to shore. Seaghan MacNamara had returned with her father.

CHAPTER
21

Wearing her emerald sword, Arrah went to the beach to greet her father's ship when he landed. The flags from the masts flew brightly, the brilliant red and green banners of the O'Donnell signalling that victory had been won.

Arrah had wanted to tell her father about the midwife and the underground passage, but seeing Seaghan MacNamara, all her senses focused on him as he stepped out of the currach behind Reevnarg. Despite the fall air and the chilly sea Seaghan's arms were naked. He was muscled and thick and hard as oak timbers. If they'd been alone, Arrah might have reached out her hand and touched him, wanting to feel that protective aura she'd sensed in him after the de Burgo battle. She wanted to do that now, feel the hard knot of arm muscle against her fingertips. But something about the way he looked at her suddenly frightened her. *You've sailed the Dragon's Mouth and defeated de Burgo,* she told herself. *Surely you're not afraid of a man who dressed your wounds.* She stood taller and touched her sword.

Reevnarg was in high spirits. "Aye, daughter," he said when he hugged her to him. "It'll make my heart sad turning her over to you. She's a fine ship, the *Skatha.*"

The green velvet dress with a large ermine collar draping over her strong, pliant figure made Arrah look soft and seductive, sultry as an eastern cat. Reevnarg, with his hands on her shoulders, held her at arm's length and looked at her with paternal approval. "Aye now, isn't that the way a daughter should meet her father? Dressed as a woman. Not with blood on her hands. She'll make a fine wife for Carbri O'Connor, don't you think, Mac-Namara?"

She saw dark anger in MacNamara's eyes. She saw his lips part slightly, felt her breath quicken. Not knowing what else to do, she spoke the obvious. "Did you put down the rebellion?"

Reevnarg answered. "Aye, we did that! Five of their leaders, I sworded off their heads myself. Two got away. Ran off to the hills, they did. But we've seen the last of this nonsense now. They'll be paying their tributes without a whispering. Isn't that right, MacNamara?"

MacNamara said nothing. He let his eyes travel down Arrah's body, allowing them to rest on the undercurve of her breasts, on her waist, and on her hips. There was something indomitable and fierce and strangely imprisoning about Arrah's posture and the jeweled sword at her waist. She became more powerful each time he saw her. When she was in bed and wounded, he had thought that perhaps he could sway her from marrying Carbri. Now he wasn't sure. If he wanted to escape her spell, he had to leave now. He had to turn around and get back in the currach and row back to the ship. Yet he couldn't. He sensed the danger in loving her, the same danger he had sensed when he fell in love with Tiltiu, yet Arrah was even more dangerous, for she was fierce. Tiltiu had been fragile. He wanted Arrah to yield her fierceness to him, to open her mouth to him. He wanted to unbuckle that sword, pull the dark soft velvet from her breasts, and knead the nipples between his teeth.

Reevnarg, who was already walking toward the castle, took MacNamara's silence to be sullenness. "Aye, he gives dark looks about everything he does. Must be the influence of that damned French temperament on him. Tell the cooks to stir up the fires tonight. Call up my pipers and drummers. We'll have a feast and dance till the sun shines on our bellies tomorrow. Will you be coming, MacNamara? I've want to take my eagles out before the eve's feast." He strode up the beach toward the castle.

"In a moment." Seaghan's eyes on her were black and hard. She held the tiger in one arm. Its tail was curved up over its head and the beast batted it playfully. "Does the sea witch take off her sword when she makes love?"

His voice touched her like a tongue, as if he were kissing her freely and malevolently. Her cheeks grew hot. The hotness moved to her lungs, as though she'd just breathed in close to a hot fire. She'd sensed the presence of his formidable and intense virility before, but now she was overpowered by it in a way she never thought possible.

"It depends on the man," she challenged.

He took her arm, and she allowed him to lead her down the beach a way, behind a large boulder. She stopped there, leaning against it. Seaghan was in front of her. She knew she shouldn't be here with him, yet the force of him was as unrelenting as the whirlpool into which she had sailed. If she didn't move away from him, he would draw her in, and yet she didn't want to go.

"Do you know that the great storytellers of old once said that land and sea, evil and good, dark and light, man and woman were one?"

"What does that have to do with me?" she asked.

"You're a woman of great courage. You dared to take a pirate's ship from him, and to navigate the Dragon's Mouth, and you dared to take on de Burgo. Now I give you another dare."

He reached out and touched her face, caressing her lips with his thumb. She didn't draw away. "Dare to dream. Dare to dream of love. Not just a lad's love. But a man's love. Dare to dream of what it is like to make love with a man until you feel completely and utterly possessed by him. Until he comes into you deeper and deeper until you lose all sense of yourself. I dare you!" He looked straight into her eyes.

"I'm betrothed to Carbri."

She saw the flash of anger light his eyes. "Then why don't you draw away from me?"

There was a silence between them. A kind of subtle hostility.

"Because at night, I've dreamt of you doing this."

He abruptly pulled the tiger from her and dropped it to the ground. "It's not a beast to be treated like a lap cat," he said angrily. "You had better make your choice."

"It's my tiger. You gave it to me and I'll treat it as I wish. Otherwise take the beast back!"

She knelt beside the animal. As she did so, MacNamara reached to his sword belt. Her eyes were near the same level as his groin and she grew aware of the violence in his hands and the power of his loins beneath them. She heard the unbuckling of metal from leather. MacNamara's dark eyes gave her a look that went into the deepest marrow of her bones. His potential for violence made her blood run hot. She couldn't look at him any longer and began to stroke the tiger.

MacNamara lifted Arrah with rough quickness. Then in one brusque movement, he tucked his sword beneath his arm, and looped his belt about the tiger's neck. He handed the loose end to Arrah.

She refused to take it. "Carbri saved my life."

MacNamara's eyes narrowed with a dark malevolence. "In India they use them for sport. To eat men."

"Is that why you gave it to me? So that it would eat me?"

He grabbed her shoulders with a power that made her wince, then kissed her. Never had she been kissed the way he kissed her. The kiss was all things she had ever imagined in a kiss: passionate, and tender and demanding. He kissed her as though she were the first woman in the world and the last woman in the world, as though he lived for that kiss, as though she'd lived for that kiss. The kiss took her breath away and sapped her strength, all the while piercing her with a greater and more powerful desire than she'd ever known.

"The ocean is cold, Arrah, but in it is the hottest blood of all."

He grabbed her hand and tied the loose end of the belt about her wrist with a sharp, tight pull. "Control the beast while you can, Arrah O'Donnell. Or it *will* eat you."

He turned from her and walked in the direction of the castle.

She couldn't hurt Carbri. He had risked his life to be with her, had gone with her through the storm when Reevnarg's sailors wanted her thrown into the sea. He was kind and gentle, and his hazel eyes sparked with mirth. And yet she knew her body would never forget the way MacNamara had just kissed her. Damn him! Damn her for allowing him to do it.

She tore the belt from about her wrist. The scent of him was on the leather and she unlooped it from around the tiger's neck and threw it into the surf. She picked up broken pieces of clamshells and threw them into the sea as far as she could. It was still not too late to turn to Carbri, to turn away from the maelstrom of dark sensation that MacNamara whirled her in.

At the point where she could no longer be seen from the bay, she tied the tiger to a scrub bush. She pulled off her clothes, and running into the sea, leaped headfirst beneath its surface. Its sharp chill took her breath away. She welcomed the numbing cold, allowed it to sweep over her limbs, wanted it to penetrate every part of her body and wash Seaghan Mac-Namara from her. She wanted the chill of the ocean to wash all of his damned penetrating heat from her, and to cool her again, to fill her with its clean cold. She swam and swam, dove deeper, and drove herself and pushed herself to the limits of her endurance, to a point where mental consciousness was gone, to a point where she was merely a creature of the sea.

As the sun set in the west and a full moon rose on the other side of the horizon, Seaghan MacNamara watched Arrah O'Donnell walk out from the sea. Her legs, as she emerged, were hidden in the blackness of the water. The tops of the waves were brightened in that phosphorescent moment of color that lasted only at sunset when the white foam was no longer white but a luminous green-blue. Her breasts still caught the last rays of sun and were turned into a magnificent shade of red-gold, like the red-gold of Ireland itself, except for the undersides, which were shadowed. He saw her breasts heaving with the exertion of her swimming. Her high, proud head was thrown back, her mouth open. Behind her was darkness. In front of her was the still-brilliant red-yellow of the setting sun. The last rays of sunlight caught the droplets of water on her breasts, and she looked as though she were at once carved from gold-colored crystals and ebony. The lines of her limbs were hard and firm and yet the swell of her breasts was soft and beckoning. She was darkness and shadow. Softness and power. She was sea queen and sun goddess. He'd tried to forget her from the first time he'd seen her dance, but she was like a succubus haunting his dreams. He felt the ache rise across his lower back.

Arrah had not been aware of the storm coming, and now she saw a jagged fork of lightning in the distant sky. She moved to her clothes. The tiger rose, putting its paws far in front of it and stretching up its back legs. She spoke in low words to it. Already from the castle she heard the riotous laughter of drink and feasting and heard the boisterous rollicking drums and pipes.

She shook the sea from her hair, felt the chill of the night air on her body, and shivered. She felt invigorated and intensely alive as though each fiber of her body had been reawakened to some deep sensation.

The night was filled with the sounds of the sea. This was what she enjoyed most. Not the boisterous, drunken laughter of men, but the surf crashing easily and rhythmically against the distant cliffs, then falling away and surging again against the rocks.

The weather was uncertain, strange. In the shallow distance that was the cliff top, she could see mist beginning to envelop the hill. She heard a gull wail, and then a seal bark.

Eagle Bay shimmered to Arrah's left. The night tide lifted; waves rose to the sky, then fell back, only to rise again in foam.

MacNamara watched the beautiful sinuous movement of her body. She bent down to put on her sandals and he caught his breath as he glimpsed her moon-splendored buttocks. The color had faded from the sky and here, as he saw her from behind, she was like an open rose to him, white and inviting and perfect. He knew he should show himself, but she moved without timidity or self-consciousness. One movement on his part and she would grab her clothes and the moment would be spoiled.

Arrah heard something and started. Spinning about, she grabbed her dress in front of her. She grasped her sword and peered into the ever-darkening shadows.

"Arrah O'Donnell!"

The waves rolled and she couldn't recognize the voice that spoke. The sailors said that sometimes the mer people came and tried to lure people on shore into the sea.

"Arrah O'Donnell!"

This was no merman's voice. At the edge of the beach was a grouping of low granite boulders, worn round by the sea. She saw a shadow move behind them.

"Show yourself!" she ordered. Her voice had grown accustomed to commands.

The shadow moved and she recognized the powerful build immediately as that of Seaghan MacNamara. He came closer. The memory of his kiss returned. That slow spin of sensation began to whirl again through her blood. Somewhere in the distance she heard the rumble of thunder. It was at that moment she knew she had no choice but to hurt Carbri. The gown, held up like a careless triangle in front of her womanhood, did nothing to hide the lithe curves of her thighs. Both of her breasts were bare. She made no further attempt to cover herself.

She looked at him, but a cloud crept over half the moon. MacNamara stood in shadow. "Is that how you amuse yourself,MacNamara, by scaring women?"

"Is the sea witch frightened of the dark?" he mocked.

She tried to look at him more closely, but the heavy cloud completely darkened the moon just then, and MacNamara's face grew even darker. Standing there, he looked as though he had been formed from the rocks themselves, as though he had been quarried and not born. *Yes, she wanted to say. I'm frightened of you. But more than that, I'm frightened of myself, of my desire for you.* "You answer questions with questions," she said.

"Only because you do."

She answered with sarcasm. "Is that how a *man* takes his amusement? By hiding like a small boy behind a rock and watching women?"

He smiled. "I think you knew I was there all along. I think that's how the sea witch seduces men—by showing her breasts above the waves like a siren."

She looked at him directly. "Were you seduced?"

"The first time I saw you." He removed his cloak and put it about her shoulders. She welcomed the cloak, and welcomed his body heat in it. She'd begun to shiver from the night air. In the darkness she still couldn't see his face, but could smell the warm, masculine smell in his clothes and, too, there was the unmistakable smell of the sea on him, the pungent iodine of salt and seaweed. She tried to look at him more closely, but the darkness grew deeper as another bank of clouds crossed the moon. There were nothing but dark hollows where his eyes should have been.

"There are sharks in that water. Someday Arrah O'Donnell will tempt the Fates once too often."

"Perhaps, perhaps not," she said and turned to walk to the castle.

But MacNamara took her arm. "Wait, Arrah. Your body invites men like no other woman's body. Your movements. The way you carry yourself. Yet your eyes defy. Your words push away. My father's wife played with me. I won't be played with again."

She was caught in a enormous duality of feeling for him. The heat from him moved up along her forearms, making the backs of her arms shiver. He was enormous and powerful and he intoxicated her. Desire for him flowed through her body. She ached for him, yet she was afraid that the essence of Arrah O'Donnell would be subsumed in his power. She wanted to move close to him and yet knew that if she allowed herself to do so, she would never again be able to escape the hard heat of his body.

She stepped back, but he reached and grasped her behind the waist and grabbed her to him and closed his mouth over hers with a fierceness that demanded that not only her mouth surrender, but her body as well. She felt the blood drain from her. It seemed to be flowing into this huge hot mountainous man who held her. He pulled her harder against him. She was powerless in his grip, for one vicelike hand held her chin while the other held her waist. His tongue was hard and knowing and demanding, and she wanted to tear herself from him, yet wanted, needed to press herself against him. She knew the danger of his violence and pulled away. "I'll be mistress of my own soul. I want to make love with you, MacNamara. But I'll not belong to you or any—"

He grabbed her to him and his mouth claimed hers. A remembrance of Carbri told her that what she was doing was wrong, but her body betrayed her. She allowed him to press her down to the sand. She felt the solid hot heat of his body on hers, warming her from the night air. He grabbed her hands and pushed them above her head. She realized that it was his strength that had excited her from the very beginning, and that he knew it, and that made him even more dangerous. She wanted him to take her and take her and do with her what he'd promised. She felt the roughness of his fingertips, too gentle against her nipples, and she grasped his fingers in hers and pressed them more tightly against herself. His hot breath, his lips grazed her nipples. She pressed his head harder against her breasts, and felt his teeth and moaned out her desire. She was hot, open, and waiting for him, elemental in her lust, and spoke in the hoarse whispers of intense desire. She felt the power in his arms and in his loins, now pressing against her. Her body demanded.

He raised himself from her and she felt the cool air where his body had been warm against hers. She opened her eyes; saw him struggling with his satin hose and helped him pull them off from his muscled buttocks. And then she saw him, moon-silvered, erect, and splendid. For a moment she thought the moon had deceived her; he was enormous. She cried out, seeing him. He quieted her with a deep, dark kiss, but she had no desire to be quieted and his kiss only increased the urgency of her body. He had opened a tremendous ache in her and now she needed him to fill it. She tilted her hips to him, and grasped his buttocks to her. He drew back momentarily and inserted his fingers. She moaned her impatient want and arched her back to him and thrust herself against him. The hard enormousness of him touched against her own softness and she lifted herself to that glorious penetration and cried out, but her cries were silenced by his mouth, as he pushed in and pushed in, slowly and relentlessly and deeply into her. And she moved with him, pressed her body higher to his and spread her thighs farther so she could take his hugeness deeper.

He took her, but she took him as well, the softness of her want demanding more and more from him, and still more, her throaty obscenities urging him on to greater fierceness. She felt his largeness fill the sides of her and block out her senses. As thunder crashed, he penetrated to the very marrow of her bones. He possessed her deeply, and fiercely, the solid, enormous flesh thrusting pleasure into her again and again, and just when she thought it impossible, once again.

She felt as though he had merged into every corner of her being, as though each time he thrust into her body he also entered her soul. Her body no longer seemed to belong to her. It had been transformed into foam like the waves of the sea, but made from pure lightning; and each time he plunged into her, her body rose higher and higher like the waves of the sea, and when her body could take no more sensation, it seemed to explode and fall back to earth in a shower of pure white stars.

CHAPTER
22

Seaghan and Arrah were so engrossed in each other's bodies that they didn't notice the storm coming on them. The wind hit and rain pelted down on them. They rose quickly. MacNamara grabbed up his cloak and slipped it over her shoulders. She picked up the tiger and started to run toward the castle.

"This way!" said Seaghan and quickly led her to one of the longboats. He pushed out and began to row in the direction of the *Skatha*. MacNamara pulled hard against the waves, his skin like sculpted ebony in the darkness. Lightning slashed across the sky and seemed to run down Seaghan's body, illuminating the dark muscles to steel. With each pull, she felt the enormous strength in his arms as the boat lunged forward in the water.

They reached the *Skatha*. Seaghan, standing in the prow of the boat, steadied it for her. He was tall as lightning as the sky lit him in a shocking blaze of silver. There was no lag in the thunder now, but it rolled instantly and Arrah felt the vibration in the air about her.

She allowed Seaghan to guide her in the darkness to the captain's quarters.

The moment she was inside, he grabbed her to him, kissing her hungrily. She felt his hardness rising against her, and welcomed his easy power when he picked her up and carried her to the berth. Without seeming to ever let her go, he was on top of her, his knee pressing between her legs. She opened to him willingly. He was totally in darkness, so dark that she could see none of his features. He took her hand and pressed it against himself, and she felt the heavy swell of his desire. His breath grazed her right nipple, his lips first, then kneading tongue and teeth teased it to tautness. He bit her erect nipple gently. His mouth left a trail of cool kisses as it travelled to the other breast.

She bent her body up like a bow to him. "Wait," he whispered. Cool caresses from his tongue made a line down the skin of her stomach and down the inside of one thigh. He kissed the inside of one knee and then the other, then began to kiss his way up her thigh again, his lips soft against her soft skin, up, up, moving little by little, coming closer and closer to her nether lips, until the soft pleasure of his tongue parted her. His breath blew hot into her. His lips and tongue and teeth tormented her, touching her, kneading her, lapping at the edges of her sensation, making her body so fierce with desire that she grabbed his hair and pushed his head deeper between her thighs. But he was powerful, and he refused to yield to her, giving her nothing of himself but his breath. She cried out in an agony of want. "Please! Please!" He slowly inserted one finger, brought it to that small peninsula of paradise. Speech stopped and became pure sound as her body was shaken in spasms of pleasure. He cradled her and kissed her eyelids until she stopped shaking.

She felt his largeness nudging against her. He inserted only the head of his thickness to her, and she, still in the after-contractions of her first pleasure, tried to pull him in, but he permitted only the head of himself to penetrate against those gentle contractions tugging at him like a soft mouth. He was like a snake, circling and circling its burrow, and slowly going in and then changing its mind and sliding back, until he felt her body stiffen beneath him. He grasped her hard to him and plunged in, catching her in the throes of her highest pleasure so that her body shook as though lightning itself had touched her. He cradled and kissed her, but he had not taken his pleasure yet, and so he began again, this time moving farther inside her.

His huge hands pushed under her buttocks, lifting her to him so she could accept all of his length. He began to thrust, first slow and solid and careful and in complete control, then he began to move faster and faster so that she contracted around him. His love was like thunder, his mast-hard flesh conjuring a storm of sensation so she cried out and cried out, and after an eternity he cried out too, "I've drowned inside you," and she again was overcome by that rising wave of time when he exploded into her, powerful and potent as the sea.

Lightning struck repeatedly and they were both caught in the brilliance of its illumination, both of them clinging to each other like drowning bodies, both of them shuddering in the tremors of love.

When the tremors stopped, they held each other and listened to the wind and to the rising and falling ocean and to each other's skin. Outside, the storm was severe and on land the wind blew with such ferocity that the gravestones seemed to shake, but in the ship's quarters they were oblivious, wrapped in a cocoon of love. They spoke of the sound of the stars turning and of the moon whispering to them, and of love. Arrah was caught in a sensation as though she were floating away into nothing, like foam on the top of the sea, and in that splendid feeling of nothingness she fell asleep in Seaghan's arms.

The next morning Reevnarg was preparing to leave for the mainland to do a count of his cattle. MacNamara and he both stood in the main hall. Bridgett, who had taken a liking to MacNamara, was in the hall pretending to be filling sconces with oil.

Reevnarg grabbed his sword and buckled it to his large girth. "So you've decided to stay here, MacNamara?"

MacNamara and Arrah had returned to the castle at dawn. "Yes. I'm off myself to France in a few days. I'll take some leisure before I leave."

Reevnarg put his hands on his hips and stood with his legs wide apart. "You know that Arrah is to marry young O'Connor."

MacNamara narrowed his dark eyes but said nothing.

Reevnarg turned and looked out to sea. "I'm not one to be listening to idle chatter. What you do with women is your concern." Reevnarg turned back to MacNamara. "You're a damned fine soldier! A bloody sailor. I'd rather have you at my back in battle than a thousand other men. But she's already repudiated one marriage and it was costing me dearly. That cursed Glundel was behind the MacDayat uprising, I'll wager on it. You'll not lead her to repudiate another."

MacNamara met Reevnarg's gaze fully. The answer came back level and without emotion. "Her marriage is assured. You'll not suffer the loss of any bride price."

Reevnarg seemed relieved. "Take the serving wenches. Take Bridgett there. She'll be an agreeable lass, won't you now, Bridgett? You'll always welcome a big handsome bull."

"Oh yes, MacNamara, sir!

As soon as Reevnarg had stepped into his longboat Seaghan MacNamara and Arrah O'Donnell were entwined in each other's nakedness in Arrah's chambers in the castle. Afterward, he lay on top of her and she felt the solid rhythmic pressing of his stomach muscles on hers as he took breath. She kissed his neck and felt the dampness of his exertions against her lips.

He rolled off of her and then pulled her close to him. His eyes mocked

her. "Reevnarg made me promise that I wouldn't lead you to repudiate
another betrothal. I said that I wouldn't."

"My father! He cares only for his eagles and his damned bride price."

"Marry me, Arrah!"

"I'll marry you!" She knew her marriage to Seaghan would disappoint
Carbri, but Carbri was no fool. He would be able to see that marriage
between them was not the right choice.

She had gone through all the reasons in her own mind several times and
would tell him gently.

First, there was the question of Carbri's marriage to Agneis. Arrah had
never anticipated that marriage to Carbri would cause such havoc.
Seaghan had told her that Geralde de Burgo would convince the O'Connor
septs to name someone else other than Carbri as the O'Connor tanaist. De
Burgo's influence was everywhere. The sight of dead men and dying men
returned to her. Phillipe de Burgo lying in a pool of blood. There would be
no peace if she married Carbri.

Second, Seaghan was right that Carbri would want her to leave her
sailing. On shipboard he had always wanted her to stop asking questions.
He had tried to prevent her from becoming bosun, and from sailing the
Dragon's Mouth. Love was accepting another person's desires, not trying
to change them. Seaghan understood her love of the sea, and her need to
sail it.

Third—although she couldn't tell Carbri this—there was the question
of pure, carnal lust. She had loved Carbri, probably would always care for
him and carry a fondness in her heart for him, but never would her blood
rise to him as it rose to Seaghan. Seaghan made her feel things in the way
that Carbri had never been able to. She was strong and needed a man about
her who was as strong as she was. The very thought of Seaghan excited her
in ways she had never known. She had never felt that way about Carbri, and
never would.

"I have chateaux in France. Gardens, the likes of which you can't
imagine. You can do whatever you want there," Seaghan said.

"No! We live here!"

He ran his thumb down the edge of her jaw. Her tanned face and neck
had turned pink-gold with the flush that came after love.

"We'll make love without end!"

"We do that here!"

He pulled her to him. "My arms have ached for something, never
knowing what it was until I found you. I'm at peace when you're here

beside me. It's as though when God took the rib from Adam he left a great aching hole. I feel that ache. All my life I've been looking for something to fill it."

They existed in an enchanted paradise of love and more love. They made love with the pounding of the sea echoing in their veins, and the sun's rays gracing them, and the light of the stars streaming down on them through the open window, burning their bodies to look like heavenly creatures of fleshed starlight, their splendid anatomies stretching and straining in the efforts of love. At night she fell asleep with his member still in her. When she rose from her bed, she would feel his love liquid run in thin streams down her leg. He would run his hands along her long, limber limbs, never tiring of the feel of her curves in his hand. When he was away from her, he carried the memory of her body in his fingers, the feel of her skin, the hot wetness between her legs.

They walked hand in hand along the beach, stepping over the tide pools left by the receding water where the tiny mud sharks lingered. They took the tiger with them on a leash now, and he put out his claws and tried to catch the little fish and sniffed at the crab holes in the dark gray sand. The gulls lifted in small flocks ahead of them as they walked, and then landed again a short distance in front, only to fly off as the lovers approached.

Back at the castle, Mary gave Arrah stern glances. As soon as Seaghan left the room she harrumped. "I seen the two of you out on the beach. Lookin' happy as two clams at high tide. You wasn't listening to a word I was tellin' you."

"He loves me!"

"Yea'd be better off if the devil loved yea."

One afternoon, as Seaghan and Arrah walked along the beach and she saw his hard chiselled face in profile against the bay, she asked him why he lived in France. He stopped walking. She saw the dark strength of his eyes falter. There was a silence between them.

He took a long breath and spoke. "My mother died and two wives followed her. My father remarried a woman named Tiltiu. She was beautiful, with hair so long that it brushed the dew from the grass when she went out in the morning. I was barely a man, and I loved her, with the deepness of feeling that only a youth new to manhood can feel for a woman. But she was my father's wife and I rebuked her advances. Nothing came between us until one night.

"A group of us engaged in drinking and brawling. We were young men, and like young men, we talked only of two things, women and battle. We drank much and recounted our exploits with all the color of youth. My father was hunting the roe deer, which was his passion, and was not expected back. She came to my bed in secret, and I, in drunkenness and half-dream, but mostly in desire, for I had desired her . . . I took what she offered.

"My father had suspected her for some time. He was much older than she, and jealous of her every glance. His hunting absence was a ploy. He returned in secret in the middle night and not finding her in his bed began to search the castle."

He looked at Arrah again, drew breath and continued. "Her body was on mine, my hands raised up to her breasts when he opened the door. Our pleasure was tempestuous and we didn't hear my father enter my chamber. My father shot an arrow and pierced her heart. He could have killed me as well, but Bres stayed his hand. I was not the perpetrator of the act. And unknown to me, I was not her first encounter. Carrying Tiltiu, I ran out of his castle. She died in my arms. I buried her myself. Bres told me later that I was to leave Ireland. If I ever returned, my father would kill me."

He continued speaking. "At first I raged. But necessity teaches us all new passions. I think there are some men who are born with soldiers' hearts. Battle gets in your blood. Fighting becomes like food. You can't live without it. Life is an unbearable tedium without conflict. I find now that I miss the excitement of the battle when I'm too long from it. The sea is most magnificent when it is tumultuous. Perhaps a man's life is like that as well.

"I traveled to England. Fought as a soldier for her on the mainland against the French. I advanced well in ranks. On a second expedition, the ship on which my soldiers and I were being transported was fired on by a French galley. They took us prisoners, as galley slaves.

"I was put into the service of a wealthy French count. Jean Pierre de Montreuil was a recluse. It was rumored he was a monster. But no crew member had ever seen him, and rumors are always rampant on a ship.

"We came under heavy attack by an English galleon. The Fates work in strange ways. Some men call it luck, some the will of God. By whatever name you know them, the Fates play with us. The man in front of me was killed. My shackles broke loose. I jumped free of the burning ship and climbed onto a piece of wreckage. I saw an object clinging to a smaller piece of wreckage in the water. It was a body with a drapery-like covering on its head.

"I pulled the drapery off. You cannot imagine my repulsion at what I saw. It was a monster-headed creature with skin paler than any I had ever seen, so white in fact that it was like bleached bone. Protuberances swelled over the entire skull so that the face was not at all the face of a man as much as a bizarre brute, part dog, part bull, part lion. I drew back horrified, convinced that some monster from the deepest regions of hell had come for me.

"But the monster begged me not to be afraid and to assist him in his weakened condition. I helped him up onto my board, and as we floated about there, he told me his story. He was Jean Pierre de Montreuil.

"Until he was five or six, he had a beauteous and delightful childhood of the kind that a child can only have in the gentle climes of France. He was betrothed to the daughter of one of the counts of Normandy, a match which would have made his family both richer and even more powerful than they were. But he began to suffer unbearable torments of the head. His head was bled, and he was given infusions of countless medicinal herbs. Mud was pressed to his skull. Doctors, magicians, surgeons, all were called at one time or another but no remedy could be found to eliminate the pain. His head began to change in strange ways. Protrusions appeared on his forehead. His nose became pushed to one side. As time went on, his skull became even more deformed, like a bull's with a wide, swollen forehead. He was kept in a room completely by himself and was never allowed to be seen by anyone except his old nursemaid. He studied voraciously, for study was his only pastime.

"There was no choice for his parents but to cancel the betrothal. There were no other children in the family. Both his parents took a fever and died when Jean Pierre was a youth. He grew into adulthood, all the time suffering from excruciating headaches that continued to push his visage into more and more frightening configurations.

"I succeeded in fashioning a small square of sail from a length of canvas and we sailed to the coast of France. From there, we continued on our way to Damme. Jean Pierre, contrary to the aspects of his terrible face, was a man of immense kindness and intelligence who had a brilliant mind for commerce. From the isolation of his castle, he directed his lands and his ships. He was loved by his servants, but I was the only one to ever see his face unhooded, except for his old nurse and two dear friends. We spent many happy hours sitting in front of the fire discussing the Greek and Roman writers, theology, and philosophy. In the summers we would take a light cart and horse and go into the forests. He raised magnificent horses, Spanish blood. Most of these monsters do not live very long. He was a man of middle years when I met him. He died, naming me his heir. I took the title of the Count of Montreuil.

"For a time I played the part of the French nobleman. I attended the court and"—at this point Seaghan looked down, before continuing—"and for a time I amused myself there. But I disliked the affected manners and the gossip. Courts are places of foppery and idleness. A half-dozen men concern themselves with matters of state. The remainder are toads and fawns caring for nothing but intrigues of the bed. I chose not to live there.

"I, too, have ships. A dozen carracks. Some of the fastest on the seas. Hunting—my lands are forested with fine oaks, filled with deer and wild boar. Horses—hot-blooded creatures of Moorish breeding with fine fetlocks and wide, flaring nostrils. Control of a ship is one thing, control of an Andalusian stallion is another. The power of the beast between your thighs is almost as exciting as that of battle, almost as exciting as making love with you. I love you, Arrah. For the first time since I was cast from my father's house, I know peace."

That night he woke and found that she was not in bed. He went looking for her, opening the door of her bedchamber quietly. She was working, bent over a table, her fine profile a half-dark and quiet silhouette beside the candle. She wore a cloak of the winter fur of ermine about her shoulders, but her breasts were bare. She was so beautiful that he wanted to weep.

"Why are you awake?" he asked.

"I'm thinking about my new ship."

"I think your men are correct when they say you're a witch. Half in light and dark you look like one."

"Perhaps there's a little of the devil in all of us."

"Come back to bed, my devil!" he said.

"I've work that needs attention!"

"You've a man that needs attention!" He lifted the quill from her hand, laid it on the table, and brought her hand to himself. She bent and took his heavy tumescence between her lips and began to suck, making that vigorous dragon of flesh slippery and wet with life. She loved the hugeness of him, the taste of him. He clutched at her hair as his body shook in a spasm. Then he blew out the candle, its smoky smell momentarily overcoming the fragrance of her skin and hair. He lifted her from the chair and carried her to her bed.

Then it was he who could not sleep. She had to belong to him. To be without her would rend an impossible chasm in his life. After he'd lived in darkness for so many years, she was his only light. To be without that light now would be . . . he couldn't do it! He was to leave in four days. He needed a promise from Arrah that she would leave with him.

Fall came on the lovers as a surprise. They had walked much on the hills, but had lived their world reflected in each other's eyes and remained oblivious to the subtle changes of colors in the leaves. One afternoon Seaghan lay down his cloak for her and loved her there on the hill, and after, she looked up and suddenly noticed that the leaves in the top of the ash trees had turned to red. The wind smelled vaguely of the north. Arrah felt the chill of the ground rise through her back, but on top of her she felt Seaghan's warmth, his breath on her neck, and she felt as though she could stay beneath him forever.

His head lay on her breast. "You see the way the haze forms on that large hill on the mainland? And behind it. See the way those two mounds look like perfectly overturned bowls? Did you know that the Greeks of long ago said that the first bowl was made in the shape of Venus's breast? And did you know that in our own tales from the ancients, the first spear was made from the man piece of the god, Crom? Needing a weapon, something to kill his enemy with, he tore a piece from himself because it was so long and heavy."

"I remember when I shot Captain Whip. I felt the same as the first time I was going to make love."

"You, Arrah O'Donnell, lust for power in the same way that you lust for pleasure."

"Pleasure me now!"

"Is that an order, Captain Arrah?"

"Yes!"

During the day, when she wasn't with Seaghan, she planned another ship in her head, and began to sketch drawings. It would have four masts to capture the wind, but it would have oars, too, so that it would never be becalmed. She sent Patch to shipyards at Galway and Portugal to inquire about having such a ship built.

At night she and Seaghan loved and held each other until the moon moved across the sky.

Trying to find the essence of Arrah O'Donnell was like trying to find the heart of the sea. She was mysterious, and challenging and fascinating. For every detail he learned about her, there was more that he would never know.

Seaghan had been welcomed into the beds of the daughters, wives, and mistresses of some of England's and France's most powerful men. Some men made a living by gleaning information from torture. He used pleasure and traded his information for power and wealth, which increased his substantial estate to ever-widening areas of influence. A well-pleasured woman gave everything, and often had knowledge that her husband or father never suspected she possessed. He had even learned how to pleasure virgins without spoiling them. But in his dealings with women, he had come to scorn them. Inevitably he cared for them more before he bedded them than after. In love a woman lost her secrets.

But Arrah was wicked, for every encounter left him crazed for more. Sometimes when he loved her she was like a near mad creature of darkness, a succubus, sucking breath from him. Sometimes he thought he wanted to die on her breasts so he would be free of the torment of losing her. Her sensuality knew no bounds. Yet she held something back. She would shudder long and hard in his arms after love, but even when their bodies seemed melted into each other, some part of her remained outside his grasp. He needed her to yield to him completely so that he was certain of never losing her.

They made love on the beach. And after, she ran naked into the sea and swam down under the waves. The slanting sun turned the water's surface into a jeweled splendor of green, gold, crimson, and diamonds. When Arrah came out, he saw the light fall over the curve of her breast and shadow the underside, and he saw the sun reflected in the droplets of water on her skin so that she seemed to be made of particles from a rainbow fallen to earth.

He realized then that unlike all the other women he'd had, Arrah O'Donnell would never completely belong to him. He threw his cloak over her and tried to rub her dry. But she threw the cloak off and began grabbing up small bits of sticks and twigs from the driftwood, then built a fire and sat naked by it. She changed there in the firelight to a raw and primeval creature that he did not recognize. As she sat there naked, ignoring the wind, the fire casting its hues on her shoulders, he knew that Arrah would never love any man as much as she loved the elements. She was a creature of the sea and wind and fire. The knowledge made him desperate and angry.

"I belong with you," he said. His face was very serious when he spoke. "I'm taking you to France with me when I go."

Now she grew angry, her eyes seeming to ignite in the growing darkness. "I'll go with no man, unless I wish it!"

He grabbed her and pulled her to him. His breath came in short bursts like that of a runner after a race. "That's what you want, isn't it," he whispered, "not love, but power!"

"Yes!" she said. "No one will make me vulnerable again. You are not a woman. You don't understand what it is to have your body used as property.

To have a man have power over what or who will enter your body. No one will tell me whom I should marry or when I should marry or where I will live. I will not give up what I have gained. Not to you or my father or anyone."

He felt himself losing ground and grew angrier. "Do you know hell, Arrah? I've been in hell for years, the death of Tiltiu ever torturing me. When I'm with you I feel as if I've been allowed to heal. I feel happiness. You're my salvation. De Burgo will attack again. It's only a matter of time before Glundel Joyce arranges some alliance with him. I won't see you destroyed."

She turned from him. "Those rocks and that sea. They're mine. They're what make me! No one will take them from me. Not you, not de Burgo, not anyone."

He exploded in a violent flame of temper. "I curse your rocks! I curse the wind! The sea! I curse your eyes and your lips. And I curse the moon and the sun for making you so beautiful to look upon." His voice broke. "And most of all, I curse myself for falling in love with you. Arrah, come with me!"

"I love you! But I won't let you own me! This is my home."

"Love!" He spit the word. "Love is allowing yourself to be vulnerable. You know nothing of love. You know lust. Your body lusts for pleasure. Your nature lusts for power. You have two ships now. You're having another built. How many do you want?" But he didn't wait for her to answer. "A dozen. And after that you'll have two dozen. And then twenty. And then twenty-five! It'll never be enough for you. And you'll put fifty men on each. That's what you want, isn't it? Men whom you can order about. And when you've established yourself and have dozens of men like rutting stallions whinnying about you, what will you do then? Order them to pleasure you?"

She slapped him, the sound bursting like a gunshot.

"Do you not like the sound of those orders, Arrah O'Donnell? Here are more. 'I order you to climb on top of me.' "

She slapped him again.

"Will you say that, Arrah? 'I order you to put it into me. I order you to thrust.' "

She slapped him again.

" 'I order. I order!' That's how Arrah O'Donnell will live her life. Ordering men. Because men will be afraid to make love to you. This is one man who is not afraid of you."

He took her then, punishing with a fury, trying to thrust the sea and wind from her veins. While evening fell and the sea grew red and gold with the colors of the setting sun, and the sky above him grew dark, while the fire lightened her skin to a golden-tawny shade and the sea grew darker, while the sky grew black, and there was no color but the moon and the white phosphorescence of the waves, all the time, he loved her. And still she escaped him.

When he finally let her up, her eyes, her bearing still challenged him. "I love you! Why can't you love me?" His voice was quiet.

She looked at him squarely, her eyes dark in the night. "I love you, but here I stay strong. I'm master of my own soul, not dependent on anyone." She turned and walked back to the castle.

The next day was a still, sunless day. The sky did not appear so much cloudy as merely a uniform, pearly gray, like the inside of a seashell. The sun behind the clouds was like a perfect, round pearl, silver like the full moon. The bay was as gray as the sky, like a polished metal mirror in which the reflections of the lead-gray mountains were clear and motionless. It was an unusual calm. There was a small scrub forest ahead of where Seaghan and Arrah walked. The trees were motionless, gray, and drooping. She and Seaghan seemed to be the only two people alive in the world. So intense was the quiet that when a small mouse ran across their path into the dry leaves and twigs, it sounded loud as a stag crashing through the bracken.

Neither Seaghan nor Arrah talked. Both of them were deep in thought. Arrah was planning to take a ship to Spain. The Spanish were fine weapons makers. If de Burgo attacked, she would be prepared. She would not allow her island to be taken.

Seaghan spoke, interrupting her thoughts. "When you open an oyster, sometimes you find a pearl inside. It's the most beauteous part, and yet it's the part that brings the oyster the greatest pain. That's how you are to me. I need you. I need you like the tides need the moon! I can't stay here in Ireland. My father will kill me, or I will kill him."

"I won't allow you to possess me."

His face was enormously tender and soft, all the volatility and dark anger of yesterday was gone. "I love you. Come! It's going to rain. Let's return to the castle."

As soon as they were in her chambers, he reached behind him and locked the door. She wore a dress of a deep blue, soft, and exotic wool, and he began to undo the pearl-gray buttons down the back. His hands were gentle at her neck as he gently swept up her hair so that he could undo the first buttons. He kissed the back of her neck, and then went down her back, breathing his warm breath on her spine as he undid one button after another. He slid the dress from her, then picked her up and carried her to the bed and lay her on it as though it were an altar. His hands slid beneath her silk camisole. He was taking great care with her as though she were a maiden about to be deflowered. His hands as he parted her thighs were gentle.

His eyes were very black and she saw her own reflection in his pupils, small and black. He circled her lips with his finger as he spoke. "There are moments when a certain thing is at its pinnacle." She felt his finger run down her throat, down her breast, along the line of her stomach. He stopped then between her legs and parted her as though her nether lips were petals on a rose. "It's the moment that a flower is opened to perfection. It's the moment a matador thrusts his sword and knows he's hit the heart of the bull." He plunged his finger into her then and twisted his hand in such a way that he went deeper and into a place she'd never felt before. "There's a moment like that in the pleasure between a man and woman that is beyond ordinary pleasure, beyond any pleasure you can imagine." She felt his finger circle far inside her. "It's called the secret of Venus. I'm going to show it to you." His voice had a strange quality, gentle, soft, his breath was slow and close in her ear like the roll of the sea crashing softly in a shell. She wanted to say something, ask him what he was going to do, but his tongue prevented her from speaking. He kissed her slow and long, masterfully and darkly, and then he moved in. There was nothing she could do to prevent him. He was too skillful in his knowledge and he pushed himself slowly and relentlessly into her, and when what he did frightened her, he spoke gently. "You're not afraid, are you," but he commanded more than asked. "Hold on, Arrah, we're nearly there in the ocean of pleasure. Be courageous in love as you are in battle." His voice was as imprisoning as a hand, pushing deeper, and afterward when she lay crying and trembling in his arms, he cradled her and spoke in quiet words. "Hush!" he said. And the softness of his voice was even more unnerving than what he had done to her body, for there was an unearthly gentleness to it. She was afraid of the place where he had taken her, for she knew she wanted to be taken there again and again.

"You'll come to France with me now?" he asked softly.

She nodded and without speaking fell asleep in the seductive and dangerous harbor of his arms. Her body exhausted, she slept as though she were dead.

When Arrah awoke, Seaghan's arms were about her. He was kissing her back. She languished for a moment in that state, half dreaming, half waking, but it was his soft mouth that kept bringing her back to reality. What had happened during the previous night seemed to have happened in another world, in a dream.

He turned her and smiled at her. "The sun will be shining high soon. You've a lot of preparations to ready before we sail to France."

"France!" And then she remembered her promise, but it was like a dream. The gentle ache between her legs was the only reminder that it hadn't been a dream. Her body no longer seemed to belong to her.

Just then, she heard a shout from the watch. "The *Belle Étoile*." Arrah got up slowly and went to the window. She saw the ship and a longboat being lowered from it. She saw Carbri climb down to the longboat and reach up and help Finola descend from the ship.

CHAPTER 23

Carbri was so overjoyed to see Arrah waiting for him that he vaulted out of the currach even before it touched shore. He ran through the water, his arms open wide, his legs spraying water about him. "Arrah! Arrah!" he shouted as he ran. Sebastian and Hirple and a few other of Arrah's sailors stood about her. The arrival of a ship was always an occasion, for they brought cargo to be unloaded, and news.

Carbri grabbed for her exuberantly. "Christ, I missed you!"

Although she smiled at him and allowed him to throw his arms around her, her hands were placed on his chest, keeping a distance between them, and when he tried to kiss her, she turned her head so his lips caught the side of her neck.

"Carbri," she said, "you look like you had good journey." Finola sat in the boat. Since it was she, Finola, who had arranged Carbri's betrothal to Agneis de Burgo, Arrah assumed that she had arrived to try and talk Carbri out of marrying Arrah. Arrah had never cared for Finola: Finola was fifteen years older than Carbri, and had a character that liked to direct everything. Arrah didn't like to be directed. But now Finola might prove to be a valuable ally and Arrah resolved to be pleasant to her.

"Why aren't you kissing me?" asked Carbri.

"I am kissing you." She gave him a perfunctory brush of the lips on the side of his cheek.

" 'Od's blood! That's not how you'll be kissing a man you haven't seen for nigh a month," and he grabbed her again and tried to kiss her once more, but again she gave him only the side of her face. "What's the matter?" he asked.

"Nothing . . . I'm just surprised to see Finola. I imagine she's here about . . . your marriage," Arrah said.

"Her husband is dead," Carbri answered. "She heard MacNamara was here."

Arrah remembered the first time she had danced with Seaghan. It was
Finola who had touched his arm. "What has he to do with her?"

"She's bloody daft on the wencher!"

The boat had just touched up on the shore, making a grainy, dragging
sound as its prow was pulled onto the sand. Carbri strode to meet it and
helped his sister to step out.

Arrah's resolve to be pleasant to Finola vanished. The dislike she had
always felt for the dark-haired, heavy-lidded woman returned and intensified.

Carbri's sister wore the traditional Irish dress of a laced bodice and a rich
blue gown over a shell-colored long shirt. She wore a matching cape
decorated with a very large gold pin. Arrah had put on her dark trews and
jerkin. She wore a silk shirt beneath the jerkin, but had laced it nearly to the
top of her neck so that her bosom didn't show beneath. She had wanted to
wear nothing that would arouse Carbri.

Arrah felt Finola's eyes go down her body with condemnation. Etiquette
required that the two women embrace and kiss on the cheek. Finola
reached out for her and Arrah saw the glint of jeweled bracelet on her thin
wrist. But Arrah drew back, her eyes smoldering and gray.

"Arrah, child," Finola spoke in a kind of singsong voice. "How absolutely delighted I am to see you again. How . . . strange you look in that
garb. Like a galley sailor!"

The air between the two women bristled. "I can't move about ship in
garments like yours," Arrah replied.

"Ship? Oh yes! I'd heard that you were taking up ships. Fishing, is it?
Certainly, Carry, as tanaist you're not going to allow your wife to go about
smelling after herring, are you?"

Carbri, sensing the hostility between the two women, took Finola's arm
and led her toward Mary. "Will you be seeing that a bath is prepared for my
sister and that she's made comfortable?"

"I'll do that. Come along, Miss Finola, and leave the lovers to sort out
themselves."

Arrah gave a harsh look to Mary, but said nothing.

Carbri noticed the tiger that Arrah had by her feet on the leash. "Where
was it you was picking up that thing?"

Arrah smiled. "His name is Kian. How was your trip?"

"Much the better now for seeing you, me love," he said with an attempt
at heartiness. He wanted to jump on her, had been thinking of nothing else
for days, but she was behaving in a strange manner. Perhaps the cause of

her distance was Finola's presence. He knew Finola's directing temperament and Arrah's resistance to it. Once Finola was out of sight, Arrah's disposition would improve. He was certain of it.

He reached into the longboat and brought up a bolt of white satin. "Look at this. I'll even be bringing you a cloth for your wedding dress. Come now, love, and show your man how happy you are to be seeing him home." Once more he took her arm and tried to lead her in the direction of the castle. "Don't worry," he said, "she'll be gone in a day or two. For my way of thinking she's a goose for coming. Chasing after that rake like a bitch in heat. She sent a messenger that I was to come and get her and bring her here. What was I to do? She's me own bleeding sister."

Arrah was confused and irritated. Seaghan and Finola? What were they to each other? She needed to find Seaghan. He would explain this business about Finola. "I've things that need tending."

"What is it you've got to be doing that can't wait?"

"Bridgett needs some help with . . . cloth dyeing . . . and she's waiting for me."

"For the love of Christ, woman. Cloth dyeing on your mind when your man's plums is swelled to the size of cabbages?"

"I didn't know you were coming today! I promised Bridgett!"

"Bridgett! Not once in your life was you helpin' with cloth dyeing unless it was under duress from your mother. I used to hear you arguing. What the devil is getting into you?"

He tried to clasp her shoulders, but Carbri's hands felt strange on her body and she drew away. "Carbri, I . . ." He couldn't know how her feelings for him had changed. She wanted to tell him everything, to have it all out in the open. He had always been honest and truthful with her, and she wanted to be honest with him, but when she saw the bewildered look in his eyes, she couldn't bring herself to say anything else. Later she would explain everything to him, and warn him that if he married her, he would be displaced as tanaist.

She would do both things tonight at the feast. With a pretty serving wench and plenty of spirits, he would soon forget his disappointment. For now, she had to find Seaghan and distract Carbri with other things.

"You've brought some cordwood with you, I presume," she said. Because of the windswept nature of Eagle Island, the wood that grew there was not good for the big feast fires. There were some stands of strapping willow and alder as well as pine, but the best fires were made from the hot woods of beach and ash and even oak. Turf was used in everyday fires, but for feasts the aromatic, crackling fires made from the mainland logs were most desirable. Whenever a ship returned from the mainland, it brought wood with it.

"Cordwood!" said Carbri. "When I haven't held you in my arms for weeks. Arrah, what's gotten into you?"

She remembered the happiness on his face when they had been children and sailed their small ship together on the bay. For a moment she regretted everything that had happened with Seaghan, wished she could turn back time and see Carbri carefree and laughing again. But there was no going back. "We'll need it for the feast fires tonight, Carbri," she said. She addressed her sailors. "The rest of you row out and help him unload."

Hide-covered currachs slipped into the water.

"Aye," said Carbri. "That's a fine way to greet your man. He comes home from the sea and you send him back out!"

"The cook's ailing. And Bridgett is such a simpleton. She doesn't know how to boil water for the barber. She was wailing like a banshee when she saw your ship come in."

Trying not to allow his disappointment to show, Carbri shrugged his shoulders. "Aye, lads, well, that's the way she is." He walked back out into the waves. Hirple and Sebastian guided their small craft toward him.

Arrah watched the boat for a moment and then turned and walked toward the castle.

Sebastian steadied the boat and Hirple grabbed Carbri by his lean buttocks and helped pull him in. Sebastian and Hirple, rowing silently through a few long, easy waves, sat facing toward center. There were oars at Carbri's position but he left them alone and simply sat, shoulders slumped forward.

Hirple and Sebastian didn't like each other, but for the moment they needed each other's help. Each had watched the ensuing romance between the dark-bearded MacNamara and Arrah with uneasiness, for it foiled each of their plans. Each knew that even if Arrah married O'Connor, she would continue to be her own master. Both Sebastian and Hirple thought it was only a matter of time before their own plans came to fruition. Sebastian had continued to be of assistance to Arrah in any way he could. She had even smiled at him favorably. Hirple had since found a couple of sailors who were willing to participate in overthrowing Captain Girl. He, as Captain Hirple, would soon be in charge. In the meantime Eagle Island made for pleasant enough shore time.

But then MacNamara had returned and Sebastian saw his own hopes of becoming Arrah's lover dashed. Hirple, too, had seen his hopes vanish. The sailors would rise up with a little prodding against the woman, but not against the rough-mannered, huge-armed MacNamara. They'd seen him fight against the de Burgo swordsmen. There wasn't a man on board ship who would dare raise so much as an eyebrow against him, let alone a sword. Now O'Connor had returned, and Sebastian and Hirple listened and watched with interest.

Hirple listened with particular care to the statements about Finola and MacNamara. He had had enough experience with jealously to recognize that the green-eyed monster had bitten Arrah. Sebastian and Hirple rowed in unison. Hirple winked at Sebastian, then spoke to Carbri. "Well, that ain't exactly a warm welcome that Captain Girl was givin' to you!"

"Women," said Carbri. "They've always something about to take them away when a body will be wanting them."

"Aye, somethin'."

"Damned flux. Keeps their natures cranky as a speared shark," said Carbri.

"You say your sister has a feeling for MacNamara?"

"Aye. Damned blackguard, he is! He left her, the way he does with 'em all."

"*She* is not so disagreeable when she is close to him," said Sebastian carefully. They would have to proceed with caution. One never knew what a man's reaction was when it came to his women.

"No! He'll be having a way with them."

"They are capricious, no? One day yes, one day no."

"Well," said Hirple, "*she's* had her share of playing."

"Aye, she's not had luck in marriage."

Hirple took a breath and spoke gently. "Wasn't your sister I was—"

"What are you saying?" Carbri's shoulders straightened.

"A woman. She play when her man is leaving," said Sebastian.

"What the devil are you saying?"

"MacNamara's been stirring your stew!"

Carbri leaped at Hirple, sending the boat rocking crazily.

Sebastian shouted. "Captain! What Hirple says is true. Your woman . . . she is your woman no more. MacNamara, he—"

Carbri turned and slugged Sebastian so hard he fell backward into the water, making a large wave that splashed over the other two men in the boat. The boat itself nearly tipped.

"Rest easy, lad," said Hirple, cringing backward and grabbing both sides of the currach, trying to steady it. "Don't be pissing a storm at the Frenchy. 'Taint him been doin' the goat's jig in your mutton."

"Still your filthy tongue."

" 'Od's plums. I'll still it. I don't give a herring fart he's done your duty twixt your sheets. But he's done it, he has. Been droppin' anchor day and night, night and day!"

"Quiet!"

"Aye, aye, sir. But we was just thinkin' you should be knowin'."

Carbri felt numbness and pain at the same time. He was undone in a single stroke. He saw the wood spines of the boat and a dowel sealed with tar in a knothole. He felt like that knothole without a dowel, without anything.

"Give us a hand then to bring the Frenchy back in. He looks like a drownin' rat, he does," said Hirple.

Carbri sat motionless while Hirple pulled Sebastian into the boat. Sebastian sat on the seat, water dripping from his clothes and hair, collecting in a small pool at his feet in the bottom of the boat as Hirple took up the oars again.

"Come around!" ordered Carbri.

"What the devil for?"

"Turn around, I say."

"Rest easy, lad. Don't be getting your cords in a knot."

"I'll kill him."

"Now don't you go doin' somethin' foolish, sir."

"It's true, Captain Carbri," said Sebastian, wiping at a drop of water that was trickling down his nose. "MacNamara, he is a very good fighter. I have seen him with my own eyes."

"The Frenchy here's right. It would be takin' six men at once. And she'd be hatin' you for it the rest of your life. I've an idea, Captain Carbri. There's a better way to win your lady back than to try and kill the bedpresser."

Arrah had not liked what she heard about Finola and Seaghan. Again the words from the garden came back to her: *From princesses to serving girls.* He had been a lover of his father's wife. And what of it, she rebuked herself. He was a man, and a man was a man. And it didn't matter how many he had loved. He loved her now. She wanted to see him, wanted to feel his arms about her so that he could reassure her.

But Seaghan was not in the castle anywhere. He had gone and taken one of Reevnarg's eagles out to the hunt.

Be damned. She had the pearl dress she found in her mother's wardrobe. Without even trying, she was a hundred times more attractive than Finola. And if she wore that dress, Seaghan wouldn't so much as look at that pan-voiced creature again.

She began to shout orders for Bridgett in the kitchen, and busied herself with preparations for the evening feast.

The castle had been expecting Carbri, so the cattle had been butchered and hung in quarters. Now the meat, which had been basted with honey and salt and pressed garlic, was brought in and speared on the spits. The fires in the huge fireplaces were all bellowed and the meat put into place over the flames. Walnuts had been soaking in brine for nearly a week. Cowberries had been made into sweet and succulent spreads, then baked in sweet pastries, and these were carried into the great hall. Jugs of ale were set out. The entire castle was filled with the bustle of feeding and the anticipation of feasting.

Arrah bathed. Her shoulders were like ivory in the falling light of afternoon. She made small frothy nests with the soap and creamed her shoulders and breasts. And as she emerged from the bath she rose like Venus, beautiful and sensuous and desirous of love.

Mary rubbed her with towelling and Arrah's ivory and gold skin flushed. Mary harrumphed a great deal and cleared her throat several times and finally said, " 'Tis a great mistake you'll be making. Carbri's a fine lad. But yea won't be listening to anything I'll be telling yea."

When Arrah saw her image in the mirror, she cursed herself for cutting her hair. She remembered Seaghan's words about his stepmother's hair. It would take years for it to grow back to where it was before, down about her waist.

She lifted the silver dress from her wardrobe and slipped it over her shoulders.

Mary looked at her. "Yea'll be breaking that poor lad's heart when he sees yea."

The dress seemed to catch the torchlight and candlelight and reflect it in a hundred shades from green to purple to silver. The light from a torch caught a small ruby in the sword handle as she girded it to her waist, and it shone for a moment, liquid as a drop of blood.

The heavy wooden door swung open and Carbri entered the room. "Christ, Arrah!" was all he could say when he saw her, and then he was struck speechless, his mouth hanging open.

She stood looking at him for a moment, his lithe build, and the comely face, handsome in a boyish, slender way. She would have to tell him now, but when she opened her mouth to speak, the words caught like small hooks in her throat. She skirted the subject, cast out for a way to approach it. She went to the window and saw the oyster catchers and gulls along the beach. Overhead she saw the migrations of birds, the white-fronted geese and redwings, and barnacle geese that made their winter home in Ireland. She heard the sea and saw the seals in the distance, their glossy coats like slabs of black butter on the rocks. Because she couldn't say what she wanted to say directly, she said other things. "The barnacle goose is returned for winter."

"Aye," said Carbri.

"They've come early this year," she said.

"Aye." His voice was flat, without emotion.

She felt the discomfort, turned, and spoke slowly. "Do you know your clansman who goes by the name of Murrough?"

"Aye."

She waited for him to say something else, but he remained quiet. "He's causing some trouble," she said to break the silence.

"So I've heard."

She hesitated, then spoke carefully and formally. "MacNamara says that if you marry me you will be displaced as tanaist." Now that she'd said his name, the rest would be easier. She faced Carbri again. "MacNamara says that Geralde de Burgo is using Murrough and plotting against you."

"Do you know how the blackguard came to his knowledge?"

"He says he has spies."

"Women spies!" Carbri retorted. "Chambermaids and the wives of other men."

She had meant to tell him gently, but now she blurted the statement out in a single breath. "I don't want to marry you!"

"I suppose it's MacNamara you want to marry."

She was startled by his knowledge, had threatened Bridgett and Mary with banishment if either of them breathed a word of MacNamara to Carbri. Still, now that he had said it, she was relieved. She nodded. She could see Carbri's clear hazel eyes cloud with an expression of pain. She felt tears well at the back of her eyes. "Carbri, I didn't mean to hurt you."

"MacNamara said he loves you, and you believe him?" And then angrily he answered his own question. "Of course you believe him. Every woman believes him." Carbri looked at her and reached out his palms, then drew them back as if his hands hurt. He walked to the window and looked out. "MacNamara is a taker. He charms women and leaves them."

MISTRESS OF THE EAGLES

Arrah found Carbri's anger easier to deal with than his pain. Regardless of how many women Seaghan had made love to in the past, he couldn't have made love to them in the way that he made love to her. "I don't care what he's done before. I know he loves me."

"Do you know he loves Finola as well?"

"He may have her loved once, but he loves *me* now."

"He loves himself."

"We all love ourselves. You, too, Carbri O'Connor."

"You're many things. But I've never thought of you as a fool. Finola is the same with him. He's a bawd and a blackguard and a traitor to his own father."

"You're jealous of him. Because he's a better swordsman than you."

"Arrah! I was seeing what he did with Finola. I know what he's done with the wives of others. He takes everything from a woman, then he'll be leaving."

"It's not true."

He reached to take her hand. "Arrah, I love you. I've loved you from the time we were children. I don't care what happened between you and MacNamara. The devil take him. I want to marry you. I want to wake in the morning and know that you are there beside me. It's his way. He uses and casts off. He changes women more often than he changes his damn satin shirts. Marry me! Forget MacNamara!"

"I can't!" she cried.

"Do you want me to show you!" he shouted suddenly. "I'll show you how much MacNamara loves you. He's with some woman now! I heard laughter in one of the chambers."

He grabbed her hand and pulled her. Arrah came down the hallway eagerly with him. She needed to see Seaghan. If she could speak with him, he would clarify everything.

They went past several doors, then heard a woman's voice.

"You can't marry that French woman!"

The words made Arrah stop. *Marriage to a French woman.* No, it couldn't be Seaghan in there. Seaghan had never mentioned a French woman.

Carbri looked at her. His face was serious.

The woman's voice came again. "Seaghan. I always liked it when you touched me . . . there."

Arrah took the handle and pushed the door open silently.

Nothing could have prepared her for what she saw. Seaghan, his back to her, bent down over the bed. Finola lay on the bed, her skirts pulled up about her waist, her thighs splayed. Seaghan's head was down between Finola's thighs.

"Well, well," said Finola. Her voice before had been strange, serious, now it reverted to its singsong. "If isn't Little Miss Captain of the Herring Fleet."

Seaghan leaped up and turned around. The falling light caught the moist sheen of Finola's sex, which lay open and gaping like a wound.

Arrah had listened to this man's quiet, persuading voice; had made her body vulnerable to him, and her soul; had tasted him in her mouth; had known him so intimately that she could never imagine that she had lived without knowing him. She tasted betrayal now, a taste like iron.

"She leads quite a life, your wife to be, Carbi. Betrothal to the Joyce to start. Then betrothal to you. And in the meantime, a liaison with this stallion here, am I not right?" smiled Finola.

Arrah felt desperately cold, as though winter had come upon her.

Finola lay back, voluptuous and inviting as a harem princess, her mouth slightly open. She slid one knee closer to the other to close herself, and turned from her back to her side. She had had enough experience with love and physical desire without love to know that both MacNamara and Arrah were vulnerable for the moment. "Tell me, Arrah. Did he tell you that he would open your thighs—"

"Silence, Finola!" said Seaghan. "Arrah! It's not what you think. It's—"

"Did he say that he would make love to you like no one has ever made love to you before!" sang Finola again.

Arrah felt the blood leave her legs. She felt the floor come up. Damn. No! She wouldn't give in to the weakness. "Get out, both of you. Leave my island!"

Seaghan stepped toward her and reached out, but her hand went to her sword. Somewhere from within herself she had pulled out a sea-cold shell of control. "You'll go straight to hell, MacNamara."

"Arrah, listen."

"I won't listen."

"Damn you, you will listen." He crossed the room in two strides.

But Carbri pulled his sword. "Leave her!"

"Damn you, boy! Put your sword away!" And MacNamara kicked the weapon from Carbri's hand. It clanged across the stone floor. He gripped Arrah's shoulders with both hands. "I love you!" Seaghan shouted.

Carbri leaped after the sword and took it up. "I'm no boy. On guard!"

"Do you want to die, young fool?"

Carbri's sword menaced. His bright eyes were hard. "Leave or draw your steel!"

MacNamara released Arrah's shoulders and turned and faced Carbri. MacNamara hesitated, but when Carbri took a step toward him, he pulled his own sword.

Arrah stepped between the two men. She faced MacNamara. "Do you want to cause yet another death?" she asked. Her words were weapons; her aim was flawless. "Wasn't the death of your stepmother enough?" She felt her weapon find its target, saw the bright burst of pain in his dark eyes. Her words were devoid of all emotion. "I don't ever want to see you again. I'm mistress of Eagle Island. If you ever set foot on her shores, I'll order you killed."

MacNamara sheathed his weapon. His face was pale. The massive shoulders looked like a wall which was about to crumble. She had a final weapon and aimed it as MacNamara left. Her victory would be total. "Carbri," she said. "You and I will be married. Send for Father Thomas immediately."

PART III

CHAPTER 24

Bres was terribly unhappy living with Naira. He was, for all purposes, a traitor. He had betrayed his uncle, Brion, the very man who had raised him as a son.

It was customary for chieftains and other important personages to send their sons into fosterage to other families. Bres's father had sent him to Brion MacNamara. Normally Seaghan also would have been sent elsewhere for fosterage, but Brion loved Seaghan too much to part with him, and had insisted on raising him himself.

Seaghan and Bres had grown up as brothers. As young boys they had slept together in the same bed, like puppies from the same litter. As youths, they were virtually inseparable. Brion himself had taught them to ride together, to fight with swords together. He had even instructed the boys in the ways of love together.

Betraying Brion had been the most difficult choice of Bres's life and he had agonized over making it.

At the time he'd believed it was the right choice. His first loyalty had been to Seaghan, whom he loved as a brother, and Brion had been unfair in his treatment of Seaghan.

Seaghan had not been Tiltiu's first conquest. She gathered men to her, like a small flame gathers moths, flattering their maleness with her air of womanly fragility. She had such small hands, they could fit into the mouths of small jars.

Seaghan had been away, fighting in battles for his father's troops, when Brion first married Tiltiu. Bres had not gone to battle because he was recuperating from a thigh wound. He had fallen from his horse during a hunt and a wild boar had attacked him, ripping open his thigh with its tusk. At the wedding everyone had been stunned by Tiltiu's beauty.

Within a fortnight of her marriage to Brion, Tiltiu was making sheep's eyes at the guards. She was very beautiful in that delicate way, and few men could resist the need to protect her. She would ask for a guard's arm if she walked up a set of stairs; or if she rode a horse, she would ask another guard to lead it for her, for she was afraid that the horse might leap unexpectedly and throw her off.

Tiltiu had made eyes at Bres as well, but he had four sisters, and when he returned home to visit his mother and father, he saw the manipulations of his sisters as they primped and played with would-be suitors, affecting feminine frailness, seeming to be soft as flowers, when earlier he had seen them scrapping like tigresses over the attentions of a particular suitor. Bres was not deceived by Tiltiu's pretended delicateness. She was like a poison flower.

Seaghan had achieved a formidable reputation with the servant girls, but the raunchy bawdiness of kitchen wenches proved inadequate training for the soft smiles of Tiltiu. Bres had tried to warn Seaghan, but the warnings were lost in the light of Tiltiu's downcast eyes.

Later Seaghan had told Bres that Tiltiu had come to his room, telling him she was afraid because she'd had frightening dreams. She asked him only to hold her for a while.

When Bres learned of Brion's plan to attack Reevnarg O'Donnell and kill Seaghan, he had decided to warn Seaghan of the impending attack. Considering Brion's unfair treatment of Seaghan, it was an honorable thing to do—perhaps not wise, but honorable. Over the years Bres had tried to reason with his uncle to forgive Seaghan, but the old man had bellowed at every mention of Seaghan's name, and cursed him instead like a devil, vowing to kill him if he ever returned to Ireland.

And then Bres had met Debrogail, and in the light of her smile, and in the magic of her healing hands, the memory of his betrayal had faded. Had he been able to travel to France with Debrogail, he could have forgotten his treasonous act.

With the companionship of Seaghan and Debrogail, he could have tolerated being an outcast.

But he could not tolerate it living with Naira. Even though Debrogail was dead, he couldn't forget her. When he made love to Naira, he always thought of Debrogail. Naira wanted him to keep the candles lit when they made love so she could see his handsome body, but he always refused. Once he'd opened his eyes and seen Naira's contorted face beneath him, and then suddenly he had not been able to continue what he'd started.

When he remembered Debrogail, he always felt empty, like half a man, and after he made love to Naira, he felt like no man, like a coward, like a traitor, to himself, to his uncle, and Debrogail.

And in the eyes of the O'Donnell troops, he saw mistrust. He was a MacNamara, the enemy to them, even though he had married Naira O'Donnell. And when he saw MacNamara men chained as prisoners, he saw nothing but hate in their eyes for marrying the daughter of the enemy. Hatred was around him on every side.

He wanted to go back to Brion MacNamara. It wasn't too late. Brion didn't know that it was he who had alerted Reevnarg of the MacNamara attack. Taking part in the attack had masked his complicity.

He had also led two successful battles against the family of Naira's former husband, and beaten them back. She was now in firm control at Glen Head and could no longer use the excuse that she needed him to lead her soldiers.

When he had been defending Glen Head Castle, he was swept up in the movement of battle. But now that peace had been reestablished, he felt not only the wearying loss of his love, but also of his MacNamara companions. He wanted to drink again among friends, to engage in hurling matches with them, and to recount the victories of war with kinsmen.

"Naira," he said, "there are some men who can live as an outcast. I'm not one. I'm not happy at Glen Head. I want to return to MacNamara lands."

"Happy," she said, her blue eyes hard. Her eyes were always hard. "What man is happy? Happiness is for the cows chewing their cuds in the pastures, happiness is not for men who feel and breathe and think. Men fight, and win battles, and men kill other men. You mope around here like an old woman."

"Naira. You're beautiful. Why must you be so hard with all your words?"

"Because life does not like gentleness. The doe is gentle and she's slaughtered by wolves. The world is a place of fang and claw."

"Even the cruelest animal has places of softness, even the soft underbelly of a tiger is soft. Is there no place in you that's soft?"

"I was soft, Bres, obedient, the kind of girl my father wanted, yet he always saved his smiles for Arrah. It was she whom he took riding and eagling, and damn him, he even gave Eagle Island to her. He always said he wanted softness in a woman. Yet, me, who was soft, he never favored. Even her mischief he favored.

"When she let loose his damned eagle, he took her and he beat her. She was crying when she came home, but afterward, when she returned with that bird, he said, 'Aye, there's a tough-hearted girl for you.' So don't talk to me of softness. Do you know what it does to a girl to have her father bestow his smiles on one sister, while he treats the other as if she doesn't exist?

"Finally, I decided that I would be like Arrah. She had built a small boat and sailed it around Eagle Bay. She and Deb—" but she didn't say the rest of Debrogail's name. "She and Carbri O'Connor. 'Come, Naira,' they called. 'Come join us.' And they were laughing and giggling so much on their sailboat that I did join them.

"I wanted to please him. And Reevnarg smiled when he saw us, and I was pleased, for he had smiled at me also. Except that he took both our heads and plunged us into the sea. 'So you want to be sailors, do you?' he asked. It was the one time I joined in, and I thought I was going to drown. And after that I grew afraid, and now, Bres, I'm afraid of losing you."

"Do you know, Naira? Sometimes when you are soft, I could care for you."

"And if you were a little harder, Bres, I would care for you more."

"I've seen my own uncle kill his wife because of hardness, and I've seen him cast out his own son because of hardness, and I've seen him scream like a man wracked with pain because of hardness. I want to leave before I see that happen to you."

"Bres. There's something you should know." She smiled. It was the first time he'd seen her smile in a long time. He thought of Debrogail's smile. Naira rarely smiled these days, and when she did, she smiled with cold eyes. But now her smile had a different quality, almost warm. "Bres," she said softly, "I'm carrying your child. Are you going to play the traitor to your own child as he grows this very minute in my womb?"

The news stunned Bres. He had performed his husband's duties with Naira, but they were loveless couplings, a mindless duty, during which he thought of Debrogail. It never occurred to him that she would get with child. He remembered Debrogail laughing, singing, dancing. How very different things would have been if Naira had not discovered them that night. It might have been Debrogail telling him she carried his child. He would have been overjoyed, and would have swept her up in his arms, high over his head.

Naira came close and took both his hands in hers. "Forget Debrogail! She was being porked by another man when she died." Naira began to cry. Two great tears trickled down her cheek and stopped at the corners of her mouth. "Debrogail's dead. I'm your wife. I was soft enough to allow you to put a child into me. Will you hold me as if you're pleased?"

Debrogail's dead. Debrogail's dead. He had an image of her squeezed to death by a tree, while she was being fucked by another man. He had betrayed her by marrying Naira and in turn she had betrayed him. Tears sprang to his eyes. He didn't love the woman who carried the child, but the child was his, and would carry his name and he would stay.

Naira noticed his tears and reached up her hand and wiped at them. "My darling Bres. I'm so wonderfully happy. I've finally done something to please you."

For a long time he thought the longing for Debrogail would never pass. And yet after time, it did pass.

And with Naira's growing pregnancy, her temperament softened. She became good-humored and she smiled often, and he began to feel some affection for her as he saw her stomach swell with child.

To try to forget the image of Seaghan MacNamara bent between Finola's thighs, Arrah threw herself into the rigors of sailing with a fury. Memories of Seaghan abounded at Eagle Island—the chamber where they had made love, the beach where they had walked, the grove of trees where they had lain together, so she absented herself from these places and went where there were no memories of him. She was always on the sea, en route to Portugal, Spain, and Africa, trading, carrying goods, bartering. Climbing the masts, fighting the wind, fighting the sea, furling and unfurling the sails, these were the means by which she tried to blot out his betrayal from her mind.

It never occurred to her that something might be amiss at home. Arrah had never seen her father in any state except one in which he exuded power and robust health. While she was away from Eagle Island, she simply assumed that his power and strength were assured, and that as long as he was alive he would remain chieftain of the O'Donnell and in firm control of Eagle Island and his territories on the mainland.

But Reevnarg, crossing a bog on one of his excursions on the mainland, was bitten by mosquitoes and developed malaria. He was given an infusion made from wood avens and feverfew, but nothing seemed to help him. News passed that he would soon die.

As news of Reevnarg's imminent death spread, leaders of lesser O'Donnell septs began vying for power. Like sharks in a feeding frenzy, they began to attack Reevnarg's more vulnerable mainland positions. Some of Reevnarg's men deserted and went with other O'Donnell clans who had made alliances with Glundel Joyce and refused to pay their tributes to Reevnarg.

Other of his land troops, lacking strong leadership, fell into disarray on the fighting field and were defeated.

With Reevnarg's illness, Seaghan MacNamara's predictions about Carbri losing the title of O'Connor tanaist came true.

Murrough, Carbri's clansman, who had been jealous of Carbri's being named tanaist, formed an alliance with Geralde de Burgo, and they took Dunmore Castle from Carbri. Carbri managed to escape with his life, but without Reevnarg's troops coming to his assistance, he lost his title to tanaist and therefore all possibility of becoming chieftain.

Arrah was in Portugal when news of Carbri's defeat came to her. She had no choice but to return at once.

At Eagle Island she found Carbri, downcast as a whipped dog. The loss of the position of tanaist was a terrible blow to him, and he had sought solace for his defeat in the ale jug and for six weeks had been drunk as a boiled owl. Reevnarg had had a relapse, and lay shivering in his bed, his face gray as if death waited, hiding beneath his bed.

When Arrah learned that not only the O'Donnell properties on the mainland were under threat of attack, but Eagle Island was in jeopardy as well, she flew into a fury. No one was going to take her home from her. She grabbed Carbri's ale jug and smashed it on the floor so the ale ran in a stream about her. She ordered him locked in his chambers for three days until he sobered up.

With Arrah's spirited return, a sense of purpose was rekindled in the soldiers at Eagle Island. Glundel Joyce had formed an alliance with O'Donnell septs who wanted to control the island. He attacked, but Eagle Island, because of its cliffs, was a difficult location to take. Arrah ordered archers and swordsmen out to the beach. Glundel Joyce and the O'Donnell septs were beaten back.

Arrah set immediately to regain some of her father's position on the mainland. If men's loyalties could not be counted on on the basis of blood, then they could be bought with gold. She had no choice but to hire mercenaries.

She sent to Rathlin Island for the Scottish mercenaries called galloglasses. They were heavily armed fighting men, each of whom was always accompanied by an arms bearer and a boy. They carried six-foot-long heavy battle axes, and wore long mail coats, but were skilled with other weapons as well. They demanded very high wages, and cost a great deal to billet.

Captain Whip's gold, which had once seemed so abundant to a young woman running from an arranged marriage, was quickly diminishing as she paid out mounds and mounds of coinage to the mercenaries.

With Reevnarg's illness and the subsequent turmoil, tributes had fallen on the mainland. She had no revenue. No one had even exacted tolls and steerage fees from the merchant vessels that traveled back and forth along the coast.

Arrah took up the activity that her father had once overseen. Many captains were surprised to see a woman exacting steerage fees and refused to accept the terms of her toll. She ordered their ships attacked and took possession of them herself.

Within weeks of her return she had established herself in firm control of Eagle Island and the seas around it.

Reevnarg made an eventual recovery, but he was not the Reevnarg of old. He no longer strode. Instead, he walked like a man who was afraid of falling. Sometimes he would sit in his chair for days, wrapped in sealskins, and shiver.

On land, unfortunately, her mercenaries were suffering defeat. Arrah was fighting on two fronts: on one side she fought the alliance of the revolting O'Donnell septs who had linked forces with Glundel Joyce, and on the other side she was confronted with the combined forces of Murrough O'Connor and Geralde de Burgo. The enemy armies consisted mainly of kern, which were unarmored foot soldiers. They were not very effective soldiers, but they outnumbered her mercenaries.

She needed more men. If she tolerated defeat on the mainland then with time her enemies would again attack Eagle Island.

This time she sent to Scotland for large numbers of the galloglass mercenaries, but to pay their high wages she had no choice but to plunder.

Patch was against her idea to resort to piracy. "Sailing is one thing, lass, but plunder another," he said. "They'll hang ye for it."

"If I don't attack my enemies, they'll attack me. They were jealous of my father's power, but as a woman they hate me. They think I have no right to Eagle Island."

She attacked vessel after vessel. She would swoop unseen out of the mist like a ghost ship, and plunder the ponderous merchants and then disappear into the mist again.

The merchants carried fine cloths, heavy brocades, taffetas, lace. But these were inappropriate for her active life shipboard, so she sent them to continental markets and ordered them sold secretly. She had her own women sew her knee-length breeches and jerkins of the softest skin of the red deer. These she ordered lined with satin. She wore silk shirts. Her hips and thighs were sleek. Mary told Arrah, "Bare yer breasts to the wind, lass. It's what yer sailors believe work magic for them." And so Arrah unlaced her shirts, and like the figurehead of a ship, showed the tawny bare mounds of her breasts.

Spurred on by her complete and utter lack of fear, the spirit of her men was high. They raided with a vengeance, fighting with as much fury as twice their number.

Arrah drove her men, but most of all, she drove herself. She was active in every waking minute of each day so she wouldn't ever have to worry about Eagle Island being attacked again. She worked long into the night, sometimes falling asleep at her table, and Carbri, who had sobered up and returned to his old self, would come and wake her. "Come to bed," he would say to her gently when they were on shore together, but she would push his hand away and begin at her work again—tallying, planning, drawing charts for her men.

One day she overheard Patch and Mary talking. "MacNamara's in France," she heard Patch say. "He's fighting against the English."

Arrah stormed into the room where the two stood. "If I ever hear you mention his name again, I'll have you sent from Eagle Island, do you understand?" Not only had MacNamara betrayed her affections with Finola, but it was because she had been trying to forget him that she had been absent from Eagle Island. If she had been present, she would have had the sense to make certain that none of her father's troops deserted on the mainland. The O'Donnell would not have lost many of their vast properties there. As far as she was concerned, MacNamara's entire wooing of her was nothing more than a ploy to undermine O'Donnell power.

"He didn't mean you any harm, lass," said Patch.

"I mean it, Patch. You've been loyal to me, but no one will ever put my home in jeopardy again."

Patch looked at the floor. "I understand," he said quietly.

Naira labored through childbirth an entire night, through the day, and through a second night. It was a boy child, she was certain of it. Boys were more difficult births than girls, but the pain would be worth it. With the birth of a son, Bres's loyalty to her would be assured.

Because it was a difficult birth all the doors at Glen Head Castle were opened. But as Naira's travail continued and the child still did not emerge, other household articles were opened: trunks were unlocked and the mid-wife gave orders for bottles to be uncorked. Four of the strongest men in the castle were called to shake the birth bed to help bring the child.

Finally after midnight a child began to emerge, not head first, but buttocks first, folded in half, her thighs and buttocks bruised from the long labor. The women in attendance crossed themselves and whispered prayers. A breech birth was an omen of ill luck. But the worst was yet to come. The baby was born with an enormous birthmark that covered half her face and chest. Never would a girl find a husband looking like that.

"You have a baby girl," said the midwife to Naira. She did not tell her about the birthmark.

Exhausted from her labor, Naira smiled weakly.

The midwife rubbed the child with goose lard so that it would be strong, and then to countervent the effects of the birthmark, she wrapped the child in a boy's nightgown so that she would have plenty of men about her. Then the midwife took the child and put her in a shovel and took her to the chimney and held her over a low flame. All the women were convinced that the child was a changeling brought by evil fairies, and that the fire would make the evil spirit rush up the chimney. The midwife began to chant: "Burn, burn, burn! If of the devil burn, but if from God stay safe from harm."

The child began to cry loudly. There was the smell of heated cloth. The child began to scream. The midwife pulled the shovel from above the embers and carried her to her mother.

Naira looked at the child and cried out when she saw the birthmark.

"I've wrapped her in a boy's gown," said the midwife. "You'll have no difficulty finding a husband for her."

"I don't want her," said Naira. "She'll be a burden to me all my life."

"God has sent her to you," said the midwife.

Exhausted, Naira turned her head to the side and fell to sleep. The midwife lay the child next to her mother.

In the middle of the night, Naira woke, groggy from her labor. For a moment she was disoriented. Candles burned low beside her bed, wax dripping in bizarre shapes. Then she remembered she'd given birth. She looked down. The horrid-looking baby with the terrible purple face slept beside her. The midwife snored softly in a chair beside the fire. Naira gently lifted herself for she was still in pain. Groping behind her, she pulled the pillow from behind her head and pressed it over the baby's face. The child struggled softly, like a kitten in a sack. It made a soft mewing sound and after a few minutes it lay still. Naira looked at it with cold eyes.

She put her pillow back under her head, and then taking the child to her breast, she began to scream. "My child is dead!"

The midwife jumped in her chair.

"My baby! My baby!" wailed Naira.

The midwife, hands clutched as though she was praying, approached the bed. "Don't cry so," she said. "It's the will of God that she be taken from you."

"You killed her," screamed Naira. "It's your fault!"

As time passed, Finola realized that marriage to Seaghan MacNamara was an impossibility. She had not seen him since that day in Eagle Castle. He had left for France and had never returned, and when she sent a messenger to him, the messenger came back saying that MacNamara was on the battlefields and that he had no wish to receive any more communications from Finola.

Finola began to search actively for another husband.

She had heard of Geralde de Burgo's strange prowess. She made up an excuse that she wanted her son to be put into fosterage at the de Burgo castle as an act of atonement for her brother's marrying Arrah O'Donnell.

Debrogail was present in the main hall when news arrived that Finola O'Connor was asking an audience with de Burgo.

De Burgo flew into a rage. "Throw the treacherous minx into the dungeon and hang her tomorrow."

Glundel Joyce, who was also present, stroked his white beard and stepped forward. "If I may," he said, "I think you might find it of interest to listen the woman out!"

"Cursed bit of Eve's flesh!" De Burgo's naturally florid face was even redder than usual. "I'll wager she manipulated Carbri into running off with that O'Donnell woman. My Agneis still weeps."

Glundel Joyce touched de Burgo's arm. "Calm yourself. Agneis, gentle soul that she is, will weep less after she's wed to me." Glundel's first wife, the daughter of Reevnarg's kinsmen, had died. In fighting against Arrah, Glundel had noticed that many of the O'Donnell septs were losing their courage. Many had decided to revert their loyalty back to Arrah. Glundel had abandoned the O'Donnell septs and decided to marry himself into a stronger family and asked for Agneis de Burgo's hand. De Burgo had granted his permission.

De Burgo seemed somewhat mollified by Glundel's comment. "Aye,

Glundel, it'll be good to have you as my son-in-law. A man wants reasoned men about him as he grows older."

Glundel continued, "I have a secret source at the Castle of the Eagles. She tells me that there has been great hatred between Arrah and Finola because of Seaghan MacNamara."

When Debrogail heard the name MacNamara, she caught her breath. She had never forgotten Bres with his handsome face, Bres with his long, lean limbs, lithe as a stag. Geralde de Burgo had treated her kindly, and accepted Magnus as her brother. As de Burgo's songbird, she was no longer a common servant and didn't have to accept the attentions of men the way she once had. But when she sang her songs of love, she thought of Bres. The heavy solidness of his manhood in her, the tender touch of his fingers on her chin. At nights in her bed she ached for him.

Glundel went on. "You might find it advantageous to speak to Finola. One never knows when a family rift can bring good luck to outsiders."

Finola bowed low to de Burgo when she entered his main hall. She had reddened the cleavage between her breasts and scented them with water of rose. She was everything his wife had not been: intelligent, blatantly sexual. She looked directly at him when she spoke. She formed her lips around each syllable of each word languidly, sensually, as though she was sucking his cock. When she yawned she made it look as though she was bringing him to climax.

Within an hour of meeting each other, Finola and de Burgo were in bed. De Burgo had rubbed his secret powder on his phallus and by the time he could no longer hold back the rush of pleasure, she was wailing like a pleasured banshee beneath him.

Night after night Debrogail heard the feral whinings of Finola as de Burgo ploughed into her. Night after night Debrogail dreamed of Bres.

Arrah lay on a bed of yellow leaves, the sky clear overhead. Seaghan MacNamara lay beside her, his wide chest exposed. She kissed Seaghan's cheek. But the kiss woke her and she realized she was kissing Carbri.

He woke. She accepted him, felt the thrusts of his want. When Carbri was finished, she rose immediately from her bed, threw on a robe and rowed out to her ships. It was then that Arrah stood on the deck and vowed to herself that never again would she dream or think of MacNamara. He had nearly cost her the loss of her home. Never again would she allow Eagle Island to be made vulnerable.

In battle she was able to forget MacNamara. She threw herself into acquiring territories with even greater vigor. The more territory in her control, the less chance of an attack of her enemies against her home.

She was very beautiful, but with an edge to her that was chilling. Some people said that her body had become inhabited by the spirit of the war goddess. It was well known that Arrah O'Donnell never left her chambers without three daggers, as well as her sword and two pistols. She handled her swords and pistols as well as any soldier. Battles were fought, and with her large number of imported mercenaries, she was victorious. The war goddess was on her side: her area of influence continued to push farther south, reaching to St. Brendan's Sea.

The tiger grew into a sinewy and magnificent beast. When Seaghan betrayed her, she had thought of getting rid of Kian, but realized she had become too fond of him. Once he chewed through his hemp cord leash and she awoke to find his yellow eyes staring at her, his head close to hers, his tiger breath hot on her cheek. He frightened her so badly that after that, he was attached with a golden chain at the foot of her work table. Sometimes when she worked she would rest her bare feet on Kian's side, digging her toes into the soft fur.

Hirple and some of the other sailors attempted a mutiny, but Sebastian alerted her to it, and it was quashed. The conspirators were hanged from the yardarm, all except Hirple, who managed to jump overboard. But the sharks caught him, and for a brief moment the water about the ship reddened with his blood. For his loyalty, Sebastian was made captain of his own ship, a captured Portuguese caravelle called the *Saragossa*. Patch was offered the captainship of a bark, but he refused, telling Arrah that he preferred instead to sail with her. Hook and Mute stayed with her as well.

Because the old woman had tried to kill her, Arrah was afraid to use the nutlets of the gromwell plant to prevent conception. Twice Arrah was with child and twice she miscarried. The first time she was involved in a battle on board ship; the second time, a battle on land. The second time her recovery was long in coming. Mary sat beside her bed night after night. The child, had it come to term, would have been a boy. Carbri took to drinking for several weeks, in turn mumbling then shouting that other men's wives were content to walk carefully and to sit on pillows when they were with child, but his wife went into battle.

By this time Arrah's hair had grown long once again so that the chestnut tumult fell midway on her back. Her assets also continued to grow. She now had twelve ships at her command and nearly a thousand head of cattle and horses. Horsemanship was the one thing she enjoyed almost as much as sailing. She loved the control, the power of her stallions between her thighs. The serfs eyed her in complete awe as she rode across the hills, her hair flowing about her arms, the tiger running beside her.

She had given Carbri two of his own ships. But there were whispers among the sailors about his ability as a captain. "Forgot the pull of the current . . . We had to claw like the devil." But the whispers always stopped when Arrah was about. Her fury regarding lack of loyalty was well known among them.

There were always pitchers of ale in front of Carbri when he sat at the table, or usquabaugh. And as the evening wore on, Carbri wouldn't bother to fill his own tankard, but drank straight from the jug so that the liquid spilled from his mouth onto his jerkin. He would wipe his hands down his chest and on his thighs. "Arrch!" he would say. "The meads of Murrisk make a man proud to be an Irishman." Sometimes his nature would change with drinking. Then he would look at Arrah. "Aye, there is my wife. She can be sailing a ship around Ireland blindfolded, but can she be giving a man a son?"

But the next day, he would revert to his old self. "Aye, Arrah," he would exclaim. "You'll be having the damned nicest arse this side of hell."

After the death of her first child, Naira had been afraid to conceive again for fear that a second child would be born with a birthmark. Originally she had put all her hopes on the child she carried, thinking that as a father, Bres would become more aggressive in the acquisition of lands. But he had remained remote, and he had no interest at all in fighting. He seemed to be held prisoner by some misguided sense of conscience.

Other men flipped their loyalties from side to side as easily as a stone was flipped over, but not Bres. Often at night he spoke in his sleep, uttering words such as "traitor," and "pardon, Uncle, for my betrayal."

He was not the husband his comely, vigorous looks had promised when first she had lain eyes on him.

When Reevnarg had been struck ill with malaria, she had tried to persuade Bres to go and take control of Eagle Island, or go and collect the tributes on the mainland, but he had refused, saying that he was a Mac-Namara, not an O'Donnell. Eagle Island was not his island, and O'Donnell tributes were not his tributes. Then Arrah had returned, retaking control of Eagle Island.

When he learned of the child's death, he simply sighed and said, "It's God's punishment against me for betraying my uncle." He had fallen again into torpidity and total lack of interest. It was as though his spirit had left him, and she found herself wishing that he would leave Glen Head so she could be free to marry another man, someone who would assist her in her ambitions. But Bres didn't even seem to have the vigor in his bones to take up and return to the damned MacNamara lands, which he seemed to pine for endlessly.

The only time he came to life and acted like a man was when that fool Carbri O'Connor came to take him hunting for deer. Then some of his former manliness returned. He smiled when he returned, his face brightened with fresh air and color, and he and Carbri would sit for hours drinking and talking. But as soon as Carbri left, Bres would return to his dejected state.

If spirit had left Bres, it burned in the form of envy in Naira. Over the years, Arrah had regained control of everything Reevnarg had lost, even gaining substantial amounts of territory. Arrah, with her ships and army of mercenaries, became wealthier by the day.

All Naira had was a single castle on Glen Head. Arrah had tributes all down the west coast. She had countless dresses in her wardrobe as well, robes of the kind that Naira could never obtain. Arrah had pearls, rubies, and emeralds, and when Naira went to visit her she was fed on plates made from pure gold.

Whenever Naira saw Arrah, Naira smiled her warmest sisterly smile, but inside she seethed.

When Naira first met Bres she had gone to the old fisherwoman, who had given Naira something which made Bres fall in love with her. The old fisherwoman had moved to a deserted hovel not far from Glen Head. Naira saw her as little as possible. She had learned to hate the old woman as much as she hated Arrah. Each time Naira saw the old midwife, with her hideous birthmark, Naira was reminded of the terrible secret the midwife had told her.

And then mercifully the old woman had died. Naira was glad to get rid of her. Her love potions, her attempt to kill Arrah by tricking her to swim some stupid underground passage had all failed. The midwife had been nothing but a silly old fisherwoman with a fisherwoman's mentality. Naira was tired of the pathetic revenge of the fisher people.

She had to seek someone with greater power to destroy Arrah. This time Naira went to see a woman who had a reputation as a witch.

She lived in a decrepit house on the edge of Lough Crosse, surrounded by honking geese and scurrying pigs.

Naira wondered why it was that witches chose to live in such deplorable surroundings when they had the power of prophecy and magic.

Naira hadn't even dismounted when the old woman said in a voice that scraped like the dried skin of a shark against wood, "I know why you've come."

Under the old woman's red skirt, wide blue-veined feet splayed outward.

The witch led Naira into her house. "Nothing comes without a price. I require your gold as well as three drops of blood from your left breast."

Naira swallowed, but agreed. She took her gold bracelet from her wrist and put it into the witch's shrivelled hand. The witch tucked the article into her pocket, then went to a side cupboard made of wicker and brought back a wooden cup.

"Take your gown from your shoulders."

Naira did as she was told. She shivered in the cool air.

The old woman touched Naira's breast. Her hands were like slivers of ice.

Naira caught her breath sharply.

"Your hatred," continued the old woman, "is carved on your face and has turned your eyes to stone. Beware of what you ask me to do. Vengeance is one thing; envy another. When the devil sees it, he makes it grow."

"I want Arrah O'Donnell dead," said Naira without hesitation.

"Very well," said the old woman.

She brought a dagger and a stone and a bowl of water, and she began working the knife against the stone, back and forth, back and forth, first one side of the dagger and then the other. A gray, grinding paste began to form on the stone. Naira shivered and pulled her robes up more closely over her shoulders.

But the old woman reached out with a cold, scrawny hand and pushed Naira's robe down again. "You must sit with your shoulders and breasts bared; otherwise, the spirit won't come to your blood."

Naira loosed the cloak, but she couldn't stop herself from shivering.

Now the woman lifted the knife to Naira's breast on the underside. Naira felt the cold metal there. "I warn you," said the woman, "don't cry out, or the spell will be broken."

She slowly drew the knife point along the curve of Naira's breast. Naira swallowed against the cold metal but she didn't cry out.

The old woman took the blood that ran like a small thin line and scraped it into the cup. This she mixed with some water and ash from her fire, then added a secret sight powder. She went to some jars on her shelf and mixed in some of their contents: dried cat's flesh that she had powdered with the use of a mortar; bat's tongues; a frog's skin, removed while it was alive; and the black, congealed blood from a two-headed pig. These things she mixed and heated over the light of a fish-oil lamp, and then drank.

Naira drew back in horror. The witch began to speak, jibberish at first, then more clearly. "Don't draw back from me in repugnance, for you with your envy are more evil than I. You've already suffocated one child. You must sacrifice a second if you wish success.

"The golden eagle lays two eggs. The stronger of the eaglets pushes the smaller one out of the nest so that he alone will survive from the nourishment his parents bring him. It is the way of all things. On a flower, if there are too many blossoms, they all take from the stalk and none grow large. But remove all the other and the single blossom that's left will grow large and strong. If you want to be strong, you must first kill Arrah. But to do so you must first weaken her.

"She is with child again. She will travel to Portugal, and will be in a weakened condition on her return. You must kill her child before the child touches land, otherwise she'll grow yet more powerful. Nothing takes the strength from a woman more than the death of her child. If you wish to defeat Arrah O'Donnell, kill her child."

When Naira returned to Glen Head, she called her messenger to her, and paying him with gold sent him to Portugal, to the port of Lisbon. "Keep your watch for a ship captained by Arrah O'Donnell. Keep your wits about you. When she docks, hire a corsair to follow her. There will be a newborn on board. The child must be sworded and hurled into the sea."

CHAPTER
25

The third time Arrah had become pregnant, Carbri had pleaded with her. "Please, I beg you, take care of yourself and our child. Refrain from the life of the sea." She sat in her chair; he took her hands in his and knelt before her. "I love you, Arrah. You're so lovely I want to have another like you—a small Arrah that I can hold in my arms and bounce on my knee. I want to be able to love our child as well as I love you." She saw the sadness in the clear, pale hazel of his eyes.

Arrah no longer felt the hurt of MacNamara. Love was like a bruise, a dark-blue coloring that disappeared with time. It was a lesson to be learned. She took Carbri's hand in hers. He was a gentle, good man.

"All right, I'll do as you ask."

His smile seemed worth the sacrifice.

"If you want to sail, sail with me. I'll take you wherever you want to go."

For a time she had stayed on land, taking walks along the sea and picking sea shells. But then the sea began to beckon to her distant eyes again, and she decided that Carbri or no, she would sail for Portugal. She still had two months before her pregnancy came to term.

Carbri, angry with the pointlessness of talking to her, took up drink again.

Arrah had advanced a Galway builder a sum of money for a new ship, but there had been many delays and the ship still wasn't finished. Arrah knew it was time to abandon the *Twilight Moon*. Teredo, the shipworms, had done terrible damage to the hull and there was only so much patching and filling with pitch that could be done. Nonetheless, she loved her first ship the best of them all and planned to take it on its last voyage.

In Portugal Arrah saw the brightly tiled roofs and the magnificent flowers, huge as a man's palms, in the market. In the hot, busy streets she heard the noisy cackle of the vendors and the raucous music of the gypsies.

She tasted the sweet wines of its sun-covered hills. Arrah was beautiful in her pregnancy, like ripe fruit. Her skin, always radiant, now took on even greater luster. But Portugal did not clear the cobwebs from her brain as she had hoped. The heat made the heaviness of her pregnancy unbearable.

She wanted to leave, but a fortnight of storms followed. Each day she awoke to a wind- and rain-pelted dawn. Under different circumstances, she would have dared the storms, but now she had another life to think of. Carbri had extracted a promise from her that she wouldn't sail if the weather was bad. Each movement of the child in her womb reminded her of that promise. So she waited. She was irritable and hot with nothing to occupy her. She tried to sleep to take away the boredom, but sleep wouldn't come. At night she turned from side to side, the sheets on her berth clammy with humidity. During the day, she paced the deck of her ship like a tiger in a cage.

In the middle of one night's storm, the aft mast snapped off. Arrah was furious with herself. It had been stupid to sail an old ship because of sentiment. Another delay would ensue. Arrah felt her child move inside of her.

Finally the *Twilight Moon* was sailing again. The mast had been stained with pine resin to keep it free from the effects of the sea water, and was still a golden color in its newness.

The ship carried silks, Portuguese wine, and salt, as well as fruits and coffee, the new drink from Arabia, which Arrah particularly enjoyed. She found its dark, strong taste more invigorating than the yellow flag seeds which her servants roasted and made into a hot drink, or the thin mint and camomile infusions her mother used to drink. And then one night when the moon was full, Arrah was taking a sip of coffee when she suddenly let the cup slip from her hand. It crashed to her cabin floor with a rattle, spilling the dark liquid. Mary came running and helped Arrah to her berth.

There was a knock on the door, and Patch burst into the cabin. He saw Arrah lying in bed, her face so pale he almost didn't recognize it, and for a moment he thought his captain was dying, but then he remembered his own wife, and when she had her children. "There'll be a sail silhouetted against the moonlight. Far on the horizon," he said.

"Fool!" yelled Mary. "We're busy now," and without another word she slammed the door in his face.

Like her mother's parturition, Arrah's, too, was difficult and long. Mary held Arrah's hand during the labor, and bathed her face in cool water. Mary, who'd never had any experience as a midwife but who'd had two babies, tried to cover her own fright and concern by talking the entire time. "Aye. It's just like when I was birthing me own. Aye. Stubborn, they was, the both of them. Had to push like the devil."

The child was long in coming. Arrah cried out repeatedly.

The sailors were quiet, growing progressively frightened each time they heard her cries. The sailors felt a vague uncertainty about Arrah. She had a kind of weariness in her body that they'd never seen in her before. They glanced at the master's cabin and dark thoughts rose from their hearts to their minds. They remembered sayings they'd heard on land. *A woman giving birth was an evil thing. Devils were about her.*

Patch touched his pistol. He knew what was on their minds. They would kill him first before they went to the cabin. Mute, too, was heavily armed and stood close by, and Hook kissed Angel. "Aye, Angel, darlin'. We'll look after our captain, won't we?"

Mary wrung her hands and prayed to God, while cursing him for making birthing such a difficult thing. "Aye, that's a damned man for yea! He'll be taking his pleasure and then leaving the woman with the pain. The good Lord in heaven, he weren't no different. Leaving Mary to be lying in a stable to be giving birth, while He was up there in heaven. Cozy on His high throne with His feet up, I'll be wagering. Comf'y as fleas on a dog. Yea got hips on yea, lass. Damn it. Yea got plenty of hips but what's a body to do when a babe is to be birthed bottom first. Lord, if He was ever to be birthing, He'd be making it a lot easier, I'll tell yea!"

At dawn the waters were silent, the air heavy and oppressive; the crew sensed something nearby. There was on the air a particular odor. Some of the men recognized it. Others sniffed, trying to determine what it was.

"Sperm whale," someone said. But the matter-of-fact tone belied a certain anxiety. All the sailors had heard the stories of whales attacking ships. Then, too, their captain was still in the throes of labor. The sailors kissed their talismans, made crosses on themselves. Tied double monkey fists and looked for good omens.

The sun was rising, its rays like the lip of a cauldron of liquid lead.

"There she blows!" one of the crew shouted.

A thundering big school of whales appeared, perhaps two hundred of them, frolicking on the surface of the waves, thrashing their tails, throwing themselves quick as dancers in the air despite their enormous size.

A giant whale was in the lead. But he had turned and was coming toward the ship. He had a spout as high as the main yard and it was blowing like a chimney. He approached the ship, his great tail thrashing like a tiger's. A monster like that, longer than the ship herself, could smash the ship in a single charge. And it was swimming directly for them. The leviathan was white as a mountaintop, his back crusted with white shells, barnacles, and harpoons. The scars of his old wounds were pierced with fresh wounds. Harpoons, many of them rusted, stuck out of his back like needles from a woman's pincushion. The glossy-white membrane of his mouth looked like a coffin's satin lining.

There was nothing the crew could do. The ship had no harpoons for whaling. Nothing.

"It's time, mates," somebody shouted. "The devil's come to get us."

The whale suddenly turned and changed direction.

The crew stood dumbfounded and silent, staring at the monster as it swam back toward the main pod. A cry came from the master's cabin, the cry of a wee wain, and the sailors broke into a cheer, for they were convinced, unequivocably and certainly, that their captain had somehow been responsible for the whale's turning.

Mary quickly wiped the child and rubbed its small body with fat to bring good luck to it, before wrapping it in a bundle of linen.

Arrah ran her hand down her sides and her stomach. She could feel her bones again. She felt thin as a wire. "Where's my baby?" she asked. As Mary placed the baby in Arrah's arms, its dark-blue eyes locked Arrah's in an intense stare. Arrah felt some invisible hook lodge under her heart and pull at her with a violence. She saw her child's small hands, the tiny, perfect fingernails like miniature pearls, the small fingers folding and unfolding like baby starfish. She kissed the baby's hands, and the soft, soft cheeks. Never had she felt such soft skin. Never had she known such overwhelming love.

Mary said, "Well now, I ain't ever seen a prettier wain. And born at sea she was too."

Arrah knew she would call the child Milly. The light came in and slanted across Milly's face and she began to cry. Instinctively Arrah opened her breasts to her child. She ran her fingers down the smooth, smooth skin of the child's forehead. She remembered what her own mother used to tell her. "I love you higher than the sky and as wide as the ocean." For the very first time Arrah knew exactly what her mother had meant. She would suffer anything, do anything, to ensure the life of this child. She would kill or be killed without a moment's hesitation. That's what it meant to be a mother.

And as the child attempted to suckle, Arrah called for something to drink, for she felt an enormous thirst.

Mary brought her a tankard of ale. "It'll be bringing the milk, it will. Make the wain strong."

Arrah held the child close, feeling her soft, soft cheek against her own breast. She kissed Milly, her hair falling forward throwing a shadow on her daughter's face. Words from a lullaby came back to Arrah from a place before memory. Words that her grandmother had sung to her. Arrah tried to sing the words but exhaustion defeated her. With her child's name on her breath, Arrah fell asleep.

Behind the *Twilight Moon*, another ship had also noticed the pod of whales; a corsair, captained by an evil-looking Turk. He gave the order for his fore and aft sail to be unfurled and his ship began to pick up speed.

CHAPTER
26

Three times Patch came to the captain's quarters in an attempt to warn Arrah of the approach of the corsair, but each time, Mary had chased him out. "Won't yea be leaving her alone to get her proper rest. And her having such a difficult time of it and all!"

Mary was afraid to look out the window of the master's quarters. She'd heard the shots and shouting and finally the clash of weapons. She swallowed frequently and pulled her neck in and made funny biting motions with her mouth. She looked at Arrah sleeping on the bed. There was an expression of peace and tranquility on Arrah's face, an expression that Mary had never seen there before, an expression that said Arrah was oblivious to what was going on about her. And so she should be.

Mary had been to a Portuguese apothecary and had bought some sleeping powder from him, some of which she'd secreted into Arrah's wine. She, Mary, was having nothing to do with being awake in the middle of the night. It was the change of life coming on her. Well, change of life or not, she was needing her sleep, and a little powder helped her to get it. And a little powder was helping Arrah O'Donnell sleep as well.

Arrah had lost a lot of blood during birth. There was the pile of sheets in the corner to prove it. Mary had had no experience at being a midwife. All she knew was that if Arrah continued to bleed the way she had been bleeding, she would die. After Arrah had fallen asleep, Mary had inserted a packing. Now with Arrah staying quiet and restful, the blood would stop.

Mary had no notion how many men were on board the corsair. Nor did she want to know! Besides, pirates weren't such a bad lot. She'd seen enough in her tavern. On land, pirates didn't seem much different from other men. They drank and pissed and wanted their pleasuring the same as any other. But damn! Did they have to be so noisy? She'd told Patch especially not to make any noise.

*   *   *

Arrah had been hearing a strange noise in her dream for some time. A baby crying. It was her baby. She knew that. She'd called it Milly, but it was high up in a tower, and she had no way of climbing up to it. She climbed up into a beach tree nearby, but the beach tree turned into a gallows, and Arrah fell down from the gallows, and hit the ground, and still her baby cried. Somehow in her dream, Arrah knew that she was asleep. There was the sound of fighting. She tried to get up from the ground, tried to break out of sleep, but the sky and the dream weighed too heavily on her shoulders, and she couldn't lift herself from it. She managed to force her eyes open, but her lids were heavier than her head, and they closed again and she fell back into sleep. But still her baby cried. The sounds of the battle were real. Her baby's crying was real. Her baby was in danger. She had to wake up. She forced herself to sit. She forced her eyes open.

Even before she had a chance to ask Mary what was going on, Mary began a steady scolding chatter. "Now, don't yea go worrying yerself about it. Patch and them others will be looking after them heathen Turks. A new mother will be needing rest." Already Mary had pulled a couple of heavy trunks in front of the cabin door so that it couldn't be pushed open. She continued talking without hesitation. "Yea've no color in your face, Arrah lass. Yea lost a fearful lot of yer blood. I was having to pack your insides. Yea should stay quiet and drink spirits, and that'll be bringing yer color back in your face. Ale and mead is being good for a woman come from the birth bed. And parsley. Now don't yea go and worry none!"

Arrah felt weak and heavy-headed, so she didn't argue; she wanted nothing more than to lapse back to sleep, to allow its comfort to carry her off on its dark wings. But something made her distrust Mary's appraisal of the situation. The tiger, his yellow eyes intense, paced the floor in the corner where he had been tied with his gold chain. His fur stood straight over his powerful shoulders as he took short, listening steps. Arrah turned from the tiger back to her child, and sat straighter in bed.

Milly's lips, perfect, pale arcs, made a small sucking motion. The noise from outside grew sharper as steel clashed on steel. The noise disturbed Milly's sleep and she fretted. Immediately Arrah was overcome by a fierce tenderness, so intense that she felt her breasts grow hot. Milly yawned, and then her pale fists, delicate as shells, rubbed across the small face. One of the small thumbs found the lips and Milly started sucking on it, and for the time of a breath she was quiet, but then she began to cry again. Arrah lifted the child to her breast, and Milly began to suckle. Arrah felt the tug of motherhood deep in her womb. She felt sleep pulling at her.

But Mary's voice jarred her.

"Finn, damn your stinking hide! I've told you plenty o' times the linen's not for you." The goat had been chewing on the bed covers. Arrah looked at Mary. She'd heard Mary scold Finn often enough, but never quite so sharply. Finn went to a chest and began to lick at its marble top.

Mary was tearing up linens for diapers. "Yea've nothing to worry about, lass. Patch and the others will not be letting any harm come to us."

A halbred shattered the lead window. The huge cat froze. Arrah instinctively sheltered her baby with her shoulders. But Arrah was still in a kind of cloudy disorientation from the exhaustion of her labor, and moved more slowly than she normally did. A shard caught Milly's cheek, cutting it. Blood began to collect on the perfect smooth skin. Milly began to cry shrilly. Glass lay on the covers of her berth. Holding her child, Arrah leaped out of bed.

"Yea've got to be keeping still." Mary tried to lead her back to bed.

"Quiet! How can I be still while there's battle about me? Why didn't you wake me?"

"Yea've birthed a wain. And yea was bleeding the whole time. Yea've got to stay quiet."

Arrah took a corner of the swaddling cloth and wiped away the blood from the small face. She tried to quiet the baby, held it and rocked it, but her cries were turning into shrieks. Arrah offered it her breast, but Milly refused to take it. Arrah had never felt so helpless. Sailing, fighting, planning forays—none of these had prepared her for the heartbreaking cries of a newborn. She held and rocked and kissed and cooed, and still her baby cried, cried as though its very being had been split in two. Arrah wanted to shout at the crew to stop fighting, to put an end to the ear-splitting noise. She tried to shelter Milly from the noise by holding her close to her breast.

Mary kept looking from side to side, so far that the whites showed in her eyes. "Damn that Patch," she kept repeating. "I was telling him to keep it quiet. She's just a wee afraid of the noise, she is. Them newborns will be needing quiet. And what a devil of a way for a bairn to be brought into the world, but with a fight of pirates on board."

There came a knock on the door. Patch yelled through it. "Arrah, the battle's against us."

"Damn you, Patch," shouted Mary back through the door. "Wasn't I telling yea to be leaving us in peace? She'll be needing her rest, she will."

"Arrah, if you'd just was to show yourself. It might make the men rally!"

"I know'd yea shouldn't have come, but yea'll never be listening to anyone but yerself," scolded Mary.

"Hush!" ordered Arrah.

"Arrah," called Patch again. "Please be hurrying, lass."

Carrying Milly, Arrah looked out through the curtained window. She ascertained from the bloody bodies slashed with halberds and pikes lying on the deck that what Patch had told her was true.

Arrah handed her child to Mary.

"If yea go out there, yea'll kill yerself."

"If I don't go we'll all be killed," Arrah answered. But something was the matter. A darkness kept coming over her eyes. She didn't feel well.

Mary cooed and rocked the child. "Hush! Hush, darling."

Arrah grasped the table edge for balance. She threw a robe over her chemise and pulled on her boots. She picked up her brace of pistols, as well as a single one from beneath her pillow. She handed it to Mary.

"And what the devil am I to do with that?" asked Mary.

"If anyone comes through that door, shoot him."

"Yea make a fine mother looking the way yea do!"

"Will I make a finer mother if I'm dead?" Arrah began to drag at the trunks in front of the door. She felt a surge of blood leave her body and the darkness came up.

"Arrah, for the love of God! Yea shouldn't be . . ." Mary put the baby down and rushed to help, pulling with one hand, trying to hold Arrah with the other.

Arrah felt the weakness. She would go out on deck, show herself, and come back in. "Why didn't you call me earlier?" she said to Patch as soon as the door opened.

"Mary there wasn't allowin' me to wake you!"

"Damn you, Patch! Can't yea be fighting like men out there instead of bothering a mother?" shouted Mary. "Hush! Hush, child! Hush, darling."

Arrah did what she did more from habit than from thought. She shouted at her men. "May the devil take you that you cannot do without me for a day." Two Turks were astounded to see a woman holding a brace of pistols. They knew there were women on board, but they never expected to see one fight, and so stood dumbfounded and still for a moment. Arrah fired both her pistols at one time. Both shots hit true, hitting one Turk squarely in his dark face, the other in the throat, so that blood bubbled there. Arrah felt the darkness. If she wasn't strong, Milly would die. She took a breath, then shouted. "Cowardly lubbers. Are you men or spawns!"

A cheer went up from her crew. "Men!" they shouted in unison.

"Then fight! Damn you! Fight!"

The incident with the whale pod and the birth on board ship had frightened the crew, but now seeing their captain up and about and full of courage herself gave them zeal, and they fought the Turks with renewed vigor.

Arrah felt Patch's arm around her shoulder and wanted to lean into it, but was afraid if she showed any weakness, her men would lose heart again.

The Turkish pirates had orders that they were to kill the baby on board. They could do with the women as they wished. A Turk hiding on the other side of the cabin door watched Arrah leave.

Mary, meanwhile, had turned her back on the locked door to lay the pistol on the table. She had no use for the bleeding things. They were loud, noisy, and heavy, and she couldn't hold the pistol and the baby at the same time. The baby was crying, and she was trying to soothe it by walking with it back and forth in front of the berth.

The door was kicked open and a swarthy-skinned heathen, his sword drawn, stood there.

"And what the devil do yea thinks yea'll be doing here?" Mary yelled. "Get out of here! Yea've no cause to be here!"

The pirate gave her an appreciative look.

From the time she was young, Mary had learned to use the power of her body. "So yea've taken a liking to what yer seeing, have yea?" She pulled open her bodice showing him the heavy whiteness of her breasts.

He sheathed his sword and smiled. He had only one tooth and very red gums that looked even redder because of his dark skin.

She put the baby down on the berth.

The pirate knew what it was that he had to do to the little whelp, but in the meantime, he found the woman's breasts more than he could resist.

Mary had never known what it was to have a man take time with her and this encounter was no exception. It was over so soon that when Arrah came back she discovered the pirate with his parts still hanging naked between his legs.

He looked at her, made the connection with the baby, and remembered what his mission was. He went at the baby with his sword. Mary and Arrah screamed at the same time. Since Mary was closer, it was she who rushed him. The pirate slammed her aside with his fist. She hit her head against the table, grabbed futilely at a map and slid to the floor.

Arrah went at him like a creature possessed, half leaping, half flying.

He looked at her and saw that he didn't want to kill her, at least not yet. He would have her first. On their raids of ships, some of his mates had killed women first and then used and abused their bodies in disgusting ways, but that had never been to his liking.

Arrah was in a weakened state and so he easily flung her away. He raised his sword against her baby. Arrah screamed and grabbing the map from beneath Mary's fingers, flung it at the Turk. Since it was made from the skin of a sheep, it had some weight, and fell over his head, blinding him momentarily.

Arrah grasped the table and tried to get to her feet, but the violence of the Turk's shove had made her hemorrhage. She slipped on her own blood and fell facedown on the floor, her hand outstretched in front of her.

The Turk swung blindly with his sword, slashing through the fabric on her bed. Arrah wailed, but not from pain. Now she felt nothing but helplessness. She had to get to her feet. She saw her own sword beside her bed. She had to reach it. She crawled like a wounded beast, half dragging herself, for her strength was fast leaving her. She slipped and clawed and felt the wood beneath her fingernails. She picked up whatever she could from the floor: a shoe, a glass jar. She heaved everything, and missed, for her judgment of distances was impaired. She saw her astrolabe. It was heavy enough to do damage. She reached for it, felt the crunch of his boot on her fingers, and howled. She tore at his boot with her other hand, and screamed. She saw a rat scurry out beneath the bed, and for a moment her eyes and the eyes of the rat met. Arrah tried to hold on to the Turk's boot, trying to keep him from Milly. She saw his other foot step back, getting ready to kick her. She saw the red velvet of her bedcover and the pile of bloody sheets on the floor. She waited for the impact of that foot in her face, but just then Mary, having managed to get to her feet, grabbed a chair and smashed it over the pirate's head.

Arrah screamed for Mary to give her her sword, and when she had it, Arrah sat up on her knees and began to stab the stunned pirate. He made a few feeble attempts to stop her, but his hand fell away uselessly after her second thrust. She stabbed him and stabbed him and stabbed him. She stabbed him as though she were afraid that he would come back to life again. Milly was crying, screaming, but Arrah heard nothing. All she saw was the sailor with his sword outstretched, aimed at her child, and she stabbed.

Mary lifted Milly from the bed. "He's dead!" she shouted at Arrah, but Arrah heard nothing. Mary screamed again, but still Arrah heard nothing. As long as there was a square of flesh that wasn't blood-covered on this foul heathen, there was a chance that he might come back to life.

The door flew open again. There stood a second Turk. Mary screamed. "Does the Lord not hear our prayers that he sends these heathens to kill us?"

The Turk came in and saw the goat heading toward him. With one swing of his sword the goat's head was severed from its neck. The body stood there for a brief moment, headless, blood spurting from its neck like a fountain. The Turk looked pleased with himself.

"Lord have mercy." Mary was sobbing and holding her hand to her breast. "Is almighty Christ a lunatic that he puts hope in us one moment, then kills it the next?"

Milly was screaming. Mary was screaming. Through the broken window there was the vicious clang of battle, the sharp shatter of glass as another window broke. Arrah felt blood flowing from her. Her arms were weak. She tried to lift her sword . . . she had no more strength. It slipped from her fingers.

She had to get up. Her body was too heavy. She had to get between the Turk and Milly. Had to. She touched her bed, tried to help herself up. Everywhere there was blood. The floor was greasy with it. She put herself between the sword and her child, and pleaded. "No. No! Won't you leave us in peace!"

He slammed the hilt of his sword against Arrah and she toppled again.

Mary grabbed up the baby. "Look at yea," she shouted. "Sword and all, going to slaughter a poor helpless babe. Won't yea be ashamed of yourself." The Turk ripped the baby from Mary's arms and held it out ready to stab it.

Strength came to Arrah from somewhere. She leaped at him, trying to gouge out his eyes, but clawed down his cheek instead, felt the spaces under her fingernails fill with his flesh. He dropped Milly. Mary grabbed her up. The baby was screaming, and as Mary pushed it roughly like a hurling ball into one of the trunks, it screamed even louder. But at least there it was out of the way of the pirate's sword. The Turk flipped Arrah off his back. As she fell, she saw the pistol on the table. She had no strength, yet had to reach it. She lunged up one last time, and as she fell back pulled the trigger, catching the pirate in the spine, so that he dropped screaming and squirming to the floor.

Arrah felt the blackness reach up for her, and this time she couldn't fight it.

Another figure filled the door.

Mary cried. "Lord, no mercy? We kill one! He sends another."

The figure held a pistol aimed directly at Mary. She screamed. Without warning, he dropped his pistol to the floor, and then fell himself.

Stepping over the Turk's body, Patch entered the cabin. "We've defeated them!"

"You damn fool!" screamed Mary. "Help! Arrah's bled to death!"

CHAPTER
27

Debrogail became a favorite with Geralde de Burgo's grandchildren, especially with the children of his dead son, Phillipe. De Burgo harbored a sense of conscience for the death of his illegitimate son. Phillipe had been a splendid land tactician, but he had had little experience at sea. De Burgo knew he should not have let Phillipe go to fight Arrah O'Donnell, and yet he knew that something had to be done about the growing hostility between Phillipe and his brother over the question of inheritance of de Burgo properties.

That question had, at least, been settled by Phillipe's death. But Phillipe's son, Nevil, a beautiful child of three years, had grown difficult after the death of his father. The child cried constantly as if his very heart had broken, and sometimes he was given to a wild, raging screaming that seemed to go on for days and days. Everyone was afraid that Nevil had inherited his grandmother's madness.

But Debrogail and her singing seemed to have a quieting effect on him. She would rub his head and sing to him. Eventually it came that the child would spend almost all his waking hours with Debrogail.

Nevil was de Burgo's first grandchild, and he loved the cherubic little child dearly. It had pained him to see the boy nearly driven mad with an unnatural grief.

Originally de Burgo had wanted to send Magnus away. De Burgo had little use for men who had been crippled and could not assist him in battle. But Debrogail said that if her brother was sent away she, too, would leave. Little by little de Burgo realized that his grandson cared for Magnus almost as much as he cared for Debrogail. None of the other men seemed to have much tolerance with a boy who cried and screamed, but Magnus, if Debrogail was not about, had a kind and patient character and was able to quiet the boy with silly games and grimaces.

Debrogail and Magnus and the children spent hours together. They would often go down to the beach together and build pretend castles in the sand, scooping and digging and piling and turreting.

One afternoon de Burgo walked down to the beach. Debrogail and Magnus were with his grandchildren.

They had made a shark from the sand. It was a huge shark, longer than a man. They used bits of twigs for the teeth and they hollowed the places where the eyes were. They rounded the hump, and scooped the tail and curved it like a shark's tail. Nevil was laughing. It was the first time de Burgo had seen the child laugh since his father had died, and de Burgo was genuinely moved. He stood back at a distance, not interrupting the play.

Then Debrogail began to sing. She took Nevil's hand and de Burgo watched her walking barefoot in the sea, the surf splashing up about her ankles. All the while she sang.

Once again de Burgo was struck by her beauty. There was something about her that was different than that of the other servants. She didn't have the same subservient carriage that the other serving women had. Her skin was finer, and her hair, although a tangle of curl, had a softness to it. She moved him in a way that no other woman ever had. She moved him in a way that went beyond lust.

His heart was overwhelmed with joy, particularly since he saw his grandchildren's eyes filled with wonderment as they looked up at Debrogail.

When she finished de Burgo approached her. "Christ, dear girl," he said. "You charm the wildness in a man and all his cares disappear when he hears you sing."

"Thank you, my Lord," she said.

"Is there anything you want for?" he asked.

She thought of Bres, for despite her relative happiness at Galway Castle she had never forgotten him, but then she saw Magnus sitting on the sand. With his crutches he had been unable to follow them. She had heard of de Burgo's magic often enough. "I wish for a good leg for my brother," she said.

"Alas, dear girl," he said with genuine sadness, "even I with my magic cannot give your brother a new limb."

"Then I wish for a harp," Debrogail said. "A harp to accompany my voice, so that I may please you even more."

"You shall have it," he said.

*   *   *

The *Twilight Moon* sailed with all possible haste to Paris. As soon as the ship docked, Mary sent out for a wet nurse. Patch ran to the house of Seaghan MacNamara. The big man came without a moment's hesitation to the ship.

Arrah had lost an enormous amount of blood. Mary was certain she had died. It was Patch who had detected Arrah's faint heartbeat. Arrah remained weak, a body who moved in and out of consciousness as though in a dream.

The woman that Seaghan saw was just a shell of the woman he remembered. Her skin was so pale it looked almost translucent, like the wing of a moth. He knelt beside her berth, stroked her forehead, took her hand and kissed her fingertips.

He told Patch to go with all possible haste to the clinic of a Dr. Sylvius. Patch was to tell Sylvius that Seaghan MacNamara requested his presence *immediately*.

Seaghan MacNamara had been a tortured being ever since he had been cast out by Arrah O'Donnell. The memory of her had lingered in his arms and in his loins. Nothing could take away the ache. He was driven by a mad recklessness brought on by the piercing finality of her words: *I don't ever want to see you again.* The words were in his mind at the beginning and the end of each day, and in his dreams. He taunted death at every turn, would have welcomed it had it come. He sailed into a hundred storms, fought a hundred battles. And momentarily in the middle of the action he could forget, but the moment he stopped he remembered, and the ache opened in him again hungry as an archway. He had cursed her name a thousand times and cursed himself for falling in love with her. He had taken women and then hurled abuse at them for no other reason than they were not Arrah O'Donnell. After, he was filled with remorse and spoke tenderly to them and wiped away their tears. But it was no use. It was Arrah O'Donnell's face he saw each time he looked at a woman, Arrah O'Donnell's limbs he felt each time he embraced a woman. The ache was only intensified after each encounter and so he abandoned women completely for a while, living instead the life of a celibate. Such imposed rigors made his aggressive nature even more hostile. His eyes were wild with a volatile, pained expression. A long scar along his left cheek further added to his appearance of dangerous unpredictability.

But the hostile wildness disappeared now as he sat beside her bed, kissing her fingertips and smoothing the hair back from her face. His huge shoulders were slumped with palpable pain. He brought her fingertips to his lips. "Arrah!" He whispered her name over and over again.

Meanwhile, Patch had been told by a servant that Dr. Sylvius was not at his practice and could not be located, that he didn't know where he had gone, or when he would return. The servant suggested that Patch seek out Dr. Carnet, whose house was close to the bridge.

Dr. Carnet took one look at Arrah and said, "She must be made to drink ox blood. Much of it. Go to the butchers, and bring back a bucket of it."

Arrah was dreaming. She was suffocating. She was dreaming that blood was being poured down her throat. She didn't know who, or why they were doing it. She choked and they pulled her tongue forward and held her mouth open. The blood kept coming. She was drowning in it. There was blood on her hands and on her clothes. No, they couldn't make her drink any more blood! They tied her hands and pressed her nostrils shut. They pried her teeth open with a stick. She was suffocating and she opened her mouth for a gasp of air, and then the blood came in and she was choking in it. Everything was blood—all the faces, her clothes, her hands. She was drowning in blood. She heard the crying of a baby, her baby. A pirate held her baby on the point of a sword and the blood of her baby covered everything. Her mother came to her, her hands reaching out to her, and Arrah called her name, but then her mother's face turned into a skull, and she began to pull at Arrah. She reached up and pulled Arrah into the grave with her. Arrah screamed. She was unconscious, but in a deeper consciousness she kept seeing the dark face of MacNamara. She had forgotten him. But he kept coming back. He kept touching her forehead. He kissed her forehead. "Leave me!" she screamed. But he covered her mouth with his hands. "You mustn't waste your strength. You must get stronger now. You must drink more blood." "No more!" she screamed. They tied her hands, put sticks in her mouth again, made her drink more blood. The blood tasted the way his love fluid tasted years ago. "I hate you," she screamed, "I hate you."

Dr. Sylvius cut an imposing figure wherever he went. He was white-bearded and white-haired, but with very dark eyes and dark, dark eyebrows. He was a grand man with an enormous girth and wide, dramatic manners. He was the foremost anatomist of his day and immensely conceited.

When Sylvius received the message from his servant that Seaghan MacNamara had been asking for him, the famous doctor came aboard the *Twilight Moon* and flew into a rage as soon as he saw what Carnet was doing.

"*Merde!*" swore Sylvius. "What are you doing to *my* patient!" and he flung Carnet out of the way. "Beast! Incompetent! Idiot! You know nothing!"

Carnet, who was as white-bearded but shorter and more slender than Sylvius, shouted back, "And you! What do you know? You never put your hand to a single body. It's always your assistants, butchers, and barbers who do your work."

"Barber, yourself. Take your bag and return to cutting hair. Get away! It's fortunate you didn't kill her. I've seen them drown in blood. Their lungs fill with it!"

"What do you suggest? The great Sylvius. It's easy enough, your work. Corpses! Death! When was the last time you touched hands to a *living* thing!"

"No thanks to you, this will be the first of the day. The way to put blood into a body is not through the stomach, but through the walls of the veins themselves."

"The veins themselves! My God, you're deranged. How do you propose to put the blood in? With a spoon? Hah!"

"Fool! You make an incision in the vein!"

"I always knew you for a madman! The blood will run out!"

"But, no! Not if it's done properly. You there, One Eye. Go to the street and find a dog. Any dog. Lively, but not vicious. I've no wish to be bitten."

To his assistant, Sylvius gave the order to return to his clinic and bring back some of his wooden tubes and his blood-letting stand. "And hurry," he shouted to both of them.

Sylvius had been called in to treat the Count of Montreuil for the headaches that had agonized him. It was there that Seaghan MacNamara had made his acquaintance. Sylvius had a great love of beautiful horses and fat roast goose, both of which were in abundance at MacNamara's estates.

Sylvius looked at the woman whose hair, neck, and face were covered with blood. "Is she your mistress?"

MacNamara sadly shook his head. "She's another man's wife."

"You'll never change, will you, Irishman?"

Sylvius noticed the baby with the wet nurse. "Is that your whelp?" he asked.

Again MacNamara shook his head. Suddenly, Sylvius seemed to notice his surroundings. "Is she the captain's wife?"

"It's her ship," MacNamara said. "She's captain."

Sylvius lifted the blood-caked hair with the tips of his fingers and looked at the face of his patient for the first time. For Sylvius, living patients were not of interest most of the time because he couldn't open them to see what was inside. He wiped his fingers on the bed covers. "Under that blood lies a beautiful woman. Why does she choose a life . . . like this?" He stretched his fat arms out like a priest before the eucharist.

"Because she has the sea in her veins."

"With so much blood lost, it's good she has something in them. Why don't you marry, Irishman, and stop pursuing other men's wives? I thought you were to marry the Countess de Villon."

"After I met Arrah, I could think of no other woman."

"That's not what I heard! I heard you were a devil between the sheets." Sylvius noticed the tiger lying not far from Arrah's bed. "Did you give her the beast?"

MacNamara nodded.

"Always in search of the exotic and dangerous, eh, Irishman?"

Sylvius's assistant came back with several lengths of wood and some cord, and soon after Patch returned with a brown, spotted dog, a thin, mangy creature, lively enough in a kind of nervous, frightened way.

Sylvius stood, giving orders, swinging his arms, and gesticulating in his superior manner. The assistant muzzled the dog with a piece of cord. He then tied the dog by its snout, shoulders, haunches, and back legs to the vertical pole. The dog's head was about halfway up the pole, his back feet nearly touched the ground.

"You see, primitive," said Sylvius to Carnet in a voice dripping with condescension and disdain. "you make a puncture in the vein of the dog and in the vein of the patient, and you allow the blood to run into the patient through one of these hollow sticks."

"Where did you ever get such a preposterous idea?" asked Carnet.

"You're preposterous, and stupid, and a fool for your doubt. And I'm a bigger fool for sharing my brilliance with you. Nonetheless . . . if I don't show you, you'll continue with your antiquated methods."

He spoke to his assistant. "Take your dagger and cut the dog's throat." The assistant bent to do as he was told. "Not there, fool. On the side. There," he said, bending grandly and directing as though he were a painter at work on a very large canvas.

But just as the assistant was finding the vein, Seaghan MacNamara stepped between the assistant and the hapless, whining dog. "Stop," he said.

"What is it, Irishman? Not pity, for misery's sake. It's miserable enough, this cur. Bag of bones. Better dead than making it scrounge for food! Less flesh on it than the pope's nose."

"Take my blood!"

"I think that is too risky. The blood of a man might prove too strong and kill her."

"Isn't it true that at the moment of conception a man's and woman's blood mingle. The woman doesn't die then, does she?"

Sylvius ran his fingers through his white hair and then scratched his white beard. "Yes, that's true enough. But what if she were to sprout a beard. You would love her less with a beard I think, and if her voice grew deep like yours." Sylvius smiled at his own wit.

MacNamara exploded. "And what if she were to grow spotted like that dog?"

Sylvius worked his lips and jaws rather vigorously. "You make a point! But sometimes, there are complications when a man's veins are opened. The green rot can set in."

"I'm willing to take the chance."

"Very well, Irishman. Open his vein," Sylvius ordered his assistant.

"If you do this, they'll tie you to the stake and burn you as a witch!" protested Carnet.

"Carnet. Merde!" Sylvius drove Carnet up against the wall of the cabin syllable by syllable. "Fool. Half-wit. Nincompoop. Idiot! Another word and I will use *your* blood. Stop interfering. Go home. And you, fool," said Sylvius, speaking to his assistant. "Make the incision there! There! Higher on the forearm. The same place on her arm. Now put in the tube. Damn you, man, what are you waiting for? The angels to land? Quickly now. Don't let the blood go to waste. You there, Irishman. Hold your arm higher. There's no magic in blood. It can't run uphill."

CHAPTER 28

The dreams faded. Arrah woke slowly to the voice of a woman singing. A lamp was lit on her table. There was the sound of a child fussing lightly. Arrah called Milly's name.

Mary appeared from the darkness. It was she who had been singing. "All the sainteys in heaven be praised. Patch! You bloody one-eyed salt! Are yea deaf that yea can't hear? She's awake! Our Arrah's awake."

Mary moved back.

"No, don't leave me."

Mary came back like a vision from the darkness, holding Milly in her arms. She handed her to Arrah. "You was without milk. But we found her a wet nurse, and look at the likes of her now."

Arrah took her child. The small lips opened into a yawn. Arrah brought her face close to Milly's. For a moment, they were held there in the halo of the lantern, mother and daughter ringed round with light, their faces golden.

Mary gave a little cry of excitement. "In the name of all the sainteys what ever lived. But there ain't nothin' more beautiful in this world than a mother and her child."

Arrah felt lightheaded and weak, but at the same time she was again caught up in a fierce overflowing of love. She remembered the battle with the pirates. Remembered the killing, but the rest . . . was it a dream? Her mouth tasted like dried blood.

As if Mary read her mind, she brought her a tankard of ale. "Drink it," Mary said. "It'll be bringing back yer strength." She continued. "We almost lost yea, yea know. Arrch! What a crew of cutthroats they was! They killed me Finn." Mary wiped at her eye with a corner of her skirt. "He was like a lad to me. But look at the both of yea. When I see that me heart is glad again."

Mary brushed Arrah's hair back over her ear and touched Milly's cheek. "He was here, yea know, MacNamara. If it hadn't been for him sending for that witch doctor. The other one kept feeding yea blood. Christ, it was awful! I couldn't be standing to look at it. Yea gagging and biting your lips so hard to keep them closed. And then MacNamara offering his arm. Yea've got his blood in yea now, lass. His blood coming into yea right there—" Mary poked at Arrah's forearm, where a dressing had been applied.

"Him?"

"Methinks it's the work of the devil. I was saying me prayers back there in the corner, thinking God was a-going to strike us all dead. But yea would've died. I ain't never seen no way of healing except for leeches."

She hadn't just dreamt it, then.

"Patch is in his employ, you know."

"Patch?" Arrah was overcome with a dark dizziness. The bed seemed to be spinning beneath her. MacNamara had betrayed her in love; now his blood ran in her veins, to be carried there for the rest of her days. Her man worked for him. Betrayal was around her, thick as air, spinning and spinning. Would it never stop? She wished that another dark wave would sweep her away so that she would never again have to think or feel. But Milly fussed. Arrah forced herself to open her eyes and confront the reality of her situation. "Tell Patch to come in here!"

"I'll do no such thing. Yea've come back from the arms of the devil. I'll not have yea leaving that poor wain an orphan because of some silliness now. Yea'll wait until yer well before yea starts asking things that are of no harm."

Sylvius had been right about the effect of the transfusion. Once the new blood took effect the body returned fairly quickly to its former vigor.

"Patch!" Arrah shouted loudly.

Patch entered.

"Are you in MacNamara's employ?" Arrah demanded. Her voice was cold as stone.

"I was in his employ once. Before I knew you the way that I know you now."

"How could you do this to me? All this time. Betraying me."

"I was never betraying you, Arrah. There was a battle once, not between soldiers, but between soldiers and serfs. Brion MacNamara, Seaghan's father, was trying to take the land about Gort, where I was living. Seaghan was a youth. Not him in command, but another. It was frightening and horrible. Rape and pillage and burning. I was home with a wound in me thigh and couldn't move. The soldiers coming in and me wife and daughter there. Me daughter just a lass and screaming and me powerless as they dragged her out. They set the torches to me thatch, and me still inside. Seaghan arrived, turning on his own men, saving me own daughter from violation. He came through the fire and carried me out. Me hands was already burned from the fiery thatch falling around me. 'Tis the reason me hands are so white, because of the scars." He paused then added with great feeling, "I never betrayed you. He paid me to look after you. And I looked out for you."

"I don't need you to look out for me!"

Patch felt the hurt of her words. He and Arrah had grown over the years to have a close and loyal camaraderie. He loved her, not in the way a man normally loved a woman, but as a fellow seaman and as a friend. "No. You're right. Arrah O'Donnell won't be needing a single body to watch for her. I'm asking to take your leave. I've a family I ain't seen for some years. Me boys will be nearly men, and me girl, a woman."

"You need not ask my permission. You're not in my employ anymore!" She saw the power of her words go through him.

"Patch!" cried Mary. "Don't be a fool. Don't be leaving."

"It ain't like this old salt to be staying where he ain't wanted. Good-bye, Arrah!" He left.

"That was a damned fool's thing yea was just doing."

"Quiet," said Arrah, "or you'll go too!"

"I'll not be quiet. I've not lived all me days to be quiet when I see fool's things done! He's done nothing but good things for yea, Patch has. Or is yea forgetting so soon already? Now that yer a sea queen 'tis easy enough to be forgetting the help of others and be taking all the glory for yerself."

"He betrayed me!"

"'Twasn't Patch betrayed yea! 'Twas your own heart. What the devil's the matter with a man taking a taste of two women at the same time? If yea take a taste of roast mutton, there ain't nothing preventing yea from taking a bit o' pork as well. Love ain't no different! I'll tell yea something. I ain't never seen a man love the way MacNamara loves yea. Never left yer side the whole time. Wouldn't eat. Wouldn't sleep. Just sat there in that chair, his face hanging lower than a snail's diddle. One hand holding yer hand the whole time. The only time he was ever getting up was to be giving me a pack of cards to be playing with so I'd stop bothering him with me talk. I was talking too much, he was saying. Waiting he was, for a word from yea!

But then, after when they was taking blood from him and passing it into yea, then yea was cursing his name when yea was out of your head. Worse than anything I ever heerd. And I've heerd the best and worst o' cursing. Lord, it was like the devil hisself speaking from your tongue. He got up after that. Not so much as looked back! I was mistaking about him. He's like the ones I knowed, but not like them. Oh, Arrah. Me heart broke for him."

"And my heart broke when I saw him with Finola!"

"Mark me words, lass. 'Tis a bloody sad life yea'll be leading if you keep on wounding with your shield."

Already Arrah was deeply sorry about sending Patch away. Mary was right. He had been her friend and teacher, and she had no right to speak to him as she had. She sent Mary running to bring him back, but Patch had left. She sent Mute and Hook to look for him along the docks, but he had disappeared, and there was no trace of him anywhere on the quays or in the numerous taverns that lined them. She gave orders for messages to be left in each public house for the sailor with the tattooed eye, but no response came.

Her strength returned and she herself went looking for Patch, but there was no sign of him anywhere.

As Arrah returned to the ship she thought of MacNamara and of what Mary said. What kind of man allowed his veins to be opened so that another could live? But then she remembered the sight of Finola, her bare thighs open on the bed, and the knot of hurt tightened again in her breast. She would never allow herself to be vulnerable again.

When she returned to the *Twilight Moon*, Arrah discovered Mary playing with a deck of cards. Arrah had seen plenty of cards before, but none quite like the ones Mary showed her. They were made of thin wooden pieces about the size of a man's palm, and were beautifully and brightly painted in reds, blues, and golds, with pictures of men, women, swords, cups, stars, and rods on them.

"They're fortune-telling cards," Mary said. "MacNamara said he got them from a gypsy woman. Does yea want me telling your fortune?"

Arrah went to her bed and picked up Milly, and kissed her face. Arrah was not in the mood for fortune-telling. She believed people made their own fortunes. Her servants and sailors were always consulting cards and omens of good luck and ill luck. Her mother, too, had always been busy looking for omens of good luck and bad luck in the flights of birds, in the call of the crow, and in numerous other things. To Arrah, it seemed that as often as the omens of luck pointed to good things, bad things happened and vice versa. In her years as a captain, she had learned not to trust in luck, but in her own skill, learned not to trust in omens and prophecy, but in the straightness of her shot. Nonetheless, Mary had been morose since she'd sent Patch away. There was no point in making her even more belligerent: Arrah agreed to Mary's request. Mary spread out the cards facedown in a half circle and asked Arrah to draw out one card. Arrah halfheartedly did so. As she turned the card over, she was confronted with a picture of death. The figure, a skull with a long black cloak and a dark metal helmet, carried a scythe. The figure had red, fluid, bloodlike hair showing beneath his helmet.

Mary blanched, jumped back in horror, and crossed herself.

Arrah quickly turned the card back over. "I don't have time for such silliness," she said.

But Mary was obviously shaken by the card and came close to Milly and made the sign of a cross on her small forehead, and repeated, "God bless it," over and over again.

Arrah had waited four days in an attempt to try and find Patch. It was time to sail home.

She ordered the anchor lifted. Just as the ship was pulling away from the dock, Arrah looked out and saw the man she had been looking for. She leaped off the boat.

"Patch! Patch!" She ran at him, grasping his white hands in hers and holding them. She said nothing, for she was too ashamed to speak.

Mary was shouting from the ship. "Patch, yea bloody one-eyed fool. Where was yea getting to?"

Patch smiled at Arrah, his tattooed eye blinking as he spoke. He saw that she was crying and smiled gently. " 'Twould never do if your sailors saw you!"

"Please come back!"

"No, lass!"

"Can't you forgive me? Please?" She looked directly at him.

Her eyes were bright with tears. She was very beautiful in this moment of shame. "Surely now if Christ forgave them that nailed him to the cross, I can be forgiving you, lass." He wiped her tears. " 'Tisn't a question of forgiving. When you look like that I could be forgiving you for taking the sun from the sky. But 'tis a question of my own life. You've been my captain these years. Now 'tis time to be master of my own soul. I've a family. I want to see them."

Arrah threw her arms around him. "Patch!"

"I'll miss you, lass. But my girl's near a woman now, I ain't seen for some time."

"Will you come and visit me?"

He grasped her by the shoulders and looked at her. "Arrah, lass. You're an eagle. You can soar. Don't let the bitterness in your heart weigh you down. He loves you!"

Arrah looked down. The pain was still too great.

As Arrah was rowed ashore in a currach to Eagle Bay she was greeted at the shore by both Carbri and her father. Carbri embraced her stiffly, but she found him cool and withdrawn. She smelled his strong ale breath and knew he had once again been drinking. He had taken to bouts of heavy drinking ever since he had been displaced as tanaist by Murrough O'Connor. Despite her mercenaries, she had never attempted to retake Dunmore Castle for Carbri. She always assumed that someday he would do that himself, but up until now he hadn't.

Her father seemed stronger than when she had left him. Reevnarg was absolutely besotted with his granddaughter. He took her immediately from Arrah and tears filled his gray eyes, and despite his large arms, he was gentle with her. When he handed Milly back to Arrah, he said, "Arrah, I remember when you yourself were . . ." and he held his hands out helplessly, as if they were trying to remember the size. "Aye, daughter, you were so small . . . and now you're a mother yourself. And I remember your mother holding you."

Carbri looked at Milly briefly, but said nothing about her, nor did he hold her.

Mary was virtually bursting with eagerness to tell her story. "Yea should'a seen her. This bunch of cowardly spawns. Hook and the rest. Fighting like old women until Arrah went out on deck. Two muskets she fired into their damn heathen faces. And that was it." But Mary didn't include in her story the part about MacNamara giving his blood to Arrah, although she gave a graphic account of Arrah being forced to drink ox blood.

"Looking for battle, as always," said Carbri.

"I didn't attack them. They attacked me."

"You could have been killed," he said.

"If we hadn't fought, we would've been killed. What was I to do? Allow them to take me and Milly?"

"You could have stayed at home!" and he turned and walked back toward Eagle Castle.

Reevnarg looked at Arrah. "He's been like that ever since he came back from the mainland." The news of events that her father related was not good. Glundel Joyce as de Burgo's son-in-law was inciting fighting and rebellion amongst many of the border clans from whom O'Donnell exacted tributes.

In addition Glundel had linked forces with Murrough O'Connor, the new O'Connor tanaist, and they had attacked Carbri when he was at Naira's castle at Glen Head. He'd been out hunting with Bres and the two were drunk. Carbri had fallen behind a bench, where he went unnoticed. If it had not been for Reevnarg arriving unexpectedly with his troops, the castle would have been lost. Unfortunately, both Glundel Joyce and Murrough O'Connor had escaped to the hills. "Carbri's been sullen as a shark, his tongue red with drink ever since," concluded Reevnarg. "Aye, it's queer men my daughters have married. Carbri and Bres, instead of fighting men, they fight the ale jug."

Naira couldn't contain her fury when she learned that Arrah had returned safely with a baby girl. "Incompetent half-wit," she screamed at the messenger, and grabbing a thin dagger from a table, she plunged it into his heart before he even had a chance to defend himself.

Jealousy, envy, and fear of discovery had turned Naira into a monster, fed by dissatisfaction, bitterness, and plotting. Bres was the biggest disappointment of her life. He cared nothing for power but was always off hunting roe bucks like a common stalker. She had tried to talk him into taking Eagle Island from Arrah's control. It would have been easy, but Bres had merely looked at her like she was mad. "I don't think I heard you say that," he had said, and then walked away from her.

She had thought of using poison, but Arrah had one of the servants taste everything. She would have stabbed a knife into Arrah's breast herself, but Arrah had more skill with knives and daggers than did many men.

There had to be some other way, and then suddenly, purely by accident, it presented itself to her.

Bres had never been more than a mediocre lover, and when she stopped reaching for him at night, the love-making had stopped completely.

One day he returned in a jovial mood from hunting with Carbri. "We stalked three deer," he said.

"I don't give a pig's grunt for your hunt," she said. "If you'd put as much energy into love-making as you do into hunting, you'd be of more interest to me!"

Bres said nothing, and he would have let her words lie there and retreated off himself, but Naira, in a foul mood, taunted him. "You're nothing but a limp fish. A limp fish in bed, a limp fish when it comes to fighting. Eagle Island should belong to me, but you're too much of a coward to help me take it."

Always Bres had held his tongue or lied in front of Naira, but he'd been drinking with Carbri; his tongue was loose, he felt invigorated from the hunt, and Naira had never been as cruel with her words as she was now. Bres flamed with the pent-up resentment and anger of years. "It was you who wanted me. All these years I've been a traitor to my uncle, and in return you have not given me one kernel of happiness. You don't interest me in the least! The only reason I agreed to marry you was because of Debrogail."

Naira was as angry and bitter as Bres. "Well, you could have saved yourself the trouble." She savored the words she delivered next, wanting to hurt him. "Because I ordered her buried alive, the night I sent her from Eagle Castle. You fool! You stupid, spineless fool! If I would've known you were such a coward, I would have saved myself the trouble!" She began to laugh hideously.

Bres's hand went to his sword and he raised it, then stopped. It was not in his character to kill a woman. He left her there, her awful laughter echoing the walls, and he returned to Brion MacNamara.

She was relieved that Bres was gone. Fearing that he would leave her, she had always hidden her true motives from him. His presence had been nothing but a hindrance to her. For years she had tried to keep his sensitive, gentle nature appeased through careful cajoling and inoffensively cloaked lies.

She no longer had to hide anything from Bres, and she plotted against Arrah with single-minded vigor.

She considered seducing Carbri, but Carbri was a mutton-skull of the first order, stumbling-drunk half the time, and merely loudly drunk the rest of the time.

One night while visiting the Castle of the Eagles, Naira noticed the dark, sullen handsomeness of Sebastian, who kept himself aloof from everyone else. Naira called him to her bed. She was certain he would help her kill Arrah.

He had a well-muscled chest, with a large amount of wiry hair. He had practically no hips at all, but a respectable member, stubby but wide, nuzzled between his thighs.

Naira climbed on top of Sebastian. Keeping her breasts low, she slid down Sebastian's torso, so that the wiry hairs of his chest grazed against her nipples. This excited desire in them both. She slid farther down, so that one nipple brushed against his groin, then allowed her nipple to stroke the shaft of his phallus. Meanwhile she cradled the underside of his testicles in her fingers, lifting them and caressing them lightly.

"I'd like you to do something for me," she said.

She breathed on his phallus, but when he grasped her head in his hands and tried to push her face down, she resisted. "I want you to help me," she said. She ran her tongue tip up and down the length of his member.

"To do what," he responded.

She nibbled lightly at the skin at the root of his member just above his testicles. "First promise me you'll help me!"

He tried to pull her onto himself, but again she resisted. "You and I are similar," she said. "We both want what we don't have."

"What do you want?" he whispered.

She put her whole mouth on him and drew her lips up and down, then removed her mouth.

"I have a plan that could benefit us both," she whispered. "You're ambitious too. I see it in your eyes. You will help me, won't you?"

"Naira!"

She took him again in her mouth. When she heard him moan, she knew she had her answer.

Because Debrogail was de Burgo's favorite songstress, she was royally treated by all. Debrogail was given a bed with sheets, unlike the other servants who had only a pallet that they pulled close to the embers at night. Even Finola, who was not given to generosity, gave Debrogail gifts. She gave her a small box inlaid with gold and decorated with the circles and intertwined bodies of birds and animals.

But no gift pleased Debrogail as much as the harp that de Burgo gave to her. It was a plain instrument, of simple wood without ornament, but she grasped it to herself eagerly and spent long hours learning how to play it.

She composed a song about Magnus's wife, which she called "Cathlin's Ode," in which she described the harrowing account of being imprisoned and the gentleness of the woman who had saved her life.

Since neither had any family left, Magnus and Debrogail were devoted to each other as brother and sister. They were down on the beach together one evening after Phillipe's son had gone to bed, when Debrogail first sang

"Cathlin's Ode" to Magnus. Behind them the wind whispered in the leaves, a soft accompaniment to the harp and Debrogail's voice. The waves of the sea lapped gently against the shore.

When she finished her song, Magnus had tears in his eyes. He took Debrogail's hands in his hands and kissed them. "Debrogail, I love you with all my heart. When I hear you sing, you give me hope. I realize that a God that had given you a voice as beautiful as yours could not treat my Cathlin and my child cruel in the hereafter, but that he would take them to his bosom in heaven. There she knows no suffering or heartbreak. I remember the way that she smiled when she heard you sing."

But along with Magnus's enthrallment of her song came words of warning. "Don't sing your most beautiful songs in front of Finola."

Debrogail was surprised by his warning. Finola had always been kind to her, not friendly, but kind enough with her small gifts, and she found Magnus's warning strange. "I don't understand," she said.

"You're very beautiful. Do not trust anyone. Men, and women, call us friends one moment, and as with the flick of a finger, so soon they change their words and call us foe. I'm not afraid of death, Debrogail, I will be with Cathlin. But I'm afraid for you, Debrogail. You are so beautiful. You will always be vulnerable to the desires of men and therefore the jealousies of women who love those men. I sometimes see the way Finola watches Geralde when he listens to you sing."

"Geralde has never even taken me to his bed. Why would she be jealous?"

"Because de Burgo loves you in ways that he will never love Finola. Beware of her. Beware of how you act toward de Burgo."

Ladders of mist seemed to rise from the trees and the moon shone through them. "Why must I always be put in jeopardy because of the jealousy of other women?" asked Debrogail.

"Because jealousy knows no boundaries," answered Magnus.

CHAPTER
29

Two years came and went. The hawthorn was in bloom, and the bold yellow gorse flowered the same color as the tiger's pelt so that when he lay down in it, he disappeared. There were newborn lambs that played everywhere on the hills, bounding in the sunshine and kicking up their sharp black heels at butterflies. Cows licked the necks of their calves and the young badgers came out and sunned themselves on the sunny side of the hills. Young seal pups, black like dark shiny butter, slithered down from rocks into the sea and barked noisily.

Milly was a delightful child. She had her mother's thick tumble of chestnut hair and her father's laughing, mirthful eyes. She charmed everyone with her laughter and bright eyes, everyone except Carbri.

Just after Arrah had sailed for Portugal, while she was expecting Milly, Carbri had gone hunting with Bres at Glen Head. Naira had made a comment about Arrah. "Carbri," she had said, "It's none of my concern, but you're my brother-in-law and I love you like a brother, which I never had. How is it that you allow your wife to sail off time and time again with so many men? Bres would absolutely turn green with jealousy if I did such a thing. And think, too, of the kinds of activities she engages in with her crew. All those men, all those ports. I know my sister. She is a woman of intense vigor; a woman like that has intense desires. I would wonder at the kinds of activities she engages in with her crew." Naira had reached out and touched his hand, "If I were you, dear brother, I would keep her home."

Carbri was drinking at the time, and angrily he had dismissed Naira's comments. "I love Arrah, and she loves me."

Unknown to Carbri, Naira had cultivated her ability to focus on a man's weakness. With her honeyed voice, speaking in seeming innocence, she manipulated that weakness for her own ends. She had been successful with Bres; and now she was successful with Carbri. He, too, had often wondered the same things. Because he drank substantially he was often unable to rise to Arrah's desires.

Although he denied Naira's comments, her words stuck in his craw, needling him. He drank to forget them, just as he drank to forget losing the title of tanaist to Murrough O'Connor. Unfortunately when Carbri drank, Naira's words grew even sharper in his mind. By the time Arrah had returned carrying Milly in her arms, his intoxicated mind had convinced him that Milly was not his child. He was cool and distant toward her: if she looked at him he would look away. In two years not once had he picked her up or held her.

Arrah had gone to take delivery of another ship, and Carbri stayed at Eagle Island. Mary had caught a cold and coughed nonstop. Between coughing, she alternately wiped at her nose and cursed God for bringing down such an illness on her. Milly wanted to go for a walk, Mary scolded her.

Carbri turned on Mary. "It's what you're bloody well here to do, and you'd better do it."

Mary had never been one to mince words. "Well, if it isn't the crow calling the kitty black. Well then, yea're her father. Yea can take her!"

"Father!" Carbri spit the words like a curse.

"So that's the reason yea've been avoiding this child. Where's the eyes that God put in yer head, man, that yea can't be seeing she's yours."

"My spawn, or the spawn of some sailor?" scorned Carbri.

"Carbri, Carbri. I never took yea for a fool, lad. Yea drinks too much, 'tis true. But damn, will yea deny yer blood? Look at her looking at you!"

Milly was looking at her father with a look of hope and bewilderment. She'd seen this man about her and hadn't in her young heart ever understood why he never smiled when she smiled at him or why he never hugged her. Now Milly reached up her little hand and held it out, "Walk, Papa?" she asked.

Carbri looked at Milly.

Mary erupted. "For the sake of Christ will yea forget your cursed ale jug! I'm with Arrah when she sails, and she's never been but faithful to yea! If yea're a man at all, stand up to the truth. Take the child for a walk on the beach."

Reluctantly Carbri did as he was told.

Milly was playing in the sand when suddenly she dropped her straw doll and ran sobbing to Carbri, her small shoulders quaking, as she threw herself against her father's legs.

When Milly finally stopped crying enough that she was able to tell Carbri what the matter was, she talked of a great black monster chasing her on the ground.

"Where?" asked Carbri.

"There on the sand," and Milly pointed, and then shrieked in terror as her own shadow seemed to leap up at her.

Impatiently Carbri laughed at the silliness of it. " 'Tis nothing but your shadow chasing you. Everywhere you go, your shadow goes. Look, I have one too." Carbri was going to pull away and show her. "Look at it," he said.

But, terrified, Milly clung to his legs.

"Turn around here," he said.

She stayed where she was, hiding her face.

He bent down to her. "You don't have to look with all your eye, just part of it," he said.

Slowly she turned her face.

"See—when I wave my hand, my shadow waves his hand."

Milly looked at the shadow. She lifted her own small hand and waved it, and when she saw that her shadow moved she smiled hesitantly. When she looked at her father, her face grew serious again. "Papa, why don't you ever smile?"

With her question Milly touched some deep-rooted sadness in Carbri. He remembered how he had held Arrah shaking in his arms after the pirates attacked Reevnarg's ship, how hand in hand he and Arrah had jumped into the waves together, and how much joy they had felt in France, and how it had all disappeared. Tears sprang to his eyes.

"Papa, why are you crying?" Milly asked.

She stood absolutely still, then touched his cheek where tears streamed down. "Papa, please don't be sad."

Shame and regret filled him and his heart seemed to break. She was his daughter, and for two years he had not held her. He put his arms around Milly, and choked out his words. "Heart of my heart." And he began to sob.

"Papa," she said, "please don't cry."

After a time he stopped. "I'm not sad anymore."

"Then make your face smile . . . please!" she said.

She was his daughter who needed him to shelter her from her own shadow, and he would shelter her. He wiped at his face with his sleeve. "See how big a fool your father can be!" And he spread out his arms so they made a large shadow and he began to laugh through his tears.

And Milly began to laugh, and then she spread out her arms, and giggling wildly, she tried to run from her shadow. When she couldn't, she collapsed on the sand in ecstatic laughter.

Carbri went to her and half laughing, half crying, he hugged her and kissed her hair. This child needed protection, and he was filled with a happiness he had not known in years. She was his daughter. He couldn't protect Arrah. She wanted no man's protection. But this child needed him.

That night, as Carbri tucked Milly into bed, she played the same game she played with her mother. It was the same game that Margaret had played with Arrah.

Milly made Carbri hold out his hands and say with her, "I don't love you this much. I don't love you this much. How much do I love you? I love you high as the sky and wide as the ocean."

Arrah named her new ship the *Mōrrīgan*, after the Celtic goddess of war and love. The *Mōrrīgan* was a magnificent bark, hewn from the finest golden oak of Ireland, with long, straight aged timbers and a stout beam. The mainsail was thirty paces high and drawn with the O'Donnell eagle, fierce and proud, his beak open, seemingly prepared to rip the sun from the sky. Beneath his claws the words in Latin: In this sign conquer. With twenty ships and two thousand men, Arrah O'Donnell was the most powerful woman in Ireland, a veritable queen of Tir Conail.

Inside the stateroom everything told of power and wealth. The black polished ebony walls were shined like mirrors so Arrah could see her face in them. Her captain's table was decorated with gold leaf on the legs and about the edges of the green-dyed leather that formed the top. The sheets on her berth were of Italian satin, the curtains of painted silk. The globe that showed the dome of the heavens was formed in pure gold. A solid gold phoenix stood beneath it, its beak encrusted with pearls, its wings filled with emeralds, its ruby eyes raised to the North Star. The enormous wardrobe was filled with a greater number of dresses than Arrah would ever wear. Embroidered silks with gold threads, fine satins decorated with pearls and precious stones. A white ermine throw covered the large oversized berth. Thick Persian rugs lay on the floor.

Naira smiled when she finally saw the ship. "Arrah, dear sister. What a marvellous bark you've built for yourself." Deep down Naira burned. It was time for Sebastian to move. He had been sent off on first one voyage and then another for months at a time, and had never carried out her plans but kept putting them off. Well, he had returned now, and Arrah was docked.

"We should order a feast to celebrate this splendid event," lilted Naira.

Arrah had never seen Naira in such a good mood, and she welcomed the idea of a feast. Carbri had defeated Glundel Joyce and managed to wrest substantial territories from him in Kilmaine. Arrah couldn't remember when she'd seen Carbri in such good spirits.

Orders for feast arrangement were given eagerly.

There was much laughter and dancing, and the O'Donnell name was heard again and again in cheers and victory songs sung by the bards. Carbri was in a jovial, amorous mood, reminiscent of his youth, and he made Arrah laugh. Laughing and holding hands, they retired to their chamber early to make love.

In bed, Arrah could feel the movement of his breath coming in small waves across her bare shoulder and across her left breast. His breath smelled after mead wine, a fruity, bitter, pungent aroma, but not unpleasant.

His hands slid down the side of her hip, familiarly down the side of her haunch, and then up inside her thigh. His hair smelled of peat smoke, for Carbri had sat in the place of honor close to the fire, along with her father.

But now, instead of continuing with what he had begun, he fumbled. "Arrah," he groaned. " 'Tis the drink. It'll be exciting the desires, but taking the wind from a man's sails. I'll be needing a little of your help to raise the mast." He rolled back flat on his back, and in a moment, he started to snore.

Arrah had wanted to be taken quickly, almost violently. Earlier she had danced with many of the soldiers. All night she had been surrounded by the warm smell of sweating men, had felt their hard shoulders brush against her arms. She needed pleasure now.

"Damn your drunkeness, Carbri O'Connor! How can a woman love a man when he comes to her with a limp fish!"

He started awake with a jerk of his arms and a loud snort. "Arrah. Patience."

"How can I be patient with this happening time and time again?"

"It's not happening all the time. Be helping me along." He made a move to grab her.

Her desire was gone; only anger was left. "No. I'm not doing that anymore for you."

"All I ask is a wee help. I've had a wee much to drink."

"It's all I've been giving you, Carbri, is help. You can't be thinking of anybody but your own drinking. How can a woman go on loving her man if he can't pleasure her?"

"I can pleasure you. Come here, Arrah Girl!" He made a move to grab her, but she pulled back. He looked at her. Now his voice changed abruptly to the ugly tone that frequently came with drunkenness.

"You're not a wife at all to me! Always off sailing you'll be. Never home! Never in my bed. A woman's duty is to care for her husband!"

"I owe duty to no man."

"One child! What kind of woman is giving her man one child!"

"I'm not a brood mare or a cow to be producing for you year after year!"

"What's the worth of a woman if she can't be giving a man children?"

"Damn you, Carbri. If it weren't for my soldiers and ships, you'd have nothing."

"You're a dog's bitch. You care for nothing but yourself. Your pleasure! Your power!"

"If I waited for you to pleasure me, I'd wait a long time, would I not?"

"Whore! Sailing off with your sailors. MacNamara was just one of many, wasn't he? How many times did you allow old Patch to climb on you? Mute? Hook? The others?"

She knew that tone. The unreasonableness, the self-pity. There was nothing more she could do now. She grabbed her velvet robe.

"Where the hell do you think you'll be going!" He lurched to a standing position, grabbed her wrap, and threw it across the floor.

"Out for a walk."

"I'm your husband, and you won't be going anywhere unless I say you can be going."

"You can't tell me what to do and what not to do."

"I say you'll not be going anywhere!"

"Let me pass!"

He blocked her way. But when he reached out and tried to stop her, he collapsed in a drunken heap on the floor. He shuffled vaguely in an effort to get up, but collapsed back into sleep.

Arrah stood and looked at him for a moment. Tomorrow he would be sober. Tomorrow he would be good-natured again.

Moonlight from a full moon streamed in through the open window of the castle, turning her lean, strong shoulders to ivory. Her fine-sculpted cheekbones were high and hard in the moonlight. Her hair was long and thick and fell in a mass of curl past her hips in a splendid fan. She wore a strand of pearls that she had neglected to take off because she had been in a hurry to have Carbri make love to her. She wrapped her robe about her and walked down the darkened stairway.

It was a stairway she had traveled frequently in the middle of the night, for she was often given to bouts of sleeplessness, particularly just before the time of her moon. She was always restless then, often walking in the surf in the middle hours, then returning to bed.

In the feast room, bodies were strewn about haphazardly, men and serving wenches who had fallen asleep beside the low trestle tables and beside chairs. She heard snoring, and the whistling of air through hairy nostrils. She heard the smacking of lips. There was the unmistakable smell of stale ale hanging in the air, even though the window was open. With that many men sleeping in the same room, the air was always stale.

Out in the courtyard Cuch raced up and touched his wet nose to her feet. The guards at the gate nodded to her silently. They were accustomed to her late-night wanderings. The day had been warm and she could still feel the heat in the stones beneath her feet on the path to the beach.

She looked out on the black and silver sea. Were women always doomed to be disappointed by their husbands? People came to expect certain things from each other, from husbands, from mothers and fathers, and from children. Only the sea didn't disappoint. Changeable in its constancy, the steady timeless rise and fall of the waves, the sea didn't fall prey to too much drink.

"Arrah!"

Arrah stopped walking. Surely Carbri hadn't wakened and come looking for her. She hoped not, for he was often in a foul mood when he woke from drunkenness. Ahead of her stood the low round grouping of limestone boulders where so many years ago Seaghan Mac— NO! She wouldn't allow herself to think of him. "Carbri?" she called, but no one answered. It was her imagination, the night playing tricks on her. She walked to the boulders, touched them. Again she felt the day's heat at her fingertips.

At the top of Eagle Cliff she could see mist beginning to unfurl, inching its way, creeping with silent fingers closer to the sea. Bad weather always began with mist at the top of Eagle Cliff. The fisherfolk said that there was a storm fairy who lived beneath the hill. He brewed up bad weather in a cauldron deep inside. The mist began to form when his cauldron was beginning its first boil. As yet there was no indication from the sea that a storm was coming. The surf splashed gently against the shore. Somewhere a seal barked.

Feeling irritable and hot, she walked to the surf. She pulled open her robe at the neck, hiked her skirt over her knees, and allowed the surging waves to cool her feet and ankles as she walked along the shore. Farther along she opened her robe, dipped her hands to the sea, reaching in as far as her elbow, and lifted the water to splash it on her face and neck. The coolness trickled down her breasts.

"Arrah!"

She started, pulled her robe close and peered into the severe shadows. There was silver and black in the night, no other color. The castle in the distance was silver; the rocks, silver; the moon, silver; and sometimes the sea, but everything else was black. She tried to peer behind the blackness, but it yielded nothing.

The waves crashed gently, and again she heard the voice. "Arrah!"

She saw a shadow move behind the rocks from where she had just come.

"Show yourself." Her voice was imperative. Nonetheless, she was uneasy, for she had left the castle without any weapon.

"Don't be afraid," said the voice, and now the shadow showed itself to be moving amongst the rocks, but it was still too far in the distance for her to recognize it.

"Who are you?"

"Don't you know me?"

The shadow came closer.

She looked at him, but a cloud crept over half the moon, a heavy-looking cloud, full and dark and voluminous. The night was still calm, but a storm was coming. All that she could see was that the approaching man walked with the unmistakable gait of a sailor.

She recognized Sebastian and relaxed. Since Patch left, Sebastian had become her second in command. He had proven himself a capable commander and captain, but his own ship, the *Saragossa*, had been recently wrecked. An iceberg, an edge of which jutted far out below the water's surface, had ripped an enormous hole in the hull of the ship and it had sunk. Sebastian was sailing with Carbri now on one of his ships, until another could be seized. Arrah knew enough of the natures of men to realize it would have been unwise to take a ship from one of her other captains and turn over its command to Sebastian. Any captain would resent Sebastian if she took away his command, even briefly. Soon Sebastian would have his own ship again. In the meantime she thought Carbri could use the help of an able seaman like Sebastian to assist him.

"Why is it you're about when all the others are snoring in their beds?" she asked.

"The dance, I think. My head is dancing still," he said, pointing to his head and laughing. "And you?"

Arrah looked up at the moon, her bold exquisite beauty caught in a stunning silhouette. "I've never been able to sleep when the moon's full. My grandmother used to tell me that the fairies lived on the other side of it. 'At full moon you could see them skipping across its face,' she said. As a child I would stay awake looking for them. The habit has stayed with me."

"And did you see them ever?" he asked.

"No." She smiled and looked down at the surf. Sebastian came beside her and together they stood looking out at the sea, at its constant, ever-changing silver and black waves rising and falling to the moon. "It's a magnificent thing, an ocean, isn't it," Arrah said more than asked.

"When it's calm it's a beautiful thing."

Clouds covered the moon again, and the sea was a pure black thing except for the edges of the waves, which were like lace fringed with silver at the moment that they crested. Sailors and the fisherfolk believed that the phosphorescence was scales from mermaids who had died.

Sebastian stood closer to Arrah than custom allowed. His arm didn't touch hers, but she was aware of him, aware of him as a man, and aware of the longing she'd felt earlier in the feast hall. She was aware that he was aware of her too. New sailors would look at her with obvious, lewd eyes, but she tolerated none of their suggestiveness and reacted immediately. "Look at me like that again and I'll have you flogged. I'm your commander, not your doxy!"

It was unthinkable to indulge herself with her own sailors, the same sailors that used Bridgett and Mary with as much casualness as they drank a tankard of ale. Dance with them, yes, she had danced with them for the fun of it in lighthearted amusement, but allow them to make love to her—never!

Nonetheless, as Sebastian stood close to her, she felt a vague stirring of desire in herself. She moved away from him.

"If you were my wife, I wouldn't let you from my bed at night."

His presumption stunned her. Occasionally she had caught him looking at her in strange ways, but always he'd talked to her as his commander. She attributed his boldness to the festivities. She had danced with him earlier and had found his closeness pleasant. He had not taken any liberties with her, nor would he have dared, but she had allowed him to hold her closer than any other sailor. She answered, "If you were my husband, you would know that you would have no choice. I come and go as I please." She walked away from him.

He caught up to her. "Can I walk with you a little?"

He was being far bolder than he should have been, yet she found her desires being stirred by it. "And if I said no?"

He looked at her directly. In his voice there was challenge. "Would a woman who's just fought with her husband refuse another man to walk with her?"

She felt the blood in her cheeks prickle. "The disagreements of your commander and her husband are not your concern." She strode away.

He caught up with her. "The behavior of a ship captain is always of concern to those who serve him."

"You're not at sea now!"

"The way a man acts on land follows often the way he acts at sea."

"Carbri has moments of truculence. It won't be long before you have your own ship again," said Arrah.

"Carbri's sailing is involving more than myself. The safety of a ship and the crew, all this depends on the skill of the captain. You are knowing he must put to memory the landmarks and the sea depths. All the currents that could smash his ships against the rocks. Three Fathom Pinnacle is on a direct course from Valentia Harbor to Blasket Sound. To the west southwest are the Stromboli Rocks and the Scollage Rock. They are very dangerous. On account of the strong tides, a great precaution must be taken to avoid these rocks. The moon was full. The tide stream was at its most strongest. Navigating through Blasket Sound, Carbri was forgetting completely to think for the added strength of the streams. It is a danger when the wind is blowing. We were nearly wrecked. We were saved only by a calming *miraculeuse* and the sweat of oaring."

"He's not so incompetent as you say! He sent Murrough's troops fleeing like rabbits."

"I helped him. He has not the head for strategy."

Arrah had heard rumors long enough, but to hear them directly from Sebastian just after Carbri had disappointed her in lovemaking made her angrier than she already was.

She turned on Sebastian, partly because he had articulated her suspicions and frustrations, and partly because he had aroused in her a feeling of desire that she didn't want to feel. He was her best captain; nonetheless, he was still in her employ. If she admitted Carbri's weaknesses to Sebastian, then she would have to admit them to herself. She loved Carbri, she told herself. Sometimes he was disagreeable, but most of the time he was kind and good-humored, and he loved her. She told herself all these things, but inside she was afraid if she stopped loving Carbri, she would start thinking about Seaghan MacNamara again, and she couldn't, wouldn't allow herself to do that. She grew defensive. "Carbri's one of the best sailors on the coast. He knows more about his men than they know about themselves. Sailing close to those rocks saved him voyage time. He expected his oarsmen would be able to pull his ship away."

"Once, several seasons ago, perhaps it was true. But your husband is losing his memory for sailing directions. This wasn't the first such happening."

"There is nothing the matter with my husband!"

"It goes little by little, a man's memory. And a man who begins to lose his memory, he falls prey to other weakness also."

She saw Sebastian's eyes go to her breasts; she ignored the obviousness of his remark. To answer to it would admit its truth and she refused to do that. "He's not losing his memory. Carbri is as good a sailor now as he ever was! You're envious of his position."

"It is true. I am envious. I am envious because he has the right to love you and I do not. And yet, he is failing at love in the same way he is failing at sea. You are a woman with much passion. You have need of a man who can love you!" Sebastian hesitated for a moment, then continued, "And the same man who's given to drink . . . loses his abilities. . . . Is that why you can't sleep, Arrah, because your husband couldn't love you tonight?"

"I'll have you flogged! Particularly since I know you share my sister's bed as well."

"My relations with your sister have no bearing on my abilities as a captain. You know what I say is right. You know that a captain's memory must never fail him. Drink makes your husband forget. It's a place he's sailed a thousand times. When I reminded him, he flew into a fury like a mad dog. It was only by the grace of the winds that we were saved."

"Is that why you came out here, to tell me this?"

"I heard the two of you arguing. Like many drinkers, Carbri finds it difficult to keep his voice calm. I find it sad that a man can't make love to his wife. Especially when she is so beautiful."

He approached her again and reached out as though to touch her. She stepped back abruptly.

"Return to your ship immediately!"

Arrah spun on her heels and left him standing there. The wind's fingers grew sharp, and poked and prodded with viciousness at any exposed skin on her chest and breasts; nonetheless, she was overheated with anger, anger at herself for listening to him, and anger for desiring him.

With each step the wind increased, a full wind that had swept the Atlantic, and which seemed to hurl salt and sand at her. Clouds rolled across the sky like heavy, dark ships across a sea, like heavy dark cannons across a hill.

Eagle Castle looked strangely vulnerable, almost as though it was made of a thin, pale shell, as though it could collapse at any moment. Arrah pulled her cloak closer, for the wind was picking up. Tumult now seemed to be only a few minutes away.

Sebastian watched her walk away from him. He enjoyed being the lover of his captain's sister. There were certainly perks that came with it. Fine sheets and the fragrant aristocratic limbs of Naira. He had indulged in women on the continent when he was there, but at Eagle Castle he disdained the other serving wenches, knowing full well that if Naira knew he frequented them, she would never have anything to do with him. He liked Naira's hunger for power. He didn't love her, but he, Sebastian, didn't love anybody.

He would have preferred to have been Arrah's lover. There was a kind of raw vigor to Arrah that Naira didn't have. Tonight, had Arrah been nice to him, he was planning to tell her about Naira's plot to murder her. But Arrah had turned on him like a cat and shown her claws. Well, so be it. He had refused to kill Arrah outright. She was his captain after all, and he owed her some loyalty. But if her sister was to kill her, that was something different. He had nothing to lose by Arrah's death and everything to gain. As Naira's lover, the two of them could rule Eagle Island.

Naira had planned to put some sleeping potion into Arrah's wine and then kill both her and Carbri as they slept. Normally Arrah went to bed alone because Carbri fell to sleep in a drunk stupor somewhere. But tonight Naira's plans had been foiled when Arrah and Carbri left early. Tomorrow Arrah was planning to sail for Spain and Portugal and it might be weeks again before she returned. Naira would not let opportunity slip from her again. She, too, had heard the argument between Arrah and Carbri. Now, dagger hidden in a pocket, she stood hiding in the corridor in the castle where she knew that Arrah would pass.

Arrah pounded on the wooden pedestrian gate leading into the castle walls. Both of the wolfhounds let out an energetic bark and came running.

Inside the castle she heard other dogs join in the barking. The guard let her in, nodded to her, and returned to his post.

As she walked toward the main door, she caught her small toe on a sharp projection of rock. In her anger when leaving Carbri, she hadn't thought of shoes. When she bent to rub her toe, she saw a pale form in the castle yard. She thought it was a finger of mist, like the shadow of an unfurling flag.

But Cuch and Bran both began to growl. Their hackles rose and their heads went down. They stood beside her. It wasn't a flag, but a vague shape like a small person. Arrah wanted to shout to the guards behind her, but she was powerless to turn around. Her eyes were fixed, held by some power, to the apparition that she saw in front of her. Vague and misty, a seeming mixture of light and smoke, it came closer. A chill moved across Arrah's back, as though someone had run a sliver of ice across the back of her shoulders.

The apparition began to cry. "No! No!" came its voice like a howling wind. It began to take a more defined shape, that of a young woman. A length of rope was tied about its neck, a length of rope that fell nearly to its ghostly knees. The dogs both watched it and growled. Neither dog moved. Neither dog barked. It came closer, dragging its one leg as though it had been broken. Arrah couldn't move from the ghostly form, couldn't step backward or forward. She was afraid to breathe, afraid to swallow, afraid to blink her eyes, afraid that if she blinked the ghost would pull her into the deep place whence it had come. Through its hazy body Arrah could see the castle wall behind. Now she could see its ghastly eyes. They were egg-sized, hollow and dark, and yet frighteningly white at the same time, like an old man's eyes with white skin growing over them. Its milky eyes were most terrible, for they beseeched. They were bruised and desperate and haunting. It turned its back and then she saw that behind its back its hands were tied, and she could see smears of what looked like dried blood where it had worked so hard at rubbing its wrists free. The ghost turned to her again, beseeching with its eyes to undo the ropes behind its back, but she was afraid to touch it. It knelt down in front of her, and lifted its horrible, anguished face to her, those impossible, shadowed milky eyes. A cadaverous smell came from it. "Please!" it pleaded. "Please don't let them drown me! Help me get away. Untie my hands!"

Arrah's blood seemed to congeal. She wanted to pull her hands in close, wanted to pull her skin in close, afraid that if some part of her touched the thing, she, too, would become an apparition like it. It cried again, "Please!

Please! Won't you help? I'm with child. They'll kill my child too! They're coming for me!"

The words were like a spear of ice through Arrah's heart, and she screamed, throwing her hands up in front of her face, hiding the horrible vision. Inside the castle a dog barked and then another. "Go away! Go away!" Arrah screamed, but when she lowered her hands, the ghost was still there.

The apparition stood, moved right up through Arrah's hands, and she could see her fingers through its white, shadowed eyes. "It's too late now," it said. "They're coming to take me back! Please don't let them take me!" Already it was disappearing. "Please!" Arrah heard on the wind, but the courtyard where the apparition had been was completely dark. The two dogs set into a furious barking, their hackles high on their shoulders.

"Milly!" Arrah screamed and ran as fast as she could back to the castle, up through the kitchen, up the stairs, and threw open the doors to Milly's room. According to legend the appearance of the ghost meant there would be a death of some member of the castle.

Milly lay on her bed, bathed in moonlight. Her small face was angelic. No, it was too still, like ivory, so still, absolutely still. "God! God!" Arrah wailed, but Milly was so still, there was not even a sigh from her. Arrah reached to touch her, and felt the brush of Milly's breath against her fingertips, and she collapsed on Milly's chest with a great outpouring of relief and thanks. She crossed herself, and made the sign of the cross on Milly's forehead the way her own mother had made the sign of the cross every night on her own forehead when Arrah was a child. "God bless and protect you," Arrah said.

Mary's ale-thick snoring came from a pallet at the foot of the bed. Arrah knelt beside the bed, lifting one of Milly's small hands to her lips, then the other. Milly sighed in her sleep and breathed in deeply. Arrah kissed her forehead and lay her head on her child's chest and listened to the heartbeat. She couldn't get the anguished apparition from her mind. For a long time, Arrah knelt beside her daughter's bed.

Naira had moved ahead in the corridor and stood outside the door to Milly's chamber, her dagger poised. She heard the rustle of Arrah's robe as she approached. It took a long time for Arrah to walk from Milly's bed to the door, perhaps two seconds. Naira's heart drummed in her ears. She saw the moon come out.

CHAPTER 30

Long ago Arrah had learned the way to protect herself was to keep moving and to keep moving very fast. She saw the gleam of moonlight reflected in the knife, and in one motion grabbed the knife and plunged it into the chest of her attacker. Only then as she felt the soft hand beneath hers did Arrah realize it was a woman who had tried to kill her.

"Guards, guards!" Arrah still could not see the face of her assailant.

The guards came running with torches. Arrah cried out with bewilderment as she realized that she had stabbed her own sister. Naira clutched at her breast. Blood came from her lips.

"You always won!" said Naira.

Incredulously, Arrah held her sister's dying body.

"Jewels. Power! Men! You always got what you wanted!"

"Is that why you tried to kill me!" Arrah shrieked. "Because of jewels. You want jewels!" and she ripped the pearls from her neck, and thrust the broken strand into Naira's palm. "Is this what you're dying for? Answer me!" screamed Arrah, shaking Naira. Blood rose up from Naira's breast and spilled on Arrah's hands.

"No," gasped Naira. "The old midwife was my aunt. The servant with the birthmark was my mother. Debrogail and I were exchanged as babies. Your sister is dead. I ordered her killed. I repeat the curse of my family on your family. There'll be no heirs until a woman is hanged by her lover. I fooled you! I fooled all of you!" and she began to laugh, spitting up blood hideously.

Arrah released Naira's body. A raw, overwhelming hurt began to throb inside her as if the dagger she had thrust into Naira had pierced her own heart as well. Exchanged at birth! Thoughts whirled around her. That's why the old woman had spoken of the passage. She had wanted her, Arrah, to die there.

Debrogail had been her sister. Debrogail, who had helped her carry the

bucket of whelks to the sea! Debrogail, who had told her to go back to the
hills and retrieve Reevnarg's eagle. She was the girl whom Arrah should
have called sister, and yet her mother had forced Debrogail to call her
Mistress Arrah. And now Debrogail was dead.

But it was this woman she had grown up with as her sister. When they
were small they had shared the same bed, she and Naira, kept each other
warm at night, their feet touching in the wind-cold nights of winter. Naira
had turned evil and bitter with envy, evil enough to order Debrogail killed.

Arrah needed to talk to someone about the terrible thing that had
happened. She released Naira's body and called for a guard to remove it.

She needed to feel the comfort of arms around her, she needed the
assurance that all of humankind was not terrible and dark in their hearts.
Crying for Carbri, she returned to her chamber.

Outside it was still dark, but on the horizon, the black had lightened to
dark blue and would soon redden. Her husband lay exactly where she had
left him, sleeping in a drunken heap on the floor. "Carbri! Wake up!" She
shook him gently. "Carbri, please wake up. I need you!" The walls could
crumble around him and still he would sleep.

At that moment the moon emerged from behind a bank of clouds. She
saw Carbri's lip move. Moonlight streamed in briefly, lighting his face. His
nostrils quivered as he took breath, as did the scar under his nose where a
dagger had caught him so long ago when she had run away on her father's
ship. It was Carbri who had come to her defense that fateful day. She went
to the bed, and pulling the cover from it, draped it gently over him.

Tomorrow, after the sun had crossed halfway across the sky, his phrases
would be like a charmed necklace of words, one following another. "Ah,
Arrah, my soul, heart of my heart. How I'll be loving you!" And there
would be apologies. "Arrah, my girl. Will you be sending me angry eyes
when you know that I'll be loving you as much as the earth loves the sun?
Don't you be going and staying mad at a man because he had a wee much
to drink and was saying things he didn't mean. Give your man a smile. Will
you be sending him off to sea without the memory of your fine haunches in
his hand here?"

"Carbri, Carbri." She whispered as she bent to him. She felt the softness
of his hair against her cheek. The first time he had made love to her there
had been sand in his hair. She kissed the top of his head and brought the
cover up under his chin.

She pulled a chair to the window and sat looking out into the darkness,
waiting for dawn. The distant ships, laden with full cargo, were drawing

deep in the water. In the storm, they bobbed like huge corks tossed in the windy bay. The wind rose. Would the killing in her family ever stop? They were cursed, all of them. Her family cursed, the world was a place of betrayal. Christ, they were predators feeding on each other. Her father had killed his sister. Now she had killed a woman she thought was her sister. And Naira had killed her real sister, Debrogail. Arrah pressed her hands against her skull. Death was a swirl of bodies behind her eyes. Would the killing ever stop? Tumult whirled in the sky like black, frenzied sharks, and Arrah wept.

The moment that Arrah screamed, Geralde de Burgo was consummating his marriage to Finola. She had become his only mistress, but he had been long in marrying her because his wife, although clam-brained, had the health of a horse. But one day she was pushing one of her grandchildren in a swing, and the wooden seat came back and hit her in the head. She had died within minutes. De Burgo had mourned her briefly as the mother of some of his children, buried her, and then immediately married Finola.

He kissed first one breast and then the other, bringing her nipples to a delightful hardness.

"You have splendid breasts," he whispered between tongue touches.

"Stop talking," she said, "and fuck me!"

"Wicked woman!" he said, closing his teeth lightly on her nipples, and sliding his finger into her. She moaned and kissed him deeply, seeking out his tongue eagerly. "Is this how you celebrate your wedding night," she derided him between kisses. "Your bride expects a hard cock and you present your miserable finger."

"I was simply checking to see if m'lady was wet enough."

"She's wet enough for your old thing!"

He rose above her. In one motion she felt the hardness find her, then enter.

CHAPTER
31

Glundel Joyce was disappointed with Geralde de Burgo as a father-in-law. He had married de Burgo's daughter, Agneis, in hopes that de Burgo would mount an extensive attack against Arrah O'Donnell for marrying Carbri O'Connor. But de Burgo, despite frequent prodding from Glundel, had been reluctant to attack her with all his forces, instead preferring to mouth such empty phrases as "There has never been a protracted war from which a man has benefitted," and "Victory is the main object in battle. When this is long delayed, weapons are blunted and morale is depressed."

After Phillipe had been killed, de Burgo had mounted a series of offensives against Arrah, and they had met with success, but then Arrah O'Donnell had imported many mercenaries, and they had fought back de Burgo's troops, killing large numbers of his men.

De Burgo decided that as long as Arrah didn't make any more forays into de Burgo lands, he was prepared to ignore her. Finally he had told Glundel to stop haranguing him with his tedious talk of attack.

Over a three-year period, Glundel continued to periodically blacken his hair and face with walnut brine and disguise himself as a poor vendor of saintly relics and good-luck charms, and travel to Eagle Island to glean information from Bridgett.

Mostly what he learned was day-to-day gossip and things of little interest to him. She recounted the quarrels of Arrah and Carbri because Arrah refused to have another child, and she described the frequent relapses of malaria that plagued Reevnarg.

But the latest bit of information Bridgett gave him was of considerable interest to Glundel.

Carbri had been drinking again and Patch had returned temporarily with a trained horse called Harlequin that could do tricks. The horse could pretend he was sick, could count with a stick, bow and kneel on command

and nip Patch in the rear end playfully. It was a splendid gray-silver beast with hot Spanish blood. Mistress Arrah had thrown her arms around Patch when she'd first seen him. But after Patch came, Carbri had grown jealous of the attention Arrah paid to him. Arrah had left for a short trip to Galway and while she was gone, Carbri, in a drunken anger, had forced Patch off the island along with his horse, threatening to kill them both.

When Arrah returned there had been terrible fight between her and Carbri, worse than Bridgett had ever heard. Carbri had said he wished he had never married Arrah. Arrah said she, too, wished she had never married Carbri. She was going to dismiss him, throw him off Eagle Island, and keep him from ever seeing Milly again. Carbri had apologized, and had promised Arrah he wouldn't drink anymore. Carbri for the most part had kept his word. There was a kind of peace between them and they were soon going to Deer Castle to hunt together. They were leaving in three days.

Glundel Joyce left Bridgett immediately. He did not indulge in any intimacy. He had no time to waste in planning his ambush. And in addition he was beginning to dislike her more and more each time he saw her. Once he'd made an idle promise to marry her. Now each time she saw him, she asked him when he was going to take her away. She had even grown stubborn sometimes about giving him information. He would have killed her except that he needed her.

Carbri was in jovial spirits as they began their trip. For once Arrah was doing as he asked. The area about Deer Castle offered some of the best deer hunting in Ireland.

Arrah, too, found the journey on the mainland pleasant. She and Carbri traveled with a party of nearly two dozen retainers, including Mary, Sebastian, and Hook. Bridgett had stayed back at Eagle Castle with Milly. The western extremity of the mainland was covered with rocky outcrops. As the hunting party traveled, the heather-covered granite hills gave way to low amphitheaters.

The river alternately flowed between steep, thick woodsy banks and an open valley, the water looking smooth as quicksilver. The water peppermint grew among the rushes, and because it was the beginning of summer, the purple orchids and yellow wild iris were both in bloom. Trees arched over the pale, fragile green of water lilies in clotted ponds, and the breeze, shimmering the leaves above, made sun-dappled patterns, green and light-green and dark-green, on lily pads.

The party passed an enormous flat stone supported on three lower stones. There were many such groupings throughout Ireland. They were known as lover's beds because of two ancient lovers who lived in the time of giants. The ancient lovers fled a jealous old king, and wherever they went through Ireland they brought stones together and made their bed on them. The stones were supposed to have magical powers and could cure women of barrenness if they were to lie on them.

As they traveled past the large flat stone, Carbri said, "Arrah! Why don't we be stopping here, and I'll put a strong son into you! Or have you figured out a way of doing it yourself, since you don't seem to be needing me for it?"

"Carbri, you made a promise."

"Aye, I did. But can you be blaming a man for forgetting?"

It was Reevnarg who had persuaded Arrah to put off divorcing Carbri. "There'll be the division of wealth again, Daughter," he had said. "You'll lose some of your ships, and lands. Give Carbri O'Connor one more chance." And so she had agreed to wait.

But Carbri's comment at the lover's bed made her realize that regardless of lands, regardless of ships, she and Carbri had no more life together.

A man like Carbri needed a woman who would give him a dozen children and who would knit trews and embroider pillow cases for each one of them. He had need of a woman who needed him. She had never needed him and he had grown resentful. There had been a brief moment in the hold of her father's ship, when he had reached down his hands to help her up from behind the pile of frieze. That was the first and last time she had needed him. She remembered the time with sadness, and with a certain regret. But one didn't lead a life because of past sadness. Carbri was still young and handsome and would easily find a wife.

As soon as she returned to Eagle Island, she would see the ollamh to have the divorce divisions settled. Father Thomas would be furious, but she was living her life for herself and not for Father Thomas.

When Carbri and Arrah arrived at Lough Gill, the sun was setting. It was a splendid sight, the surrounding hills reflecting in the mirrored stillness of the lake, and when the sun descended behind the mountains the glassy water seemed to turn into a mirror of rainbows. Trout jumped at sunset, red light edging their backs as they leaped out. The slanted rays of dusk turned the tree trunks into glorious colors of orange and yellow and red.

The hunting party had to lead their horses onto rafts that transported them to Deer Castle itself, situated on a small island roughly a cable's length from the coastline. It was a beautiful island, with small crystal pools overhung with willows and alders. Swans floated among the lily pads, their long necks graceful as the arms of a harp.

Arrah and Carbri were greeted by Lugh O'Connor, a hazel-eyed man with reddish blond hair who suffered from gout. He didn't walk but was carried about on a couch held on the shoulders of four servants. He embraced Carbri and Arrah with many words of welcome and offered them a bath and a feast in their honor.

Back in Arrah's chambers, Mary decorated herself in bows of every imaginable color. She pinned them in her hair and on her skirt.

Arrah had brought four trunks of dresses with her. When clansmen visited each other it was custom to have a feast every night of the visit. She chose a gold dress made of silk, embroidered on the bodice with pure gold thread.

When Arrah entered the main banquet hall, the men grew still as flags. The bodhran player dropped his stick in mid-beat when he saw her.

Some dancers crossed themselves, for they thought that they were seeing an apparition. Arrah O'Donnell, in her dress of gold silk, was beautiful beyond words. She seemed not to walk, but glide. The light from a torch caught in the emerald of the sword handle she wore girded to her waist and shone for a moment like a green flame. As she moved down the center of the banquet hall, men parted on either side to let her pass.

Arrah took the chair beside Carbri, who clapped his hands and ordered the music to begin once more. Many of Lugh's men had been drinking since afternoon and the fifes and drums made their blood leap with boisterousness and joviality. They danced jigs and hornpipes and double reels.

Arrah and Carbri sat on one side along the middle of the long wall. Lugh O'Connor lay between them on his couch.

Arrah watched Hook dance with Mary. With Angel he teased Mary, pulling a red ribbon from her hair and lifting it high above his head. Mary tried to reach up to grab it back, but without success. Mary laughed and pleaded. Hook laughed and pulled Mary close and planted a kiss full on her cheek.

Sebastian sat in a corner by himself, playing with cards and watching Arrah.

"Come, Arrah. I've a feel for dancing," said Carbri.

She danced a rollicking high-spirited hornpipe with him, but then he complained of thirst and returned to his seat and held out his tankard to be filled with ale. But when the serving girl offered a third time, Carbri declined.

Sebastian asked Arrah to take a turn. She was agile and sinewy as a gold cat in her silk, vibrant as a ray of dancing light. She felt the music in her veins and closed her eyes to feel it better. Sebastian held her about the waist. She felt the skin between her breasts grow moist from exertion. Her face was flushed and misted. She laughed and smiled, and Sebastian smiled back at her, his face filled with admiration. He drew her closer to him; immediately she stiffened.

She stopped moving, and giving Sebastian a look that forbade him to follow her, left the dancing area.

Outside she watched the moon reflected on the still lake water. There was the delicate, suck-suck sound of the lake washing on the shore, so unlike the surge of the ocean. A fiery arrow shot like a comet into the sky. It arched, then fell dark to the ground. A signal arrow.

Inside Arrah told Carbri, "I think we should cancel the hunt tomorrow."

Lugh raised himself on one elbow on his couch. His very large, red-veined nose looked larger than ever. "But the hunting is excellent now!" he protested.

She explained about the flare.

"It's likely enough," said Lugh. "My own troops are in the hills. There's nothing to worry about. Come now, Carbri, drink up with your clansman. I've some of the finest wines ever brought to Ireland in my cellars."

"I'm not at ease with the hunt!" Arrah insisted.

Lugh looked at her with glassy, bloodshot eyes.

Carbri was still in a good mood. "Arrah Girl. You've come so far, and made me happier than I've been for a long time. I've kept my promise. Can't you keep yours?"

She wanted to tell him now that she was going to divorce him. She wanted to tell him their life together was over. She wanted to return to Eagle Island and to Milly and to her ships, and she wanted to tell him she didn't give a tinker's damn for the hunt, and yet his look was so hopeful and full of anticipation that she couldn't bear to see it change.

The hunt the next day did not get an early start; the sun was already well past midday when the hooves of the party set down on the shores of Lough Gill. Lugh had already given his apologies and pointed with his cane to his swollen feet. "Nonetheless, I go with you in spirit. You'll find my trackers and dog handlers most able."

On the hills and along the river edges and in the forests that they traveled, Arrah saw a hundred shades of Irish green: there was the sage-green of rushes, the pale, delicate green of fern, and the rich velvety green of moss, the glistening darker green of watercress in a stream, the yet darker green of somber ivy clinging to a ruined tower, the almost black-green of the Irish yews, and the strange blue-green of the mountains, which seemed to have borrowed color from the sky. The earthy odor of fresh-cut bog for turf, and the heady fragrance of wild thyme and of foxglove scented the hills.

The horns blew: the stalkers had scared up a handsome buck, and the hunt began.

Hunters pursued the deer on horseback through the brush. Arrah was exhilarated by the excitement of the chase, the speed and gallop of the horse, the dodging of the tree branches, and the jumping of ravines and streams and logs. She wondered why she had never engaged in the sport with Carbri before.

They came to a low ravine where the pursued stag stood cornered and panting, surrounded by hounds leaping at its magnificent flanks and neck, drawing its blood with every noisy jump, so that the creature seemed to be put together with ribbons of blood. The buck's sides were heaving and blood ran from its nostrils. The buck fought valiantly, dropping its head and catching a hound on its antlers and throwing it over its back, but another hound had leaped to its withers and clung there, its fangs sinking into the flesh of the buck.

Arrah became disillusioned and angry. A dozen hounds and two dozen men with bows and arrows and pistols against a single buck? There was no sport in this. This was butchery.

Carbri leaped off his horse and drew the target with his arrow. Some of the hunters carried firearms but Carbri still preferred his bow, claiming that it was more accurate and could shoot farther. The hounds master called off the dogs. The arrow caught the deer behind its front leg. The buck leaped, trying to escape the burning in its heart. It leaped up at the side of the ravine, but stumbled and fell on its back, its front hooves striking at the air weakly.

Carbri was smiling broadly as though he'd defeated an army. He offered the assay to Arrah. But she shook her head. She wanted nothing more to do with the hunt except to have it over as soon as possible.

"It's a great insult to decline the assay when it's offered," Carbri said. "And very bad luck."

All the men of the hunt were watching her. Arrah turned away. If it was meat they were after, why not just kill an ox? If it was sport they were after, why use so many dogs? Why not pursue the deer on foot? She would have no part of it.

"You'll never do anything for anyone but yourself, will you?" Carbri said bitterly as she walked away.

Carbri took the assay of the deer grease, inserting the dagger under the animal's foreleg into its chest to determine how much fat it contained, hence how flavorful the kill would be. The fallen beast had a full thumb's length of fat and everyone congratulated each other, for it would prove to be a tasty morsel of venison.

Carbri bent and pulled his knife across the animal's jugular and cupped his hands beneath. He drank deeply from the fresh blood. All the other hunters did the same.

Arrah walked to a stand of trees. She saw a group of partridge take flight through the trees, and there behind them in the forest, saw the movement of metal. A pistol taking aim!

"Ambush!" she screamed. The hunters scurried for shelter among the trees. A shot rang out. Then another. One hunter dropped. Carbri ran toward Arrah, his bow in his hands. Another shot rang out. Carbri fell. Sebastian, who was running behind him, ran right past him.

Arrah shouted at him, "Pick Carbri up."

Sebastian stopped, then turned quickly and did as he was told. A trail of blood followed Carbri. Sebastian deposited him behind a fallen log.

"Arrah Girl!" Carbri reached out to take her hand but he couldn't quite reach it.

Shots rang back and forth across the clearing. Already Arrah's pistol was drawn and she waited for some movement across the clearing. She saw men running through the woods but they were still beyond range of her weapons.

Carbri was lying flat. "Come close to me. Lift me up!"

One eye still on the clearing, Arrah reached behind and lifted him. She felt the warmth of his blood on her hands and forearms.

"We shouldn't have come."

"Lugh's not a traitor." Carbri talked in short bursts. Blood was foaming in the corner of his mouth like pink lace. "Escape! Go! Give me your pistols. Brace me up against this trunk. I'll hold the ravine while you run."

"I've never run from battle before, and I'll not start now!"

"Arrah! When the pirates shot me . . . You said to me if I loved you, be brave. Now I ask you! Be brave for Milly. Run! I'll shoot your pistols."

"Don't talk."

"Flee to the castle. I'll hold the ravine."

"You can't hold it alone."

"Load your weapons. Leave me here."

She'd been thinking for weeks and perhaps even months about leaving Carbri. Now he lay in front of her telling her to leave him, and something prevented her. She reached for his hand.

"Arrah, all I ever wanted was for you to love me as much as I loved you. But it's hard to hold the hands of someone who's always reaching for the sky. And because I could never reach, I kept trying to pull you down to where I stood. Remember, it was I who first taught you to take a sounding. But you surpassed me a thousand times. I love you. I love you as much as the earth loves the sun."

"Carbri—"

He stiffened with pain. "Let a dying man have his words. I know you've loved MacNamara all this time."

"I don't love him."

"Lift your eyes. Remember how we were in France. Oh Arrah, how I loved you! After MacNamara it was never the same. I had your body there beneath mine. But part of you was missing. I hated you for it. And I hated him too."

"I was never the wife that you needed or wanted."

"All I ever wanted was for you to need me a little. Do you know what it's like for a man not to be needed by his woman? It kills him little by little."

"I am who I must be," she said.

"You're an eagle. You were meant to soar. I could never fly as high as you," he said.

She saw the blood pooling beneath him in a frightening quantity. "Don't try to talk."

"Arrah, listen. He wasn't . . . we . . . Finola and I . . . we planned it. He was her lover once, but he . . . MacNamara. It was a ruse. She tricked him . . . We tricked you. We planned it. She had a bracelet. She loosened a stone on it, then wanted him to look at it. But she hid it inside herself and told him it got stuck there. That's what he was doing when you saw him. Trying to take it out! Forgive me! I loved you too much. I couldn't stand to lose you to him." Carbri stiffened painfully. The pool of blood beneath him suddenly grew larger and spread to a pile of dry leaves.

Arrah looked at him with disbelief. There was gunfire and shouting all about her, and men crashing through the trees, and despite the noise she felt she could hear his blood seeping into the ground.

"What did you do to me?" she cried out.

"Forgive me."

Seaghan, it had all been a ruse!

"I thought I could make you happy. But I could never take you as you were. Always I was wanting you to be someone else. But making you into something else was like trying to change the wind."

"You played with my life!" she shouted. "How could you? How could you?"

"Frenchy!" Sebastian bent down, and Carbri grabbed him by the red scarf that Sebastian always wore about his neck. "Look after her! Promise! You're a good seaman. Better than I gave you credit for. Go now. Both of you!" Carbri lowered his head and gasped and was very still for a moment. Blood dripped from his nose and mouth onto the front of his jerkin. He swallowed with difficulty, collected his waning strength, and spoke again. "You never needed me. But Milly needs you. Go to her! Tell her I love her as much as I love her mother."

She remembered France. The way they had laughed with each other. The way they had loved. It seemed to her that that was the last time she had really been happy. She grasped his fingers in hers. "Carbri," she cried. "I . . . Oh, Carbri, I wish we could have made each other happier."

"Lift your eyes to the stars. It's where they belong. Look after our daughter. I love . . ." He stiffened, clasping her hand fiercely. "Frenchy! Get her out of here!"

His body went limp and he released her hand. The blood pool spread farther beneath him and reached out to touch her knee. She'd seen it countless times before, that moment when life left a body. Carbri O'Connor was dead.

PART IV

CHAPTER
32

Lugh was asleep when Arrah, Sebastian, and the others fled into Deer Castle.

Arrah ordered that the weapons room be opened and the weapons be broken out, but when she and Sebastian examined the store of arms, they discovered it in a badly depleted state. There were only a few chains, some pikes and halberds, many of them rusted and broken.

When she climbed up to the ramparts she could see the enemy. From the distance she saw the pale-headed figure of Glundel gesturing and giving orders on the shoreline of the mainland. In the forest she could hear the steady felling sound of axes. The enemy was building rafts to come to the island as well as scaling ladders to climb the castle walls.

The troops on the opposite shore outnumbered them by about five to one. Many of Lugh's kern on the mainland had been bribed by Murrough O'Connor to join with him and Glundel.

Disturbed by the sound of the chopping, the swallows swooped about the turrets of Deer Castle, their flight, gray quicknesses in the air. Fires were lit on the shoreline as the enemy troops began preparations for the evening. In the castle, there was little to do but wait for the attack. Arrah and her men wouldn't even be able to do more than take a few shots at Glundel's troops as they scaled the walls. Her men had their powder horns, but no other supplies. Gunpowder was one of the other things that Lugh had neglected to keep in storage.

Lugh was oblivious. He had briefly woken, chewed on a drumstick, drunk some more wine, and then fallen into another slumber.

Night was falling. Arrah stood on the ramparts, staring out on the water, watching, making certain that they weren't victims of a surprise attack. The moon was a perfect crescent, tipped upward in the sky. Her mother had a saying: *It's a good lucky sign when you can be hanging your hat on the moon.*

Good lucky! Bad lucky! One man's good luck was another man's ill luck. What luck had Carbri had? The luck of a relatively quick death.

She had closed his eyelids with her fingers. Poor Carbri. He had died better than he had lived these past years. His only fault was to love her.

The scars on her wrist were like fine carvings in the moonlight. Carbri, too, was a part of her past as surely as Reevnarg and Margaret, all of them forming her in some way.

Seaghan could be anywhere now. He could be dead. She learned to hate him so intensely because she had loved him so intensely. In the short few days she had known Seaghan, he had taken a part of her soul. She'd given everything to him, and then saw it disappear that afternoon with Finola.

Three stars glistened over the top of the dark purple hill on the opposite shoreline. *Two stars—evening; three stars—nighttime.* That had been her mother's saying. There was no way of forgetting the past, ever. But now she had to look to the future. *Lift up your eyes, Arrah.* That was the truth of the moment.

She had no idea how long she stood on the rampart. Time passed without her realizing it. A fish leaped out in the lake, its back edged momentarily with silver starlight and moonlight before it fell back to the water. Arrah looked up and saw that the lead roof was the same color as the fish in the moonlight and suddenly had an idea.

She and her men had to act quickly. She ordered them up to the roof to strip the lead tiles down. Lugh was snoring loudly beside the fire and didn't even notice the bustle about him.

"Stoke up your fires!" Arrah shouted to the cook.

The cook, an enormous, keglike woman with crossed eyes, rose up on one elbow in the kitchen and blinked her protruding eyelids. "But it's the bleeding middle of the night."

"If you don't get up this moment, it'll be the bleeding end of your life," Arrah retorted.

Arrah climbed back on the rampart, grabbed an axe, swung up onto the roof of the castle, and began to rip up the tiles with the axe. Sebastian was beside her, helping her.

Arrah threw the tiles down into the courtyard and began to shout orders for the men to carry them into the kitchen. "Tell Cook to empty all her pots and put lead into them."

The cook came out into the courtyard wiping a large smear of milk from around her mouth with her apron. "Lead in me pots! Are ye daft? We can't be eating lead for the morning meal. It'll be givin' us all the runs!" Cook, who prided herself on her sense of humor, was quite pleased with this remark.

Arrah shouted down. "And Glundel Joyce. You'll be giving him sour stomach. He'll roast your hams if you don't do as I say."

Cook's eyes uncrossed as she swallowed hard on the thought of this remark. Then her eyes recrossed as she ordered her scullion to pick up the lead tiles.

The lead-filled pots were hung in the fireplaces. The billows were brought out and the embers from the night's fires fanned into flames. Cook's eyes uncrossed as she shouted. "And for the love of Christ! Put wood on it. I could spit on it and put it out. More bellows. More wood."

Mary, who'd had some experience with pots in her husband's tavern, tried to help, but cook refused to share her station. "Nobody but me is telling nobody what to be putting where in *my* kitchen."

"Have it yea way, lass," said Mary. "I don't mean to darken me hands with any pot black if it ain't necessary." She sat down at a table in the corner and took out her tarot cards and drew them to determine the outcome of the battle. "Yer gonna be winning this one, Arrah," she said. "The King of Cups is turned."

"Stop that nonsense," Arrah said impatiently. "If it's winning you want, help bring tiles off the roof."

"Me, on the roof! Are yea daft, lass? I begins to swoon when I stand on me own tippy toes."

The flames rose in the fireplace at Deer Castle to nearly as tall as a man could stand. Great, huge roaring flames so that Arrah imagined herself to be in hell each time she walked into the kitchen, and everywhere there were pots of boiling, bubbling lead. Lugh continued to snore obliviously.

The dogs had long ago moved away from the fire and lay in a corner, their black muzzles resting on their paws, their eyes following the movement of people back and forth across the kitchen. One of the hounds got up to go outside where it was cooler, but as he walked across the floor, a large spark about the size of a man's thumbnail flew out of the fire and fell on the floor in front of him. He stepped on it and yelped wildly and bolted into the backs of one of the scullion's knees just as he was lifting a pot of hot boiling lead.

The scullion fell back on the dog's back, spilling the boiling lead on his face, neck, and chest as well as on the dog. The youth shrieked, an unearthly sound such as Arrah had never heard in her life. The cook's eyes floated in horror as the scullion grabbed at his face, trying to pull the scalding lead away from his eyes, but as he did so he burned his hands with the terrible burning liquid. He flew about the kitchen in a blind, burning fury, crashing still more pots down so that melted lead pooled.

Everyone watched in silent horror, then screamed and leaped as the melted lead ran in streams on the floor. The scullion still ran blind and burning.

"Stop!" shouted Arrah. But the scullion was mad with pain.

Sebastian grabbed a poker from the fire and hit the youth sharply on the back of the head, sending him collapsing in a pool of the boiling liquid. He writhed there on the floor like a lobster in a pot of boiling water.

"Christ, help him!" Cook screamed.

Sebastian struck the poker a second time across the servant's skull, and a third time, and finally the youth was mercifully still. Everyone stood stunned into dumbness. No one could look at the smashed, scalded head of the scullion.

"Pick him up," ordered Arrah. "Take him out to be buried."

"You're not a woman!" said Cook. "You're a monster."

Sebastian drew his sword. If the youth had been allowed to continue stumbling through the kitchen, he very well could have overturned all the pots of boiling lead. "Do you wish to die also?"

Cook's eyes crossed and uncrossed, and she pulled her neck down into her shoulders, but said no more.

Arrah suspected the attack soon. "To the ramparts," she ordered. "Everybody stay down and be as quiet as you can."

Arrah was thankful for Sebastian's help. He was everywhere she needed him, anticipating her commands even before she had uttered them. What powder there was had already been carried up to the ramparts.

It was still dark when the first ladders thudded against the castle walls. "Wait," Arrah whispered, "until there are several men on each of the ladders."

On the ramparts everybody waited.

"Now!" shouted Arrah. Pots of boiling lead were dumped over the side on the attackers. Many of the attackers climbed holding their shields above them, for they had been in other battles where boiling water had been dumped on them, but the boiling lead had such holding power in terms of heat that attackers' hands were burned by the heat of their shields. They dropped them, then fell shrieking to the bottom as more molten lead was poured on their heads and backs. The screaming of men came from all sides of the castle, and men ran into the lake trying to take off the terrible scalding metal from themselves. One of those burned was Glundel Joyce.

Arrah didn't remember how or exactly when she and Sebastian came to be naked in her bed. She remembered being desperate in her need to forget: the need to forget the sight of Carbri lying there in his own blood, the need to forget the young scullion lying in melted lead, the need to forget the screams of the enemy as she gave the order to dump more and more melted lead down on them.

CHAPTER
33

Sebastian had proved to be as valuable an asset in planning Arrah's campaign on land as he had been on the sea. He had a good head for tactics, and after Carbri's death, Sebastian's ideas had helped Arrah take the four Joyce castles on the mainland.

In bed Sebastian was a competent lover, but there was never any question as to who was in command. Most often she would straddle him, and begin to rock herself slowly on him, taking him higher and higher into her. Her head would be thrown back, her mouth open, and she would order him to touch her nipples and to press them hard between his fingertips. "Harder!" she would order, and then again, as her pleasure increased. "Touch me," she would demand, and he would rub his thumb against her to increase her pleasure. Sometimes she would allow him on top of her. She would make him slide his member up and down her, making him touch her pleasure point again and again, only allowing him to thrust in totally after she had taken her own pleasure and he was crazy with desire.

The flesh on Glundel Joyce's face and neck had melted like wax to form a shapeless, pulled mask. An infection set in and he nearly died. For months he hovered at the edge of life and death and then finally he recovered. His face had become so disfigured that he smashed mirrors whenever one caught his reflection. He had been married to Agneis de Burgo since she was fourteen, but even she was terrified of the way he looked when he returned, and screamed when she first saw him. He had been forced to strike her a few times to make her stop her infernal wailing. He hated her as he hated all women.

He would have left Galway Castle and the refuge of his father-in-law Geralde, but there was no place for him to go. In retaliation for the death of

Carbri O'Connor, the O'Donnell bitch had taken his lands and castles. She was more powerful than ever.

Glundel again began to urge his father-in-law to attack her. But de Burgo stubbornly refused to risk anything unless he was absolutely certain of winning, and O'Donnell was too powerful for such a win to be guaranteed. Instead of making war against O'Donnell, de Burgo had maintained his stance of an unspecified truce with her.

Murrough O'Connor, despite prodding from Glundel, also refused to take arms against her. Murrough had suffered defeat at the hands of O'Donnell and wanted no more battles. But Glundel Joyce refused to admit defeat. He secretly went to another Irish lord, Brion MacNamara.

MacNamara had a long-standing hatred of O'Donnell. Glundel lied to MacNamara, told him that de Burgo was ready to attack O'Donnell, but that de Burgo needed the assistance of MacNamara. They would divide O'Donnell's vast wealth between them. MacNamara agreed to assist de Burgo. Glundel Joyce rushed back to Galway Castle and lied to Geralde de Burgo, telling him that MacNamara was planning to attack O'Donnell and that MacNamara requested de Burgo's assistance. Then Glundel Joyce arranged a persuasive meeting with Murrough O'Connor. They would form an alliance of four: de Burgo, MacNamara, O'Connor, and Joyce against the O'Donnell.

The alliance had to move with care. The first attack would be crucial. O'Donnell yearly drew tributes of five hundred pieces of the scarlet cloth of Aranmore as well as the woolfells. That's where the alliance agreed it should first attack.

Brion MacNamara and Glundel Joyce waited in ambush as Reevnarg stepped from his boat in Killeaney Bay.

Reevnarg had had another bout of fever, a relapse from the malaria that overcame him sometimes. His mind clouded with fever, Reevnarg was careless as he entered the inlet. Brion MacNamara fired his crossbow, aimed directly at Reevnarg's heart.

MacNamara's aim was true, and Reevnarg died within moments. Brion MacNamara looked down in triumph over the body of his old enemy. The battle ended quickly, for without a leader Reevnarg's men fought badly and were easily defeated.

Those who survived wished they hadn't. Glundel Joyce, driven mad by hatred, took them to Dun Aengus, an old fort site, and there away from the earshot of Brion MacNamara, tortured them hideously before casting their mutilated bodies into the sea. The tide had turned against Arrah O'Donnell.

                                *   *   *

Debrogail was out in the garden at Galway Castle with Geralde de Burgo's grandson when Geralde came to her. It was a small garden filled with roses and hyacinths and the fragrance wafted on the air. The falling sun touched the bowers. The leaves glimmered like wafers of beaten gold. He approached unnoticed, holding something behind his back.

Debrogail's plain wooden harp, the one that Geralde de Burgo had presented her with some time before, stood on the ground. She knelt on the ground playing a game of *togaim* with the boy with small glass marbles of green and red and blue. Debrogail's head was lowered, the sun touching her hair which fell like burnished gold, like beautiful, delicate wings around her face. The boy laughed as he knocked one of Debrogail's blue marbles from the circle, and Debrogail laughed, too, throwing her beautiful head back. De Burgo had never seen anything so lovely and he stopped and watched her.

Debrogail noticed him and stood. "My Lord," she said, "welcome to our game."

The boy, too, leaped up and ran to his grandfather, throwing his arms around de Burgo's ample girth. "Grandpapa, will you play with us?"

With his free hand de Burgo rubbed the boy's curly locks, and smiled. "Later, my lad. First I have something for Debrogail." He drew his other arm forward and presented her with a splendid harp, golden strings; wood-gilt body and gold filigree. Debrogail's profile attached to the body of a mermaid was encrusted into the wood with pearls. "A woman with the voice of an angel deserves the harp of an angel, not some plain thing like that." He nodded at the wooden harp on the ground.

Debrogail fell to her knees and began to weep, not just merely crying, but sobbing as if her soul had broken.

Geralde de Burgo's breath caught. He knelt down beside her, putting his arm around her quaking shoulders trying to stop her crying. "What is it, my angel? Don't you like it?"

"My Lord!" She continued to cry.

Perplexed, de Burgo's grandson came close and he, too, bent to her. "Please don't cry," he said, tears springing to his own eyes. "Grandpapa, why have you made Debrogail sad?"

"I'll have my craftsmen make you another. Anything you like! I'll smash this one!" said de Burgo.

Debrogail grabbed de Burgo's hand, and the boy's hand, and held them up to her cheek. "You don't understand," she said. "Neither of you understand." She dropped their hands, and wiped at her tears. "All my life people have taken from me. I was a servant. They took my body when I was a child, and when I was older, they took my hands and put them to work. Later they took my voice for their amusement. You're the first one who's ever given me things. First that harp"—she pointed at the plain wooden harp standing near the edge of the circle—"and now this one. I'm crying because of happiness." And weeping again she threw her arms around de Burgo and his grandchild.

De Burgo put his arms around her and around his grandson. "Christ, dear girl," he said, kissing her hair. "It's such a small gift for someone who has brought me so many hours of joy, and my grandson as well."

Finola, who was looking for Geralde, entered the garden in a soft rustle of skirts. Across the rosebushes she saw something that stunned her. She had never in her time with Geralde seen him on his knees. Furthermore, his arms were around Debrogail.

Debrogail drew back from him. "Thank you, my Lord."

He smiled, then kissed her wet cheek. "Now, stop crying, or I really will think you don't like it."

Finola couldn't hear what was being said; all she knew was that she had seen enough—Geralde kissing Debrogail, and smiling at her in a way he had never smiled at Finola herself. She spun on her heel and left silently.

Geralde's aging knees on the stone had begun to get sore. "Help me up, dear girl."

Debrogail stood and reached down her hands to help up Geralde. "Now, play for me, and show me how much you like your new harp."

Finola's voice carried across the garden. "Geralde," she called. "Geralde. There you are!" Finola swooped into the garden. She smiled sweetly at Debrogail, then bent to kiss Geralde. "I was looking for you."

"You're always troubling me with something," he said, pinching her cheek.

"A messenger has just arrived from Glundel. Reevnarg O'Donnell is dead."

De Burgo made a clicking sound with his tongue. "Well, my son-in-law has finally had success."

De Burgo had never forgotten that Arrah O'Donnell had killed his son many years before, and he had planned revenge. But Arrah O'Donnell's strength had surprised him. He had never been a fool, and he soon realized it was a foolish man who put all his wealth and family in jeopardy because of the death of one member. His son had been a soldier, and had died like a soldier. When one had sons, some were lost in battle. It was a fact of being a father, but an eye for an eye, a tooth for a tooth, a hand for a hand—that sort of unreasonable revenge could destroy an entire family. A wise man knew when to keep his sword sheathed.

Despite Phillipe's death, Geralde had enjoyed a relatively happy life with Finola and his grandchildren around him. Now there would be more fighting. He was confident of a victory. However he had done it, Glundel had arranged a strong alliance against Arrah O'Donnell. As powerful as she was, even she couldn't win battles on four fronts.

But there would be time enough for battle plans tomorrow. For the remaining daylight, he wanted to enjoy the tranquility and peace of his garden. "Sing for me now, Debrogail. I'll think of fighting in the morning, when my body is rested. See," he said to Finola. "I've just given Debrogail a harp," he said.

"And a very pretty harp it is too," Finola said in her lilting voice. "A very pretty harp."

Arrah didn't feel sadness as much as a kind of vague regret about her father's death. Reevnarg would not want her to mourn him. Since his relapses of malaria he seemed to have lost his vigor and frequently expressed his longing for Margaret. Often he had said, "When I die, don't keen for me. Celebrate the living." So be it Father, thought Arrah.

But when she learned that de Burgo and Glundel Joyce had taken part in the attack that killed her father and cost the loss of Aranmore, she planned retaliation. She planned to raze de Burgo's lands.

She always plotted her forays as carefully as any general. She could put the castle under seige, but that would take too long, and she was impatient. She was drawing a detailed map, indicating the approaches she would make to Galway Castle. Sebastian was with her and bent over her shoulder as she marked off landmarks on the bay, when the horn sounded from the watch. Arrah went to the window. Her father's flagship, the *Maeve*, was sailing into the bay. But the *Maeve* was the ship that was taken when her father was killed.

Then as she saw the men climb down into the longboats to come to shore, she realized that the first man who descended from the ship was Seaghan MacNamara.

CHAPTER 34

The sea had splashed up the kelp called mermaid's tresses on the shore. It had been twelve years since MacNamara left Eagle Island. When he left, Reevnarg had been vigorous and healthy, and the O'Donnell lands in his control. Arrah had not been married and she wasn't yet a mother. She had been a young woman, naive, impetuous, powerless to the infatuations of love. She was older now, the victor of dozens of battles, the strongest force in western Ireland. Her body was no longer an eighteen-year-old's body that moved with the wild, untutored abandon of youth, but a woman's body, a powerful woman's body, erect, every movement calculated so no action was wasted.

Sebastian stood beside her as the longboat carrying Seaghan Mac-Namara rowed in. Sebastian was tense and apprehensive. "I'll go and order MacNamara from here," he said.

"No," Arrah replied. "Let him come."

The tiger lifted its magnificent tawny head and sniffed the air with its quivering, moist nostrils. The beast began to pad back and forth in front of her.

"He killed your father," Sebastian said.

"His father killed my father," Arrah corrected.

MacNamara's boat seemed one with the fabric of the waves. She felt her breath catch with each forward paddle stroke, saw his bare arms harden and relax with a rhythmic, repetitive sureness. His were arms of skill. She shivered involuntarily as her body remembered things that MacNamara had made her feel, things that had long ago been forced out of her mind. The air about her seemed to turn to a clear, blue-gray crystal. Behind her were crystal mountains and on their tops stood green crystal trees. No, she wouldn't allow herself to feel such things. She didn't want to struggle again with the intensity of loving him. Loving him was like being in heaven and hell simultaneously. Always he had pushed her to the extremes of her sensations. She had controlled and ordered her life exactly as she wanted since he had left, and now she didn't want anything to disrupt it. Three thousand men in her control and the wind in her hair when she was at the helm. But with MacNamara she felt weakened and powerless. She was strong, but he was stronger, and she was afraid of his strength.

"I'll handle him," said Sebastian. "You can go back to the castle." Sebastian stood with his legs wide apart, his hand on his sword.

"No!"

She regretted her garb, for she wore not one of her splendid robes garlanded with pearls, but only her black leather jerkin and black leather boots, trews, and cream silk shirt opened at the neck. She smoothed her jerkin and tugged lightly at the front. But it was Mary who said to her, "Don't you be worrying none. There ain't a woman what wouldn't sell her soul to look as lovely as the likes of you."

"But of course she looks lovely," said Sebastian angrily. "She has lovely looks always. Why should she be less lovely today?"

She didn't feel lovely. She felt frightened and ashamed. MacNamara's blood ran in her veins now, yet years ago she had sent him away in anger.

She noted his easy, strong movements as he stepped out of the boat, the beautiful curve of his powerful flank as he helped push it onto the sand. As he approached she saw the full curve of his shoulders, strong and hard. He wore no shirt, only a leather jerkin which showed off the bronzelike hardness of his chest.

He, too, was older and there was a hostility in him that hadn't been there when he left. He was broader than she remembered him. Hours of swinging a sword in battle made a man's body like that. The lines in his forehead had deepened and there was a long scar on his cheek which hadn't been there before, giving his face a ruthless, brooding, and dangerous expression. She owed Seaghan MacNamara gratitude for saving her life, for giving her his blood. She still had a scar on her forearm where the wooden tubes had been inserted. It was a scar that Sebastian did not know the history of. It had been kept a secret from Carbri too. It was her secret and Mary's and Seaghan's.

Sebastian stepped forward as if to take charge. "What are you doing with Reevnarg's ship?"

MacNamara walked past the Frenchman as if he were invisible.

Arrah saw MacNamara's eyes like two darknesses. She saw that the scar was there on his arm too. She twisted the tiger's golden chain over her hand.

MacNamara spoke. "Your father . . ." His eyes were noncommittal. "Bres, my clansman, brought Reevnarg's ship to me. I return it to you." As he talked, his dark, chiseled features were unyielding.

"I'll order a bath readied for you."

"I'll not stay. My own ship will put in before the sun falls. I'll sleep on board tonight and leave tomorrow."

"It's inhospitable to decline an invitation," she said.

"Let him go, Arrah"—at Sebastian's mention of her name, she saw the dark-cropped hair of MacNamara's beard move as though his jaw had tightened—"if he wishes," continued Sebastian. "I'm certain MacNamara is very occupied."

"And you! Are you well occupied these days?" retorted MacNamara.

Arrah, attempting to divert an altercation between the two men, changed the subject. "Carbri is dead!"

"Do you expect me to mourn him?" Seaghan's words seared like red-hot metal thrust into a pail of water. He bent down and grabbed the tiger's collar and twisted the animal's head up roughly as though he were going to break its neck. But all he did was open the jaws to examine the teeth. He stroked the animal's neck, his strong fingers disappearing in the fur of the cat.

Arrah watched his fingers, remembered the feel of them inside her from long ago. She turned her eyes from his hands to the far mountains on the mainland.

Seaghan continued, his voice suddenly softer. "When Reevnarg died, my father's men took his chieftain's brooch. Bres found it on them and gave it to me. Reevnarg would have wanted you to have it. I've forgotten it on the ship. I'll take you now to retrieve it."

Arrah moved toward MacNamara in silent acknowledgement. As she did so, her shadow crossed his thighs and the heavy curve of his groin. She remembered the hugeness and power of his loins and his thighs.

"I can go to the ship and get it for you, Arrah," said Sebastian.

MacNamara exploded like sparks thrown from a fire. "Is Arrah O'Donnell no longer mistress of Eagle Island?"

"A woman cannot do everything," said Sebastian, pulling himself straighter. "I assist her when she has need."

Seaghan MacNamara's eyes were two dark points of contempt and he spoke in ugly mockery. "When she has need! Has she need of your assistance often?"

Sebastian moved toward Arrah as though he were going to put his arm about her shoulder, but Arrah moved away. "This is not the time, Sebastian."

"Why not? You think since MacNamara returns, I can no longer attend you?"

"I'm your commander! You'll not speak to me like that!"

"I am not of your common sailors."

"Because the cockerel tops the hen, is he called Master Hen?" jeered MacNamara. His eyes were hot and dangerous.

Sebastian grabbed for his sword, but Arrah covered his fingers. If Sebastian pulled his sword he would die in a moment. She saw Seaghan's eyes follow her gesture, felt as though they burned a hole in her hand.

With ugly persistence, Seaghan repeated his earlier words. "Has she need of your assistance often?"

Her eyes rested on him. "Seaghan MacNamara, I owe you my life. For that I thank you from my heart." Her voice was strangely soft and smooth, without challenge, and belied an inner turmoil. She felt her soul exposed. There was a longing in her veins—as if his blood that now beat hot and thick in her longed again to be with him. She felt the surge of the same old danger. This time if she yielded there would be no respite from his power. "I'll tend to it, Sebastian. It's the O'Donnell brooch. Return to the castle, please. I'll join you shortly."

"Yes, Sebastian. Please!" said Seaghan, his voice cruel with mockery.

The two dark-haired men stood: Seaghan, huge and brutal like a dark block of steel; and Sebastian, tall, insolent with his long, slender limbs.

"Sebastian. It's an order." And in the same breath, she said, "Seaghan, will you accompany me to my father's ship?"

Already she had yielded some of her position to Seaghan. She saw his eyes flicker from Sebastian then settle on her again with that hot, triumphant strength.

But Sebastian spoke. "Arrah, I don't think that—" Even before Arrah saw movement, MacNamara was there. His powerful fist had grabbed Sebastian's shirt, his dagger blade pressed against Sebastian's jugular.

"Seaghan!" screamed Arrah, leaping at him and trying to pull the brute strength away from Sebastian's throat. She felt the terrible, implacable force of Seaghan's arm. He might well have been cast from bronze, so unyielding was he. "He's done nothing. Let him go." She stopped pulling at Seaghan's arm, and touched his hand. She felt the violence of his fingers beneath hers. "Come," she said softly. "I'm going with you!"

Seaghan released Sebastian.

Leading the tiger, Arrah walked toward the boat. But the tiger seemed reluctant to come. He raised his broad head and sniffed. A shoal of seals lay on the rocks. He watched them intently with his hot yellow eyes and then wouldn't move. MacNamara slapped his hand hard on the animal's flank. The tiger turned and growled at MacNamara, his white fangs bared, but MacNamara hit him again and the beast leaped ahead, its muscles moving like velvet-covered steel.

As soon as Arrah and the tiger were in the boat, MacNamara pushed it out then leaped in himself. He picked up the oars and without speaking, began to row. She picked up a set and began to row with him. With a brutal gesture, he struck her oars down. "I'll row!"

"It's my boat, my bay. And I'll row too."

He said nothing. She could feel his fury rising in the silence, the way that thunder rose from the silent air. They rowed in perfect unison, she matching him stroke for stroke.

"I owe you for my life," she said in a breathless way. "Won't you allow me to ask forgiveness?"

He rowed so vigorously that the water from the oars splashed her. She rowed harder to keep up with him. Her breath came faster; she could feel the moisture gathering between her breasts.

This was like a battle. They were against each other stroke for stroke. She watched the hard curve of his muscles move like wet bronze as he rowed. She remembered those powerful arms about her. She remembered, too, his tenderness. His hands were gentle and therefore all the more dangerous. She remembered how she had been explored by his fingers, parted, probed, pleasured in such a way that she was powerless to refuse him anything. He was a dark lover, tenderly ruthless in his secret violations of her. Since Seaghan, no one had pushed her to her limits: not Carbri, not Sebastian. She could feel the overpowering male fury mounting in him. Could almost smell it like the air before a storm.

She rowed more slowly, so their rhythm was broken, then with a deliberate and slow motion she dropped her oars. She let her hand slide to the water. The curve of his muscles moved like slick bronze as he continued rowing.

"Too hard for you?" he scorned.

"I don't want to row anymore," she said. She didn't look down but held his eyes in the challenge.

When they reached the *Maeve*, the tiger bounded up in one fluid leap to the deck. MacNamara's eyes ordered Arrah up the ladder but he did not touch her as she climbed it.

Her father's cabin held the evidence of another person's occupation. Reevnarg's compass, the magnetized needle floating on a straw in a bowl of water, stood on the table, but Seaghan's green mantle with its rough woolen exterior and satin lining lay on the bed. Charts and maps lay on the table. Her father had never used maps, but kept all landmarks memorized in his head. And the quill pen. She had never seen her father write. Perhaps that was why he had insisted she spend so much time learning with Father Thomas.

She lifted a map looking for the brooch, but MacNamara pulled it from inside his trews and threw it on the table in front of her. She picked it up. The metal was still warm from his body.

The chieftain brooch of the O'Donnell was a palm-sized artifact crafted of the red gold of Ireland, decorated with intertwining snakes swallowing their own tails, which formed a series of concentric circles. Normally the brooch would have gone to the new O'Donnell chieftain. But no one else amongst the O'Donnell clan was as powerful as Arrah. "You could have given it to me on the shore," she said flatly.

"With your rooster watching? Aye, I suppose it was just a matter of time before the sea witch found some goat to mount to her lust."

She put the brooch down. "Before he died Carbri told me it was all a ruse."

"I've been sent to hell on account of a ruse!"

"I've come to give you my apology."

"Apology! After all these years with your denial piercing me every moment? Apology! Damn you! It's easy for you to apologize!"

"Do you know what I felt seeing you with her? Her thighs gaping. All of her open and you bent down to her."

His hot eyes were dark and swift. "You didn't love me enough to listen to what I had to say."

"I loved you, Seaghan. I was destroyed."

"Love! You know nothing of love! I've lived these years with my veins lacerated. How many others mounted you?"

"That's not your concern."

"Your entire navy, I wager! That's what you wanted, wasn't it? Not one man, but power over many men. And in foreign ports, different men again?" He swept his hand across her father's desk, knocking the maps to the floor.

She felt the ship's deck slide beneath her feet. She felt darkness slip through her veins. She was frightened by the violence in his eyes but at the same time she was excited by it. Her blood rose to it.

"Please accept my apology!"

He exploded. "Damn your apology and damn you! Save your apologies for your cockerels. I don't care about you! I only came because I owe your father a debt."

Despite his words the twelve years seemed to disappear. Arrah wanted Seaghan more than she had ever wanted him. In the light of the cabin, her eyes looked almost yellow like the tiger's. She had to get him to react or he would be gone from her again. "So you don't care! You don't care then what I said to my cockerels. You don't care that I ordered them to make love to me. Do you remember your own words, Seaghan? Once a long time ago you said them to me. I ordered them to take my clothes off. I ordered them to climb on top."

"Enough!"

"No, it isn't enough, Seaghan!"

He grabbed her shoulders. "Arrah, don't."

She felt the hard restraint in his fingers. She pulled away from him, knocked her hand across the far side of her father's table, sending the compass bowl spilling to the floor with a clatter. "I ordered them to loosen my jerkin. I ordered them to slip their hands under my shirt." She hesitated for the full impact of her words. "I ordered them to slip their palms into my trews."

There was a violent pounding of blood in his chest. "Bitch!" He felt black passion rise in him like the slamming of a hammer on an anvil. He grasped her wrist and, mad and furious with want of her, threw her on the berth, crushing her terribly to it. His body was a weapon. If she denied him anything, he would kill her with his desire. He ripped away her trews, and ripped away her jerkin and ripped away her shirt. He found her and savagely and punishingly plunged in. She gasped with pleasure and he moaned against the intensity of keeping himself from exploding inside her. He felt her hot soft woman-secret tighten around him, tug at him like a great dark goddess, her urgent cries like the songs of the sirens. His flesh drove, hard and pumping; the hot pulse moving up his phallus, a dark, urgent devil. If he succumbed, it would be she who won. Beneath him, her moans grew deeper and then her body arched, and she froze there for a moment the way she always did just before climax and he drew back and then grabbing her tightly plunged deep, so her soft muscles contracted around him like a soft mouth sucking him in. It was an act of will not to burst into her. But . . . he would control her. His soul had been ripped asunder when she cast him aside. Now he was cleaved, however violently, to her once more. He paused, fighting the pushing pulse, driving it back into himself, so he cried out, too, with the effort. He was deep inside her and forced himself into absolute stillness, stillness against her contractions, absolute stillness, and he was in control now, in complete and pure dark control, thrusting and drawing back, then thrusting again, then thrusting again, pumping once more till she began to climax, her voice growing deeper and deeper, to almost a growl, and then she came to climax again beneath him, shuddering as though she had been pierced, and he knew that he held control, not only of himself, but her as well. Three times he brought her to pleasure, and still he had not yielded to his own climax. He turned her over, drawing up her buttocks with his huge demanding hands so that her back was arched submissively and she was in direct line to his want, and he pulled her onto that massive thing, and he stayed there, in her, pushing himself further. He took all of her, not resting until her body collapsed into exhaustion. Only then was he satisfied that she belonged to him once more.

Arrah woke to find Seaghan watching her. He cradled her head softly in the curve of his arm.

"My God, you're beautiful. I love you!" he whispered, then gently kissed her lashes.

"I thought I had stopped loving you. But I have never stopped," she said.

"All these years I've been fighting on the edge of a dark abyss, hoping that someday I, too, would be swallowed up in that darkness, that I would find peace in death from the torture of not having you. You're my soul." He kissed her long and tenderly and then spoke again. "If I were Adam and you were Eve and I knew the horrors which were to befall me, I would still taste the apple if you were to offer it to me. I couldn't be without you, even in paradise."

"I need you!" she replied.

She felt a tremendous well of freedom open up in her. And she began to cry and he cradled her, then crushed her to him, and he, too, felt that pain of need, that terrible flame of hurt which was life to him. He couldn't live without it. Without her, he was a man aching for his soul. He clutched her to him, and for a long time they lay perfectly still, lip to lip, ankle to ankle, as though their souls had fused.

And then, gently, he rose above her again and she saw the strong power of his shoulders loom against the dark. She felt the beautiful violence of his possession, needed it, and welcomed it. She was a chalice, which was filled again, that had been empty and not even aware of its emptiness. In the edges of her mind she knew that sailors believed that when the world ended, the stars would fall from the sky. They seemed to be falling now, bursting in soft white flashes about the bed. It was only here, in the loving harbor of his arms, that she forgot control, forgot power; that she found tranquility, found peace.

Always images had haunted Arrah's sleep, the cries from battle, the half-dismembered bodies of men, the empty eyes of skulls, the pleading of a ghost. She would wake in the middle of the night and not be able to fall back to sleep. Now the love of Seaghan put all senses from her and she fell into the complete peace of dreamless sleep.

When she woke a second time the moon had swung over and was no longer visible from the cabin window. She saw Seaghan sitting at the table. She sat up in bed and called him back to her side.

He came to her and ran his thumb down along the edge of her jaw. "Arrah O'Donnell. How beautiful you are, your cheeks flushed with sleep. You've made me the most miserable man alive, and now you've made me the happiest!"

He kissed her gently.

"What are you doing?" she asked again, looking at the charts and maps on the table.

"It is never long before your thoughts return to the sea."

"The sea is my life."

"And you are my life, my darling. Will you marry me now?"

In response she kissed him.

"Will you come to France with me?" he asked.

She frowned.

He took her chin gently in his fingers and turned her face so that she was looking directly at him. "Arrah, listen to me. I know that you love Ireland. I know that you love your cursed rocks and sea. But I can't stay here with you. My father will attack the moment he learns that I'm here."

"We'll defeat him."

His face grew very serious. "You don't understand. Once I took his wife from him. Either he kills me or I kill him. There can be no peace between us if I'm in Ireland. And there can be no peace for me, unless you are with me."

"France is not my homeland!"

"I cannot kill my father! When I was a boy he showed me how to track my first deer and kill it, and after the hunt he brought me my first woman and told me how to ensure that she was pleasured first before I took my own. He ordered the servant to lie on the bed and there he spread her thighs in front of me, and showed me the places to touch. And then I used what he had taught me against him. Like a traitor. If I stay, he'll kill me. You promised once that you would come with me. If you love me, you'll come with me now."

"I'll go and I'll stay a fortnight with you," and she kissed him again.

"Arrah O'Donnell, for now it is enough. In all God's creation, there isn't a man who is happier than I at this moment."

For most of her life Finola had felt powerless. She had not been able to choose her own husband; she'd not been able to win Seaghan. Aside from Seaghan, de Burgo had been the only one to make her happy. When she saw Geralde with his arms around Debrogail, and when she saw that he kissed her, she grew jealous. She was afraid that she would lose him too.

She'd known of de Burgo's affection for Debrogail for some time. She'd seen him watch Debrogail, his eyes filled with an expression of fascination and total enchantment, a kind of look he never bestowed on Finola herself. But she'd never had any reason to suspect that Geralde carried on with Debrogail, and as only his mistress, Finola had been more or less powerless to do anything about it even if he had carried on with her.

But now she was Geralde's wife. She was also getting older, and while she took great care of herself to keep her skin supple, and her face line-free, there were the telltale marks of age that she had noticed in herself. The skin on her upper arms had started to sag a little, and her breasts weren't as high as they once were. Geralde told her he loved her body, and he seemed to get lost in it often enough. But Finola was older than Debrogail by more than a decade. There was only so much that nettle creams and oils could do. She decided that she had to get rid of Debrogail before Geralde's kissing of Debrogail turned into a full-fledged love affair.

She'd spent her time over the past few days spying on Debrogail and Magnus and having them spied on, gleaning as much information as she could. Finally she had what she needed to incriminate Debrogail.

She and Geralde had made love; she rested her head on her elbow and twirled the gray hairs on his chest with her fingers. "Geralde, I have something to tell you," she said.

"What is it, my wicked woman?" he said. He was always in a good mood after he'd made love to Finola.

"There's something you should know about Debrogail," she said.

"Debrogail? What do I need to know about Debrogail except that she makes me happy as any man alive when she sings?" he asked.

"I know that you won't believe me," she said, looking at him earnestly. "But you must listen to what I have to say. I'm your wife and I love you more than I have loved any man alive. These past years that I've spent with you, I've been happier than I've ever been before. I wish no harm to come to you. Debrogail and Magnus are not sister and brother."

"Not sister and brother! But why would they say they are?"

"Because Debrogail is a spy."

"Finola, I never took you for anything but a clever woman, but I think you're losing your mind."

"Debrogail used to be a servant at Eagle Castle."

"I don't believe it!"

Finola continued. "I should have recognized her. And sometimes when I looked at her, I thought I did recognize her from the times I was at Eagle Island when my brother Carbri was still betrothed to your daughter. But servants, who notices them when one is a visitor?"

"That was a long time ago, Finola. How can one be sure of a face after twelve years?"

"Geralde, I love you. I wouldn't lie to you. Listen to me. I heard Debrogail and Magnus talking. I heard her say plainly to him, 'When I was small, Arrah O'Donnell's grandmother and I sang songs together.' "

"Are you sure?" Geralde asked.

"I know what I heard. Her voice is so sweet because she sings the harmonies of betrayal." Finola hesitated. She had not in truth heard anything more, but given how Geralde felt about Debrogail, the information she had given him was not enough to make him get rid of Debrogail. Finola continued, "I heard her clearly say that she planned to tell Arrah O'Donnell everything she knew about Galway Castle so that Arrah could attack it."

Geralde lay in bed thinking about Finola's words. There was little point in doing anything about it now. But he stayed awake all night, thinking about what she had said. Debrogail and Magnus had come begging to be taken in and he had allowed them to stay. They had taken shelter with him all these years, food, and Debrogail had accepted the gifts he had given her. But of late he had helped kill Reevnarg, and Arrah O'Donnell would attack again. If Magnus and Debrogail were traitors, he would punish them both with all the severity of his power. He would not be made a fool of.

The next morning he called Debrogail to him in the main hall. He sat in his chair, the ermine coat of arms behind him.

When he saw her smile at him, her red-blond hair cascading down her shoulders, he realized how easily a beautiful woman could make a fool of a man. He remembered how he had lusted after her, and how her beauty had even turned his lust into something else, a kind of veneration. She carried the mermaid harp he had given her. At the depth of his heart, he didn't want what Finola had told him to be true. If Debrogail confessed and told the truth, he would be lenient with her.

"You look very beautiful this morning," he said.

"Thank you, my Lord," she said.

"Will you sing for me?"

"But of course, my Lord. What would you like me to sing?"

"Some tune from when you were younger . . . But tell me, where was it you learned your songs?" It was the first time he had ever asked her that. Until now the origin of her songs had not been important. What mattered was her melody and the silver clarity of her voice.

"Learned my songs? Why, from my mother."

"Who was your mother?" He stood and came close to her.

"A servant woman . . ."

"And she didn't teach your brother to sing?" he asked, plucking a string on the harp.

Debrogail laughed. "She tried, but Magnus has a voice like two spoons in a cup."

"Where was your mother a servant?"

"My Lord, why all these questions so suddenly? Why does where I grew up affect the pleasure that my songs give you?"

"Answer me honestly. Where did you and Magnus grow up?" Despite the tide of anger and hurt that was arising from Debrogail's betrayal, he was trying to maintain a sense of calm. Maybe she would still tell the truth.

"Why . . . why in . . . Ballynacargy, at the O'Reilly castle, north of Clonmacnoise. As I've told you, my Lord. My brother and I . . . We were servants for Eochan when his brother attacked. We had no choice but to flee for our lives."

De Burgo exploded as he realized that she had led him by the nose down a path of songs, sweet smiles, and lies. "You're not Magnus's sister!" he yelled.

"I love him as my brother," she said firmly.

Geralde was past the point of reason. If she lied about Magnus, she had lied about other things. "You used to sing duets with O'Donnell's grand-mother!" he shouted.

When she didn't answer him, he bellowed at her again. "Answer me! Damn you, answer me!"

"Yes," she cried, "but you don't understand!"

"I understand, you traitorous minx. I understand. I loved you! I loved you so much I wouldn't even touch you when you said you loved someone else. I lusted after you, but more than I lusted after you, I loved you! And this is how you betray me! You knelt in my arms and wept your traitor's tears on my cheeks!"

He grabbed her by the shoulders and shook her, so the harp slipped from her fingers and clattered to the floor. "I always believed you. I always thought that I treated you well! And in return I expected only honesty and loyalty."

He grabbed up the harp and smashed it on the floor, again and again so wood splintered. Pearls rolled across the floor.

"My Lord! My Lord!" cried Debrogail, grabbing a splinter of what was once her harp. "What have you done!" She sank to her knees, clutching the shred of wood to her breast. "My Lord, what have I done!"

"Guards!" he shouted. "Guards," he bellowed.

"My Lord, please, tell me what I've done?"

"Save your pleas for the gallows, minx! You'll not serve Arrah O'Donnell under my roof."

Guards came running, swords drawn and axes ready.

"Take her to the dungeon. Find Magnus and throw him there too. They'll hang as soon as the carpenters finish the gibbet."

"My Lord. Please tell me what I've done!"

"You've betrayed me, whore! That's what you've done."

"My Lord, I beg you! I don't know who's plotting against me, who told you those untruths, but I never betrayed you. I swear to God!"

"I've heard enough!" said de Burgo. "Take her away!"

CHAPTER
35

The next day when Arrah and Seaghan rowed to shore, Milly ran to them, her hair flying in the wind. Like her mother, she wore trews and a jerkin instead of a dress. Bright-cheeked and out of breath, she looked up at Seaghan, her hazel eyes wide. She had to look a long way up to see all of him.

Arrah bent to Milly, and from the profile of their faces it was obvious that the two were mother and daughter: the wide, high cheekbones, the fine forehead, the determined, almost sulky set of the mouth, and the thick mass of chestnut hair. The two of them were silhouetted with the sea and the distant mountains of mainland behind them.

"Where were you?" Milly asked.

"On your grandfather's ship. Seaghan MacNamara brought his chieftain's brooch to me."

Milly looked at the stranger again. Often when she sat in her grandfather's lap as he told her stories, she would run her fingers over the circles of the chieftain's brooch. "Oh." She reached out and patted Kian's head. The tiger's head, the girl's head, and the mother's head were just about at the same height. The tiger sniffed at the girl's hair and then drew back. Milly glanced at Seaghan again. There was a vague look of discomfort in her eyes, and Arrah sensed that her daughter was intimidated by the size of the stranger.

"Seaghan MacNamara is the one who brought me Kian," said Arrah.

Milly was accustomed to gifts. Since her father had died, almost all the sailors looked on her as their own and were constantly bringing her small things, wooden painted dolls from the Cossacks, dark little monkeys carved from ebony, or small fans edged with starched lace. She looked at the stranger with different eyes, a child's appraisal, a kind of awe for this man who had given her mother Kian. "Could I have a tiger, too, someday?" she asked, more of her mother than of Seaghan.

"A tiger's a dangerous thing," he said. His dark eyes were intent on Milly. "You have to have a lot of courage before you can have a tiger."

"What's courage?"

"Doing something even though you're afraid," said Seaghan, looking at Arrah.

"Like going into dark places?" asked Milly.

"Yes," said Seaghan. "Your mother has a great deal of courage."

Mary called from outside the castle. "Milly! Father Thomas is here for your lessons."

Milly wrinkled up her nose.

Arrah hugged Milly, and wrinkled up her nose as well. "I know, I hated it too. But we all have to do things we don't like, and we all have to learn new things. The world's changing. You don't want people to think of you as a ninny."

Milly shook her head slowly, and set her lips in a resigned line, then seemed to think of something. "Why don't you have to learn?"

"I'm learning all the time. About the sea, about the wind, about people, about the world."

"But you don't have to sit close to Father Thomas and his bad smelly breath."

"When I was smaller like you, I did."

"When I get bigger"—she glanced up at Seaghan—"does that mean I don't have to sit beside him anymore?"

"Yes!"

"When I get big, will I have courage?"

"I hope so. Some people, even when they're big, are afraid."

Seaghan bent down. Even bending down he looked solid and unyielding as a granite boulder, yet Arrah was amazed at how his hard features had softened. This was an aspect of him that she loved as much as his strength. He didn't show this softness often. She'd only seen it in intimate moments. He smiled at Milly and spoke. "If you grow up and you have courage and you learn your Latin, then I'll bring you a tiger as well. Not as big as Kian, but a little one."

Milly smiled at him.

If only Arrah could have seized this moment. She wanted the world to stop turning. Her heart felt as big as the sky. She wrapped her arms around these two people whom she loved, pulled them close to her and kissed their hair. "I love you both," she said. "I love you both so much."

*   *   *

From the window of the main hall, Sebastian watched MacNamara, Arrah, and the child. He saw Mary walk out and fetch the child, and then he continued to watch Arrah and the Irishman as he picked her up in his arms and carried her from the shore to the castle.

Later, when Sebastian tried to see Arrah, Mary blocked the way. She sensed, rightly, that Sebastian despised her because of her low position. She planted her hands firmly on her hips and told him, "She's not wanting to be bothered by the likes of you anymore!"

"Old whore!" Sebastian pushed Mary so she fell down, her legs flying up in the air.

"Guard!" she shouted.

Mary was popular with the guards, and instantly three of them came to her protection.

"I shared Arrah's bed for over two years!" shouted Sebastian.

Mary, an obvious look of gratification on her face, shouted back. "Well, looks to me she's found someone else. And with MacNamara there, there won't be room for the likes of your wee thing!"

Sebastian would have killed her for that remark, but the guards pinned his arms against him and tried to take him away.

He struggled against them. "I still give orders around here! Let go of me, you fools, I'll go peacefully." The guards looked at him and released him, and although angry, he left quietly.

At Galway Castle, Nevil, de Burgo's grandson, had learned that Debrogail was to be hanged. He ran through the rooms screaming and tearing at his clothes, and knocking candles and vases to the floor, and pulling banners and tapestries to the floor. He threw a rug into a fireplace and when one of the servants tried to take the rug out, the boy grabbed a poker and, his eyes wide and wild, struck the servant. He was finally subdued, and brought thrashing and howling to his grandfather.

Any attempt to ask him questions or reason with him was fruitless. He listened to nothing, answered nothing, did nothing but scream Debrogail's name over and over again, without stopping, until he collapsed on the floor, and still he continued choking out her name.

De Burgo ordered Debrogail brought from the dungeon immediately. She calmed the boy, speaking to him softly, rubbing his head, calling his name and finally singing to him.

When he was calm again, and had fallen asleep from pure exhaustion, Debrogail picked him up and carried him to de Burgo and placed him in his grandfather's lap.

De Burgo looked at the boy's face, now cherubic again in sleep. He had been undone by the wailings of a little boy. Sometimes battles were lost for the smallest reasons. "You've bewitched my grandson," said De Burgo coolly.

"No, my Lord! It's you who've bewitched him. You with your lack of trust for someone who's never done a thing except bring you pleasure in a voice that God gave to her."

"I've decided to give you a stay of execution."

"My Lord's generosity never ceases," she said ironically.

De Burgo ignored the tone of her voice. He, too, was tired from the unceasing screaming that had gone on about him. "These are difficult times and they make for difficult choices. You'll be made comfortable in your dungeon. Nevil can visit you there when he wants."

"What about Magnus?"

"It's you who calms the boy, not him."

"If Magnus hangs, you might as well kill me now. I'll not help your grandson again," she said.

De Burgo looked at her. "What is it about Magnus that he inspires such devotion in you? Look at you. You could choose any man in this castle as your lover, and yet you save your devotion and prettiest songs for a man with one leg."

"You have sons, daughters, and grandchildren. I have no living person that I can call family. Magnus saved my life. He has become my brother and I have become his sister. I didn't lie to you about that!"

"But you lied about being at O'Reilly's castle. I won't be undermined in my campaign against Arrah O'Donnell because of lies. Guard!" he shouted. "Take her back to her cell."

CHAPTER 36

When Mary told Arrah of Sebastian's dangerous mood, she knew she had to end her relationship with him fairly. With Seaghan at her side, she ordered Sebastian brought into the main hall.

"Sebastian," said Arrah, taking a seat beneath the eagle coat of arms.

She was resplendent. She wore more jewels than he had ever seen her wear. She wore a thick choker of emeralds that turned her eyes a brilliant green. She wore a longer strand of pearls that settled just at the tawny mound of her breasts. Her dress was a green flowing fabric. Her face was dazzling. "You've served me well over the years, but the time has come for a parting of ways. I'll give you the Portuguese galleon, which you've captained the past months, and a crew of twenty men. You'll find there's a comfortable living to be made on the sea with a good ship."

"You cannot dismiss me like this!" Sebastian said.

"I can and I do."

Never had he seen a look like that in a woman. Her eyes held a look of absolute cold dismissal, negating everything that had passed between them, every night they had lain together.

"This will make your leaving easier." She cast a bag of gold at him.

He caught the money and held it incredulously. Did she think he was to be cast off like an old donkey? A single bag of gold when she had trunks of it? Gold that she would have shared with him had it not been for the return of that whoring Irishman. A single ship and a handful of men, after he'd been elevated to her second in command? This was his reward after waiting for years? "You think you can buy a man's affections with a rotting ship and a bag of gold?" he said to her. "I love you," he added.

"Don't pretend," she replied. "I know better. I saw your insolent eyes appraising me from the start. I'll have my ship escort you from Eagle Island."

It was true. He did not love her. He loved the power she exuded. Just being close to her made him feel strong. Commanding an army of a three thousand men. He threw the gold on the table and drew his sword.

MacNamara in one leap was over the table, pressing his sword against Sebastian's throat.

Arrah leaped to her feet. "Let him go!"

"Let me kill the ungrateful vermin."

"No! He's served me well."

"It's a mistake, I warn you. I see bitterness like venom on his mouth."

"He's done nothing to warrant death. Let him be." She picked up the gold bag and handed it to Sebastian. "If you don't take the gold, I'll distribute it to your crew. The choice is yours."

He grabbed the gold from her hands.

She spoke to a guard. "Escort Sebastian to his ship." It was an act of generosity which Arrah would live to regret.

For Arrah and Seaghan the preparation for their marriage began. Arrah wanted to get married in Ireland but Seaghan insisted that they travel to France because all marriages of importance had to be sanctioned by the French King.

Arrah challenged him. "Does Seaghan MacNamara need another man to tell him who he can marry and cannot marry?"

"Would you have me to lose my lands?" Seaghan queried, and then added, "When a man has a beautiful wife he wants the rest of the world to know that she is his."

"I'll go," she said, "but only to be with you. I'll not have some king tell me that I can marry you. I'll take orders from no one."

He held her chin in his fingers. Her head was high and proud, her eyes gold with flecks of anger. "Aye, Arrah of the Eagles. It's because the rest of the Irish chieftains talk as you do that Ireland shall be doomed someday. There are too many chieftains in Ireland, and no one strong enough to unite her. It won't happen in my lifetime or in yours, but it will happen. And all the pride of Ireland will not be enough to keep the damned English from here."

"You speak like a traitor to Ireland," she said.

"No, but I've been in England. The English are loyal to a strong king. I know the character of English men."

"And women?" asked Arrah.

Seaghan caught the edge in her voice. He put both his hands on her straight shoulders. His eyes didn't waver from hers: he loved her too much to be dishonest. "Yes," he answered flatly. "I took joy in making every woman want me. I made it my personal triumph, like a small battle. And I kept winning and winning. But I didn't know what I was looking for until I found you. To quit your arms is death. I love you, Arrah." Then he pulled her to him and kissed her.

Arrah returned his kisses, taking his tongue passionately. Love was as close as two individuals could ever come to the harmonious union of paradise. They found their lost years in each other's arms: they made love on the seashore. After consummation, Seaghan lay for a long time on top of Arrah, feeling her heart beat against him. The lovers were so peaceful that gulls came and scratched at the sand beside them. The sea came and touched their ankles when the tide came in. They made love on the daisy-spotted meadows and in the green fields and beneath the alders with the shade of the leaves dappling Seaghan's powerful back as he rose above Arrah. And after, when he held her, he kissed her hair gently, her nose, her eyelids. Then with skilled lips and fingers she would make him want her again, taking him deep into her mouth and sucking him into firmness, so that he was slippery and hard, throbbing and thick, alive in her mouth. She loved the smooth power of him in her mouth, the feel of him against her tongue, the taste of him.

He cursed as he pushed her head down farther and then exploded in her mouth.

With fingers and lips, tongues and teeth she brought him to hardness again.

"A man could kill himself making love to you. That would please you, wouldn't it? You would love that kind of power."

"What's the matter, has Seaghan MacNamara lost the steel in his sword?" she taunted.

"Temptress!" He pushed her down to the sand. She was wet with want. He covered her womanhood with his mouth, drank deeply of her intoxicating fragrance, his tongue seeking her dark secret pleasure, touching it in stealthful, skillful strokes until she shook in spasms beneath him, then he thrust into her wet quiver, pumping his manhood into her. Together they lay in the complete and total peace that comes with sexual exhaustion.

Arrah and Mary bustled about ordering dresses put into trunks—dresses of finest silk, embroidered with gold and silver thread and decorated with pearls and gemstones. Always at the back of Arrah's mind was the vision of the woman in the red dress who had stepped out of the carriage in Paris into Seaghan's arms.

She took her jewels: her pearls, her gold bracelets, her necklaces of rubies and emeralds that her ships had plundered from the lumbering merchants. Arrah of the Eagles would not be made to look like a peasant by the French court.

This was supposed to be a happy, joyful time, but there was an uneasiness that hung on the air.

The mist gathered strangely on the cliff of the Eagles. In the afternoons it would roll and billow as though it were going to storm, but by evening the mist would disappear, only to reappear again the next day. Kian sensed something and he paced relentlessly up and down the length of his chain.

Seaghan felt it, too, and he would frequently grab Arrah and push her back against a wall and take her standing there. But these were quick, almost anonymous couplings, frenzied as if from some kind of desperation, as though he were preparing for battle.

Shortly before Arrah left, Milly came to her as she worked at her desk. "Can I go with you to France?" Milly asked.

Arrah grabbed Milly to her. "No, darling."

"But why can you go and not I?"

"Because I'm bigger and older."

"Are you afraid?"

"No," Arrah said, but she, too, had felt the uneasiness, and then added, "I'm always a little afraid before I start a journey."

"I get afraid at night. I dream that you go away and that you won't come back."

Arrah brushed her daughter's hair back from her face. "Sometimes dreams play tricks on us. They make us believe things that aren't real."

One night Seaghan stood behind Arrah in her bedchamber as she talked and brushed the moonlight through her hair.

"When you marry me, I'll give you a wedding gift worthy of such a splendid neck. Something worthy of the Mistress of the Eagles."

She looked at him in her mirror, standing behind her, his hands on her neck, and suddenly a shiver went through her, an unexplainable cold, as though she were lying on a gravestone.

Seaghan frowned. "Is something the matter?"

Arrah shrugged. "A sense of something," she said. "I'm afraid."

He smiled and kissed her neck. Their eyes met in the mirror in front of her. "Arrah O'Donnell, afraid?" His eyes and voice questioned her. "I've never known you to be afraid of anything, not of a man, not of a ship, not of a wind."

"You used to frighten me," she said. "I'm still afraid of you sometimes. I need you too much! A woman who needs a man as I need you becomes vulnerable."

"And do you think that I'm not vulnerable to you? I love you, Arrah, and yet I know nothing of you! You're like an iceberg. I see only the surface of you. You give only with your body, but not of you. You talk of nothing but your ships or battles or currents or cargo. Talk to me about you. Talk to me about us!"

All night he made her talk about herself. He wanted to know everything about her, everything. He wanted to know about the scars on her arm, and about Milly, and about her escape with Carbri, the time they spent in France, everything, yet behind her words he could always hear the sea. It was as though the sea were in her body, flowing in her veins along with his blood. Trying to keep the sea from her words was like trying to stop the tide from coming in. But he, too, sensed something, and remained apprehensive. He was still afraid of losing her.

Glundel Joyce had been absent from Eagle Island for a goodly long time. Now he came once more disguised as a seller of good-luck charms and talismans. He carried vials of holy water from sacred springs on the mainland and bits of wood that he said were the pieces of the cross of Jesus, and he had a child's caul, which kept sailors from drowning.

When Bridgett first laid eyes on his melted face she was terrified, and he could barely keep her from screaming, for she was truly convinced he was a creature come from hell to take her there with him.

Eventually Glundel quieted her, and he learned that Arrah and Mac-Namara had left for France and that Milly had been left behind. Glundel Joyce rubbed his melted, disfigured face with his hands. This was better news than he could have ever hoped for.

He reached up under Bridgett's skirts and pressed his hands between her warm thighs. Bridgett kept her thighs pressed together and looked at him with level skepticism. For years he had been promising to take her away, but all he had ever done was bring her a few dresses.

"Come now, Bridgett," Glundel said seductively. "Be a friendly lass." He pushed his fingers higher, coming in contact with her hair. He stopped for a moment, gritted his teeth and continued until he touched the moistness of her sex. "I'm going to return for you in two days." He would get what he needed from Bridgett and by the time she learned the truth, it would be too late for her to do anything. He moved his fingers and she loosed her thighs, just a little. "I'll marry you, sweet chuck." Galway Castle was a long way from the Island of the Eagles and she had no way of knowing he was lying.

Glundel could see the rise and fall of her breasts; she opened her thighs and he inserted two fingers into her. He saw her head lift and her nostrils flare as his digits penetrated and began their work. What he really wanted to do was to plunge his fist into this dumb stoat, but he smiled. "You like that, don't you, Bridgett?"

She nodded, for her eyes were closed. She licked her lips and her mouth fell open. Her pelvis began to move rhythmically against his fingers.

Glundel continued talking. "The others, they don't take time with you. They just jump on you, isn't that right?"

She nodded again, her breath coming faster now.

He took her hand and, pulling open her bodice, pressed her fingers against her own nipple, squeezing it. She moaned as her body began its journey to that place of pleasure. He drew out his fingers.

She opened her eyes, disappointment and resentment making them dark and sullen. He lifted his fingers and smiling, outlined her lips with her own wetness. "I'll finish you in two days. But first I want a promise from you."

"What do you want?" she asked.

He hated her breasts. He hated breasts of any kind, but he had become a master at actions that belied his true thoughts. He closed his eyes, and thought of the daughters of the servants at Galway Castle. He lowered his mouth to her nipple and sucked her for a short but firm moment. He felt her stiffen beneath his mouth, and then he sucked a moment longer. "I want you to bring Arrah's child with you."

"What do you want with the child?"

From the tone of her voice Glundel realized he would have to go carefully. Bridgett had no feeling for Arrah, but she obviously felt protective of the child.

"I plan to send Arrah of the Eagles to the gallows. I want to lay a little trap for her, and my bait will be her own daughter. Then you and I, my little chicken, will lie night after night in the master chamber of the Castle of the Eagles."

Bridgett smiled her wolfish smile. "Promise you won't hurt Milly."

He outlined her lips with his index finger again and then pressed it between her teeth. "I give my word."

CHAPTER 37

The first thing Glundel did when he reached Galway was to send a man to the docks looking for Sebastian's ship. Bridgett had told him how angry the Frenchman had been when Arrah had cast him out.

The ship was there: a heavy galleon the same as all the Spanish and Portuguese ships. Glundel learned that the ship's captain was in a tavern called the Red Lion, had been there for nigh on two days, drinking and swearing and falling asleep and drinking and swearing and falling asleep.

Glundel went to the Red Lion and there he saw the Frenchman lying with his head on the table. He had found the means by which he, Glundel Joyce, would finally send the O'Donnell bitch to hell.

In Debrogail's dungeon, it was dark. She had been thinking about Bres. During the day when she was with Nevil, playing with him, watching him laugh, she had fleeting thoughts of Bres, imagining him with children of his own, children that he had sired with Naira. Would he lead them on a pony, or teach them to sword, or would he have had girls? These were the thoughts she had during the day, and they came and left fluttering about her mind, like butterflies.

But at night she remembered him intensely. Sometimes she couldn't bring back in her mind the outline of his face, or the exact shape of his nose when she was falling to sleep. But in her dreams he was vivid, and handsome, and they were laughing together.

She woke to the sound of a strange noise, coming from some other part of the dungeon. For a while she couldn't recognize it, but then she knew it for the terrible sound it was—a man crying out horribly.

"Magnus," she called to the cell where he was. "Magnus! Are you awake? What's going on?"

"Someone is being tortured," he said. His voice still carried that dejected tone. Regardless of what she'd said to him, or what songs she sang, she had been unable to bring him out of his melancholy.

"Who?" she asked.

"I don't know," he answered.

"Something's happening, Magnus," she said. "In the years I've been at Galway Castle, I've never known de Burgo to torture a man."

"Your heart is too good, Debrogail. I've heard torture often enough!"

"It's not de Burgo's way. He uses magic spells and potions to learn what he wants. When he's displeased he orders death, not torture. Magnus, something terrible is happening. I know it!"

Glundel sent word to Brion MacNamara to join him in Galway. Brion found Glundel in the Red Lion Tavern, holding the daughter of the proprietor on his knee. The younger man was playing with the ends of the ribbons that were looped in the child's shirt. Glundel held the two ends and slowly drew them back and forth across each other. Occasionally, he let his hands lie flat on her chest. Brion MacNamara spoke curtly with a repulsed tone. "Must you paw at that child?"

"What's the harm?" asked Glundel. "When they grow older they become intolerable with their shrill tirades."

"Where's the Frenchman you spoke of?"

"In de Burgo's dungeon."

"Take me to him."

"Surely you know the way. It's in the—"

"Leave off with your damnable fondling! Get up like a man and show me the way."

They descended into the dark damp confines of Galway Gaol. Brion MacNamara and Geralde de Burgo knew of each other only by name. To each of them in private, Glundel had promised killing the other, once they had attacked the Island of the Eagles. De Burgo and MacNamara seized each other's forearms in supposed greeting, but each man felt the strength in the other's grasp.

The three men passed into the room where the Frenchman was being held. He hung naked from the ceiling, his hands chained together above his head. There was a large pool of bloody water beneath the prisoner. A fire burned in the center of the cell. Irons of various sizes projected from the fire. Already there were large blisters on Sebastian's stomach and legs where he had been tortured.

An enormous man with arms like anvils and a leather apron stood throwing dice with a shark-faced man. The prisoner at first appeared dead, but on closer examination his chest could be seen moving weakly up and down.

MacNamara was instantly repulsed by what he saw. "Cut him down."

Glundel Joyce intervened. "It has been our experience here that extreme situations sometimes call for extreme methods. Hirple here has his own crow to pick with this Frenchman. Besides, he'll give us information about Eagle Island which will make it easier to attack."

The shark-faced man called Hirple limped toward MacNamara. "Aye, this bitch's dog. This Frenchy. Betrayed old Hirple. He pretended to help me. We was plottin' to overthrow that Captain Bitch. Then he turned on me. Told Captain Bitch I was the cause of the mutiny. I jumped overboard. Sharks just about ate me. But I had me dagger and slashed open the belly of one. The rest fed on it. I was headin' back to Eagle Island to get this scum bucket when I ran into Glundel. Been workin' for him ever since. Sebastian ain't nothin' but a scoundrel's dog. Deservin' he is of whatever we do to him."

In a single, swift movement, Brion MacNamara plunged a dagger into the unconscious man's heart. "That's my word. I'll brook no torture!"

Glundel Joyce smiled and put his arm around Brion MacNamara's shoulder. "Sometimes our underlings are swept up in their own zeal."

Brion MacNamara cast off Glundel's arm. "I'm attacking Eagle Island because my traitorous son is there. I swore I would kill him if he ever returned to Ireland and I am a man of my word."

"There's . . ." Glundel hesitated. "There's had to be a slight change in our plans. Your son has left for France along with his wife-to-be."

MacNamara exploded in anger. "Why wasn't I told earlier?"

Glundel's voice was charm and persuasion. "I knew nothing of their plans until most recently. Our attack must be delayed, but only for a short time. He'll return soon, I'm told. But if you're patient, we all stand to profit from taking Eagle Island."

Brion MacNamara held his hatred for Glundel Joyce in front of him like a sharp stick. "Necessity makes unwilling bedfellows. Very well. I'll wait."

Glundel smiled as he walked up the dungeon steps out into the night air. The moon was new and it was very dark. He was very happy. He knew that MacNamara despised him, and that soon he, Glundel, would be able to kill him. That knowledge made him feel immensely superior.

*   *   *

Arrah's ship sailed past Land's End and the Isles of Scilly and Wolf Rock, and past the white chalk cliffs known as the Seven Sisters, and headed north toward the estuary of the Seine.

It was bright and sunny the day that the *Mōrrīgan* moved up the Seine past the formidable walls of Paris. At first, people who were on the dock didn't pay much attention to the craft approaching the docks, for there was a constant traffic of carracks and galleons. But little by little a wave of wonderment ran through the dock people.

The burnished hues of the bark caught fire in the sunlight. Even though the ship was moving upstream, a kind of profound stillness enclosed it, a dreamlike quality, as though it had been frozen on the waves. One hundred strokes of the oars, fifty on each side, rowed in perfect unison. No sound came from the craft except the incantatory tom, tom, tom of a great drum that beat out time regular as a heart. Not one oar stroke was a moment's delay behind the other, yet the ship seemed a paradox of stillness in movement. Droplets of water appeared transformed as rare and liquid jewels falling from the oars, themselves seemingly encrusted with emeralds and pearls and topazes. The very water where the ship moved seemed a metamorphosis of silver. The brilliant white sails edged with purple hung magically still in the whispered air while the gold eagle on the main mast seemed poised to strike the sun with a kind of motionless fury.

A woman stood at the helm of the ship, a woman with waist-long chestnut hair so brilliant in the sun that it seemed to be brushed with gold. She wore a robe of the finest tissue, shimmering as if threaded with crimson and purple. In the long fluid lines of her dress, she looked like a mer queen come to shore. She wore a jewelled sword that caught the light of the sun and splintered it back in rays of scarlet and green.

A magnificent tiger stood beside her, his tawny head raised, the fur parting over his sinuous shoulders. The creature wore a collar of emeralds and rubies and was absolutely still except for the quiver of his nostrils and the blinking of his yellow eyes.

On the other side of the tiger stood a huge, godlike man, bestially masculine and arrogant, the ridges of his muscles gleaming like copper blades in the sun.

In the French court, news spread quickly of the ship that was sailing from Ireland.

One woman in particular listened with interest. She was the king's mistress now, but once had been Seaghan MacNamara's fiancée. A witty woman with an acerbic tongue that could reduce even the king's wife to tears in minutes, she was the woman Arrah had seen stepping out of a carriage into his arms.

The years had been kind to Countess Jacqueline Chopin de Villon. There was gray in her hair, but each week she would have her women henna her thick, rich locks so they were highlighted with silver-red.

A battle of fashion raged between the Queen and the Countess de Villon. The Queen was a pallid creature who suffered from too many leech bleedings. Because her hair was gray, lifeless, and spare, she covered her head with a hennin and veil that fell nearly to the floor. She was known to have a bony hen's chest covered by dark moles; therefore she wore gowns with a high, decorative doublet front, collared by a revere. The Countess, on the other hand, whom Nature had endowed well, chose open bodices with jeweled kirtles.

The King systematically ignored the hostilities between the two women. But they presented a frightening dilemma for the court ladies. If they followed the fashion of the Queen, they were snubbed by the Countess, who was the more influential power at court. If they followed the fashion of the Countess, they fell prey to the shrill and bitter anger of the Queen, who had been known to send her spies into the wardrobe of other women and have them rip their prized dresses to shreds.

No one knew exactly how old the Countess was, but she was more active than many of her younger counterparts. She began each day with a brisk walk accompanied by panting, wheezing attendants. She would take lunch and then spend her afternoon engaged in the activity which was her real passion—riding.

She had met MacNamara years ago when her husband, the Count de Villon, was alive. His properties adjoined those of the Count de Montreuil, with whom she and her husband had been good friends. They were the only two people, aside from Seaghan, a nursemaid or two, and doctors, who had ever seen the Count without his head cover. The four of them, the two Counts, Seaghan and Jacqueline, had spent many an evening together engaged in spirited discussions.

It was Seaghan MacNamara who had put into her the passion for splendid horseflesh. He had also put into her the passion for splendid manhood. The sexual appetites of Seaghan MacNamara were legendary. When Seaghan had called off their engagement, Jacqueline set out to become the mistress of the King. She succeeded in doing so. As his mistress, Jacqueline Chopin de Villon had access to vast influence. But Charles VII was a chinless, spineless, contemptible creature who wheezed and sniffled constantly. If he had not been King, the Countess would have held him in unmitigated contempt.

When the *Mōrrīgan* docked, Seaghan sent word to the palace that he was waiting for an audience with Charles, King of France.

In preparation for her audience with the King, Arrah ordered a bath in her cabin and Mary lathered her hair and her splendid shoulders. She then dressed Arrah's hair, plaiting it in thick braids interwoven with pearls, and pinning them with large ruby and pearl encrusted combs. Seaghan was out on the docks seeking news from the captains.

Arrah had never forgotten the woman in the crimson dress who had stepped from the carriage into Seaghan's arms and she had ordered her seamstresses to sew her such a garment. It was fashioned from emerald satin, taffeta, lace, and ribbons, with a doublet of mint gauze and wide, slashed funnel sleeves with fabric pulled through.

Arrah disliked the tight metal underpinnings and confining leather basquines that the dress required, but she was to be presented to the King of France as the future wife of Seaghan MacNamara. For this occasion she could tolerate the discomfort of a few bindings.

Since there was still ample time before Arrah's audience, Mary took her leave and went out on deck to be with the sailors. Arrah was left alone.

She looked through her boxes of jewels. She had dozens of necklaces and rings and bracelets studded with diamonds, rubies, emeralds, and sapphires, all taken from ships. She tried one on against her neck and then another, looking at herself in a full-length mirror of Venetian glass in a golden frame.

As Arrah looked in the mirror her reflection shimmered, and then it wasn't herself that she saw. Instead she saw the reflection of the sea woman from the dream so many years ago who had given her the instructions to sail the Dragon's Mouth.

Arrah loosened first one comb and then another, allowing her hair to fall loose on either side of her head, gleaming and fragrant. Then she took the dress that her seamstresses had made and put it back in her wardrobe. Instead she took out the fluid dress of sea-green silver encrusted with pearls that she had found in her mother's wardrobe so long ago. Arrah returned all the jewels to their various cases, and pulled out a single strand of pearls.

Arrah O'Donnell was Irish. The west coast of Ireland was not extravagant. She would not attempt to dress in the fashions of the French court. Arrah of the Eagles needed no decoration of ribbons, lace, or taffeta. She needed only the jewels of her sword, and the pearls of the sea.

Satisfied with her choice, Arrah waited for the hour of her audience with the King. She lay naked on her berth and passed the time by sketching wind roses on a map she was drawing.

Seaghan returned. She turned her head, smiled at him, and then returned to her maps. He sat down at the desk and began to make a few notes to himself.

He glanced over at the sensuous curve of Arrah's buttocks, half hidden by the cover. He saw her nipple graze the satin sheet, and he felt the hardening of desire in his groin.

He had taken her several times during the night, but now she stirred his senses again and he let his eyes rest on her. The cover made from the winter skin of ermines came to half the curve of her haunches, so that the firm swell of her buttock was readily visible. The lamp's glow slanted across her body, giving it a golden light. He put down his quill.

Arrah's hair lay loose across her shoulders. Under her left arm curved the softness of her breast, the nipple barely grazing the fine sheet. She grew more beautiful each time he saw her. Like the moon, she changed day to day.

His body, coming between her and the lamp, cast a large shadow over her that made her skin smoky and rich like musk. He slipped off his garments.

He pushed her fragrant hair away from the back of her neck and pressed his lips into the hollow at the base of her skull. He ran his tongue along the bottom of her left shoulder blade, then down along her spine, pressing his tongue into each hollow, tonguing in a soft massage, until he reached the small of her back.

He felt her breath quicken, felt her lift her sinewy back to him the way a cat would arch itself to be petted. He kissed his way up the soft hollows of her back, pressed his lips once more against her ear. Feeling the throb of desire, he slipped on top of her, pressing his knee between hers. He was still kissing her hair. It smelled as it always did, with the faint aroma of camomile flowers. His own urgency was growing now, the hard swell like bone rising almost to an ache. No longer content to just kiss her hair, he pressed her head to the pillow with his so that her shoulders were pinned and her buttocks raised to him. He could feel her readiness, and she opened to him, ready and wet. She was like a vortex, pulling him deeper and deeper into her.

He'd made love to her innumerable times, and each time he felt he was making love to a different woman. She was unpredictable and enchanting as the sea. Her variable desires intoxicated him. Sometimes she demanded that he thrust his heaviness into her slowly, like a carp caught on the hook; other times she wanted quick thrusts, the flight of birds against the wind; or inserting and withdrawing, moving up and down and from left to right . . . and then violently; or pushing on slowly, like a snake entering its hole to hibernate.

CHAPTER 38

Milly was accustomed to her mother's frequent absences, but this time a hollowness opened in her heart. The same afternoon that Arrah sailed away, Milly made Bridgett walk out with her to the cliffs above the ocean and they stood there watching to see if Arrah's ship was returning yet. Beneath them the surf crashed against the rocks, splashing up white and wet on the three hundred steps.

Bridgett said, "There ain't no way that your mother can be returning yet. She's not been gone but part of the morning." But to Milly it felt as though her mother had been gone for days and days. For a long time Milly stood gazing out on the ocean.

Each day Milly went out to watch for her mother, and each day the ache in her grew sharper and sharper, as though her own heart were exposed on the rocks at the bottom of the cliffs. In the past, when her mother had gone, Reevnarg or her father was with her. But now there was no one. She missed her father. She missed her grandfather, and most of all, she missed her mother. She began to cry on the cliff top with the Atlantic surging below.

Bridgett pulled Milly to her and kissed the soft hair of the child. As she did so, she saw a ship's sails far on the sea's horizon. She showed it to Milly. Milly grew ecstatic. Despite Bridgett's insistence that her mother had only been gone a few days, Milly was certain her mother was returning. Milly had no way of knowing that the sails that were approaching were those of an enemy.

The doors to the stateroom of the French court opened, allowing her to enter. Arrah felt uneasy: the French King could forbid Seaghan's marriage to her. She pulled the gold chain with which she led her tiger a little tighter.

Without turning her head, she looked for Seaghan in the flutter of color.

His dark head rose above the crowd, close to the throne. Without really looking at him, she knew that he no longer wore the rough mantle of Irish garb, but an elegant velvet doublet resembling those of other men of the court.

She remembered how he had made love to her a short time before. She felt the reminiscence of his love now, a delicious, dark, and secret soreness between her legs as she walked toward the throne. Sometimes when the love was particularly intense Arrah felt the small contractions of pleasure for hours after. She felt them now, those small contractions. She took a deep breath, and holding herself as straight as a ship's mast, proceeded forward.

As always, Seaghan's visits caused a flurry of excitement among the court women. He was now again surrounded by women, many of whom he had once bedded and who were eager to have him pleasure them again, or women who had heard of his prowess and were eager to experience it for themselves. He ignored the women who brushed the backs of their hands against his, or those who looked admiringly at the thick rise of his groin in the tight-fitting hose. Once, he would have taken advantage of such invitations, but after having experienced the passion of Arrah O'Donnell, other women seemed vapid in comparison.

Seaghan MacNamara watched Arrah's entrance as only a lover could watch a woman. Courtiers, men and women alike, stopped in mid-word and stood with mouths gaping when they caught sight of his wife-to-be.

In a stunningly simple dress, she made a stark and striking contrast to the court women. The women were elaborately dressed in brilliant dresses and hennins. Colored ribbons and jewels adorned them, yet they looked as fragile and frail as chalk. They were like white porcelain dolls—pretty but brittle as glass. Seaghan had the feeling their thin bones would break if he so much as grabbed one of their arms. There was not a single one among them who looked as though she might have the force to even lift the ruby and emerald sword that Arrah carried.

Unlike the women of the court, Arrah wore no metal or leather supports or corsets, and moved with a feline virility that exuded power in every stride. Arrah's body had matured in the last years. Her womanly curves were outlined by the sensuous silk of her gown, a gown decorated with nothing but pearls—hundreds of pearls, like miniature moons from some distant, miniscule world. With each step the gown lifted and floated, its colors shimmering silver and green like the sea. Arrah was not contained by the fabric, as much as emerging from it. Like Mōrrīgan, the ancient moon deity of the Celts who was both goddess of war and goddess of love, Arrah of the Eagles was a contradiction. She was temptress and warrior, silk and steel, breasts and sword, sea and moon. She moved like a huntress in search of prey. As he watched her he remembered how the warrior had become the woman; the way she had cried out, like a tigress in heat, beneath him a short while ago, when the pleasure had been intolerable. Her skin still carried that flush from love.

The crowd murmured as she approached the throne. Someone coughed.

The tiger froze in mid-step, the silver gleam of its claw caught in mid-air, its yellow eyes fixing on one face in the crowd. A woman screamed. Courtiers' hands went instinctively to their swords, but Arrah commanded the beast with the golden chain, and after a barely noticeable signal, the giant cat walked beside her once more, its muscles rippling beneath its tawny coat.

Seaghan watched her now as she moved with the cool arrogance that only power could bring. Arrah O'Donnell wore the pearls on her dress as though they were armor.

Seaghan sensed the excitement, the wonder in the crowd as though Arrah were some exotic, dangerous animal, like the tiger that walked beside her. He knew the women of the court and watched them. They found Arrah frightening and hated her. Vying for attention they brushed the arms of the men they were with, and tugged at their lace sleeves and made disparaging remarks. But the men were awed by Arrah's sensual arrogance. They politely pulled their arms from the women, straightened the lace cuffs the women had touched, and smoothed the front of their doublets. Never had the men seen such a stunning creature. Fanned on either side by lustrous brown-gold hair, her thighs invited their eyes, yet the smoke-colored chill of her eyes indicated that if any man were to lay a palm on her, she would draw her sword and slash off his hand.

Only the courtiers who stood closest to her noticed the scar that marred the skin under the right shoulder. There was more whispering, for it was unthinkable for a woman to show imperfection. The scar gave this formidable and fierce woman a vague and fleeting appearance of vulnerability.

High on the other shoulder she wore the large gold brooch ornately engraved with Celtic circles that had been her father's chieftain brooch. It pinned a floor-length mantle. Embroidered on the back of the mantle, in the red-gold threads of Ireland, was the eagle of the O'Donnell.

Seaghan stepped forward from the crowd and stretched out his hand to her. Then the two of them stood side by side. Seaghan spoke loudly and confidently: "Your Majesty, King of France. It is my wish to present you, Arrah O'Donnell, the woman I've chosen for my wife."

People murmured but were quieted, for they all knew the history of Seaghan and the Countess de Villon. Now they saw her glide silently from the crowd to the King's side and whisper something in his ear. The Queen, who sat in a small throne on the other side of the King, shot a daggered look at the Countess. "Sssshh! The King is about to speak!" A guard signalled for silence. All talking stopped. Nothing was heard except the whispered drag of pearls along the floor and rustling of gowns as women moved as close as they dared to hear.

Glundel Joyce had not been able to stop watching Milly O'Donnell. She sat in a cushioned window seat, crying for her mother. She was a beautiful child. Lovely eyes, frightened, the way he liked them. Fine skin and the loveliest of eyes. But each time he tried to talk to Milly, Finola drew her away and gave him those looks. After he killed de Burgo, he would kill that bitch, Finola. He, Glundel, saw the way she looked at him with those eyes, like he was some kind of vermin. It would give him a special pleasure to plunge a dagger into her.

CHAPTER 39

Arrah instantly recognized the woman who was standing next to the King as the woman who had stepped from the carriage into Seaghan's arms so many years ago. The woman had not appeared to age as much as she appeared to have grown more sure, composed, and yes, more beautiful. Arrah looked at Seaghan, but his eyes were forward, toward the King.

Only now did Arrah begin to take in details of the surroundings about her. The walls of the stateroom were covered in blue and gold tapestry drawn in square designs with small gold diamonds in each of the four corners. A red canopy hung over the King's head. The canopy was fringed with a band of alternating stripes of gold and blue. The King wore a red robe decorated with gold fleur-de-lis. The courtiers all wore over-mantles emblazoned with animals—lions, dragons, foxes, and eagles.

"Welcome," said the King, "you've been absent from us again."

"Yes, I had matters in Ireland which needed my attention."

The King looked at Arrah. "So our eyes tell us."

Arrah saw the woman watching Seaghan. The woman leaned forward again and whispered something into the King's ear. He cocked his head to listen to her, wiped his nose and then spoke. "You would have pleased us more if you had taken a French wife."

"I am Irish by birth. As beautiful as are the women of the court of France, I chose my bride from Ireland."

The court murmured. Half of it hated the Countess de Villon and the influence she exerted; the other half were her allies, who whispered in sympathy.

Now the Queen bent toward the King and tried to whisper something to him. When the King ignored her, she grabbed his sleeve.

"Pardon, Madam," he shouted at her. "You forget that I am King." He brushed at his sleeve.

"And a fool, if you listen to the words of that jealous harridan."

"Mind your tongue, woman!"

"I'll not mind my tongue. I am Queen. Your own wife."

The King raised his eyes so far to the ceiling that large amounts of white showed beneath them. "Alas, what she says is true."

"Allow me to speak, Your Majesty!" said Arrah, stepping forward. "You sit on the throne of a united France now. But even a short time ago, 'twas not the case. The Maid, Joan of Arc, assisted you in the claim to your throne." There was a murmuring in the court, for Joan of Arc, although popular with the peasants and soldiers, had been snubbed and disliked by court members. Arrah continued. "I have at my command fifty ships and over three thousand men. A king must be strong in order to maintain power in his own country, particularly when it has been divided with strife and war. I pledge to you, in case of further rivalries and bickering amongst your nobles, the assistance of my ships and troops."

Again there was murmuring, for the King was detested by many of his nobles. The assistance of such numbers of troops to the King would only serve to weaken their own position.

Seaghan looked at Arrah. A short time ago this woman had cried out, writhing beneath him like a she-beast, yet now she had spoken with an eloquence and dignity equal to that of monarchs.

The success of Arrah's words was evident on the King's face.

The Countess was obviously angered. Her face hard set, she tried again to whisper to the King. He swatted at her as though he might at a mosquito.

The Countess, furious with being so treated, stepped forward. "I wonder if—"

The King interrupted. "You, Jacqueline. You are not allowed to speak—"

The Countess ignored him and stood directly in front of Arrah. The two women were of the same height and the same defiant stature. The Countess spoke to Arrah. "I wonder if you know, Arrah of the Eagles, as you are called, that Seaghan is marrying you to get control of your island. He told me as much when he was here last."

Seaghan stepped forward. "That's a lie. It's—"

But Jacqueline continued. "Is it a lie that the MacNamaras and O'Donnells have been disputing the island for generations?"

"No, but—"

"What his family can't take by the sword, they will take by the marriage bed!" The Countess gave Arrah a dazzling smile. "It is MacNamara's way—to win women by the bed!"

Arrah's tongue tasted the same bronze taste of betrayal, the same taste she had experienced many years ago when she had seen Seaghan and Finola together. She heard Seaghan say something, but his words were distant and incomprehensible, like words in an echo. Was that why he had loved her, to gain control of Eagle Island? Whom could she believe? Years ago she had believed Carbri and Finola. Now was she going to believe a stranger again and see her happiness of the past days disappear, or was she going to believe in love?

She looked at Seaghan and saw the pained darknesses of his eyes as he spoke. "Jacqueline, if you were a man, I'd kill you!"

Arrah moved closer to Seaghan, and grasped his hand tightly as she confronted the Countess. "I'll not allow myself to be duped by lies."

The Queen stood and was clapping. "Bravo! Bravo! Well spoken!" The Queen's allies were all clapping now and smiling, delighted that the Countess had been properly rebuked. The Countess glared at the courtiers and immediately the clapping stopped. None of them had the courage to confront her glance directly. She spun on her heel and left the courtroom, her women following her.

The King stomped his foot impetuously. "Stop! Stop! This is our throne room, not a bull baiting! We'll tolerate none of this clapping!"

The Queen clapped louder, throwing the King a contemptuous look.

The King shouted over her clapping. "We'll give you our answer about the marriage tomorrow."

Jacqueline de Villon was furious as she returned to her chambers. She picked up a shoe and hurled it at the painted silk wall of her chamber. She had never expected him to marry anyone else. He had called off his engagement to her, claiming that he would never love anyone enough to marry her. And the King! The mention of some troops and he salivated like a dog shown a bit of bone! She flung herself on her bed and began to pound her fists on her satin cover. She would not allow herself to be dismissed so quickly. These years she had been the King's mistress, at least occasionally she had had the company of Seaghan MacNamara. That would all end if Seaghan married the Irish woman.

The King still had to give final approval for the wedding. She would think of some way to circumvent it! She would not allow herself to be displaced.

*   *   *

Arrah left the stateroom of Charles VII in even greater triumph than that in which she had entered it. She held Seaghan's arm. Courtiers smiled. There was remarkable handsomeness to the couple as though they were destined to be joined in matrimony by the Fates.

When Arrah returned to her ship, she felt a sense of doom overwhelm her. It was a feeling of intense cold, as though no fire could ever warm her. Seaghan saw her shivering and tried to comfort her, but there was no comfort now in his arms, or in Mary's chatter.

"I have to go home," Arrah said.

"But the King," protested Seaghan. "We'll be married here."

"I have to leave. Now!" she said. Outside it had started to rain. She gave orders to lift anchor. There was no talking her out of leaving. Seaghan had to stay to hear the King's pronouncement. She walked with Seaghan to the edge of the dock. Cormorants swam about in the water among some debris that had been thrown from ships.

At the end of the wooden walkway, he pulled her close. It was raining heavily, but his breath was warm against her face. He kissed her intensely and ran his thumb gently along the curve of her jaw.

"I'm afraid. For the first time in my life, I haven't been able to overcome a feeling of dread. I wish you were coming with me!"

"I must stay. I'll give you the shelter of my arms again, in but a few short days. In the meantime, I think of nothing but you. I love you. Every parting gives a foretaste of death. It is all we need of hell." He raised her hand to his lips and then turned, and pulling his mantle against the rain, he left her on the dock.

All sails were unfurled. The *Mōrrīgan* raced home.

Jacqueline de Villon had spies everywhere in the court. She knew that no marriage petition could be made formal until it was affixed with the King's seal. She had one of her clerks steal the marriage petition of MacNamara and the Irish woman from the King's chambers and bring it to her. The King was addlebrained, like a child. If he didn't see something, he didn't think of it. A marriage petition was just one more act of state he had to affix his seal to.

That night when the King came to her, the Countess smiled at him seductively. She wore a scarlet chemise of see-through silk. He was easy to please, a condition that generally left Jacqueline quite happy, for she was able to get a maximum amount of influence with a minimum investment of time. A quick turn and he would roll over snoring and drooling on the pillow beside her, leaving her alone to plot her intrigues and to find satisfaction with other men.

But this night the Countess de Villon persisted in her attentions and used every secret wile she knew to make the King perform his manly duties twice. The King fell asleep immediately after and didn't stop snoring even when she pulled his seal ring from his finger.

Over a candle she melted the red wax. She copied his hand, and wrote the word *refus* across the petition. Then she poured a little of the wax on the parchment and pressed the seal ring into the soft wax. Seaghan Mac-Namara would not marry the Irishwoman.

As Arrah came closer to Eagle Island, a mist was hovering above the sea, never rising but staying low, as if undecided what it wanted to do. The three pine trees on the tip of Beetle Head remained visible. She saw sea gulls sitting on the rocks and the words of a sailors' rhyme came to her: *Sea gull, sea gull, sit on the sand. It's never good weather when you're on the land.*

The moment the ship drew up to Eagle Island, Arrah knew that something was dreadfully amiss. Crows and ravens flew overhead in dark flocks. The gate to Eagle Castle was open and when she approached she saw that the guard had a kerchief tied about his head and there was a stain of dried blood on it. Before she even had a chance to ask what had happened, Legless Paddy cried out. "Arrah, lass. God has turned his back on us. They were here. And they've taken our heart. They've kidnapped our Milly!"

CHAPTER
40

Surely Arrah was living in a dream. She touched the lock of Milly's hair and tried to read de Burgo's letter once more. But the words were the wrong size in her mouth. "You will present your person to Galway Castle. You will arrive at said destination without accompaniment, save one woman servant. Failure to comply will result in the immediate death of your daughter. As proof that we have said child in our grasp I am including a lock of her hair."

Hook spoke. "Angel and I'll get word to MacNamara!"

Arrah put the letter down. "No, de Burgo says I must go alone."

"What guarantee do you have that he's telling the truth!"

"None. But I have no choice."

Without taking the time for further provisions she prepared to leave.

A great calm had settled over the west coast of Ireland. The sails hung slack. There was nothing on the sea but a great blanket of fog, nothing but the sound of the oars in the waves, nothing but the lock of Milly's hair and the words of de Burgo's letter.

One of the sailors stuck his knife into the mast and whistled softly for the wind, but even the wind spirit seemed to have abandoned the ship. Arrah took the mallet from the drums and began to beat it, inciting the oarsmen to row more quickly. Still the ship seemed to hang for an impossible time on each wave before it moved to the next. To try and fight the feeling of helplessness Arrah herself took the oars.

In the hypnotic movements of the oars, she found herself praying. "Our Father who art in heaven. Hallowed be thy name . . ." The numbing rhythm of the oars blurred curses and prayers so they became the same thing. Still no wind blew and the mist hung on, silent and ominous.

*   *   *

At Galway Castle, Glundel could not sleep; he rose from his bed and looked out the window. He heard the noise of swords clanging as the guards walked, but when he looked out, the mist billowing beneath him shrouded the courtyard so he couldn't see the ground. He touched the sill; it was moist with mist.

Each time he tried to talk to the O'Donnell child, de Burgo gave him angry words. "Glundel. I'm fast losing patience with you. It's not enough the children of the servants aren't safe."

Glundel slammed his fist against the stone sill. Twice he did it, so that the second time he felt the stinging where the skin on his knuckles broke. It was he, Glundel, who had kept up the liaison with Bridgett. He, Glundel. If it had not been for him, the child would not even be here, and yet now de Burgo was reprimanding him as though he were nothing but a lowly ploughboy.

What of it if he liked children? He hated women. Oh, he had learned the words well enough from that old fool who had been his uncle—the words of flattery and praise of their beauty. But he hated being in their presence. He hated the way their breasts rose up and the way hair grew between their legs. He hated his wives. Crushed columbine mixed into his first wife's food made her ill and she'd died slowly. No one suspected. His scarred face kept Agneis away so he didn't have to pay her any attention.

With Bridgett it was different. She had never changed the way that women changed. She had barely any breasts, and between her legs she had only a feather tuft of hair. But even with her, he had to close his eyes when he looked there.

He tied his dagger on and pulled open the wooden door to his chamber silently. A guard snored loudly outside his door. Without Glundel Joyce, no one would have learned of the dismissal of the Frenchman from Arrah O'Donnell's fleet, no one would have been able to get the help of Bridgett to take the child, for Eagle Island was well defended. They would have had nothing, MacNamara or de Burgo, yet now they treated him worse than a serf.

Glundel crept carefully along the stone corridor. The hallways were lit with sconces, and his body moving forward cast great shadows along the stones. He stepped over a dog that lay on the floor. The dog opened its eyes and thumped its tail up and down.

Glundel poked his head around a corner. Damn! Damn! De Burgo had posted another guard outside Milly's door. Guards everywhere. Like a prisoner. De Burgo's chamber was across the hall.

The guard was turned the other way, humming a vague, tuneless melody. Glundel crouched and in three steps he was behind the guard, dagger drawn. He put his hand over the guard's mouth. The guard stiffened as the dagger went in.

Glundel held the dagger in the man's back until he stopped struggling. The dog rose, stretched, shook himself and then came padding over to Glundel and the guard, and wagging its tail, began to lick complacently at the blood that had dripped on the floor. Glundel resheathed his dagger, pushed open the door to Milly's chamber, and very quietly dragged the body in.

It took a moment for his eyes to adjust to the light. Bridgett lay on a pallet at the foot of the bed. The child lay in the bed. Embers glowed in the chimney, for the child had taken a chill. He deposited the body in the corner and silently went toward the child.

She began to cough.

Glundel leaped back to the corner.

Bridgett stirred, smacking her lips loudly. Glundel remained motionless, hidden among the shadows. He felt the blood from the guard soaking through his soft buckskin *brocas*.

Milly was again taken with a fit of coughing, so harsh this time that Bridgett sat up. She rubbed her face and, holding the coverlet over her shoulders to keep the warmth, she got up and went to the bed. She poured some water from a pitcher and gave it to Milly to drink.

At this point the guard's body, which Glundel had propped against the wall, slid to one side and fell to the ground with a sound that only a dead weight could make.

Bridgett yelped and crossed herself. In response to Bridgett, Milly cried out and coughed again.

"Ssshhh. Bridgett," Glundel whispered. His hand was on his dagger.

"Master Glundel. What is it ye'll be doin' here?" And then through the dark he saw her smile. "Is it that what ye'll be after, sir? We'll have to be quiet then for Master de Burgo will be gettin' angrier than a rufflin' goose if he'll be finding out. He was telling me I wasn't to let you here."

Under other circumstances Glundel would have taken Bridgett and had done with it. It was a matter of little count. She was quick and accommodating. But all this time he'd been thinking of the child's fine skin and her shy eyes. Bridgett's slattern speech annoyed him.

"I've come to take her to my chamber. There's too much chill here."

Bridgett came close to him and saw the guard lying in the corner, but it was too dark to see that he was bleeding. "He's had a wee much to drink, has he? Come along and be crawling in with Bridgett. She'll take the chill from ye," and she reached out and touched his arm.

He withdrew it. "That's not what I've come for."

Bridgett realized that it was Milly he was after. "I won't allow it!"

"Stay quiet!"

"I won't have ye doing it!"

"You'll do as I say."

She stood firm. "Ye're no different than the others, ye ain't. Always promising to Bridgett one thing and then another."

"I gave you what I promised. Dresses!"

"And now ye've found something that's prettier than Bridgett and ye'll be wantin' her. All this way I come with her, so as I could be with ye. Ye and Sebastian,both of ye'll be thinkin' that ye'll be too good for Bridgett."

Milly was fully awake and called, "Bridgett!"

Bridgett moved backward toward the child. "Get up," said Bridgett. "Call Master de Burgo!"

"Get out, minx!" said Glundel.

Milly was frightened by the ugliness of the voice and began to call, "Mommy! Mommy!"

"I'll not get out. I'll call Master de Burgo! He'll put an end to your night wanderin'. I heard him scoldin' the likes of ye for wantin' to touch her."

"Out of my way, gull!" and he struck Bridgett hard across the face, sending her sprawling to the ground.

She began to scream. "Master de Burgo! Master—" Her second cry was cut short, for Glundel had plunged his dagger deep into her and the rest of the name died on her lips. He ripped the dagger down through her small, birdlike chest, into the softer flesh of her belly. Entrails and blood gushed out onto the dark stone. Glundel withdrew the knife and Bridgett fell forward, limp like an empty garment, into her own blood. He bent down, his ugly face twisted with satisfaction. Her little teeth. That's what he had once liked about her. Her little teeth. All perfectly the same size. He pulled the dagger once across her throat, threw the dagger to the stone floor and leaped onto the bed. Milly screamed. . . .

* * *

And through the fog, Arrah screamed, for she had in the nonstop hypnotic movement of the oars fallen into a kind of trance, and somewhere behind the mist she saw Milly's eyes in the darkness, wild with terror, and a pair of bloodied hands reaching for her.

Out of the mist the walls of Galway Castle rose gray and formidable. There was a stench that came up from the moat surrounding it, a smell that reminded Arrah of the dead-dog smell of Paris. At the top of the parapets she could make out the outlines of standing guards.

The mist was lifting, hanging in ladders now from the sky. The tops of oaks feathered a near hill.

The heavy timber of the drawbridge came squeaking and groaning down. Every squeak, every groan seemed to last a century.

"Give me your sword," said the guard.

Arrah handed it to him. She had lived her life by the sheer force of will, by attacking and attacking and never giving up. She wanted now to kill the guard, wanted to kill de Burgo. If they had harmed Milly in any way, she would kill de Burgo, even at the risk of her own life. She didn't care. The only thing that mattered to her was Milly.

She followed another guard through the courtyard. The mist was thick here. Imprisoned between the walls, it swirled about her, in and out of doorways and swallowing her feet. Mary followed behind, her cloak puffed out like a partridge against the mist.

De Burgo sat in the great hall. Finola stood beside him.

"Well, well," said Finola. "If it isn't Little Miss Herring Fleet."

"Where is my daughter?" asked Arrah.

"She's safe. I'll release her shortly."

"You're a worm, de Burgo. And you too, Finola. Milly is your niece!"

Finola replied in her silver voice, "She hasn't been harmed."

"Is this how Lord de Burgo does battle, by stealing away innocent children?" Arrah asked. Her outer calm belied an inner fury.

"I've grown tired of hearing of your forays and battles on land and on ship. Without you there to bewitch your men and make them fight like they were tenfold stronger, we shall defeat them easily. The O'Donnell has controlled the west coast of Ireland long enough."

De Burgo waved his hand and behind him a guard thumped on a door. Through it, Milly called, "Mommy! Mommy! Run, they want to kill you!"

Arrah rushed ahead. Two guards grabbed her. She pulled a hidden dagger from the small of her back and slashed one soldier across the arm. The second guard swung a chain at her hand and she dropped her weapon. The first man grabbed her from behind; she bit him, was momentarily free and ran to the door. Four guards came at her, and roughly grabbed her arms and hair.

De Burgo shouted. "I warn you. Struggle again, I'll kill her in front of your eyes."

Arrah stood panting like a trapped tigress.

"Mommy! Mommy!" came the voice through the door.

De Burgo gave a signal and one of the guards went to the door and rapped on it sharply. The door opened.

Milly was crying as she came running out. Her hair ran over her arms and she held flowers in her hands, dropping them as she ran. "Mommy! Mommy! Run! They want to hang you."

Arrah pulled Milly to her, felt the brush of Milly's tears against her own cheeks. Arrah touched the place above Milly's left temple where a lock of hair had been cut away. Beneath her hands she felt Milly shaking as she tried to talk.

"Glundel killed Bridgett. He had a knife. Her things inside. They fell out. And he came and he jumped on my bed. I cried for you, Mommy! Master de Burgo came. He hit Glundel. Now he wants to kill you. I heard them talking." Milly began to sob again.

A sour taste of sickness rose to the roof of Arrah's mouth. "De Burgo, I'll—"

"She's frightened, is all. He didn't harm her. Give the child to your woman. They're free to leave. I've claimed your ship for my own."

"You're a shark, de Burgo."

"We're all sharks in this land. You, too, Arrah O'Donnell. Not content with your own lands but attacking others. We've taken your ship and arranged an ambush against an English merchant to make it look as though it was you who attacked them. We have witnesses and an English magistrate and you'll be hanged for piracy. Many years ago you killed my son, Phillipe. It's your turn to die. The west coast of Ireland will be free of the tyranny of Arrah O'Donnell."

"Mommy!" Milly cried. "They can't take you." She wrapped her arms about Arrah's waist. "No, Mommy!"

Arrah bent and pulled Milly tightly to her. She felt her daughter's heart beating very fast against hers. She saw a vision, a clear vision of dark steps and gallows. A large, hooded figure stood at the top. Arrah buried her face against Milly's chest. *I'm afraid*, she wanted to say. *Afraid of dying and most of all, afraid of leaving you alone.* But she couldn't tell those things to Milly. "It's when we're most afraid that we have to pretend not to be. It's called courage. Can you be courageous with me?"

Milly threw her arms about her mother's neck. She wanted to feel her mother's arms around her so tight, so close, as though they would never let her go. "I don't want to be courageous. I want to be afraid and stay with you."

Arrah held her close and shut her eyes very tightly. She had to block out all feelings of despair. There was Milly, and her love for Milly, and Milly's love for her. Arrah of the Eagles had had them all—ships, jewels, power, and for so brief a time, Seaghan. The only thing that mattered now was trying to stop Milly's tears. Arrah took a deep breath before speaking and wiped Milly's wet cheeks with her fingers. "Come." Arrah removed Milly's arms from about her neck and led Milly toward the window. The guards moved toward her, but Arrah shook her head in a silent command. She moved with such dignity and presence that they stood where they were.

"Look up there at the sky," Arrah said. The mist was rising, the emerging sun slanting white lines of light through it. "There on the horizon, when the sun goes down, you'll see the evening star. Think of me. And when I see it, I'll think of you. And we'll be together. Remember what we used to say when I put you to bed at night? Say the words with me. I don't love you this much . . ."

Milly was silent.

Arrah took Milly's hands and spread them. "I don't love you this much." Arrah spread Milly's hands farther. "I don't love you this much! I love you high as the sky and . . ."

Milly joined her now ". . . as wide as the ocean."

"Remember those words," Arrah said. "I'll always love you! Mary! Come and take her."

Mary was crying. "Come, child!" she said gently.

"Mommy. *No!*"

"You must go now! Remember the evening star. I'll always be with you. I love you very very much."

CHAPTER
41

The jailer was a raggedy-looking man, with a rotting-vegetable odor as though his clothes were decaying. He looked at Arrah with bizarre eyes; one eye was strangely gray and clouded, the other was constantly roving.

The jailer sniffed very loudly and wiped under his nose with his sleeve, all the while keeping his strange eyes on Arrah.

He said he wanted her brooch.

"It's the chieftain's brooch," she said. "My father gave it to me—"

The jailer reached down beside him and pulled out a brutal-looking club. Arrah fumbled with her brooch, its clasp pricking her finger.

The jailer spoke again. "Hurry it up, will ya? Ain't got all bleeding day!"

She held the eagle brooch in her palm. The jailer grasped out and Arrah drew back. His fingers were black-brown, horrid looking.

"This brooch belonged to my father, Reevnarg O'Donnell, chieftain of the O'Donnell, and to his chieftain before him, and before him."

A whip hit swiftly on her back and head. Her reflexes honed by constant movement, she spun, ready to leap at her attacker. It was Hirple. "Traitorous dog! I thought you were dead."

The whip hit again. "The tables have turned, Captain Girl. Now hand over the brooch. The Joyce will reward me a fine price for it."

"You'll kill me before I give it to scum like you!"

The whip hit again.

She leaped at him, going for his eyes, ready to stab them out of their sockets with the pin of the brooch. Three guards came to his rescue and pulled her off.

Hirple ripped the brooch from her fingers. "Bitch," he shouted. "If I was havin' my way with you I'd be takin' you downstairs. There's a rack and irons and fires. All manner of things. Sebastian, he prayed for death. Right down under this floor. I'd make you feel the same thing! But de Burgo's forbidden it." He ripped her cloak from her. "There's many a soldier with a cloak not so fine as yours. They'll pay a handsome price for it."

"You'll rot in hell!"

"You'll rot before me, Captain Girl. The hangman's been given his orders. But before that. Them guards on the outside. They're just waiting to put their bit o' hards in you! Payin' me plenty to get a chance at your puddin'. I don't like the smell of woman, nor the soft buttocks. Sebastian, now, I liked him more. I used him well. Me and some of the others. So you'll prepare to entertain them when their turn at guard duty is over."

"The lowest pits in hell are saved for the likes of you!" she said.

"I don't give a herring's fart for your hell, Captain Girl. I'll take their money and let them do what they wish with you!"

Those who found out that Thomas was a hangman would ask him sometimes what it was like, putting a rope about a man's neck and watching him do a hangman's hornpipe. The truth of the matter was, death was death. Simple as that. There were no good times to die, no bad times to die. Death came when death came and there was no point in fighting it. A sword in the heart, a shot in the head, sickness or the noose—it was all the same. When God or the devil—and he wasn't sure that there was any difference between them—wanted you, there was no point in fighting them.

But this time Thomas was troubled, for there was superstition about the sea witch. People were afraid her ghost would come back to haunt them. So after the hanging she was to be shackled to four horses and ripped limb from limb so her ghost couldn't wander. Now, that was a terrible thing to do because it meant the loss of the hand of glory. The devils driving the horses would take it. There was a ready market for the hand of glory, the right hand of a criminal. It fetched a right fine price—a pound and a half, which was as much as he earned in two months doing what he was doing. It was the only way he could manage a decent living: by selling the prisoners' clothes and bits of the hanging rope, all of which would bring the buyer good luck.

The night was completely still around Arrah. The courtyard was in darkness. The rats scurried about her cell, and then she heard singing. At first she heard only a few strains of a harp, and then she heard the sweet sound of singing. It was the same song that Arrah's grandmother had sung, the song that Arrah had so loved, the song of the whelks.

> 'Tis believed that the whelks with their
>   color of purple
> Were a prince and princess who lived by the sea;
> And who often at eve, thro' the bright waters
>   rowed
> To meet on the green shore, and promise their
>   love.

The voice was unmistakeable—it was the voice of Debrogail. But Debrogail was dead. Naira had killed her, and yet she couldn't be dead for the voice was too clear and close. And suddenly in a moment of illumination, Arrah knew who Debrogail was. Arrah was manacled to the wall by a chain attached on her ankle and she began to pull at the chains and to scream. "Debrogail! Debrogail!"

The singing stopped. "Who's calling my name?"

Arrah shouted. "Don't you know me, you stupid goose of Beelzebub!"

Debrogail was stunned. There was only one person who ever called her a stupid goose of Beelzebub! "Arrah! Arrah! Is that you?"

Arrah pressed her body up against the stone wall, trying to get closer to her sister, and she pounded on it with her fists. "Debrogail! Answer me! Talk to me!"

Arrah saw a rat scurry into a hole in the wall that separated her from Debrogail and she fell to her knees, and began to dig furiously with her fingers. "Debrogail? Debrogail? Talk to me!" shouted Arrah. Her words came in a flurry now. "Naira said she killed you! She's dead. Oh, Debrogail. There was an exchange of babies. You're my sister." She dug and dug but the stone was unyielding. In a moment her fingers were bleeding from grit and mortar. There was only silence from the other side of the wall.

Debrogail couldn't believe what she'd just heard. *You'll find what's lost in the hangman's cell.* The old witch's words from many years ago when she'd wanted to get revenge on Naira.

"Debrogail. Did you hear me?" shouted Arrah.

Debrogail came to the front of her cell and whispered loudly through the bars on her door. "Don't shout so," said Debrogail, speaking in a loud whisper. "The guards will hear us. Is Bres alive?" she asked.

"I don't know. He left Naira some time ago."

Debrogail began to cry. Maybe Bres still loved her as she loved him. And then she remembered something else. "Your mother was poisoned. Our mother. I heard Glundel telling Geralde de Burgo." And then she began to cry again. She had never once put her arms around her own mother, embraced her, or kissed her.

"If she'd known what happened to you, her heart would have broken, treating you as a common servant," said Arrah.

"She made me call you Mistress Arrah."

"I hated it when you called me Mistress Arrah! You'll never call me that again."

"I always loved you, but I envied you. You were so beautiful."

"You, too, were beautiful, Debrogail."

"All the beautiful clothes," said Debrogail. "I used to think that Bridgett was a fool for trying them on, but I used to want to do it, too, but I never had the courage."

"Here in jail—it's a small matter what we wear now," said Arrah.

"I bear no grudges against Mistress Margaret. She was kind to me. She scolded you more than she ever scolded me."

"She should have scolded you more," said Arrah, wryly. "Maybe that would have kept you out of the dungeon."

"What's going to happen to you?" asked Debrogail.

"They're going to hang me."

"If I'm a stupid goose of Beelzebub, then you're an even stupider goose of Beelzebub. At least they're not going to hang me," said Debrogail.

"You always had a way of saying the right thing to make a body feel better."

"When, do you know?" asked Debrogail.

"Soon," replied Arrah.

Debrogail had managed to get Geralde to commute her hanging and that of Magnus. She would use Nevil as an excuse to save Arrah. If de Burgo hanged Arrah, she would refuse to ever sing or play with Nevil again. No, she couldn't punish Nevil. She had to think of something else. And then she had an idea.

She dipped her hands in her water pail. The water was cold, having picked up the chill from the cell.

"Debrogail?" called Arrah. "Are you still there?"

"Arrah, be quiet," said Debrogail. "I'm going to call the guard." She continued soaking her hands until she felt they were chilly. Then she shouted "Guard! Guard," and she took her wooden water cup and banged it loudly on the bars of her door and grabbed a couple of blankets and put them over her shoulders.

Magnus, who had been asleep, woke with the noise. "Debrogail, what's going on? I thought I heard you talking to someone. Who's there?"

"Magnus! I have a sister. I'll tell you later." She shouted and banged it harder against the bars.

But when the guard finally arrived, Debrogail's heart sank. He was the biggest lummox in de Burgo's troops. The man who won all the wrestling matches.

God, give me strength, she thought.

"What is it?" the guard asked.

"I'm freezing to death," she said. And she reached out her hands to him through the bars. "Feel my hands," she said. "I was playing my harp, and I got cold all of a sudden." Her harp stood beside her.

The guard, who knew that Debrogail was to be well taken care of, answered, "I'll bring you some more blankets!"

"I've blankets plenty, I can't get warm. Please do something."

The lummox opened the door and came in. If something happened to Debrogail and de Burgo's son went on a rampage again, then the guards would be held responsible.

Debrogail crossed her arms on her chest and made herself shiver violently. "I'm so cold," she said. "I feel like I'm going to die."

The guard looked at her. "I'll call the leech healer. He'll know what to do."

Debrogail collapsed to her knees on the floor. "Please help me!" she cried.

The guard knelt beside her. "What's the matter?"

Debrogail grabbed the corners of her blankets and threw them over the guard's head. In the same moment she grabbed her harp and brought its wooden body down on his skull.

In her cell Arrah heard the insertion of a key in a lock, and the opening of her cell door. She grabbed up her chains, ready to use them as a weapon, but she let them drop immediately when she saw a woman.

Debrogail ran to Arrah and threw her arms around her, and the two women held each other, crying each other's names. But there was no time for talk. Debrogail bent down and undid Arrah's manacles, and they threw their arms around each other quickly once again.

"Come," whispered Debrogail, "we have to get out of here."

But instead of turning toward the exit, Debrogail turned the other way.

"It's this way," whispered Arrah.

"I have to get Magnus," answered Debrogail.

She ran to another cell and quickly opened the door. Magnus was sitting on the floor. Surprised, he looked up at Debrogail.

"Magnus! We're leaving here."

Magnus saw a second woman standing behind Debrogail, and knew immediately who she was. He'd heard the commotion when Arrah O'Donnell was brought in.

"I'm not going with you," he said.

"Of course you're coming with us," Debrogail said.

"Debrogail, come here," he said, and when she bent down to him, he took both her hands in his.

He looked at his crutches. "Me, and all those stairs. I'll only hinder your escape."

"Magnus, you must come, please!" Debrogail stood, and pulling at his hands, tried to make him stand.

"Debrogail, he's right," said Arrah. "We have to hurry before the other guards come."

Debrogail turned on Arrah with a fury that Arrah had never seen in her in all the years they had spent as childhood friends. "What they say about you is right! You're sharp and hard as your damned battle swords. Magnus was my brother before I knew you as my sister, and I'll not leave here without him. If you want to go, then go, but go by yourself."

"I didn't find you after all these years to leave you behind now," said Arrah, approaching Debrogail and Magnus. "Grab his arm, and lift him up." Arrah took Magnus's other arm.

"You're fools, both of you," said Magnus.

The two women helped Magnus hop out of the cell and down the corridor.

They reached the stairs, the two women holding the man between them, lifting him up step by step, the arduous process slow as a snail, step by step, lifting and stepping.

They were two steps from the top when they heard voices. In one swoop they lifted Magnus onto the landing and hid behind the door as it swung open against them. Arrah whispered a silent prayer. *Spare me until Milly is of age. Then you can take me. Give me freedom now.*

Arrah grabbed one of Magnus's crutches, and from behind the door looked out. There were two guards. Holding the crutch high, she clubbed the guard closest to her on his skull. Before he had even toppled, she had clubbed the second one as well.

She, Debrogail, and Magnus passed into a second corridor. Again the torturous slow climb of right foot up, followed by left foot up, and then right foot up, followed by the left again. They reached the landing. Debrogail had her hand on the door when it opened without warning. Debrogail screamed.

Hirple looked directly at Arrah, and drawing his sword he shouted, "Prisoner loose! Prisoner loose!"

Arrah threw the crutch she held at Hirple and it hit him in the chest, stunning him so he leaned back, looking as if he might fall. But he stood his feet, sword in hand.

Debrogail, who had Magnus's other crutch, lunged for him with it, but she had no skill with fighting, and Hirple raised his sword, knocking it from her hand. He lunged at her, ready to stab her. Magnus threw his body on hers, throwing her to the landing floor, but the sword caught Magnus in the throat.

Arrah had no weapon at all. There was a torch from the sconce in the wall half a dozen steps beneath her. She leaped down for it. Behind her she heard Debrogail crying Magnus's name.

Arrah leaped back up to the landing.

Hirple's sword was bloody as he went at Arrah.

"Awake! Awake! Ho! Arrah O'Donnell's loose," shouted Hirple.

Arrah heard an alarm bell somewhere. She slashed at Hirple with the torch. Because of his lame foot he was not as fleet as she was. The landing had no railing. She had to try to somehow force him over the edge. She pushed the torch into his face and had him backed against a wall. He came back with his sword, and fire and steel parried with each other. Each time he hit the torch, he slashed off small bits of burning rags from her torch and they burned like little fires on the landing. He picked up one of the little fires on his sword and threw it against her. It caught her hand, burning her so she lost her concentration. He came at her with his sword, forcing her backward toward the stairs from where she had just come.

Debrogail, bending over Magnus, was behind Hirple. She grabbed one of the crutches that had fallen in the doorway and knocked Hirple in the back so he fell to the landing. Arrah pushed the torch directly in his face. He rolled to avoid it, but before he realized he was rolling too fast, he was at the edge of the landing. He grasped at the floor edge with his fingers, but his momentum was too great, and screaming, he fell to the stone floor below.

Debrogail was again bent over Magnus, her hands holding his hand. "Cathlin's calling to me," he whispered. "Go, Debrogail."

Debrogail pulled his hand to her lips and kissed it. "My brother! I love you!"

"You're not alone anymore. You've found a sister. I hope you find your Bres. Good-bye, Debrogail." His hand went limp.

Debrogail was crying.

Arrah had enough experience in battle to know when a man was dead. She touched Debrogail's shoulder. "Come," she said.

"He was the most honorable man I've ever met."

"There's nothing more you can do for him." Arrah lifted Debrogail by her arm.

Another guard came through the door, sword drawn, and he hacked at Arrah's torch, cutting it in two, so that the lit section fell. She kicked it up at the guard's face, and when he recoiled, kicked him hard in the groin. Arrah snatched his sword, and grabbing Debrogail's hand, was through the door.

"That way," said Debrogail in a rush. "I can't keep up with you."

"Come! I can't leave you!" Arrah pulled on Debrogail's hand again.

Debrogail held back. "They won't hurt me. Go that way!" She pointed toward a dark corridor.

Arrah heard running feet coming from everywhere and the approaching light from two corridors told her that more guards were coming. She saw a low, dark alcove and pulled Debrogail. Debrogail's skirt caught on an edge of stone and she fell forward on the dark stone. Arrah threw herself beside her.

Arrah knew the torches were coming closer. She pressed herself against the floor, felt her heart beating against the stone. She tried to make herself as flat as she could, but her bones and skin took up too much room. If it weren't for her flesh, her soul could slide into a crack in the stone and be safe. She knew the torches were probing and poking in the dark spots. She felt her heartbeat in places she'd never felt it before, in the tips of fingers, at the corner of her lip, in the pit of her stomach. The light came closer. Around her she heard footsteps on stone, the cursing of men, and their strained breathing. A light came closer. She tried to pull her skin inside itself. She didn't breathe. She felt Debrogail's fingers tighten on hers. She felt the light reach over her; she felt the cold metal of a sword at the back of her head.

The guard shouted. "Nothing here," and the light and footsteps fell away.

Arrah began to breathe again. Debrogail was beside her, her arms lifting, holding.

"There's a place at the top where we can jump into the moat. It's deeper there than in other places," whispered Debrogail.

The two women ran hand in hand down one corridor and then another, up stairs and up more stairs until they reached the ramparts. Outside the wind was blowing harder.

A guard was coming. Both women were breathless as they pressed themselves against the wall. The guard passed. Debrogail whispered, "Can you still swim, Arrah?"

Arrah squeezed her fingers in affirmation.

"Follow me!"

Debrogail led the way. Because Debrogail wore a skirt, the high step up on the wall to the shooting station where archers kneeled to aim was clumsy for her. She hoisted her skirt up around her knees. But in the darkness a corner of the ripped hem caught in the stone, and she tripped, falling against the wall. Arrah bent to help Debrogail stand, and then helped her step up again. Her skirt blew in Arrah's face.

Neither woman noticed the guard who came behind them.

CHAPTER
42

She was to be hanged at dawn. The night was completely still and dark. The moon was no longer visible to her. She heard the scraping of dry, withered leaves being carried across the cobblestones by the wind. Rat feet scurried along the stone.

She pressed her face between the bars and smelled the steel cold smell of morning. She'd fought for escape and failed. Perhaps that was the meaning of life—just struggle, and after you'd struggled as hard as you could, when you couldn't struggle anymore, then you made a decision to die with dignity.

Dawn was coming. She heard the single note of a thrush. In reply she heard the sound of metal, the clatter of a door in the corridor. She heard the insertion of a key in her cell door. The rats stopped their movement.

"Hey, you! There's a priest to talk to you," said the jailer.

She saw a second man arrive.

"Hurry it!" came the order from the jailer. "Lord de Burgo doesn't like to be kept waiting."

"Prepare to meet Him who made you," said the priest. His was a kind voice. "The Lord be with you!"

Her manacles were removed. One of the soldiers tied her wrists behind her back and led her out. Now she saw the first red banners of the sky begin to unfurl and she thought of the banners of her ships, the way they had streamed and played in the wind, of how much pleasure they had given her. Milly would be sleeping now. She heard the scrape of a sword against a wall, saw the thin crescent moon emerging from behind a cloud. A low mist clung close to the ground.

She thought of the night she had first run away from Eagle Castle to her father's ships, the way she had felt the moon in her thighs and in her arms. She had felt like she belonged to the center of the world. Now she felt simply empty, numb. The sky was turning redder now. The cobblestones were uneven and she stumbled. Somebody grabbed her elbow roughly. The priest walked beside her, his face grim.

Glundel with his melted face looked like a creature escaped from hell.

Then she saw the gallows and the hangman, enormous and black and final, a black leather hood on his face, his arms crossed on his chest. Spittle rose sour in the back of her throat. She had heard the guard on the rampart only at the last moment. Debrogail had stepped up onto the stone wall. Arrah had pushed her over in the same moment she turned to meet the guard. She'd plunged her sword into his ribs, but another guard had hit her from behind.

The guard at her elbow nudged her forward.

She put her foot on the first step of the gallows. It was a hollow sound. In the quiet morning, the hollowness seemed to grow and envelop her. The sound of death. God, she was afraid. There was another nudge at her elbow. She took another step.

She saw the four horses waiting, three dark ones and a dapple-gray that appeared shining in the moonlight. All she could hope was that she was dead when they manacled her to them.

Dawn began to color the sky, like bloody fingers reaching into the darkness.

"Restore thou them that are penitent; According to thy promises declared unto mankind in Christ Jesu our Lord . . ." The priest spoke in a low, incantatory voice beside her.

The hangman didn't move. He stood huge, still as a coffin. Only his eyes moved, dark and shining from inside the black executioner's mask. So this was the end. She herself had put on masks often enough, masks of courage. If she could hold on to her courage and dignity a short while longer, then even the hangman couldn't defeat her. He could kill her body, but the spirit of Arrah O'Donnell would not be defeated. The soul of Arrah O'Donnell would soar like an eagle. Oh God, she was afraid!

The hangman moved for the first time. He held out a blindfold.

"Do you mean to deprive me of the sunrise in my final moments?"

The executioner took her shoulders in an enormous grip and turned her around. She had never been sick on the sea, but now she felt the sea tossing and falling in the back of her throat. He pulled the hemp down over her head, scraping it against her face.

"*Dominus regit* . . . Yea, though I walk through the valley of the shadow of death, I will fear no evil, for thou art with me; thy rod and thy staff comfort me . . ." recited the confessor.

The hangman touched the side of her neck. The intimacy of the gesture surprised her for he had lifted her hair from her neck. Perhaps death was every woman's final lover. Her neck felt cool in the morning, the way it had felt cool that first night she cut her hair. Betrayal had undone her. She wouldn't think of betrayal, but of happy things, of what she said to Milly. *I love you high as the sky and wide as the ocean.* If she thought of happiness, she wouldn't be afraid. *Arrah of the distant eyes. The evening star . . . there on the horizon.* Sunrise was a signal that heaven's gates were open to receive the souls who had died in the night. Another sunrise. *Arrah, hold on.* She felt the noose tighten at her throat. She thought of Seaghan's fingers on her neck. *Good-bye, Seaghan. Good-bye, Debrogail, wherever you are. Don't be afraid, Milly. I don't love you this much, or this much, but high as the sky and wide as the ocean.*

"Have you any last words?" the confessor asked. But his voice was far and distant, like a voice in a dream.

"Answer him," whispered the hangman.

She was numb, empty. She couldn't move, couldn't speak.

"By thine Agony and bloody Sweat; by thy Cross and Passion . . . In the hour of death, and in the day of judgement, Lord God deliver us."

She looked out and saw a man wearing a heavy cowl standing beside a horse. He was waiting for her, waiting to tear her limb from limb.

"Get off, all of you, from the platform. I've had too many things go amiss with people on the gallows," shouted the hangman. There was the shuffle of feet on hollow wood.

"What the devil's keeping you?" shouted de Burgo.

"Nothing . . . she's a woman, is all."

"Woman! She killed my son. Stole my property."

Arrah felt the hangman fumble with the rope about her neck. She shivered. He was standing close to her, so close she could feel the heat of his body and still she shivered. She couldn't stop shivering.

She saw in the lightening darkness that his hands were stained with blood.

"*Ad te, Domine* . . . I lift up my soul; my God, I have put my trust in Thee." The priest's voice was strangely summoning, trancelike and seductive. "The eternal God is my refuge and underneath are the everlasting arms."

"For Christ's sake, faster," Glundel yelled.

She felt the rope pressed to the side of her neck under her ear. This was a dream, a dream from which there would be no waking, just a sinking into that deepening darkness.

The dawn was the color of blood. Arrah heard the hangman's lever, the final thud.

CHAPTER 43

Far out on the sea the mist began to rise. For a moment a ship was visible, a tiger's eyes flashed yellow on the deck. Four people were briefly visible. A huge brute of a man stood between a woman and a girl child, his arms around both their shoulders. The woman's hair was thick and unruly, as was the child's. An older man with a patched eye stood a few steps away. But before anything else could be seen, the fog rolled and fell profoundly, and this time the ship was completely harbored in the silence of mist and sea.

Milly loved the ship and stayed outside with Mary and Patch. Seaghan led Arrah into the stateroom of his ship.

Her escape had gone as he planned it. Not even Arrah had seen through his hangman's disguise. The added weight of his body broke the rope he had carefully frayed, and he and Arrah had dropped to the ground together, and they along with Patch had escaped on horseback.

But the trauma of the gallows had changed Arrah, made her vulnerable, and Seaghan felt a great overwhelming need to protect her. His heart burned each time he remembered how close she had been to death.

He had been delayed getting back from France because of the jealous plotting of Jacqueline, and had arrived barely in time. He had killed the hangman in the late hours of the night as Thomas was coming from the bed of the tavern doxy to the gallows. His heart still beat fast as he recalled fraying the rope at the last moments as the guards mumbled and complained about the delay.

He should have been joyous. He was finally going to do with Arrah what he wanted to do from the moment he had first seen her, take her to France to live with him. And yet, he was troubled—for Arrah seemed to have lost something that was as intrinsic to her as foam was to the sea. Some of the life had gone out of her, and she behaved as though she moved in a dream, as though her spirit had fled her.

When he was small he remembered picking some of the heady, aromatic blackthorn flowers and taking them to his mother when she was still alive. But the flowers had withered and died shortly thereafter. Arrah was the kind of woman who needed constant challenge in her life to keep her vital. She thrived on challenge. It was her lifeblood. As he stood there looking at her he realized he would have to somehow help Arrah get her spirit back. Without her indomitable will, Arrah would be doomed to a life of unhappiness. In France, the spirit of Arrah O'Donnell would shrivel like the flowers he picked as a child. She needed the west coast of Ireland. She thrived, was rejuvenated in the tumult of sea and wind. She needed it like the earth needed rain. To rekindle Arrah's spirit they would have to retake Eagle Island.

Never before had he been willing to change his life for a woman. Now he found himself ready to change everything for the woman he loved.

He opened the door to the stateroom and shouted to the crew, "Come about!"

Arrah looked at him. "Why are we going back?"

"We're going to retake Eagle Island."

"No, Seaghan!"

"You are of Ireland. And it's because you are of Ireland that I love you so much. Ireland is where we both belong."

"A home is where you make it. I'll carry Ireland in my heart wherever I go."

But Seaghan's eyes were set hard. "Children are conceived in passion. Your father begot you in a moment of lust. But it was the hills and rocks and sea of Ireland that shaped you, more than your father lying between your mother's thighs. Your parents have died, yet the sea and the land live on. In France there is no challenge for you, everything there ready to be handed to you by a myriad of obsequious servants. The court is a foppish place, closed, and full of the close smells of the bodies of men and women." As he talked he grew more animated and angry. "My father has stolen your home. I'll not rest until it's yours again. I, too, have been cast out of my home. I know the ache it puts into a man's heart. Your heart will be no different. I used to think I could make you happy in France, but you will long for Ireland. And if you begin to long for it, you will not be happy in France. Do you know what it does to a man to have an unhappy wife?"

"Seaghan, I will not be unhappy so long as I'm with you!"

"When one grows up with violence in the climate, one misses it when it's not present. We're going back because I love you!"

"It's nearly impossible to attack Eagle Island. With the cliffs on the west side, and the narrowness of the inlets . . ."

"When I was a boy, my grandfather told tales of a secret passage that a shipwrecked sailor found."

"I've been in that passageway. It's blocked. I nearly drowned."

"It was blocked, yes. My ancestor ordered it filled with stones, but we could open it again."

"It's too long. I can't swim it."

"Is Arrah of the Eagles afraid?"

"Yes."

He stood close to her now and touched her stomach tenderly and protectively. "I would rather die myself than see any harm come to you or to our child. But Arrah, you must reclaim Eagle Island, if you are ever to be happy again. You must reclaim Eagle Island for you and for our child that you carry now in your womb. Arrah, ordinary women can exist without spirit. They exist in the humdrum of their ordinary lives. But you are no ordinary woman. For you, living a life without challenge is like an eagle trying to fly with one wing."

"Patch used the same expression with me many years ago."

"Perhaps because it was he who convinced me to come back and return the brooch of the O'Donnell to you."

Brion MacNamara had taken the Island of the Eagles. It had been an easy enough battle. The O'Donnell soldiers were demoralized with Arrah's capture and fought without spirit.

But the satisfaction MacNamara felt quickly gave way to a dark, desperate futility. A wolfhound tethered in the yard began to bark. The great dog resembled exactly the beast that Brion remembered Reevnarg keeping when Reevnarg was still a youth. Brion remembered that dog's name— Bran—and said the name softly as he approached it. The dog began to whine. For a moment Brion thought it must be the same dog, but then realized it couldn't be. Too much time had passed. Obviously the dog that Brion saw now was the offspring of that magnificent beast.

As Brion approached him, he realized the dog wasn't vicious. Instead it whined as if greeting him, as if it knew that he, Brion, had once stroked the old Bran with friendly pats and kind words. Brion sat down next to the dog.

For a long time he sat there, stroking the dog's muzzle and scratching under his chin. Finally he laid his head against the dog's head, and then he

started to weep. He was the enemy, and yet this son of a dog from his past
remembered him as a friend. He lived with the memory of betrayal and
murder. A man without a wife, a man without a friend. He had taken Eagle
Island, but there was no one to pass it to and he wept, he wept for the loss of
friendship, and the loss of love.

The dog licked at his tears and whined, his great brown eyes looking up
at the man who had once been his dead master's friend.

Brion regained himself. He was Lord of Eagle Island now. It had been
out of his clan's grasp for too long. He loosened the wolfhound's rope and
allowed Bran to come into the main hall with him.

Already the coat of arms of the MacNamara, the rampant lion holding
the spear, hung where once the eagle of the O'Donnell hung.

Glundel Joyce was furious after the escape by Arrah O'Donnell. Not
only had the child been sent away from him, but now the whoring bitch
who had burned his face had escaped death. In the days that had passed
since the episode with Bridgett and the child, De Burgo, Finola, and
MacNamara treated him as though he were scum from a bucket of slops.

There was to be a feast on the Island of the Eagles tonight to celebrate the
victorious alliance. Everyone would be occupied. The well was in the
middle of the courtyard. He would pour poison into the well. Then
Glundel Joyce, as Lord of Eagle Island, would have reason to celebrate.

By Arrah's own remembrance and her innate sense of the sea as well as
Seaghan's recollection of where his grandfather had said the passage came
out, Arrah and Seaghan had discovered the opening, or rather the pile of
stones that had been dumped long ago to prevent anyone swimming into it.

At night, hidden in darkness and assisted by the local fisherfolk, she and
Seaghan had swum down and removed the rocks one by one. They planned
to open the gate secretly at night, and retake the castle while everyone slept.
But Seaghan's shoulders were too broad to pass through the passageway.
Arrah had to go by herself.

She stood on the shoreline, his arms wrapped around her. She was
afraid. It seemed to her that she had not stopped being afraid since she had
set her foot on the gallows. It had made her feel the great void that was the
hereafter. She tried to take strength from Seaghan's arms, but she couldn't.
She trembled. He pulled her close and kissed the top of her hair.

"Arrah of the Eagles. There are only three forces in the world that matter: the sword, the heart, and the mind. You've never been afraid of using your sword, and you've shown courage in your heart. Now you must allow your mind to guide you through that darkness of fear. When your foot touched the gallows step, you lost your trust in your own abilities. Trust me, Arrah. There is a way. Trust yourself to find that way." She saw the dark strength in his eyes.

Milly was standing beside her. "Are you going to swim the passageway because you have courage?" Milly asked. Something about Milly's words jolted Arrah. She remembered what she had told Milly: *"It's when we're most afraid that we have to pretend not to be."*

Arrah hugged Milly very close to her, drawing strength from her daughter's words. A realization came to Arrah. Ultimately, this was the meaning of life. Taking strength from yourself, but also taking strength from others. She had to retake Eagle Island for herself and the child she carried, but also for Milly and Reevnarg.

Arrah slipped from her garments and plunged into the sea. As she began to swim the secret passageway, guided by some dark inner sense, the sea on her limbs revitalized her. She found the pocket of air that had previously saved her. The last time she had been here, she was panicky, frightened, disoriented. Now she knew exactly where she was, and she touched the sides of the passage with newfound vigor. She would again become Mistress of the Eagles.

She easily located the secret stairway behind the chimney of her mother's chamber. There was nothing left to do now, but wait for the night. When everyone was asleep she would kill the two guards at the gate, then open the pedestrian entrance to Seaghan and his men and they would retake the castle.

Debrogail and Bres were in bed with each other. It was only after Debrogail had stepped up into the archer's station that she realized Arrah had been attacked by two guards. Before she could jump down to Arrah's assistance, Arrah had pushed her over the edge, and she had fallen into the moat below. It was as Debrogail climbed out of the stinking slimy water that she had encountered Seaghan MacNamara, Bres's kinsman.

He had thrown his cloak over her as, crying, she related what had happened to Arrah. He had taken her to a house where she had washed. "If you love Bres, then go to him. He's at Eagle Island. My father has taken the island. I'll take Arrah to France with me. You and Bres can come and see us there."

Only later had she learned that Seaghan had killed the hangman and taken his place on the gallows.

Since Bres and Debrogail had met again after their years of separation, they had not been out of each other's sight for more than a minute. They were to be married within days.

De Burgo was stunned and furious to see her at Eagle Island, and wanted to hang her immediately. Bres had pulled his sword on de Burgo. "Any talk of hanging and I'll kill you!" Bres had answered de Burgo.

Bres touched her and stroked her fine skin and kissed her eyes and held her as though he never ever wanted to let her go again. "When God took Adam's rib to make Eve, he left an ache in all mankind that is only stopped when he's with the woman he loves. I felt that ache all the years you were gone from me. I want to be one body with you again," he said.

She could feel him grow hard, and she slid beneath his limbs, ready to accept the fullfillment of his manhood. After, when he lay beside her panting and sweating with exertion, she wiped his body with her fragrant hair.

She took his limp member in her hair and, using her hand, slid her hair up and down his shaft. Her stroking made him want her again, and he lifted her onto his erect phallus and she was joined to him once more.

Bran, lying at the feet of Brion MacNamara, tried to stand. In a gesture of feeling for the dog, Brion had ordered fresh water and food brought close for him. Bran had drunk some of the water, sniffed at the food, and then lay back down. A cat came and sniffed at the water dish, drank from it, and then lay down in a corner.

Suddenly the dog began to whine as if in pain, attempted to rise, but couldn't. The cat had begun to meow. It, too, struggled to its feet, before falling as if drunk.

MacNamara sprang to his feet and began to shout. "The water's been poisoned. The water's been poisoned." He ran through the main hall overturning pitchers, and then into the kitchen, dumping out pots where vegetables and meats were boiling in cauldrons. "Don't touch any of it!" he shouted. "Not a mouthful!"

By the time he returned to the main hall, both Bran and the cat were dead. Brion gave orders that all activity was to cease, as though the men had been poisoned. An attack was planned; he knew that his son was responsible for the poisoning. Let Seaghan think that all were dead. He, Brion Mac-Namara, would order the main gate left open. He would wait in ambush and kill his son.

Nightfall had come, and Seaghan and his men had landed on the west side of Eagle Island, where there was a hidden sheltered cove. The mist would serve to hide his men as they took Eagle Castle. He knew enough of his father's habits to expect that there would be a great feast to celebrate the taking of Eagle Island. In all likelihood many of the soldiers and guards would be snoring drunk. It would be an easy attack when Arrah opened the gate from inside.

He had two hundred men with him, including Patch. Both Milly and Mary had wanted to go with them as they stormed Eagle Castle, and only the strongest of his words had prevented them from doing so. He had never met so many stubborn females in his life as Arrah, Mary, and Milly. And then he smiled to himself as he moved across the gorse, for in a special way he loved them all.

Damn! The boy who was carrying the standard was falling behind. "Move it ahead, boy! Faster," ordered Seaghan, "or I'll have you disciplined!"

A soft-looking soldier with a very dark face, puffing like a racing chicken, came up beside the standard bearer to assist him. "Come, boy, faster!" said the fleshy soldier.

"You, there!" shouted MacNamara. "See the boy keeps up or I'll have you both whipped."

The fleshy one hunched up his shoulders and uttered a muffled "Aye, sir," all the while trying to slink away like an egg-sucking dog.

For the first time in his life, Seaghan MacNamara questioned Patch's wisdom. "Patch," he yelled.

"Aye, sir!" The one-eyed sailor sprinted up.

"These two you insisted come along with us. That round one and the lad. They're useless as codfish on land."

Patch looked sheepishly at the two who were stumbling and bumbling ahead. "Aye, sir! I was making a mistake, sir!" He blinked his tattooed eye.

"If they get in the way, it'll be your skin."

"Aye, sir. I'll look after them!"

The troops continued walking. Finally Eagle Castle loomed ahead of them.

It rose dark, a solid square, ominous and silent as a godhead in the swirling, moving mist that rose and billowed in constant cloud around it. The gates were open.

Seaghan whispered orders to Patch. In their revelry the feasting enemy must have forgotten to close it. Attack would be even easier than Seaghan had imagined it. But they would have to be careful. There was always the possibility of a trap.

At the main gate the lad who was carrying the standard stumbled on his flag and fell forward with a terrible clatter. Seaghan leaped ahead, ready to strike the boy, but the lad's hat fell from his head and a mass of chestnut hair tumbled loose. Seaghan let his hand fall, for the lad was not a lad, but Milly disguised.

"Damn you!" he cursed the child. "You're no better than your mother."

Milly was crying. "I wanted to help! I wanted to have courage too."

The dark-faced soldier was there, scolding immediately. "Now don't ye go cursing a child."

"Mary, for the love of Christ!" Seaghan pushed Mary and Milly together. "Patch! Damn you, Patch! Get these two out of here!"

"Mary made me do it. Blackened her face with walnut brine. She weren't giving me a moment's rest!" Patch defended.

"Now!" ordered Seaghan.

Then suddenly, from high up in her mother's chamber, Arrah shouted down. "Ambush! It's an ambush! They're waiting for us!"

Men leaped out of the night.

"Prepare to fight!" yelled Seaghan.

The darkness was filled with the shadows of men killing and being killed, their victory cries, their death cries rising up to moonlit heavens. Men cried to God, cursed Him for their agony, and prayed to him to guide their weapons home. All engaged in that fight were either victim or executioner. There was room for no one else.

Seaghan, slashing mercilessly all who approached him, found his way to the main hall of the castle. There he dispensed with three swordsmen before coming on Bres. The two cousins confronted each other for a moment, swords drawn, both smiling.

"I thought you would've left for France," said Bres.

"I've come to claim this place for the woman I love."

"It's an unwise move. Your father won't rest until you're dead," warned Bres. He parried his cousin's sword lightly. "Remember how we played as boys?"

"It was you who always played the evil one," said Seaghan.

"Because you were the better swordsman. You always killed me. It's the way of childhood fantasies. Evil must always die."

"Will you make me kill you now?" Seaghan asked.

"No." Bres pointed his sword downward. "I never agreed with Brion casting you out. I remained loyal to him, but only when he wasn't disloyal to you."

"You've stayed my friend, my loved kinsmen—but I will kill him who's behind me." Seaghan spun, ready to strike the soldier behind him. But instead of killing his adversary, Seaghan stood absolutely still, for the man behind him was his own father.

The father and son, one a black-haired colossus, the other a gray-haired Titan, stood looking at each other, hatred pouring like hot lead from their eyes.

"I curse myself for putting life into the traitorous womb of the woman who bore you. On guard!" Brion lunged at Seaghan. Seaghan deflected the attack. Both excellent swordsman, they wove around each other, their swords fatal needles in that fabric of hate. Seaghan feinted, struck an octave and a second that ripped Brion's doublet. Brion stepped backward, tripped on a bench and went down, losing his sword as he fell.

Seaghan stood over him, his sword at his father's throat.

"Are you a coward as well as a traitor?" taunted his father. "You'd best kill me, or I'll kill you."

Seaghan lowered his sword and walked away from his father. Brion grabbed up his fallen sword and charged like a raging bull after his son. "I taught you the sword. Now use it, or die by it!"

Seaghan continued walking.

Brion grabbed Seaghan by the shoulder, spun him around, and slammed his fist into Seaghan's jaw. Seaghan's head snapped back but he remained standing. Seaghan turned and walked again, but Brion continued his attack, lunging his sword at Seaghan. Seaghan parried his father's thrusts, but wouldn't take the offensive. The sound of their steel echoed through the main hall. Brion lunged at Seaghan, but the younger man leaped aside, and the sword ran through the MacNamara banner, slashing the lion in half.

There were tears in Brion's eyes. He spoke breathlessly, the rhythm of his words echoing the strike of steel. "I held you in my arms! And you betrayed me."

"Father! You betrayed yourself."

"I carried you on my shoulders when you were a small boy so that you could touch the velvet nose of my stallions. You betrayed me!"

"You left her alone all the time. A woman should not be left alone."

"A woman serves her man!" shouted Brion.

"A woman needs attention, just like your damned horses, and your damned hounds, and your hunt!

"A woman does what she's told."

"Is that why she chose to love me!" answered Seaghan.

Brion picked up a chair and smashed it against his son's head, knocking him to the floor. Seaghan's sword flew from his hand.

His father loomed above him, ready to strike. "I curse you, my son. I gave you life. Now I take it—"

A silver streak of light flashed.

"Arrah!"

Seaghan leaped up and away from his father, knocking Arrah's sword from her hand just as it was about to pierce Brion's chest.

Seaghan yelled, "He's my father!"

Brion stood, his sword aimed lethally. "That was a mistake, my son. Prepare to die!"

Arrah leapt in front of Seaghan, protecting him with her body. "Look at me," she shouted. "Look at me. Blood on my hands. I've had to kill to gain back my home. And blood on your hands. And blood on the floor. Will you never grow weary of so much blood?"

"Out of my way, woman. He killed my honor!" shouted Brion.

"And you killed my father. And he killed his own sister. There has been so much hatred, here in the Castle of the Eagles. The flag of the eagle has been removed and in its place, the lion of the MacNamara. And it, too, hangs slashed. We go on killing each other because we believe in curses and fate! My father, dead. My mother, dead because of our damned Irish fighting. The woman who for so many years was my sister, dead. Is it not time for the dying to stop and the living to begin? There is a new peril growing in this land. It's the English who want our island. If we are to be strong we must be united. We can't devour each other like sharks. Father against son, brother against brother.

"Brion MacNamara, you gave the man I love life. Will you take it away from him? Will we see Ireland crumble in our hands? Will you see the unborn child I carry die, because you cannot forgive? Living your life with so much hatred in your heart is like trying to fly with broken wings.

"The Island of the Eagles will pass to your grandchild, to the child I carry now. Will you kill the man who is the father of your grandchild?"

Brion MacNamara looked at his son and at the woman who stood in front of him. Brion's arm began to shake. At first it was barely perceptible, but then his shoulders shook as well and he dropped his sword. And then he wept. Seaghan moved toward him.

De Burgo and Finola had come into the main hall.

Unnoticed, Glundel had come into the hall as well. All of his plans had gone awry. Brion MacNamara had been alerted to the poison. Glundel had begun to drink of whiskey and self-pity and now he was like a mad dog frothing with hatred. His clothes were torn and bloody and covered in feathers. He had killed anything in his sight, ally or foe. There was no difference to him now. Everybody and everything was his enemy. Even a chicken, escaped from the bawn, became his enemy, and he followed it, stabbing and hacking at it in a frenzy of hatred. Then he had come out into the courtyard and stabbed at dying men and dead men.

His lips were bloody as though he had drunk their blood. He veered dangerously toward Finola, for she was closest to him, his dagger plunging at her bosom.

Finola recoiled. With her dark robes flying, and her skin very white, she looked like a magpie trying to fly backward.

Glundel grabbed her left arm, lifted it, and plunged his dagger deep into her side. Finola tried to say something, but only coughed.

De Burgo lunged at Glundel, but Glundel swayed wildly away. Before de Burgo could take another thrust, Seaghan was there. He had grabbed Arrah's sword and now he plunged it into Glundel's side and then ripped it down so his body matter fell out like that of a gutted pig.

De Burgo slumped to his knees on the floor where Finola already lay. He lifted her head and cradled it in his lap, pushing her hair from her face.

"Geralde," she whispered. "You were good to me." Then her head fell limply to the side.

Glundel began to laugh hideously. "You were good to me! Hear that, Geralde? You were good to me!" De Burgo took a dagger from his belt and plunged it into Glundel. But Glundel, too, had a dagger hidden and as de Burgo leaned toward him, Glundel grasped him and stabbed him. The two men collapsed into each other in their dying throes, their blood running in pools and mixing on the floor.

*   *   *

There had been too much blood and too much killing for there to be any victory celebration that night. Seaghan and Arrah clung to each other in bed that night, trying to heal the bloodshed in the closeness of each other.

Even Legless Paddy had been victim of the violence. He had been killed by a wild arrow when Brion MacNamara took Eagle Island. Poor Paddy. Perhaps it was just as well he never learned that Naira had been his daughter.

From the far horizon the soft breathing of the sea rose to Seaghan and Arrah's chamber, cutting it off from the rest of the world. Around them the mist settled on the island.

The next day Seaghan and his father took the eagles that had once belonged to Reevnarg out on the hills of the Island. They were guarded with each other at first, but there with the hunt and the wind of Ireland, father and son found themselves once more.

The following day Patch and Mary, holding hands, approached Arrah and Seaghan as they returned from a walk along the cliffs. Behind them the mist was lifting off the sea, showing the purple green of evening.

"Arrah," said Mary. "You've been my mistress for a long enough time. It's time for me to be master of me own soul. I'm leaving your employ."

Before Arrah could say anything, Patch continued.

"Mary and me." His tattooed eye blinked. "With me wife dying the way she did. Mary promised to look after me chicks and me gran'children if'n I bring 'em here to Ireland, which I intend to be doing. I've tied thousands of monkey fists. The sea has had her chance at me. When I die I want to die in a soft bed on the breast of Mary!"

Mary blushed red as a lobster. "Patch here has got some money on account of the good wages you was paying him. We're going to be building a tavern. Call it the Patched Goat, after me own sweet Finn."

Arrah was on the verge of tears as she hugged Mary. "Lord God, but I'll miss you, Mary. And Milly will too. But you have my blessing, the both of you!"

"Now, don't you be cryin'," scolded Mary. "Tears is for sad times."

When they left, Seaghan pulled Arrah to him. He kissed her deeply. He looked out on the sea. The mist seemed to be weaving its own secret spell. "All about us are marrying. It's time for us as well." Debrogail and Bres were to be married, and would return to MacNamara lands, where they would live.

"And the King of France?" she teased him. "Has he given his permission?"

"He gave it, but even if he hadn't, I would still marry you. I plan to stay in Ireland. I never had the time to tell you," he said, smiling. "Jacqueline invited the King to her chambers. She made love to him and tired him out and stole his seal ring and wrote a refusal of our marriage. But the Queen, who has spies everywhere, discovered the plot and told the King. He banished Jacqueline to Normandy. The most miserable weather in all of France is there. He ordered her married to an old baronet who's spry as a lamb and will probably live to be a hundred."

"How many hearts have you broken?" she asked.

"None that I really cared about," he said seriously. "I have a wedding present for you!" From his pocket he took out a magnificent necklace which he attached around her neck. It was very large, the size of two open hands placed one beneath the other. It resembled a gold torque made in the old-fashioned style of the ancient kings of Ireland, but the necklace was in the shape of a large eagle, wings outspread. The eagle's eyes were two rubies. His wings were made of pearls, his claws, cut emeralds.

"People call me a witch. A fine witch I turned out to be when I'm powerless to your charms."

"The best is yet to come for you and me, Mistress of the Eagles. We're getting older. We want gentle winds to blow across our faces now."

"Speak for yourself!" she challenged. "I still love the violence of the wind."

He smiled, for this was the woman whose high, proud carriage he had wished to possess from the beginning. "You're a woman whose passions run high. You'll always need much of love. I know how to love you," he said, his voice confident. "I know when you want to be made love to slowly and gently, and I know when you want to be taken hard and fast."

"Yes," she said, "you've always known."

"You're my Mōrrīgan, my goddess of war become goddess of love!"

"Why, do you think, was Mōrrīgan the goddess of love and of war?"

"Because love is as powerful as death. Because only love can repair the ravages of war, of deceit, of greed. I love you."

There was no need for her to respond, for the answer was in her eyes. He saw the yellow sun of evening slanting through ladders of mist, and he kissed her again. He looked out on the bay. He watched the edges of the Atlantic wash the shore in a vivid but pale green. There was a kind of velvet softness to the air. He pulled her close in his arms and they stood for a long time looking out on the softness of the sea.